THE WIDOW'S DAUGHTER

PENGUIN BOOKS

THE WIDOW'S DAUGHTER

Nicholas Edlin was born and raised in Christchurch. He has a BA in English and Political Science from Canterbury University, and a LLB from Victoria University of Wellington. He has worked as a solicitor in Wellington and Auckland and as a legal adviser in London. He currently lives in Auckland with his wife. This is his first novel.

THE
WIDOW'S
DAUGHTER
Nicholas Edlin

PENGUIN BOOKS

PENGUIN BOOKS

Published by the Penguin Group

Penguin Group (USA) Inc., 375 Hudson Street, New York, New York 10014, U.S.A.

Penguin Group (Canada), 90 Eglinton Avenue East, Suite 700, Toronto,
Ontario, Canada M4P 2Y3 (a division of Pearson Penguin Canada Inc.)

Penguin Books Ltd, 80 Strand, London WC2R 0RL, England

Penguin Ireland, 25 St Stephen's Green, Dublin 2, Ireland (a division of Penguin Books Ltd)

Penguin Group (Australia), 250 Camberwell Road, Camberwell,
Victoria 3124, Australia (a division of Pearson Australia Group Pty Ltd)

Penguin Books India Pvt Ltd, 11 Community Centre, Panchsheel Park, New Delhi – 110 017, India

Penguin Group (NZ), 67 Apollo Drive, Rosedale, Auckland 0632,
New Zealand (a division of Pearson New Zealand Ltd)

Penguin Books (South Africa) (Pty) Ltd, 24 Sturdee Avenue,
Rosebank, Johannesburg 2196, South Africa

Penguin Books Ltd, Registered Offices
80 Strand, London WC2R 0RL, England

First published in New Zealand by Penguin Group 2010
First published in the United States of America by Penguin Books (USA) 2012

ISBN 978-1-62090-014-7

Printed in the United States of America

To Helen

AUTHOR'S NOTE

This book is a work of fiction. It is not intended to be a historically accurate portrayal of Auckland during the time described, nor is it intended to be an accurate account of the men and women of the United States 3rd Marine Division, their deployment in Auckland during the war, or their subsequent involvement in the Pacific Theatre of Operations.

THE WIDOW'S DAUGHTER

CHAPTER 1

I hesitated before taking a step inside. As soon as I opened the door I knew she'd been in there. I could feel the cautious movements she'd made, smell her faint rosewater scent, nothing more than a suggestion in the dank air. She never tells me about these little forays, but I'm perceptive enough to know when she's made one. In this dark hole of stale breath, linseed oil and turpentine she leaves an unmistakable footprint, something feline and delicate, something bright and curious. It's nothing you can see, of course, just a feeling left hanging in the air, a charge of happily disturbed particles.

I haven't always been this relaxed. If it were ten years ago, I would have flown into a blind rage. I would have spat out a stream of bile about privacy and respect. I would have played the wild, tortured, ridiculous painter. My studio was my own, went the routine; it was the black corner of my heart, and she knew it. But I'm older now, and in my old age I often forget to lock the door. This forgetting may be wilful, it may even be a gesture of some sort – I cannot say. And so she makes her sorties one by one, but for what reason I do not know. I think she is trying to find something in there, an answer maybe, an answer to a question no longer asked.

I kicked off my tennis sneakers and pulled on a pair of faded blue paint-encrusted overalls. My kit, my battle gear

– the same stinky outfit I'd been working in since the final days of the Truman presidency. As I was rolling up my sleeves I saw in the corner of the room, pinned to the frame of my second easel, the documentary evidence that confirmed what I already knew. I shuffled across the bare floorboards in my slippery woollen socks and pulled the small news clipping from the frame. Even after all her many breaches of my unwritten rule, I was a little taken by her brazenness. This was the first time she'd left something for me to notice – a message that she'd been there, a little calling card signed 'Fuck You', perhaps. She'd been carrying the clipping around for days, and now it had finally made its way into my sanctum. It was an article from Friday's paper, a small piece about a Professor Anthony Sturgis from the English literature faculty at U.C.L.A. I'd seen the article four days ago, and Missy knew that I had read it. Several times. Over and over. Putting it in my studio for me to find at seven-thirty in the morning was upping the ante, though. It was a guerrilla act, a calculated stunt. But it worked. I read the damned thing again.

Professor Sturgis had just published a novel, so the story went, about the adventures of the Third Marine Company during the war. Sturgis, now forty-four, had served in the Third Medical Battalion in the Pacific Theatre from 1942 to 1945.

Curiously, the reporter noted, the novel was almost exclusively set in New Zealand in the months leading up to the Battalion's deployment to the Pacific combat zones. Sturgis was asked why he had chosen to set the novel in New Zealand rather than in the more exotic and bloodstained islands and atolls we all knew so much about. And then the direct quote, the words from his mouth: 'Because officially the Battalion did nothing in New Zealand. Because nothing happened in New Zealand. At first the local press weren't even allowed to report we were there. We were these peculiar, highly visible, extremely loud ghosts. We were big kids with free time and guns, and no responsibility. That kind of thing only happens once in a man's life.'

Even on the sixth read I didn't recognise the answer as coming from Sturgis. The Sturgis I knew had pimples and terrible teeth. The Sturgis I knew, the one who may have saved my life, the one who had thought me a murderer and a traitor, wanted nothing more than to get laid and play five-card stud into the small hours. It wasn't just the words I didn't recognise, but something more fundamental. The tone. The voice. It was too reasoned, too assured. Too old.

I pinned the clipping back to the frame and shuffled over to my first easel, where I had erected a bare canvas. I don't have any particular method of working these days, no special ritual or tic that some of my colleagues claim to have. But I do have a way of getting started. As much to get my hand moving as for any desired textural effect, I pile on layer after layer of thin primer, neutrals or mid-tones mostly, but when I'm agitated and feeling aggressive I attack the raw canvas with a burning titanium white, searing the blistering sharpness into every fibrous grain.

Imprimaturs are painterly; I know that, I even teach it. But I've always found they've had a second, maybe even more important, purpose for me, and that is as a means of erasing. Erasing the nothingness of the bare, virgin canvas. Erasing nothingness, but deepening it at the same time. Making the nothing so thick and hostile and textured that it has to be recognised as something in its own right. I think it is this, more than the austere beauty of line, or the bleeding of God's own colours into magical shapes, that has always called me to painting. This process of filling absence, of covering up every corner of a measured world so that nothing is left behind.

Because nothing happened in New Zealand.

CHAPTER 2

Our house is situated on a few acres of land just south of San Diego. The plot used to be part of a much larger citrus orchard, which had been in Missy's family for three generations. Before he died of lung cancer in 1952, almost seventeen years ago, her father had managed to shave off large chunks of the orchard as collateral security in a variety of failed business ventures. They all had something to do with water infrastructure speculations in Los Angeles, although I never felt like I'd heard the full story. Both of Missy's brothers were killed in Normandy during the war, leaving her as the sole beneficiary of her father's diminished fortune.

The house we live in was originally built to be sleeping quarters for the seasonal pickers, lean men with hard faces sweeping in from the dust bowl, illegal Mexicans with no English. It's big and roomy and has been renovated into a proper home, but I like to think that it retains some of the itinerant spirit of the workers, a temporary shelter in a rambling world. My studio, barely ten steps from the back porch, was the original tool shed and to this day is still cluttered with dozens of items from its former life – greasy oil cans, wooden-handled secateurs, aromatic wicker baskets with worn leather shoulder straps, a dirty calendar from twenty years ago. It is in this ruin that I take pieces of myself and paint them onto canvas, slowly, methodically, one cut at a time.

It was approaching noon when I heard the familiar tap on the studio door; Missy letting me know lunch was ready. Officially, this was as close as she was supposed to come. In spite of her recent incursions, she liked to keep with this pretence, this gentle, almost apologetic tap at the door before disappearing. I supposed it was her way of reassuring me that nothing had changed, that for all the snooping she'd done, the rotten corner of my heart was still my own.

We did everything early – took our meals, woke in the morning, went to bed at night. The rhythm of our life was so taut, so well understood, that at times we could go days without talking, without uttering a single word to each other. We had met a few years after the war at San Diego State University. I had just landed a new job (a new career, a new life) teaching a freshman painting class in the fine arts department. Missy, forty-two years old, recently widowed, was the Frank E. Lessing Professor of American Pragmatics and taught history to seniors. She was the first older woman I'd ever had.

I was just coming back to life in those years, trying to learn how to walk again in a world where A-bombs fell from the sky and yet you were supposed to care how big your neighbour's car was. I knew how to paint, had known my whole life, but I was still trying to learn how to be a painter. Trying to unlearn being a surgeon. Trying to forget New Zealand and the blood and guts that followed it.

There was so much talking during those years, so much empty chattering and bankrupt rhetoric, that Missy's silence was almost deafening. I had never met another person so fundamentally incompetent at small talk. I would watch her in the staffroom as she sat in the corner alone, eating her corned beef on rye, reading a tattered copy of William James, a thick cone of silence around her that nobody dared disturb. Naturally this degree of self-possession led most of the staff at the college into thinking she was either conceited beyond the pale or just plain weird. As a fellow mute I knew it was neither.

I accidentally-on-purpose staged a series of run-ins with her around the campus – in the PHILOSOPHY (AMERICAN PRAGMATISM) section of the library where I feigned an interest in John Dewey; by the oak tree out back of the registry building where she liked to drink her morning coffee; on the side street by the student cafeteria where I knew she parked her car. I had been avoiding real contact with people for over four years by that time. Initially the painting had been enough – the fraught communication it afforded was just about more than I could handle. But pretty soon I found myself needing someone to sit with in the evenings, someone who wouldn't ask too many questions, or demand to know what I was thinking. I needed somebody to be quiet with, somebody not frightened by silence. She knew my reputation (it was the stuff of legend around the campus in those days: Peter Sokol, the spy-artist, the traitor-artist) but for some reason she didn't seem to care. Maybe it was her learned pragmatism, maybe she just found it interesting; either way, all it took was a cup of bad coffee under the shade of the campus oak tree for her to agree. I bought her dinner that night and moved into the orchard house a couple of weeks later.

The kitchen was filled with streaky orange light when I came in for lunch. Although the renovation had rounded off some of its austere edges, this room still betrayed the house's purely functional, communal roots. It was a large, square, open space with oversized amenities, a sink the size of a child's tub, bench tops that ran round three-quarters of the room. Like everything else in the house, the kitchen was a shrine to exposed timber and gluey, decades-old varnish that was beginning to chip away from the wood like toffee from an apple.

I stood in a shaft of light and closed my eyes for a brief

moment, feeling the fiery heat on my eyelids. I was particular about washing the windows on account of the quality of light that came through. When I wanted to think of New Zealand, which was not often now, I would scrub clean every window in the house so that the sun that poured through was met with no opposition, no gauzy impediment. Even then nothing could match the harshness and crystal purity of that south-sea light, the light that goes on haunting me. But now I mostly let the windows be damned.

I took a seat at the kitchen table, an old slaughterhouse relic from the property's animal husbandry days, scrubbed clean but still stained with the blood of a thousand beasts. I rubbed my eyes; at sixty a morning's work isn't as straightforward as it used to be. I'm only good for a couple of hours at a stretch now before the primitive ache in my back sets in. Missy had laid out some cold cuts on the bench, and there were some fried potatoes in the skillet. I heard a creak on the porch followed by the old familiar measured step. I turned to see her come in through the open door, armed with the day's newspapers and a stack of mail. She put the load down on the table in front of me, catching my eye just long enough to acknowledge what she'd done and that she knew that I knew and that it was just a matter of who was going to mention it first. These are the games we play after nineteen years.

'Good afternoon,' I said, staring absently at my paint-flecked, paper-dry hands.

'Good afternoon, Peter.'

Missy is tall and regal. She wears her shoulder-length gunmetal hair wrapped up in a bun at the back of her head, an eraser-tipped pencil wedged into the centre of the arrangement. She has the hawkish nose of a Roman senator's wife. Her upright bearing and her high cheekbones give her reticence the gravity it deserves. She has waited, I know she has waited, but I have yet to propose, yet to make her the

7

honest woman her dignity demands.

'Potatoes for lunch?' I said.

She caught my tone, its metallic edge. She turned from the sink to look at me. I smiled with my eyes.

'Yes. And some beef.' She looked out of the window in front of her, serene in the unfocused light. 'Were you able to concentrate this morning?'

This was a typical Missy question. She never asked any direct questions about my work – what I was painting, what media I was using, what I was trying to achieve. She had an artist's sensibility, and as such her questions were about process and process alone.

'Eventually,' I said, leaning back on my chair and yawning.

She had more than just a sensibility – she was an excellent drawer, a natural with no training. When I had first moved into her house, and she had given me the shed as a studio, she asked if I would teach her how to paint. She said she was sick of charcoal and lead, and that she wanted to understand colour. But I knew instantly that the question was not just about furthering her skills, her native talent. It was a litmus test of involvement, an oral mapping of the parameters I would concede. When she gave me the key she had no idea that from that point on the studio would be sealed-off to her; that the man she slept with every night would cut himself in there to bleed his past, a past that didn't involve her, a past we never spoke of. She had assumed, in that wonderfully unassuming way of hers, that the studio would be an extension of our life in the house, that it would be part of both our lives, and that what came out of it would be explicable to her on some fundamental kind of level.

So I said no, I would not, and she has made a pig of me ever since by having the grace to never mention it again.

As we ate Missy pored over the front section of the *Tribune*, swallowing whole articles on the troop build-up and the

Cambodian strategy in one bite. There was no encumbrance on her concentration, no mental drift to the easy static of middle-age. I ate my fried potatoes and cold roast beef in silence, watching her eyes scan the two-inch columns, careful not to scrape my cutlery against the plate. I didn't need to read the papers to know what I thought of the war.

I was beginning to think we might make it through the entire meal without broaching the subject, but to my surprise she cracked.

'Are you going to go?' She said this without taking her eyes off the broadsheet.

'Go where?'

'To the lecture?' She looked up at me, her expression cautious. 'At U.C.L.A.?'

Sturgis was launching his book with a lecture and Q and A session on war literature, apparently a specialty of his. When Missy had first shown me the article I'd made the mistake of telling her that I knew Sturgis. More than that. That he was an orderly in the Third Medical. That when I knew him he was a cocky Bronx kid who couldn't spell and who wrote sentimental poetry in free verse because he couldn't get the hang of metre. That his best friend was killed because of me.

I kept eating until the question lost its impetus. We'd lived together for nineteen years, and in all that time she'd never pursued anything as far as this. I'd dropped fragments of information here and there, of course, and I took it as a given that she knew everything they'd printed in the papers about me at the time. But we'd never directly spoken of it. She knew me as Peter Sokol, the San Diegan painter. My persistent failure to mention Dr Sokol, the United States Marine surgeon, must have counselled her against asking at first. After a time the quiet scandal that my exhibitions used to engender slowly dissipated. And then year followed year, and there just didn't seem to be any point in talking about it. I extended her the same courtesy by never referring to her late husband, who'd been shot down over Tokyo. When we met we were people exhausted by death. She knew as well as I did that no amount of talking was going to change anything, and for this I fell in love with her. I pushed my plate away and leaned back in my chair again. 'Do you think I should?'

The response was immediate.

'I think you have to,' she said.

CHAPTER 3

I was thirty-two years old when I did my basic training at Camp Elliot, California, in the winter of '42. As a medical officer, a doctor no less, the physical training I was put through wasn't half as bad as what the enlisted men had to endure, but most of them were twenty at best. I would wake at bugle call, five a.m. sharp, with legs like lead weights, the nauseous taste of sleep sticky in my mouth like a night's fill of bourbon. As a prospective captain I was entitled to take a more relaxed approach to the drills – in truth, all the Corps cared about were my highly skilled hands – but at that time in my life I almost craved the physical exertion, or at least the numbness that followed it.

I wouldn't admit this to anyone, but the Japs did me a favour that sunny day in paradise. I was coming out of a bitter divorce and had spent the past two years in a daze of empty barrooms at dawn. Somehow I'd managed to observe my professional obligations as a physician, dragging myself through eleven-hour shifts at San Francisco Public, but the off-hours were, and remain, sketchy. So running five miles a day, negotiating ungodly obstacle courses and firing pistols at moving targets was a blessing because it exhausted the living hell out of me, and because it made thinking close to impossible.

Still, I had no idea what I was getting myself in for when I signed up with the Marines. Most of the people I knew, the

11

ones that weren't 4F that is, had been drafted into the Army. I would have happily gone that way too if it hadn't been for my uncle Leo, my father's baby brother. Nine months after my father and Leo left their native Prague on little more than a whim, and only six months after being released from Ellis Island, Leo fought with the Marines in France in 1917 as a newly minted American. The two years he spent serving his new country and earning the right to be called a citizen were the defining feature of not only his, but my whole immigrant family's life. I was going to war one way or another, so honouring his memory seemed the right thing to do. It would be my atonement for abandoning them all.

And so I became Captain Peter R. Sokol of the Third Division United States Marine Corps, Third Medical Battalion, on Christmas Eve, 1942. I was horribly miscast as an officer and everybody knew it, but I was an orthopaedic surgeon. Like it or not, the bastards needed me.

The Third Division set sail from San Francisco on the USS *Mount Vernon* on a wet and bleary New Year's Day. Six weeks later we arrived in Auckland, where the Medical Battalion was to build a hospital while the Infantry Division and Engineers trained for battle. I started to notice the light as we passed over the equator and wound our way down through French Polynesia. The alizarin crimsons and dreamy pinks of the evening sunsets reminded me of Gauguin, but the brazen fire white of the forenoon was unlike anything I could place in art. The farther south we travelled the more intense it became, so that by the time we entered the Waitemata Harbour I could barely keep my eyes open for the blistering glare.

The light in California is hazy and laconic; it rests on the material world like gossamer, distorting edges, the gaps between one thing and another. In New Zealand it illuminates everything with intensely bright, crushed-diamond haloes. I was interested in the difference because, in spite of my circumstances, I was still a painter. No matter how many days and months and years I'd spent in operating theatres cutting through flesh and wiring fragments of bone together, I couldn't help but see the world as a series of colours, shapes and geometric planes, all organised in parallel lines, rushing towards a vanishing point.

One notices the light in New Zealand first. Second is the rain. The first five days it poured down with the doggedness of clockwork – every noon hour and dusk like some ancient call to prayer. We were in a foreign land and we were being rained on by a foreign sky. High summer rain too, hard and straight and furious. When we weren't taking shelter the Third Medical spent those first few days setting up a twenty-six bed general hospital in the Victoria Park camp. Victoria Park, the place I was about to call my home, wasn't much more than three or four football fields of grass on doubtful land not long reclaimed from the nearby harbour. It wasn't much of a location for a hospital. In wintertime the field turned into an unremitting bog that threatened to swallow us all. And directly across the road to the west, at the foot of Franklin Road, adjacent to a pub known as the Birdcage, was Auckland's homage to Victorian bleakness – a redbrick, municipal council garbage dump set against a great monolith of a chimney that the locals referred to as Perfectus the Destructor, and which cast a pall of ripe, incinerated trash over the camp from morning to night. But who were we to complain?

Other divisions had been disbursed throughout the country's North Island, some having to travel as far south as Wellington. We were the last Marine division to arrive in New Zealand, but there had been a regular Army presence in the country since early '42. In fact, the Army had done all the hard work for us; the digs we inherited had been an Army camp, and the new hospital the 39th had built in Cornwall Park, complete with

13

over a hundred beds, meant our workload at Victoria Park was going to be light.

What surprised me was that the brass didn't seem to expect anything else. New Zealand was a long way off Washington's radar. It was too far away from the combat zones of the Pacific to be used as a launching pad for attacks on the Japs, and it had been calculated that the country was under no serious threat of attack. Our leisured hours, our spell of purgatory before the hell began, would only be interrupted by tending to the few wounded men who were deemed fit enough to be shipped out from the field or EVAC hospitals in the Pacific Theatre, from New Guinea, the Philippines, and eventually Guadalcanal. We were also responsible for treating the clumsy leathernecks who twisted their ankles or broke their wrists during training exercises. And so we built our makeshift hospital, pitched our tents and dug our latrines in the sticky late summer heat and in the pouring rain, all under a putrid and persistent cloud of Auckland's burning waste.

Initially the war planners tended to leave the medical personnel alone. In the first week we'd been camped I hadn't had to deal with an officer above the rank of major, which suited me fine. One of the benefits of being stationed at Victoria Park was that it was close to the central city hotels, so that most of the high-ranking officers had their quarters off camp. This situation would have been ideal if Cartwright hadn't elected to stay on camp himself. After what had happened in Frisco, and the tension that had followed on the *Mount Vernon*, I would have thought he'd have wanted to be as far away from the men as possible. The incident seemed to have cost him the promotion he so dearly coveted, and so I was genuinely surprised at first that he'd chosen to stay. But as the days passed I realised it wasn't the men Cartwright was concerned about. It was me.

Looking back now it is plain to see why Cartwright felt

as though he was obligated to me, but at the time I honestly didn't think I'd done him any great favour. We were both responsible for what had happened that night, and I knew that it would just be easier for everyone if I took the rap alone. I was an outsider, a Marine by default; that sort of thing would be expected from someone like me. But if they knew Cartwright had been involved it would have had implications for the whole Battalion.

It wasn't until our second week in Auckland that I finally found myself alone with Cartwright. It was early evening, and for once the rain hadn't come. That morning a dozen casualties from the Second Division had arrived from the Solomons for treatment. They'd been whacked hard in some snake pit of a delta called Rice Anchorage, trying to get at the Jap base in Munda. They were properly banged up, several of them with injuries to multiple body systems at once – thorax, skin, bones, gut. The guys in the EVAC hospitals on the islands did the debridement and even the definitive surgery where possible. Tough cases came to Australia or New Zealand, the kids they'd been able to patch up enough to keep alive, but who, for one reason or another, needed more surgical work or critical care.

I wasn't on duty that evening but Diddle, the eighteen-year-old company clerk from Des Moines, came to my tent to tell me Cartwright needed me in the post-op. I found him standing above a patient's bed halfway down the right-hand row, clipboard in hand. There were twenty beds in the post-op and most of them were filled. The long, rectangular room was lit with naked bulbs, which seemed to constantly gain and lose strength with the labouring tide of the generator. The place stank of ammonia and the minty astringency of plaster-of-Paris.

I stood behind him and cleared my throat.

'Where's your jacket?' he said. Cartwright was tall and ruggedly blond in an actorish kind of way. The night was clammy, and he had a thin film of sweat on his upper lip. He looked happy with himself, which was nothing out of the ordinary.

'I'm not on duty.'

'You're standing here, aren't you?'

I looked at the clipboard in his hand, then down at the patient in the bed. It was Private Walker. I'd operated on the kid earlier that morning. He had a compound fracture of the tibia caused by a land mine explosion he'd been unlucky enough to get in the way of. There weren't enough usable fragments in the wounded area to do an autogenous graft, so I'd had to mine the femur for more bone. I'd fastened the grafted bone to the tibia with a collar of vitallium screws, and left the wound open for deferred suture as the *Manual of Therapy* recommended.

'How's he doing?' I asked.

'Feel his toes.'

Cartwright pointed his pencil in the direction of Walker's foot. The tips of his toes were cold to the touch and the areas above and below the wound had recently swollen. I looked up at Cartwright, who was rocking on his heels, his spare hand buried in the front pocket of his white coat. He gave me the old familiar look, the very same hardened eyes and clenched jaw he'd regarded me with for years now.

'Vascular,' he said, redundantly.

'No kidding.'

'What do you mean no kidding? Did you check?'

As far as I could tell most of the patients were asleep, but there was the distinct sound of beds creaking around us, an audience forming.

'Of course I checked.' I flicked my head to suggest we leave the room but he wasn't going anywhere. 'Come on, Cartwright. The popliteal artery was in one piece. Anyway, we can just ligate it now.' It did feel bad seeing my error in the raw, but this was the kind of miss even the most experienced surgeon could make.

'You won't be doing anything.'

'What do you mean? He's my patient.'

He rocked back on his heels again and looked over my shoulder, his face loosening into a deadpan attitude of boredom. 'Colonel Ford is aware of the situation. He's going to try anastomosis in the morning. If that fails,' he said, taking a cursory look down at Walker to make sure he was asleep, 'the leg will have to go. In the meantime, he's no longer your patient.'

He replaced Walker's clipboard back on the hook at the end of his bed, then carried on up the row to the next patient.

'You're free to go now, Sokol,' he said, his back turned to me.

It was then that I had the horrible thought, the one that I had successfully avoided since I'd signed up, but the one I knew had always been coming: that this was my life now for God knows how long; that this was how it would be.

'Cartwright?'

He looked up from the bedside where he was seated on a stool, a quick, birdlike movement.

'It's Major,' he said.

'Sorry. Major. But I was just wondering something. Why did you choose to stay on camp? Why aren't you up at the Ambassador Hotel with the rest of them?'

He resumed his examination of the patient, running his pencil across the frame of a Bohler-Braun traction cradle. 'I didn't choose anything. Colonel Ford wants me here.'

'Why?'

He looked down at the floor then back up at me. He didn't have to say anything. It was right there on the face he was pulling, a very military face, a study of militariness. It said, because you can't be left alone. It said, because nobody trusts you. It said, because you're not a real Marine.

17

CHAPTER 4

I first met Cartwright at Stanford Medical School in '34. We were in the same class, shared all the same seminars and labs, but we barely managed five words to each other the whole of that first year. Cartwright was something of a celebrity at med school, getting himself elected to every social club and student body going. He traded on his name, which came with a long history of California congressmen, United States senators, and even a governor. And from what I knew of him at the time, Cartwright, with his level gaze and modulated tone, was nothing if not a politician. Like all good politicians he had a shit-eating grin for everyone – from the professor of neurosurgery to the assistant janitor – that he could turn on and off at a moment's notice. He was a mediocre student at best, but where he finished in the class was of little importance; his future had been mapped out in advance, and all that was required of him was that he turn up to class and go through the formal motions.

It wasn't until my second year at Stanford that I began to encounter Cartwright on a regular basis. While my science grades were shaky (I just scraped by in organic chemistry and natural physics), I'd shown an aptitude for basic surgery, which I simply put down to a painter's steady hand and a stomach not easily given over to queasiness. Because of this I was allowed to take the intermediate surgery elective. It was a small class of ten students presided over by Dr Mason Kendall, a renowned thoracic surgeon who'd been stripped of his status as a diplomate of the American Board of Surgeons after he was discovered fleecing methadone from Portland General, where he'd been a visiting consultant.

To my surprise, Cartwright was among the students lined up outside the lab on the first day of the semester. I was surprised by this because I knew Cartwright had taken the elective the previous semester. As we filed into the cool laboratory with its stink of sulphur and bleach, Cartwright shook every hand and looked flush into every set of eyes, including Kendall's. He made no mention of why it was he happened to be doing the class again – he just clasped your hand firm, gave you the open smile of a ten-year-old, and dared you to ask. Which of course no one did.

At the end of the first week, a week of inspecting, incising, slicing, hacking and suturing back together an endless procession of steely-cold cadavers, we were all summoned to Cartwright's villa in Pacific Heights for a weekend luncheon. I had a sense then, confirmed later by experience, that these gratuitous acts of hospitality had little to do with Cartwright's interest in his new classmates. They were simply a way for him to impose himself on an ever-increasing circle of connections, people who might come in useful one day. Cartwright hated outsiders so much that he took it upon himself to bring everyone in. That way everything could be known and there'd be no room for misunderstanding or confusion. It was old-timey and quaint, but I had a sentient eye for amateur politicians and their politics, and couldn't help but see the terrible cunning beneath the skin.

But on that first Saturday afternoon, playing croquet on the lavish expanse of lawn at the rear of his daddy's playhouse, I didn't give a damn about anything other than the strange creature who sat chain-smoking under the shade of a paisley

19

umbrella in the corner of the garden. She was pale, blonde, fierce and magnificently alone. I thought I caught her looking at me a couple of times, and this knowledge of being watched by her, this compelling need to be watched by her, made me clumsy and awkward and ridiculous. I couldn't have been very discreet because before long Cartwright wandered over to me, croquet mallet casually slung over his shoulder, linen pants rolled up to his knees, and nodded in her direction.

'My sister. Beth Cartwright,' he said, taking my arm in his hand and gracefully, pointedly, steering me back towards the game.

CHAPTER 5

The Victoria Park Camp was a typical military hospital set-up. The hospital itself, which included a six-bed theatre, a pre-op triage wing and a twenty-six bed post-op ward, was the sturdiest feature in the whole joint, made out of prefabricated pine wood wrapped in corrugated iron. Colonel Ford ran the administration of the Battalion out of a side office attached to the hospital. The rest of the camp was olive-green canvas – the latrines, the mess, the supply tents and the living quarters. As a captain I got my own tent, as did Cartwright, who, due to the night-time absence of Colonel Ford, had assumed the mantle of acting C.O.

Just behind Perfectus and the stinking garbage dump was Freemans Bay, a residential neighbourhood seriously lined with scores of plane trees and determined rows of almost identical narrow cottages, wedged together like keys in a typewriter. And at the top of Freemans Bay, ten minutes' walk from the camp, was the Ponsonby district, home to a number of public bars, community halls and clubs, a Red Cross, and several brothels.

We'd only been in camp a fortnight but already I'd had to treat several Marines for fractured jaws, cracked ribs, broken noses and other fight-related injuries sustained on Ponsonby Road. When one of our orderlies couldn't work for three days on account of the twelve stitches I'd had to sew into his eye

21

socket, Cartwright ordered a blanket suspension of all local leave passes until further notice. The move wasn't popular, and I knew it was just a matter of time before the men came to me seeking answers.

It was Saturday lunchtime, and I was in line at the mess when Sturgis tapped me on the shoulder.

'Waiting for some chow, Captain?'

I turned around to see Sturgis's pimply face grinning at me from under his pisscutter cap, which was at least a size-and-a-half too big for his head. He had the usual touch of controlled mania in his eyes, a look that seemed to propel his face forward at you while he remained perfectly still.

'No,' I said. 'I'm going to the ballet. What does it look like?'

'Oh, that's a good one, sir. I've got to write that down.'

'Take it easy, Sturgis.'

I let the cook slop some glutinous brown stuff onto my tray and was about to head to a table when Sturgis piped up again.

'Ah, excuse me, Captain. Do you mind if we, um, had a word with you.' He looked around the room. 'In, um, private.'

I could see now that he wasn't alone; O'Keefe and Timmins, like Sturgis, both orderlies in the unit, stood just behind him like a pair of well-behaved minions. The three of them were everything nineteen should be – awkward, impish and self-amused. The only difference was that they were in uniform, waiting to be shipped off to some Pacific hell-hole where, even if they could make it out alive, they would leave the best parts of themselves and never be the same again.

'Sure,' I said. 'Follow me.'

I led them over to the far corner of the giant tent, their trays laden with formless food. As we sat at an empty trestle table I noticed that all three of them were looking at me kind of funny. It took me a moment to figure out what it was: respect. After what had happened in Frisco before we sailed, I'd obviously grown in the men's esteem. Now I had the dubious honour of being the guy they trusted.

O'Keefe and Timmins set upon their food like wild animals tearing into fresh kill, every now and then remembering to come up for air. Sturgis barely touched his, remaining calm and poised until he had my full attention.

'What is it you want, Sturgis?' I said, finally taking my eyes off the feeding frenzy happening before me.

'Well, it's like this, sir. Me and Timmins and Oki here wanted to raise an issue with you. Um, in regards to the local leave issue.'

'Why are you talking like a city councillor?'

'I was brought up to mind my manners, sir. And with you being an officer and all—'

'What he means to say,' put in Timmins in his thick Texan drawl, 'is that that son-of-a-bitch Cartwright's taken our leave passes.' He pointed his fork at me from across the table, wildly punctuating the air. 'And you know what that means, don't you, sir? No booze. No snatch.'

'Pardon me for being so crude, sir,' said O'Keefe, also from some nameless shit-hole in Texas, 'but if I don't pop my cherry sometime soon I think my eyes are gonna shoot clean out next time I sneeze.'

'You dumb son-of-a-bitch,' said Timmins, looking sideways at O'Keefe. 'You only pop your cherry once. First time. And we all of us know your ugly cherry is lodged squarely up your momma's fat ass.'

O'Keefe made to stab Timmins with his butter knife but stopped two inches short of his nose. Sturgis cleared his throat and, surprisingly, the Texan Two cut out their act and went straight back to their food.

'Excuse me, sir, I apologise for my partners' directness, but I think their eloquence just now has shown you the seriousness of the situation.'

I liked Sturgis. He was everything I would have liked to have been at his age but wasn't. He was the natural centre of the group, but somehow detached. He was cynical, but not dangerously so, and he had that special kind of winning disposition that prevented any outward display of surprise or embarrassment. This last quality made him seem older and was responsible for, or so I was told, some of his greatest feats with the opposite sex. He was the kind of kid who went out of his way to bag forty-five-year-old Manhattan housewives, and whether he was successful or not didn't seem to matter. It was all story, all narrative.

Sturgis claimed he'd met me in Greenwich Village in the summer of 1940. I had no such memory but it was difficult for me to dismiss the claim outright, as I'd come across a lot of young guys like Sturgis around that time. I was still in the fallout from my divorce, and, desperate to get out of California, I had managed to secure a locum assignment in New York for twelve months. I rented a basement apartment on MacDougal Street, did my designated hours at St Peter's, and spent the rest of my time painting or drinking at Diane's or Blue Keys, or any of the other Village dives whose doors were open. I was a ghost, stalking the neighbourhood at night, my head reeling with booze, my ears ringing with Artie Shaw tunes. I stayed up all night painting in the damp bowels of my apartment. Outside of work I barely talked to anyone. I'd come to New York with the vague notion that my divorce had set me free, not just from my wife, but from the parallel world I'd mistakenly entered into when I signed up for med school a decade earlier. I'd never totally given up on painting. I took night classes from a former student of Marsden Hartley right through my internship at San Francisco Public, had subscriptions to *Art Front* and *Outlook*, and was still in the throes of a love affair with Picasso and Braque and Gris. As a young man I'd tried to instil my pictures with commentary

24

and message, but the more I painted the more I realised that there was simply nothing beyond painting. The beauty of Cubism was its distance from the messy humanness of the world around me. As a Cubist, all of my worldly concerns were reduced to an intense focus on the geometry of nature and the wicked irony of flattened perspective. These were the only things I had to care about, and over time they came to form for me an abstract, but altogether truer reality. My discovery of Cubism heralded a retreat from life I've never quite been able to stop.

But by the time I'd made it to the Village I was falling under the spell of my countryman, Stuart Davis. I combed the city's galleries looking for his work, for *The President* and the *Egg Beater* series of pictures. What was left of my salary at dawn went into canvas and pigments, oils and sabre. I was feverish with a desire to create, to emulate Davis's modernist renditions of the street, to beat shapes down to no more than two glorious dimensions, to slash railroads of black through my oversized canvases, to describe unknowable objects and fill them in with godly primaries, cadmium reds and yellows, the ultramarine of Van Gogh's final skies. There was a vision of my own in there as well, something arresting my startled eye during dead moments of a day, a vision of ochre and gold that was like a first memory. I burned with the notion of slapping down my colours in bold, impasto strokes in real time with the chaotic images flickering through my head, but when I tried to paint, something happened. Or, rather, nothing happened. I layered canvas after canvas with primers of thick white, eight, nine, ten layers deep. Titanium white, egg-shell white. I stayed up all night spreading it on but I couldn't take it any further. Every time I mixed a colour, a safe raw umber, say, to start off with, my arm would freeze in terror.

I had yearned for the chance to have this time, this space to do my work, but when I got it I clammed. The strange thing, though, was that I could not stop painting white. I filled dozens of canvases with dozens of layers, but I couldn't stop. I was painting over, erasing, making new. Whitewashing. I walked the streets late at night, skulked in cafes and bars waiting to see something, overhear something, but in the end it all started to feel like affectation. Kids like Sturgis, well-meaning but too young to know that they had to die. Everybody in the Village seemed to have a title for himself – free-verse poet, folk musician, surrealist, Dadaist. I spoke to no one but couldn't help feeling suffocated by this hang-up with definition. And so, by the time my locum assignment was up I was glad to get out.

With his oversized pisscutter and his Texan sidekicks, it was hard to see the Sturgis sitting in front of me as part of that world. But here he was in the flesh, all knuckles and bones and crocodile smile. He had been wandering across the Midwest when Pearl Harbor was hit, and, charged with story potential, he somehow made it to San Francisco a day later to sign up for the Corps.

I took to him instantly when the Third was formed at Camp Elliot. After eighteen months of divorced life I had become too indifferent for my own good. I thought the war might bring out some life force in me, some élan, and initially it had. But the rush I got on that day in December subsided very quickly as the monotonous routine of boot training took hold, strangling everything in its path. After a while the otherness of it dissolved, and I was back to where I had started. There was a lot of hysteria at the time but for some reason the war didn't seem exceptional to me. I later put this down to genetic disposition, a European inheritance of cramped living, of strife and hardship that was too fresh to be levelled out by American equanimity, but at the time it made me a pariah. To cover for it I had to feign deep seriousness and solemnity so that I wouldn't be found out.

But for Sturgis it was all experience. He wanted to be a writer, and had quit Columbia halfway through his freshman year to wander the country in search of words and sentences. The war was his chance to realise his boyhood fantasy of living like Hemingway, driving an ambulance, drinking and carousing, gathering material. He had put a lot of thought into this pageantry, and the last thing he needed was an asshole like Cartwright curbing his field trip. I felt I understood this. I think I even envied it.

They were all waiting expectantly for my response.

'So what do you want me to do?' I said. 'Cartwright's the one in charge.'

'All due respect, Captain,' said Timmins, pointing his fork at me again, 'but after what you did in Frisco, I'd say he owes you one.'

'I'd say you have him over a barrel, sir,' said O'Keefe.

'Just like your brother had you every night,' Timmins said. O'Keefe didn't flinch.

Sturgis cleared his throat again. 'We just thought that, seeing as we're not mighty busy here and all, you might be able to put a word in to Major Cartwright. On, you know, our behalf.'

'For morale's sake,' said Timmins.

I'd never liked this sort of thing; being prevailed upon, being cajoled into doing favours, working factions one against the other. I lacked the wit, the diabolical nature.

I told them I would see what I could do.

Later that afternoon, after I had finished my rounds in the post-op, I decided to take a walk up to the Ponsonby district to see what all the fuss was about. I was still finding it difficult to come to terms with summer heat in February. The air was thick and alive with moisture, so that even mild exertion left you slick with sweat. I could feel the salty beads of it surfacing on my brow and lip as I trudged up the gentle slope of Picton Street.

It was only late afternoon by the time I got to Ponsonby Road, but already there was a malevolent feeling of too-many-drinking-hours hovering over the village. The crowd was mainly American, the joint forces all represented, spilling out of the pubs and onto the streets. Men were clutching glass jugs of amber beer, singing, shouting, and cursing the earnest souls from the Red Cross who manned the prophylactic stalls dotted along the main road. There were a few military policemen, or M.P.s, hanging around, but they didn't seem too interested in any kind of law enforcement familiar to me.

Ponsonby Road itself was a curious mix of redbrick shops, restaurants and corner bars situated between clusters of private houses, the same kind of narrow wooden cottages and small villas that populated Freemans Bay. As I walked along, though, I noticed that not all of the houses were family homes, as many of them had small plaques and signs on their fences identifying themselves as women's associations, dental surgeries and church groups. A few of these houses were conspicuously unmarked, yet seemed to be attracting a lot of foot traffic from the young doughboys and leathernecks, not to mention the white-clad sailors. I took it that these were the places Timmins and O'Keefe so desperately wanted to visit.

I decided I'd seen enough and turned down Franklin Road on my way back down to Victoria Park. I'd only gone a few paces when I heard shouting in a strange language come from within the house I was passing, a small white cottage whose front door would have been no more than three or four yards back from the sidewalk. On the door of the house there was a small gold-coloured sign bearing the legend 'Ponsonby International Chess Club and Philosophical Society'.

I hung back for a moment out of instinct, but whatever it

was that had caused the shouting must have stopped. I was about to set off again when the shouting resumed, followed by a thumping noise as if someone or something were being thrown against a wall. I was about to step over the small picket fence to peer in through the front window when the door flung open and two men in dark suits emerged, dragging what looked like a very tall, very thin Oriental man – Chinese perhaps, although I was never one for picking races or creeds. The two suited guys threw the Oriental across the sidewalk and into the hood of a car parked on the road out front of the house. I stood completely still, a little dazed by the spectacle. The Oriental lay prone across the hood for a moment without moving. The men in suits didn't say anything, but when they turned they noticed me for the first time. Both of them did a quick double take. I didn't say anything but stood my ground. They were both pale and appeared quite ruffled by what had just happened. I looked at the Oriental, who was by that time unfolding his large, spindly frame from the hood of the car, and then back to them. The one on the left looked nervous and on the verge of saying something, but his friend, who wore small wire-rimmed glasses, put his arm out to stop him.

'Don't worry,' he said to his friend, but looking straight at me. His accent was English, like the toff English you hear in movies. 'He's only an American.'

The Englishman put his hand on his buddy's shoulder and guided him back to the house. Before they were through the doorframe the other man shot me a quick look as if he had just remembered something.

'Fucking Yank,' he said in a broad, short-vowelled New Zealand accent.

I laughed involuntarily, a short 'ha' from the dead air at the bottom of my lungs, but by the time it had got out the door had slammed shut. I turned back to the road to see if the Oriental needed any help, but he had vanished.

CHAPTER 6

Colonel Ford's anastomosis hadn't been able to save Private Walker's leg. The shrapnel from the mine had taken too big a chunk of the popliteal artery to perform an adequate retraction and suture. Which meant that he became my patient again.

Cartwright and I had been assigned the amputation, the hospital's first. We'd both been called in off-duty to perform the operation immediately, as Nurse Muller had correctly identified a spreading clostridial myonecrosis infection that would have killed him if left any longer. Cartwright had received the call after me, so by the time he made it to the O.R. I was standing over the anaesthetised kid in my scrubs, waiting to go.

'We're taking it off?' he said, holding up his scrubbed pink hands for Nurse Muller to glove.

'Looks that way.'

Cartwright approached the table and stood opposite me. He had his game face on but I could see the uncertainty in his eyes. Nurse Muller stood behind him, tying the thin straps of his mask.

'All yours, Major.'

He nodded at me and held my gaze a fraction too long. He was beginning to sweat.

'Okay, then,' he said, his voice sounding a little tinny. He held out his hand to Muller. 'Saw.'

'Sir?'

'Saw, goddamit. Let's get moving here.'

Muller looked up at me in a panic.

'What are you doing, Cartwright?' I asked.

'What does it look like?'

'Don't tell me you were going to do a guillotine.'

He was in a spot, and I could see he didn't know what to do. The *Marine Manual of Therapy* was continually being amended as new techniques or better practices emerged in the field in the Middle East and Europe. One such amendment had been the shelving of guillotine amputations in favour of the circular method. Cartwright had clearly missed the change.

His icy blue eyes were leaping out at me across the patient. He wanted to say something, wanted to recover his dignity in front of Muller, but nothing would come. A different person may have enjoyed the moment, but it was making me feel nauseous.

'I've done a couple of circulars back home,' I said, unable to look at him, at his desperate stinking Wasp pride lying flat on top of Private Walker. 'Why don't you assist me on this one?'

I made an incision just below the knee in an elegant circular pattern, guiding the scalpel as it descended into the sinewy tissue, pausing only to allow the skin to retract and run like a receding tide. At the point where the skin stopped I cleaved the exposed muscle in a series of lateral strokes, waiting for each layer to retract before cutting into the gristly periosteum membrane. Cartwright finally got his saw then, cutting through the dense anterior crest of the tibia, then leaning forward to work his way through the delicate fibula. We then set about the gardening work, tidying up the exposed nerves and ligating the weeping veins and arteries. Cartwright watched as Muller and I finished by delicately dressing the raw, tender stump, our hands eerily moving through the space just vacated by Walker's discarded shank. As soon as I stood back from the patient, Cartwright snapped off his gloves and blew out of the theatre.

Aside from the personal reasons, I found it hard to have any sympathy for Cartwright on a professional level. Missing the amendment to the *Manual* was no big deal. We all knew that we'd be required to improvise, to perform surgeries out of our specialties and wing it for the common good. What I disliked was the attitude that he was above the mistakes we'd all been told we would necessarily make. After breezing through med school in the bottom third of the class, Cartwright just happened to land a surgical internship at a private Los Angeles clinic with the leading plastics guy in the country. A friend of the family, as he put it. I'd heard rumours that this so-called friend of the family found his new protégé an inconvenient and potentially dangerous liability, but couldn't do anything about it. Young master Cartwright was on his way.

When I graduated I didn't get the private clinic, but what I did get set me up beautifully for the war. I did my internship at San Francisco Public under a mildly capable orthopaedic surgeon fast going to seed. I did all my learning at the table, turning over as many as fifteen procedures a week all thanks to car crashes, bar fights, football injuries, gunshots, and plain stupidity. I could have rotated into a different practice area, but ortho appealed to the painter in me. We cut flesh and tore it back until we got to the bone; whatever we were doing, we were always heading to the bone, to the primitive element. We used bone-punches, metal hammers, five-inch Smith-Petersen nails, steel wire, steel plates and screws. We were mechanics of the body. If I was going to be doctor then this was the only workable fit.

Cartwright was methodically lathering his forearms with

creamy white soap when I came in to the scrubroom. I threw my bloody apron down into the laundry basket and took a position alongside him at the next basin, holding my hands under a limp stream of tepid water.

'If you'd identified the aneurysm he would still have his leg,' he said, scrubbing his left hand with a nailbrush in fast, hard motions that made his skin turn bright pink.

'Jesus Christ. You think I don't know that?'

'Well, I'm just saying.'

'All right. I get it.' I could have said something about what had happened in the O.R. but I'd never fared well in point-scoring battles with Cartwright. Even if I was right, I just didn't have the energy or the tenacity to follow it through. I turned off the tap and started to dry off my arms and hands with a prickly white towel.

'Hey Cartwright, I wanted—'

'Major.'

'Right. Major. A few of the men have been asking me about the local leave. They say you've suspended it.'

He didn't say anything for a moment. He calmly rinsed the frothy soap residue from his skin, hit the tap, picked up a clean towel and took a couple of steps towards me, chest square, eyes level. I was familiar with this technique. He'd tried it on me several times over the years, including once in my own home. He was slightly taller than me and was heavy across the barrel, a physical characteristic he liked to take for gravity. He stopped two feet away from me.

'That's correct,' he said. 'You saw the chaos here last week. You really think we should be condoning that kind of behaviour? Captain?'

If my experience with the Cartwright family had taught me anything it was never to take a backward step. Tom was just the same as his father and grandfather and his brothers and uncles – all politicians of some description. They had a way of physically invading your space, of standing so close that their alpha personalities could paralyse you. Like the constant dinner parties and gatherings, the endless molesting handshakes, arm pats, chest points and backslaps were just another way of reducing your individuality, your difference, your unpredictability. The more they stood in your face and poked and prodded you, the less able you were to resist them. They knew this and they used it.

Initially I had fallen victim to the Cartwright cajoling, but after what had happened with Beth I'd grown a spine and had learned to challenge these little advances, these provocations. When Cartwright took a step forward, I took a step forward. So there in the washroom I was at it again, acting out my self-taught drama of defiance.

I said, 'It's not a matter of condoning, Major. They're kids, for chrissake. And come on, it's not like we're rushed off our feet here.'

'Those bastards aren't kids, Sokol. They're Marines. They've got a code to live up to and . . .'

'Come on, Cartwright,' I said, unable to contain a bitter laugh, 'spare me the code, would you.'

'What are you implying?'

His answer stopped me dead. I'd gone too far. In spite of everything, I didn't want Cartwright to think I had anything over him. I didn't really care what he did to me – he could bust me all the way down to private for all I cared – but I didn't want him to feel obligated to me. I'd known Cartwright long enough to know that being obligated to someone or something was inconceivable to him. He was the politician after all; he was the one who was supposed to hold the cards. I didn't want to get into any games with him, because I'd seen people lose at the hands of the Cartwrights before.

'Look, I'm not implying anything, all right,' I said, stepping away from him to change back into my khakis. 'I just think the morale here is going to get pretty low if you deny the men their leave.'

He stood rooted to his spot. I'd backed down, so there was nothing for him to prove any more. He started to chuckle and shake his head as if he'd just figured something out, alighted on an elusive solution, something so obvious it was funny he hadn't seen it earlier.

'Jesus, Sokol. You're a surgeon. You're a captain in the United States Marines. You don't owe these plebs anything. When are you going to learn to accept yourself?'

'What the hell are you talking about?' But I knew exactly what he was talking about, and he could tell.

He laughed again, condescendingly, and shuffled off to his locker to get changed. 'I'm not changing my mind, Captain.'

'Then what about just the orderlies? Sturgis and Timmins. And O'Keefe.'

'No,' he said, stepping out of his whites.

I was through with the conversation and wanted nothing more than to get out of Cartwright's presence, but I knew that if I didn't get the leave I'd have Sturgis and his crew on my ass all day.

'What if they're my responsibility?' I said.

'I've heard that before.'

I bit my tongue. 'No, come on, I'm serious. You can even tell Ford that I asked to have delegated responsibility for them. I mean it.'

'I don't owe you anything, Sokol. You know that, don't you.' It wasn't a question.

'Look, I don't—'

'Because nobody would believe you anyway. Not Ford, not Colonel Green. Nobody.'

'You're being paranoid, Cartwright. Nobody's blaming you for anything.'

He stood up and threw his dirty scrubs at my feet. 'All

right,' he said, coming close to me again, pointing his index finger into my chest. I could smell his warm, slightly stale breath. 'We'll do it your way. The bastards can have their leave. But it's your ass, Sokol. Your ass.'

CHAPTER 7

The drive to Los Angeles would only take a few hours, but I had decided to take my time and make a day of it. It had been, unbelievably, over five years since I'd last ventured out of greater San Diego, and now that I had decided to go I thought I'd revisit some of the spots along the coast that I'd been so drawn to as a young man.

I didn't know why I was going. I could always read Sturgis's book in the comfort of my own home, my studio and canvases within touching distance, with Missy quietly pulling the straggly weeds from her rose garden. And even if I did make it to the lecture hall at U.C.L.A., I couldn't imagine having the nerve or the gumption to actually approach him at the end. What would there be to say? He had written the book. If writing a book was anything like painting a picture, then I know that it's the work of art that counts. The mess of life or the mystery of nature behind the work tends to dissolve, to lose its structure and coherence, its very nature as something real. I have colleagues that like to talk a storm about their unnatural relationships with nature, but the only real artists I've met have been bigots, bigots for their own work, their own perception. It's not nature that appeals to them; it's their own ham-fisted view of it that counts.

Anyway, if I were in Sturgis's shoes I don't think I would like to confront the real-life model for my protagonist, my leading player. It's a whole different person in print – more insightful, better looking, a quirkier name and a stronger jaw. Real things are inevitably a disappointment. Plus, there was still the possibility that he hated my guts; that after all this time he still hadn't found it in himself to forgive me. I know that I certainly hadn't.

So while I didn't quite know why I was going, Missy had, in her quiet way, insisted that I go. It was about a week after the news-clipping episode that I discovered her approaching my studio door one dappled morning. I usually start work at around seven, but on that particular day I had struggled to get out of bed on time. When I got up I couldn't find Missy anywhere in the house, which was strange because she usually plays the piano in the mornings while I'm out in my stinky shed. When I say usually, I mean always. The woman has a formidable devotion to routine, which has gotten even sterner since she cut back her teaching load last year. The first two hours of the morning she devotes to her Steinway baby grand, playing everything from Bach's *Goldberg Variations* and Chopin's *Mazurkas*, to her favourite syncopated Gershwin masterpieces. The piano is followed by coffee and three hours of reading, journal articles and treatises from her field, monographs of contemporary pragmatists devoted to dead ones. When we first met she used to draw in the afternoons as well, still lives of fruit from the orchard, flowers from the garden. She would wrap her hair up in a blue cotton handkerchief and work on the slaughter table in the kitchen, bent over her thick bond in total absorption, her hands stained so black with charcoal she could have been a collier. But she no longer does this.

I was standing at the kitchen sink finishing my coffee when I saw her through the window, coming up the gravel path towards the house. Just this slight deviation from the daily schedule was enough to put me on alert. I shuffled across the Douglas-fir floorboards to the French doors that look out towards the studio and the orange grove beyond it. I could see that she was carrying a parcel of some description, and that her usual measured step was conspicuously out of rhythm. She looked hunched and nervous. She continued up the path to the junction that leads either to the back porch of the house or to the door of my studio. At this fork in the road she briefly paused and stole a quick look at the house. I hid myself behind the curtain, although from her angle she wouldn't have been able to see me anyway. I could see now that what she was holding was a hardback book. When she started off down the path to the studio the penny dropped. I quickly moved to the back porch, slipped on my old leather boots, and set off to catch her in the act.

The morning was all Californian – soft air laced with nascent heat, languid reds and oranges faintly sparkling in the turquoise sky. I walked on the dewy grass so she wouldn't hear the crunch of my footsteps on the gravel. I was thrilled in that moment, stepping through the beautiful morning, sixty years old and sneaking up on the woman I loved. She was just about to twist the knob.

'You never told me you'd taken up painting,' I said, trying to sound as deadpan as an English detective.

She jumped and spun around to face me all in one movement. She was lovely in her fright, her native grace momentarily gone, all guilt and earnestness. I looked at her for a moment, biting my bottom lip, strangely relishing the anxiety of the moment. I had turned this rickety little building into a symbol of jealously guarded pain, an excuse for my distance, my feeble reluctance. Yet standing there in the glassy morning I found I didn't really care any more. She clutched the book to her chest. I could see the title and the author's name.

'So, what, you're here to evict me?'

'You gave me a fright,' she said, smoothing the front of her Egyptian cotton dress, composing herself.

'If you're going to take the studio do you mind if I have the piano? Seems only fair.'

'Don't tease me, Peter.'

I wanted to hug her, squeeze her till she fainted. Truth of purpose was as close as Missy got to a fetish, and I could see she was mortified by the situation. In all the years we'd been together I'd never had the opportunity to impeach her motives or behaviour, not even a casual remark or word out of place. The book, still pressed up against her chest, stood between us like an elephant.

'I was just going to, to leave . . .'

'The book. I know.'

'I'm sorry, Peter. It's wrong of me to pressure you like this. I'll leave you be now.'

We looked at each other and I felt the surge in my stomach, the one that comes every now and then when she looks at me in that certain way, her eyes misty with silent, buried hurt. I'd been getting this feeling in my gut more often these last few years. I knew what it meant too. It was a little plague visited upon me, a chastisement for limply playing hostage to history, to something that happened on the other side of the world almost three decades ago. I wanted to say or do something to make it go away. I wanted to take a step forward, take her face in my hands, and ask her to marry me. But I couldn't.

I creased my face into a smile as she walked past me, still holding the book, back up towards the house. I stood where I was, looking at the studio door, at the knob where her hand had just been, listening to the crunch of gravel beneath her feet.

CHAPTER 8

On arriving in New York, my father worked as an apprentice for a wheezy Brooklyn sign-writer, a dinosaur of an Irishman famous for religiously putting away a quart of whiskey a night. When the gouty old bastard fell off his ladder one day young Tobias Sokol decided not to catch him. Instead he took over the business. He worked with an immigrant's thirsty zeal, and was able to save enough money to move my mother and me out to California when I was four years old. Years later, when I discovered that it was fashionable for painters to draw inspiration from the tasteless shapes and colours of commercial signs, I liked to pretend that it was my father who had bequeathed me my painter's eye, that in some unrecognised way he had been artistic himself, and that the creature had been passed to me by blood. But it was a lie, and I knew it was a lie even as I thought it.

Tobias Sokol's one and only work of art had been the brutal reinvention of himself. He fled Prague and his family not because of any oppression, but because he was restless and indifferent. He left his yarmulke at Ellis Island because he couldn't see what good it would do him in trying to make a living. We left Brooklyn because he was sick of being just another immigrant, just another Jew amidst all the other Wops and Micks. It is this and nothing else that I have inherited from him. This inexplicable desire for reduction, this need to

41

strip everything back, to pare myself down to the gristly core. This need to run.

I was only following his lead when I eventually left them for good. I would have gone to art school had it not been for an eleventh-hour scholarship offer to study medicine at Stanford. I had no interest in medicine at all; the only thing I had ever wanted to do was paint. But Stanford was at the other end of the state, which was as good as a world away. And so I became a doctor, not out of any sense of vocation, but because I was my father's son, because it put me at arm's length.

The regularity of our life together has programmed me to get hungry at exact hours of the day. I work all morning without giving a thought to food, and then at five minutes to midday, without notice or forewarning, I get a rush of weakness which leaves me barely able to hold my brush. It is at this time, without fail, that Missy will gently tap on my door to indicate that lunch is nearly ready. I found it reassuring to experience the same onset of weakness at the exact same time, forty miles from home, driving along the sun-scorched coast road on my way to Los Angeles.

I had spent a leisurely morning working my way north from the orchard, sidestepping the San Diego freeway and taking the back roads along the coast. I had already stopped in at a couple of beaches for nostalgia's sake. After the war I spent a good deal of time along this coast, renting beach houses for weeks at a time, splendidly alone. The eight days I had spent in the stockade at Camp Elliot on my return to the States had prompted a change in my thinking about what I wanted to paint. Up until then, when I had been able to get colours on to my well-primed canvases, I'd been somewhat doctrinaire in my adherence to the geometry and formal irony of Cubism. I'd focused on elemental and technical concerns at the expense of all else. I was in love with a beautiful theory precisely because it rejected reality. I had enough problems dealing with reality in my own life; I didn't want it imposing itself into my art.

That period up until I signed on with the Corps remains hazy in my memory, and in the years since I haven't been able to quite figure out what I was trying to achieve. In any event, the war brought about its end in no uncertain terms. And it wasn't just the death and the waste of the war that changed me. I was still an aesthete after all, and the things that were burned on my mind more than anything were colour and light. In New Zealand in particular the cold light of day was enough to burn holes in your retinas. You could almost see the radiation in the pale air. When the light shines so bright on things, real things, real people, it's hard not to notice them.

When I finally got released from the can, and the Corps, I fast learned that I wasn't the only one with new ideas about painting. Guys like Pollock and Motherwell were doing something different, abandoning pure lines for whatever flowed from the capriciousness of their shaky hands, peopling their work with these strange, quixotic shapes that I found deeply troubling. But of all of them it was Gorky who broke my heart. I had an inkling of what I wanted to do, but it wasn't until I went to New York for a week of reconnaissance that I found it. When I stood before *The Liver is the Cock's Comb* I almost wept. It wasn't just the technique, the inflected, almost musical palette, the vicious swathes of cadmium red like a sea of blood, or the haphazard outlines scratched beneath the paint that seemed like anarchy defined. No. It was the primal, almost anguished scrum of figures that arrested me, so desperate and lonely in their nearness to the human form. I had no words to describe what I saw, but I understood it as an expression of something real and essential and powerful. It was an explosion of colour and shape and intensity, but at the same time it was a reduction, an ellipsis. It was a

43

stripping down to the bone, to the marrow, to the astonishing inevitability of life passing into death. This was something I could understand.

And so I headed back west to paint, and to paint alone. I rambled my way up and down the Californian coast, living on the retirement fund I'd amassed prior to the war, cashing cheques and not changing my clothes. I painted for six, seven months straight, going from one cobwebbed beach house to another, my jaw locked in dumb silence, bleeding colour and indignity and loss onto canvas.

But all that happened a long time ago. I am an old man now, or at least approaching that irrevocable designation. I have long lost the desire to know why I paint what I do, or to fit it into any sort of programme or movement. The older I get the less I want to understand. I've spent years receding from life, and, if I could, I would pare back my narrow existence even further. Perhaps this trip of my mine, this foray up the coast, might just help to seal off another closet, strip off another layer of flesh on the slow journey to bone.

It was exactly twelve o'clock when I swung my tan De Ville into the lot of a roadside diner, a low-slung white building with blazing red sign-writing. I wasn't even halfway to Los Angeles. I parked between a large rusty, run-down truck and a dirty green VW van. The day was starting to heat up, so I didn't bother with my light overcoat, a garment I tend to take everywhere, no matter the conditions.

I could see the shape of the book underneath the coat, there on the passenger seat beside me. I hadn't decided whether I would read it or not. I gently pulled back the coat, cautiously, as if it were a blanket covering a sleeping child. The cover illustration was tastefully understated, a watercolour of a man and woman standing in the middle of what looked like a windswept field. The row of trees in the background were bent in the wind, and the two figures, their backs turned, stood close together so that it appeared as though they formed a couple. But on closer inspection the distance between them seemed to take on greater significance. It was as if they had come to the field alone, but the wind and the elements and the harsh absence of anybody else were pushing them together. Beneath this picture was a thick white banner with the title in plain black font: The Widow's Daughter, by P. Anthony Sturgis.

I ordered a grilled cheese sandwich and a coffee and took a seat in one of the booths running along the front window. The joint was surprisingly busy given the remoteness of the area. I was wondering when Sturgis had turned from Tony to P. Anthony when the waitress, a redheaded woman of around forty, brought my order. Just as she arrived a loud burst of laughter issued from the booth in front of me. The waitress and I looked up. In the booth sat three young men, no older than twenty-two, with long hair and scraggly beards, all dressed in colourful shirts and vests. There was also a young woman with long blonde hair and a magenta bandana tied around her head. She had inserted what looked like hawk feathers into the bandana at either side of her head, giving her a comical imitation Indian look. I had seen a lot of young kids dressed up like this lately – most of my sophomore class at San Diego State in fact. I guess I'd been too distracted in my own work to really notice the change take hold. One minute they were in crew necks and button-down shirts, the next they were dressed up like gypsies. The four of them were talking loudly about something to do with the war. The woman kept saying 'Nixon' as if she were calling a cat, or working out a song with one lyric.

They looked fairly innocent to me, but the waitress, whom I took for being the owner's wife (she had a proprietary air), looked down at me with a scowl.

'I'm sorry about them, mister. For some reason the dead-beats like hanging round these parts.'

'No need to apologise.'

I could sense that she wanted to continue the discussion, so I opened Sturgis's book to make out like I was reading. I stared at the first page for a moment, but could see out of the corner of my eye that she hadn't moved. After a few seconds I looked back up at her. She was still eyeballing the kids in the next booth, the leathery skin on her bony face drawn taut.

'What I don't get,' she said, presumably to me but looking at the kids, 'is where they get all their money from. Here it is a Wednesday morning, middle of the working week, and these deadbeats have been sitting here the best part of two hours.'

She said all of this in a voice loud enough to be heard throughout the diner. She clearly wanted to attract their attention, but for the time being the four of them were still lost in their own loud conversation. She looked at me for support, but all I could offer her was an oblique raised eyebrow. The last thing I wanted was to get involved in any kind of scene, particularly with this woman at my flank. She looked back at the kids, who'd quietened down some.

'Nope. No sir. Money's obviously not a problem for these ones.' She looked down at me quickly, conspiratorially. 'Most folks in here, sir, are like your good self. Honest workin' people. I'd say that'd give them a right to eat their lunch in peace.'

A hush fell over the room, the only sound being the spit and hiss of hamburgers frying on a grill. I couldn't bring myself to acknowledge her, but I knew the book was a useless prop. I looked up to see one of the guys in the group looking straight at me. He had a big mop of dark frizzy hair, pale skin, and wore a pair of black horn-rimmed glasses. He plucked the cigarette from his mouth and blew out a stream of purple smoke.

'Hey, what's your problem, old man?' he shouted.

I couldn't even hear the hamburgers any more. I could feel every pair of eyes in the diner boring in on me.

'Nothing's the problem,' I said, hardly believing the words were tumbling out of my mouth.

'Do we offend you or something, man?'

I could see he was very pleased with this question, as he looked around at his friends with a smirk. I said, 'No.'

'Are you threatened by us or something, man? Think we might start shooting up the place?'

At this the waitress lost all control. She started screaming and ran towards the kitchen. People stood up from their chairs, and a deep murmur rippled across the room. I looked back at the kids. The smugness was gone and they looked alarmed. After a second or two a big, bald, hairy-knuckle type came flying out of the kitchen heading straight towards their booth, baseball bat in hand. At the sight of him the four of them jumped out of their seats and ran for the door. I watched them out the window, in the brilliant daylight, running and laughing and piling into the VW van. The owner wasn't chasing them any more, but they screeched out of the parking lot in a hurry.

A couple of people, regulars maybe, got up to shake the owner's hand as he proudly wandered back to his kitchen. I tried to bury my head in the book in all the confusion, but the waitress made a point of coming back to my table.

'Sorry for all the bother, mister. Sandwich is on the house.'

I smiled thinly and nodded, quickly turning back to the book. She lingered for another moment or two, so that I actually had to start reading the thing. When she finally left I'd read enough to know that Sturgis could write. Well. The son-of-a-bitch.

I ate my sandwich and read through another couple of pages while the place calmed down. The writing was fluid and well constructed, but as with the news clipping I didn't recognise the voice. It didn't sound like Tony Sturgis to me. As I continued to read I was almost saddened by how mature and level the tone was. I had liked Sturgis a lot; he was a special nineteen-year-old. I was glad that he'd grown to be an intelligent and talented man, but the truth of it was that what I wanted to hear was the cocky Bronx kid again, the firebrand who read Faulkner in the jungle but couldn't spell.

The redhead refilled my coffee and I kept reading. It was pure voyeurism, as if I were a pallbearer at my own funeral. One thing struck me as odd, though. He had a character that fitted the description of Cartwright, but he started the story in Auckland. If I was telling the story, and it was my story, I would have started back in San Francisco the week before we sailed. It was there that the problems began.

CHAPTER 9

Our training at Camp Elliot had finished a week before Christmas. By the twentieth of December the Third Division had been assigned to its various units, one of which was the Third Medical Battalion. I'd known for some time that it was likely that Cartwright and I would be working together, but actually hearing our names being read out one after the other left me cold. I had thought, hoped, that when my divorce finally settled eighteen months earlier that I would be rid of Cartwright for good.

The battalion relocated from Camp Elliot to Frisco on Boxing Day, 1942. We were to have four days of local leave before we sailed on New Year's Day. The only restriction on the leave was that you had to wear uniform at all times and be back at base by midnight.

I'd kept my head down at Elliot and did what was asked of me, but the code didn't come easy. I understood the basic philosophy of discipline and order, but the officer caste thing was the real problem. Some of the orderlies and drivers were as old as I was, and a few of them better educated and smarter than me by a long shot. I found it hard to swallow that I was their superior, which I guess meant that I missed the point entirely.

Cartwright's presence alone was enough to keep me from the officer club gatherings, but this other thing, this inherited awkwardness, sealed it. I couldn't fake my entitlement to the bars on my lapel around the likes of Ford and Green. They knew and I knew, so I figured the less they had to confront me, the imposter in their midst, the better. I was happy to be just another grunt on the line.

And so I inevitably gravitated towards the enlisted men. When we got to the Frisco base I had no intention of leaving it until we sailed, but just after chow on the morning of the twenty-seventh I ran into Sturgis and Timmins on the yard. They were shooting some hoops and goofing around in the wan sunlight. Sturgis had been my partner in an obstacle course drill at Elliot, and I had taken a liking to him straight away. I sat down on a bench at the edge of the court to watch their game, but as soon as I had taken my seat Sturgis fired a bullet pass at me. I fumbled it like a klutz.

'Come on, Captain,' he shouted. 'Look sharp.'

'These are surgeon's hands, buster. I can't go round catching basketballs. There'd be anarchy.'

They both laughed.

'Come on, sir,' said Timmins, waving me over. 'You're up.'

I threw the ball back at Sturgis. 'No, I'm good. You guys go for it.'

Sturgis fired the ball straight back at me and this time it stuck.

'Too late,' he said. 'Shot clock's ticking.'

At this O'Keefe emerged out of nowhere and started screaming for the ball; apparently we were a team. I started a slow dribble, hang-dog and languid. Sturgis was on me like an animal, his big bony hands waving circles in the air, waiting to pounce. I edged forward slowly, trying to find an opening for O'Keefe, but Timmins had him locked. I stepped forward then back, trying to break into the keyhole. Pretty soon the trash talk started.

'Okay,' said Timmins, elongating his Texan drawl. 'You can dribble. We get it.'

'Idea is to get it in the basket, Captain,' said Sturgis.

Timmins yelled, 'Ten seconds. Nine, eight.'

I fired a pass to O'Keefe, who took it well. He pivoted on his left foot and managed to turn Timmins inside out. He made a drive at the basket but Timmins had recovered and was back on him. His surprisingly deft move had drawn Sturgis into no-man's land, so he fired the ball back at me. I caught it clean on the free-throw line. I was open. Timmins yelled 'Two seconds!' I set myself, propped on my knees and released the shot. It felt great off the tips of my fingers, a little physical intuition that it would drop. I must have squinted or blinked in that moment because the explosion of sound as Sturgis slapped the ball in mid-flight came to me in darkness. I opened my eyes just long enough to see the black orb of the ball, surrounded by a fiery halo of sun, within an inch of my face. In the instant that I put the sound and the image together the ball hit me flush on the forehead, and I was sent flying back four or five yards, out of the keyhole, onto my ass.

I wasn't out but my head rang like hell. When I finally recovered my vision, Sturgis, Timmins and O'Keefe were standing over me. I brought my hand to my forehead to check for swelling, but there was none.

'You, ah, you okay, sir?' asked Sturgis timidly.

I looked up but all I could see were three silhouettes fringed with sunlight. I stuck my hand out to O'Keefe, who pulled me up.

'You want me to get you anything, Captain?' he said, a little sheepishly.

They looked nervous as hell. The only thing I could think was that these kids were going to be orderlies in a warzone, and yet here they were, standing around a basketball injury, looking at their feet.

'That's a foul,' I said. 'Two shots.'

'Right on it's a foul,' said O'Keefe after a brief pause.

Sturgis laughed and slapped me on the shoulder. 'No disrespect, sir, but that ain't no foul. I'm afraid you just got hit with the block of the century. You can bust me if you want, but I ain't conceding no foul.'

I looked at Timmins, who still wasn't sure whether he was in trouble or not. 'What do you say, Timmins? Contact with the head. Foul, wasn't it?'

He looked back at me with his mouth open.

'See,' I said. 'Three against one.'

'Can't argue with democracy, sir,' said Sturgis, his open hands in the air.

'Shut up and check my pupils for dilation.'

As Sturgis did this I could see Cartwright over his shoulder, marching across the yard towards us.

'They're fine,' said Sturgis. 'Hey, um, sir, me and a few of the guys here were planning on taking a night out on the town tonight. You know, last night of freedom and all, and . . .'

They saw Cartwright, and within an instant all three of them stiffened like boards and snapped salutes. I was still a little dazed by the knock, and the sudden change of attitude caught me by surprise.

Cartwright cleared his throat. 'At ease,' he said to the men. He gave me a queer look. 'What's going on here? I looked over and saw that you were on the ground. Captain?'

'I'm fine, Cart . . . Major. We were just playing a little ball and I took a knock.'

'You were playing basketball?'

'Yeah. Basketball.'

He stood there for a moment, just standing, not saying a word. At first I thought he was angry, but that wasn't it. This sort of thing had happened at Elliot as well. He'd stroll into a group of men who were playing cards or shooting the breeze and just stand there. I couldn't read it at first, but pretty soon the penny dropped. The Corps is all about order and hierarchy, sure. But an officer who can't relate to his men, who can't command the respect of his men, is a nobody. Cartwright knew this. Guys like Ford and Green, for all their brass, were admirable men, even likeable at a stretch. Cartwright had never had to deal with dickweeds from Texas before, never had to handle lippy New Yorkers, or the brooding, masturbating sons of Midwest crop farmers. They may as well have come from a different planet. The problem for him now was that in order to advance he had to be their leader, or at least be seen to be their leader. And to be their leader they had to want to follow him.

'What's this about a last night of freedom?' Cartwright asked.

The question was directed generally to the group, but nobody seemed willing to pick it up. O'Keefe coughed loudly a couple of times. It was up to me.

'It's nothing, Cartwright.'

'It didn't sound like nothing to me.'

I shrugged my shoulders. 'The men have organised a night out on the town tonight. Given that we're sailing in a few days.'

'I see.' He dug his hands into his trouser pockets, flapped his loose wings a couple of times, and stretched his face into a thin smile. 'Well, there can't be any harm in that. I reckon I'll come along, if you don't mind.'

O'Keefe had stopped coughing but kept his hand cupped over his face, now masking a wince.

'Sure,' I said. 'Why not?'

'Okay then.'

'Okay.'

If Cartwright hadn't come along when he did I would have thanked Sturgis for the invitation and politely declined. If he'd pressed me, I would have made up a half-assed excuse, something to do with my health, a death in the family, anything to avoid the responsibility of chaperoning a group of boozed-up, horny, reckless nineteen-year-olds on a last lark before the fighting started. By inviting himself, Cartwright had drawn me in. I'd spent enough nights manning the emergency room at San Francisco Public to know that last nights out have a tendency to end up in cuffs or traction, or, in some cases, both. If Cartwright was going to go, I had to keep him away from them.

The night started off awkwardly. We were the only officers in the group, and I could see that the others – three more orderlies whose names I didn't know and a couple of staff sergeants with faces like dockside toughs – were none to happy about our presence. One of the sergeants, Kazanski, was in fact a longshoreman in real life. He had a meaty forehead and nose, and deep-set lines like gashes running down the flesh of his cheeks. He was the oldest of the enlisted men, around twenty-six or twenty-seven, and I could tell by the look of him that whatever living I'd done in my life he'd done triple. The men seemed to defer to him whenever a decision had to be made – what to drink at the Dalrymple on Ashbury, when to leave the Whiskey Bar on Central – but he was benevolent in his authority, a dictator dressed as a consensus man.

The city was awash with khaki green and starched white. On every corner groups of doughboys, leathernecks and sailors leered at women, drank and sang, all to the tune of endless whistle notes blown by harried M.P.s trying to break up fights. By the time we got into Fat Sally's on Stanyan Street, the fourth sawdust-floored venue of the evening, the tension between Cartwright and Kazanski was starting to get out of hand. Cartwright, trying to be one of the boys, had gotten himself drunk and was starting to act stupid, encouraging the men to drink more and stronger shots, baiting them into doing juvenile things like fleecing the eight ball from a pool table at the Dalrymple while two Army guys were playing; like jumping on stage with the band to sing 'Bye Bye Blackbird' at the Whiskey Bar. The younger guys were lapping it up, but I could see that Kazanski had been around the bend too many times to think that this sort of thing could work out well.

As everyone was taking a seat at a large table in the back of the saloon, I took Cartwright by the arm and led him towards the bar. The booze had made him limp and pliable, and he followed me without a struggle.

'What? Where are we going, Sokol?'

The bar was in the shape of a horseshoe, and most of the clientele – servicemen of every description, the odd slickly dressed Italian, a few whores – were congregated at the bend of the shoe, spilling out across the sawdust floor towards the big, wide-open doors. I shepherded Cartwright to one of the far ends of the shoe, which was dark and relatively unpopulated. I pushed him down onto a barstool.

'Hey, what gives, buddy?'

'Nothing gives. I just wanted to buy you a drink is all.'

'Oh.'

He was a pathetic drunk, his uniform all rumpled, hat askew, his mouth wide-open and clownish. I finally managed to attract the attention of a barman.

'Two club sodas, please.'

Cartwright quickly pounced. 'Hey, hey, come on, Sokol. Get me a real drink, would you.'

'Why not just ease up a little, huh? Come on. We're in charge of these guys.'

He gave me as level a stare as possible, mouth closed, eyes focused. 'Two shots,' he said to the barman. 'With chasers.'

When the drinks were in front of us Cartwright made to head over to the table, but I grabbed him by the arm for the second time.

'Have a drink with me, Cartwright. Come on, now. It's been a long time.'

He eyed me suspiciously before clasping my shoulder. 'All right,' he said, flopping back onto his stool. 'Why not?'

I desperately didn't want to do this, but I had to keep him away from the men, and Kazanski in particular, for as long as possible. My hope was that after ten minutes or so he'd forget all about them and I'd be able to lure him out the door and back to the base.

We held up our shots and clicked them together before knocking them back. I closed my eyes as the old familiar burn passed down my oesophagus and the sweet, overripe taste of Kentucky bourbon came alive in my mouth. It was a tremendous feeling. I'd been teetotal ever since I signed on for the Marines six months earlier, and this brief foray back into the action was reminding me why I loved it so much, and why it was imperative I never touch it.

We both let a short silence fall, a pregnant pause rich with backstory and anger. There was so much to say and not to say to Cartwright that I almost couldn't bear to look at him, sitting where he was, absurdly out of place in a roughneck bar. I was about to say something – my heart momentarily full of conciliation – when the wild snap of a snare drum cracked the thick air, followed by the deep rumbling of a bass, the running water of a tinny piano, and the urgency of a gang of horns, four or five of them all at once. With one heaving motion scores of bodies surged towards the dance-floor. The band was doing the latest Benny Goodman stuff, 'Sing Sing Sing' or something like it. I looked over at our table, which had been deserted – I just managed to catch a glimpse of Kazanski pushing his chair aside and slicking back his jet-black, Brylcreemed hair, ready for action.

I turned back around to see Cartwright ogling a young blonde in a scarlet-red dress who was walking by us on her way to the powder-room. She couldn't have been any older than twenty-one, but the style of dress and the thick lashing of makeup on her face gave her a certain air of movie star maturity. Cartwright flashed a toothy smile at her, which she returned with a studied flicker of her pencilled eyebrows. As she passed she lightly brushed Cartwright's arm and said, 'Evening, Major' without stopping. We watched her as she disappeared into the throng at the edge of the dance-floor. I suddenly felt very old and tired.

'Did you see that, Sokol? I mean, did you see that?' said Cartwright, as exhilarated as a schoolboy.

I had a sudden desire to punch him in the face. 'Women like that aren't real. They're illusions.'

'That's real deep, Sokol. Anyway, I know what I saw.'

'Have you seen Mildred? Since you got back from Elliot?'

He looked up at me quickly, his blue eyes cool and sharp again. Ever since my divorce from Beth, and even before that, he didn't like me talking about anyone in his family with anything resembling familiarity or connection.

'Tomorrow,' he said eventually, taking a long pull on his beer.

Cartwright had married Mildred Shackleton six weeks after Beth and I staged our little elopement act. They had known each other as children, their families loosely coming from the same patrician stock. Mildred was as thin as a rake, with fair skin and rust-coloured hair, and was five years Cartwright's senior. Her father and Cartwright's uncle were partners in a white shoe San Francisco law firm, and the marriage was, I believe, a pure face-saving quickie, a way for the Cartwright family to restore some dignity to the line after the scandal involving their black sheep of a daughter. It was as close as you'd get to an arranged marriage in America, and Cartwright had never forgiven me for it. To make matters worse, poor old Mildred turned out to be barren.

He must have read my thoughts because he turned to me, and in the ugly body heat and noise of the bar, said, 'You're a son of a bitch, you know.'

I didn't answer. I didn't even look at him. Instead I called the barman over for another couple of shots.

'You're a son of a bitch, Sokol.' The tone of his voice hadn't changed.

The barman lined up the shots and we knocked them back without ceremony. I felt the sudden chest burn and gut surge. I was ready now. I'd been waiting for this moment for almost two years. Cartwright had never so much as mentioned Beth to me in all that time, but I had seen the indignant fury in his eyes, heard the grievance in the timbre of his voice, felt it in the backdraft of every one of his movements. I was prepared. I would let him spit out his Yankee rage and I would say nothing. And then from the moment he shut his mouth our association would be finished.

But instead he said, 'The men respect you for some reason. All of them. And, I mean, you're pathetic for chrissake.'

I looked at him with what I thought was bitter disappointment, but which he seemed to interpret as offence.

'As a Marine, I mean. I guess you're a passable doctor. But Jesus, Sokol. Come on. You're not an officer's asshole.'

I looked around the saloon, at all the kids flinging each other about the dance-floor.

'What are you doing here, Cartwright?'

He leaned in to me conspiratorially. He was about to say something and then stopped at the last minute, looking up at me as if we'd just met.

'What is it?' I said.

I could see that he wasn't sure whether he should say anything, but that the excitement was getting the better of him.

'Don't tell anybody,' he said, 'but I've been looking at the plans for New Zealand.' He looked over his shoulder to check that nobody was listening. 'It seems that Colonel Ford isn't going to be quartered with us at the hospital. Do you know what that means?'

'Tell me.'

'It means that I'll be ranking officer,' he said, tapping his chest hard with his thumb. 'And you know what that means, don't you?'

'I can think of a few things.'

'It means a promotion, Sokol.' He was down to a whisper now, like a kid at confessional who knows he has to fess up but is mighty proud of his sins anyway. 'It means I'm going to be a colonel!'

Just at that moment I felt a damp palm on my shoulder and turned to see Sturgis, his face glowing red and slick with sweat from dancing. He had a buxom brunette in a pink and white dress hanging off his shoulder. He seemed to be having the time of his life.

'Here you two are,' he shouted, his sense of pitch and volume all gone from standing too close to the band. 'Come on back over to the table.' He grabbed me by the shirt sleeve and started pulling me after him. I managed to shake him off and turned back to Cartwright, but he was gone, already two steps ahead of Sturgis on his way to the dance-floor.

Timmins and O'Keefe had clearly struck out, as they were back at the table nursing their beers, looking resignedly up as Kazanski and Quinn, the other staff sergeant, were quickly rounding the bases with their dance partners. I took a seat next to Timmins and gave O'Keefe a sympathetic nod.

'How come the sergeants get all the action?' I said, unable to resist a little dig.

'Pardon me, Captain,' said O'Keefe, 'but that limey son-of-a-bitch Quinn ain't gettin' no action. She's just biding her time till it's respectful for me to cut back.'

Timmins, noting my confusion, looked at me deadpan.

'Sergeant Quinn up there done cut in on O'Keefe,' he said, the smile only showing in his eyes.

'I see.'

'That randy bastard,' O'Keefe said, suddenly buoyed by something. 'Hey, Major Cartwright's making the big play.'

I looked over to the dance-floor, where Cartwright was trying to cut in on a young civilian who was dancing with the blonde in the scarlet dress. The young guy, dressed in a shiny bottle-green suit, didn't look too happy about having his lunch cut for him.

Timmins and O'Keefe were laughing hard, rocking back on their chairs, good old boy style.

'I'd be careful if I were him,' said Timmins.

'Why?' I said.

'That wop he just cut in on is Lucio Grasso's nephew.'

'Who?'

'Lucio Grasso. You know, the bookie. The one heading straight for Major Cartwright now.'

The kid in the green suit had skulked off to the bar and stood there pointing in Cartwright's direction. The so-called Lucio Grasso, a bear of a man in an even shinier green suit, had started walking in the direction of his nephew's pointed finger.

Cartwright, who seemed to be doing famously with the blonde, had his back turned to the oncoming bookie. Timmins and O'Keefe, who had sensed quicker than I what was about to happen, had sprung to their feet and were trying to make their way to Cartwright on the dance-floor. But there were too many swirling bodies in the way. I stood trapped behind a young sailor in his whites doing a bad version of the samba as Grasso grabbed Cartwright by the lapels and tore him away from the scarlet dress.

It all happened so fast, but at the same time it seemed that I could see every frame happening in isolation. Sturgis, who had somehow made it back onto the dance-floor with his brunette, tried to squeeze his small frame in between Grasso and Cartwright. Grasso's clenched fist had already been drawn back to a position beside his right ear, cocked and loaded. What had meant to break Cartwright's nose instead caught Sturgis flush on the jaw with a primitive, dull thud. He dropped to his knees, teetered for a stunned moment, then flopped to the floor. The band kept playing, but most of the people on the floor had stopped dancing and formed a ring around the action. Having disposed of Sturgis, Grasso now looked up at Cartwright and cocked his fist again. Cartwright stood absolutely still, a rabbit in headlights. Just as Grasso was about to deliver the king hit, though, I saw a blurred image of what looked like Sergeant Kazanski flash across the scene, and heard the watery crush of a beer bottle smash against the side of Grasso's head. Kazanski fell to the ground on the back of his victim, but was up in a breathless instant. Time stopped for a silent moment, just long enough for my brain and eyes to slip back into alignment, before somebody hollered the inevitable yelp and the brawl started. I got down on my hands and knees and crawled under a canopy of wild swings and haymakers to where Sturgis lay unconscious on the ground. He was knocked out all right, but his breathing was regular. I tried to get to Grasso but couldn't make my way past a pair of doughboys doing a pretty accurate Greco-Roman wrestling impersonation on the ground. I was thankful then for the mad screeching of the M.P.s' whistles as they stormed the saloon. When I finally got back to my feet a team of M.P.s were putting cuffs on Kazanski. Another was attending to Sturgis, who was beginning to come round.

Cartwright was nowhere to be seen.

CHAPTER 10

'You okay, mister?'

The words were like a blow to the head, and I felt myself jump like a thief. I turned to see the redheaded waitress standing over my booth, coffee pot in hand.

'You been staring out that window for the best part of an hour,' she said.

I leaned back into my seat tiredly, feeling as though I'd just been roughly awoken from a dream. I didn't know what to say to her.

'You want some more coffee?'

'No thanks,' I said.

Mercifully, she went away. I looked back out the window at the parking lot and tried to recapture the outline of my daydream, but all I could get were fragments and images that wouldn't fully realise, that wouldn't cohere. It had been the first time in years that I had consciously followed a memory from that time. Of course I lived with the flashes and shards of memory that forced themselves into my daily thoughts, but at some point I'd made myself stop following the narratives.

I closed Sturgis's book and absent-mindedly studied the cover image again. Although he hadn't started at Camp Elliot, Sturgis had got most of it right, the early stuff that I had read at least. As a painter, I understood why he would want to maintain an element of mystery in his characters' development. I like to think my own work does something similar, stripping away the glut of context. Some things are better shown than explained, as I like to tell my students. And besides which it would have been too much of a mouthful to go into why I took the rap for all the trouble that night. Why, when we got back to base, Cartwright had dobbed in everybody and whitewashed himself of any wrongdoing. Why Kazanski had been transferred to a different company and busted down to corporal. From a style perspective, for the sake of narrative flow, it was better to leave a cloud over all the background and just put us in Auckland, harbouring unnamed grudges, and only vaguely intimate the root cause.

The diner was nearly empty now. The lunch rush was over and the redhead and her husband were going about their miserable routine, wiping the tables that they'd wiped a thousand times before, scraping the animal fat from the grill, counting the disappointing takings. My instinctive dislike of the redhead started to soften as I watched her count the grimy banknotes, expertly dividing the bills into units of one, five and ten. The husband lumbered around behind her, refrigerating this, wrapping that.

I looked at the cover of the book again and wondered if the picture had been specially commissioned for the novel. I'd only read the first of six chapters, but I had a fair idea of where it was all going. And if I was right then the picture on the front, the two anonymous people on that windswept field, seemed a pretty accurate synopsis of the story. In spite of myself I opened the book and scanned through the second chapter, then the third and the fourth until I found her. The subject. The whole point. He'd changed the name, of course, but I recognised her instantly. It was like looking at an old, forgotten photograph of your first love, the pain still there, palpable, inexplicable.

He'd called her Eliza Wilson. EW. Emily Walters. Emily Wasserman. English woman.

I couldn't help but read a page or two involving Sturgis's EW. It was a thrilling, weightless experience. She was certainly much changed, this Eliza Wilson, and, knowing what I knew about the arc of the story to come, I wondered how Sturgis would make it all turn out; whether he would, in his figurative way, forgive me. But for now I was relieved he'd taken licence with her. I didn't want anyone remembering her in such detail, and I didn't want anyone to falsely bring her back to life.

Emily Wasserman. Emily Walters. The English woman.

I couldn't say why Sturgis had changed her so much – whether it was out of respect for me, which was unlikely, or because rendering her as she actually had been was just too implausible. I know that in the years following the war I'd certainly struggled with the impossibility of it, how contrived she and her family were for that time, that place. I liked it that Sturgis had made his EW a New Zealander. A local girl, a Kiwi.

It rang true.

CHAPTER 11

By mid-March we were getting more wounded into the hospital, and life at Victoria Park had started to settle into a routine. The Second Marine Company had made full-scale landings on Guadalcanal, and was in the process of trying to secure the island so they could build an airstrip. We only got blanched versions of events in *Stars and Stripes*, but the glassy, fretful eyes of the wounded gave a fairly good indication of the true story.

Cartwright had relented and given the men their local leave. Some even managed to swing two-day passes to trip around the North Island. Sturgis and O'Keefe had gone to a place called Rotorua, a stinky, geothermal wonderland of hot mud pools and stale beer.

These trips to the provinces of New Zealand, which were largely encouraged by the brass, were supposed to double as public relations exercises with the locals. In March of '43 there was still a blackout on all press reporting of the American presence in the country, an especially lame attempt to fool the Japs into thinking we weren't there. Although, as time passed, I began to learn that the censorship probably had less to do with fooling the Japs than it had to do with placating the locals. The fights I had seen on Ponsonby Road were apparently taking place throughout the country, with a couple of small-scale riots breaking out somewhere in Wellington, and one in Queen Street in Auckland. The local men were naturally pissed at the way their women were throwing themselves at the U.S. servicemen. Then there were the local Maoris, the native people, who didn't take too kindly to the attentions of the Southern elements of our presence.

In fact, on their return back to camp from Rotorua, I had to rebreak and reset O'Keefe's nose after an incident involving a pitcher of beer, a pool cue, and a forty-year-old Maori farm labourer. I had O'Keefe sitting upright on a table in the O.R. Sturgis and Timmins had come in to watch the show: Timmins just for fun, Sturgis to watch O'Keefe suffer for just about getting him killed.

'You dumb piece of shit, Oki,' Sturgis said, standing to the left of me as I gently touched at the purple mound on O'Keefe's face where his nose used to be. He had some nasty swelling over the nasal bone and septum, and the whole cartilage structure seemed to be dislocated. 'There ain't no goddamn Jim Crow laws in New Zealand.'

'How the hell am I supposed to know that, smartass?'

'Take a look around. Does this look like Bubba country to you?'

'Tilt your head back,' I said. 'Okay, now, look at me. I'm going to have to break your nose again before I can set it.'

'Aw, sweet Jesus, doc. It ain't that bad.'

'Well, it's either that or you walk around with a question mark on your face for the rest of your life.'

'I'd say leave it,' said Timmins, who seemed to be having a ball. 'A bent horn has the advantage of detracting from them beady eyes and slack jaw. Least now he'll have some character.'

'Go fuck your momma,' said O'Keefe.

'Already have. She's no good, though.'

'All right, all right,' I said. 'Now this is going to hurt, O'Keefe, so grab on to the side of the bed here and squeeze tight.'

I gripped the base of the nasal bone between the heels of my hands and shunted it to the right until I felt the whole edifice of nose and cartilage pop back into place. A few drops of ruby red blood trickled from his nose. O'Keefe was man enough not to yell or scream, but he was powerless to stop the stream of tears that rolled down his cheeks.

Timmins laughed. 'How'd this happen, anyways?'

'This dumbass here,' said Sturgis, 'called a Maori guy a nigger and tried kicking him off the pool table in a pub.'

Timmins said, 'So?'

'What do you mean, "so"?'

'I'm struggling to see the connection with the broken nose, is all.'

'There's no segregation here, you fucking hillbilly.'

I taped up the bridge of O'Keefe's nose tight and wiped away the crystals of dried blood from his upper lip.

'They don't look like niggers, anyway,' said Timmins. 'More like wetbacks.'

'Give it a rest, Timmins,' I said, walking out of the O.R. and into the scrub-room to wash my hands. The three of them followed me out and stood around the basin. The shrill stench of old booze coming off them was nauseating.

'Anyways,' said Timmins, 'the Maoris ain't the problem. It's the white guys that are the assholes.'

'You better watch out,' I said, shaking water from my hands. 'Cartwright will withdraw your leave if he hears of too much trouble. Make nice with them. Try to remember: it's their country.'

'That's a fine sentiment, Captain,' said Sturgis, handing me a towel. 'But, honestly, I don't think you know what they're like. It's like they can't talk in complete sentences. They make Oki here look like Winston Churchill.'

In fact, I did know what they were like. I'd seen them up at the bars in Ponsonby, down at the wharf on Sunday mornings.

The New Zealand men were brooding silent types, all right, as if they'd all been charged with protecting some bitter secret about the country. But I didn't dislike them for it. I just think they recoiled at the sight of American largeness. I'd seen the same thing with my parents' relations who'd come over from Prague, a bristling at unrestrained openness, a distaste for the uniquely American assumption that people are supposed to care about what we have to say. It didn't help that guys like Sturgis were plucking their women from them like ripe peaches from a tree.

'Well,' I said, 'I guess all the best ones are fighting overseas.'

'Doesn't excuse ingratitude, sir,' said Timmins.

'That's an awfully big word, Timmins.'

'We're doing them a favour, ain't we? Being here and all. I mean, what are these assholes doing about this situation with the Nips? They'd be wide open, I reckon, if we weren't here. They'd all be eating rice and speaking chink by now.'

Sturgis started clapping. 'Timmins. I'm impressed. I think Ike could do with a man like you in D.C.'

'Whatever you're doing,' I said, sick of the conversation now, 'just try not to be so loud about it.'

As far as I could tell, life in New Zealand was carrying on much the same as before the war. There was the conspicuous absence of young men, of course, but there didn't seem to be the same hysteria that had rippled through the U.S. The tension back home had become too hot in recent months. It was getting impossible to have an inch of room to yourself without some asshole bellowing clichés in your ear about sacrifice and the common good. While there was grave concern in New Zealand, it was of the understated variety. It made for a refreshing change.

In addition to this, we also had the luxury of having time

on our hands, and Ponsonby was a pretty good place in which to be bored. The district was full of bars and pool halls and card clubs. It even had one or two small galleries, showing some locally produced paintings, which I'd taken a liking to. It was interesting to see how the local painters dealt with the blistering light that savaged their country daily. To me the light seemed to define everything, every object in clear isolation, giving land- and cityscapes an almost cartoonish quality.

I'd whiled away many an hour wandering the streets of Ponsonby, taking in the life. The Red Cross had rented an old dance hall as a basis of operations, and I'd go there on Sundays to watch the U.S.O. bands and play poker with some of the Army guys Sturgis had fallen in with. Every Saturday morning, after doing my rounds in the post-op, I would head up to the Ponsonby farmers' market with a few of the guys. The market was held at the bottom of Western Park, which was a gully sloping down from the ridge of Ponsonby Road through Freemans Bay, levelling off close to Victoria Park at the bottom. It was a beautiful setting, punctuated with native ferns, shrubs, and dozens of mature oaks and maples.

I had Sturgis and his two sidekicks with me one particularly fine Saturday morning. We'd wandered through the stalls, spent a sundrenched half-hour watching a cricket game on an adjacent green, and slowly made our way up the winding paths of the park to the second plateau, near Ponsonby Road. The sun was intense and hot, so we tried to walk under the canopy of oaks as much as possible. I was lost in thought listening to an orchestra of cicadas when Sturgis's voice came to me through a fog.

'What do you think, Captain?'

The three of them had been banging on about a local girl Sturgis had talked to at the cricket game a few minutes earlier, but I had totally tuned them out.

'Think about what?'

'The women. Who's easier? Timmins reckons the women here are easier than anybody back home. Any state. I don't know why he says any state seeing as he's never left Texas, but for argument's sake I'm willing to accept the proposition. Now, seeing as you and me are travelled types – men of the world even – I think it should be up to you to cast the deciding vote.'

'What about O'Keefe? What does he think?'

'Disqualified,' said Timmins, 'on account of his only experience being his immediate family.'

'I ain't disqualified, sir,' said O'Keefe. He was breathing hard as we came up the last stretch of the rise before the plateau. 'It's just that I like to sit these debates out. I figure it don't get you none, so what's the point of talking about it.'

'You see, Captain,' Sturgis said, coming up alongside me. 'It's up to you.'

We finally made it to the second plateau, a flat expanse of rich green grass bordered by tree-lined paths. The glare was electric, otherworldly.

'I'm going to have to sit this one out as well, fellahs,' I said. 'I'm afraid to say I've never found any woman to be easy.'

The green was, as usual, brimming with eclectic activity. A saxophone quartet was tucked away in a corner, almost in the shrubbery, doing Bach pieces that I assumed must have been arranged for clarinet. Running along the path on the eastern side of the field was a row of stalls, or rather tables, with people sitting or standing behind them ready to anoint you, corrupt you, convert you, and compete with you. In the middle of the green, providing a strange counterpoint to the earnest civic directness of the church groups, women's rights associations and sensibly dressed occultists, was a vaudeville troupe dressed in gypsy garb, juggling knives, books and footwear while at the same time hoisting and flinging each other around like boneless ragdolls. They had their own little band with them as well, playing something like the klezmer music I'd heard in some of the cafes in the Village in New York. For all their noise and dramatic garishness, nobody paid them the slightest bit of attention.

I stood watching the show for a few moments, trying to figure out why nobody else was looking at them. When I turned around I noticed that Timmins and O'Keefe had wandered off to the astrology stall to have their stars read by a prim-looking woman in tweeds and moody browns. Sturgis stood beside me.

'Not interested in your future?' I said.

'Not in knowing it in advance, anyhow.'

I looked at the ground as his innocent words seemed to ripen in the summer air. Sturgis had seen the wounded troops come in from the Solomons. He'd retrieved them from the dock, carried them in stretchers to his ambulance, and driven them to our makeshift hospital. Men who would not walk again, men who'd lost arms, eyes, lungs. Men who may never make it back home. I could only assume he'd seen beyond the broken bones and infected flesh wounds; that he'd seen the eyes, wild with a sense of death so near and present you could taste it.

We silently headed off in the opposite direction to Timmins and O'Keefe, hands behind our backs like Harvard dons. The sky overhead felt enormous.

'You and Major Cartwright know each other, right? I mean, from way back.'

'We were in med school together,' I said, a little surprised by the question. 'Why?'

'No reason. It just seems that, you know, you guys have a lot of history.'

'How do you mean?'

'Just the way you are together. I don't know. Whenever the two of you are in the same room it's like there's a lot of, you know, tension, I guess.'

'It's complicated,' I said, a little pissed off all of a sudden. I looked at Sturgis's profile, his slightly bulbous forehead and his adolescent pimples, and remembered I was talking to a boy. 'You wouldn't understand.'

He didn't say anything. As we continued walking in silence I could sense his hurt; I'd cut him down at the knees about something he prided himself on. We were having a grown-up conversation away from his imbecile buddies. He was trying to get to know me better, to talk man to man, and I'd played the kid card on him. I placed my hand on his shoulder in a friendly pat but he wouldn't look at me. For all his bluster he was at heart a sensitive young man. Nobody who read as much as he did could be anything other. More to the point, though, was that nobody in the Italian army would have had the gall to tell Hemingway he wouldn't understand. I let go of his shoulder.

'It's just that it's, well, very involved.'

He looked at me now, face wide open, waiting for more.

'I was, believe it or not, married to his sister. Once upon a time.'

The wide-open face lit up like a lantern. 'No shit? His sister?'

'Yeah. His sister.'

'Jesus,' he said quietly.

'It's not like you to act all surprised.'

'It's just that, I mean, his sister? Really?'

'Really.'

Without realising it we'd almost done a full lap of the green. Just as Sturgis was about to launch into his cross-examination we literally bumped into Timmins and O'Keefe, who were staring and pointing at a prominent stall in the corner of the park, just near the exit to Ponsonby Road.

The stall was manned by four guys in stiff, dark suits. I moved a little closer so I could read the sign placed in front of the desk. The words 'Ponsonby International Chess Club and

Philosophical Society' were painted in white on what looked like a large piece of slate. The name rang a bell. I moved up closer, past the pale, neat-looking men offering Baptist redemption, so that I could get a good look at the guys in black. All four of them were unloading pamphlets from a wooden crate. When they finally looked up I immediately recognised two of them as the guys who'd thrown the Oriental against the car on Franklin Road. The other two were dressed in identical clothing and carried themselves in the same, clerkish manner.

'I've seen these guys before,' I said to the others, who had come up behind me. 'Franklin Road a few weeks back. They were having a wrestling match with this giant Oriental. A Chinaman, I think.'

'That giant Chinaman?' said O'Keefe, pointing just to the right of the chess club's stall.

I looked in the direction of his outstretched hand. Situated to the rear of the chess club's stall, buried in the shadows of a pair of Norfolk pine trees, was another desk with a slate sign. The sign was covered in inexplicable characters from an Asian language. A small Oriental man in a suit of cheap blue cloth sat at the desk, head down, engrossed in recording something in a large book. To his left, hovering halfway between this second desk and the chess club desk was the tall, thin Oriental I'd seen splayed on the hood of that car last month. He wore the same blue outfit that his buddy was wearing. For all his height he had a strange air of invisibility about him. He seemed to hover on the threshold of the chess club's space, cloven between two single-tone worlds.

I turned to O'Keefe. 'That's the very same giant. A couple of these guys in black here threw him onto a parked car. And before I knew it he just . . . disappeared.'

'He must suck at chess,' said Sturgis.

'Or philosophy,' I added.

Timmins whacked me on the arm, excitedly trying to get my attention.

'That giant you're talking about, Captain, is none other than the celestial pimp. From the cathouse up yonder.'

'The what?'

'The celestial pimp. From the—'

'What the hell is a celestial?' asked Sturgis.

'There's a celestial cathouse?' O'Keefe said, his jaw slack with awe.

'Damn straight,' said Timmins. 'Better than reasonable price, too.'

'What the hell is a celestial?' asked Sturgis again.

'An Oriental, you dumbass. Chinaman, or whatever the fuck they are.'

'There's a Chinaman cathouse?' I said.

'Yes. I mean, no. I mean, it's a cathouse with chink girls run by that giant Chinaman there.'

O'Keefe looked incredulous. 'You mean to say you've been to this chink cathouse?'

'Course I have, Bubba. Every Marine has a duty to scout his area. It's in the code.'

'Why didn't you tell me about it?' said O'Keefe, who looked close to tears.

'I don't want you infecting the place. Plus, you'd never be able to handle the opium.'

'There's opium?' said Sturgis, suddenly interested.

I looked around to see two of the dark-suited gentlemen handing out pamphlets to uninterested passers-by. They were giving them to everybody, including the gypsies who were now lounging in the middle of the green on a break. One of the guys walked past me and I put out my hand in anticipation, but he just looked at me cold and carried on by. It was the New Zealander, the one with the broad accent who had called me a 'fucking Yank'. I looked around the rest of the field and noticed that the four of us were the only people in uniform. I guessed the rest of the servicemen, American and Kiwi alike, by-passed this area and headed straight for the bars on Ponsonby Road.

The man with the small, wire-rimmed glasses – the one with the English accent – stood up behind the desk. His disciples were at his flank now. He looked as though he was about to give a speech, so I motioned to the others to quieten down so I could hear him.

'A celestial cathouse,' said O'Keefe, muttering the words to himself as if they represented some ironic tic of nature, something expected but unbelievable all the same. 'You sure you're not making this up?'

'I'll prove it then,' Timmins said. 'It's just over yonder. Not fifty yards as the whore flies.'

'Ladies and gentlemen,' said the Englishman, clearing his throat and manfully gesturing over the whole green to include everybody – the gypsies, the Mormons, and even the members of the saxophone quartet who were busy packing up their instruments. 'My name is Oscar Walters, chairman of the Ponsonby International Chess Club and Philosophical Society.'

'Take me there now,' O'Keefe forcefully whispered, nudging Timmins in the ribs. They both looked at Sturgis and me for a moment, for what I don't know, then took off through the trees like twelve-year-olds on a mad caper. Sturgis stayed at my side, a broad smile creasing his baby-fat cheeks.

'The International Chess Club Association is committed to the free exchange of ideas among the world's great nations,' said the Englishman in the halting, deadpan manner of an insurance clerk. 'The ICCA understands the nature of this conflict that has gripped the world. This is no ordinary war. This conflict is necessary, ladies and gentlemen, if we are to realise the full potential we have within us. This conflict is not about the petty feuds of princes and kings. It is about what it means to be human. It is about nothing less than our very evolution, our very survival.'

He paused after that little nugget and nodded so that the five people listening to him over the droning cicadas could take it in. I could see he was a fledgling student of oratory, and I appreciated the flourish, as one appreciates the wild swings of a college middleweight, all heart and no technique.

'Do not let yourselves be fooled,' he continued, but then had to stop as the klezmer band started up again. I looked over my shoulder to see that the juggling and dancing was back underway.

This Oscar Walters character stepped out from behind his desk to compete with the noise. Sturgis and I moved a couple of steps forward to hear his straining voice. He gestured to his right, and, emerging from the shadows, the giant Oriental stepped into the blazing light like a mythical figure out of Herodotus. He stood at Walters's side, as straight and rigid as the Norfolk pine trees behind him. He didn't look like a pimp to me, but maybe I was naïve about such things.

'People of New Zealand,' said Walters, looking expansively around the green again, 'the ICCA introduces Mr Quan of the Auckland chapter of the Chinese Chess Association. The CCA, in a show of international solidarity, has pledged its support to the ICCA in all future operations.'

At this, the men in dark suits all started clapping vigorously. Back in the shadows, the small Chinaman in the blue suit stood up and gave a deep, solemn bow. I was so enthralled by the pageantry that I almost jumped when Sturgis tapped me on the shoulder.

'Come on, Captain,' he said. 'I told Jackson we'd be there by noon.' He looked at his watch. 'He would have dealt the first hand already.'

'One minute,' I said.

'While we acknowledge our limits here, at the bottom

of the world, we do say that chess, the very benchmark of civilisation, can be our chief tactic in keeping the lines of communication open. Because chess is not just a game, ladies and gentlemen. It has the power to tell us who we are, and what is truly worth fighting for. It reminds us that culture and civilisation are gifts worth protecting.'

Another spontaneous round of applause and a deep bow. I looked around the green. By now Sturgis and I were the only people listening. In fact, we were the only people even bothering to look in their general direction.

We walked to our card game at the Red Cross in silence. The sun was becoming oppressive and I was looking forward to getting into the cool of the dance hall. I knew what was on Sturgis's mind, the reason for his silence. I'd been debating with myself ever since we left Western Park whether to say anything. I hadn't told anybody about Beth – not really, not anything beyond the bare outline. It had never seemed worth the effort. Besides, nobody I knew had shown much interest, until now at least.

I'd intended to skip through the war unnoticed – do my job, do my duty, and fade into the khaki background. I didn't want any more entanglements or obligations to other people. I knew that if I told Sturgis it would change our relationship, such that it was anyway. It would deepen it. We would share something. I would divulge something to his trust. I didn't want that kind of connection, but there I was, a hundred yards from a poker game, unable to keep my mouth shut.

CHAPTER 12

It turned out that Beth Cartwright had been watching me that day with her cerulean blue eyes, under a parasol on her father's immaculate lawn. She had a way of secluding herself on the edge of the action, far enough away to be missed, close enough to be noticed. And by the end of that day, in spite of Tom's earnest attempts to steer the two of us away from each other, she had made her presence known to me.

It was exciting for a long time. The months of sneaking around behind Tom's back, busting her out of her parents' and relatives' various mansions, and hiding her away in my dingy apartment on the seedy fringe of Chinatown were exhilarating. Cartwright had no idea. At school he was too busy with his clubs and student bodies and secret remedial surgery classes with Dr Kendall to notice the wicked smile on my face as I barrelled into class late, morning after morning. He even invited me to more of his family functions, where he would ghost his father around mahogany-wainscoted rooms learning how to press the flesh, work the crowds. Beth and I would stand at opposite corners of the room at these events, exchanging childish looks and stolen smiles, mentally preparing ourselves for the next prison-break.

She was the black sheep of the Cartwright clan. At twenty-one she had already eschewed the civic-minded family tradition of a couple of years spent nursing before gracefully retiring into stately married life with a friend of a friend. Not for Beth. Instead she'd spent two years at Sarah Lawrence reading English and American literature, and she was determined to demonstrate to everybody that the experience had made an impression on her.

The books she had read introduced her to a different way of thinking, to people she never dreamed actually existed. She fell in love with characters whose hopes were so often dashed on altars of pride, greed, lust and envy – people fundamentally destined for bad luck. And so through her characters she fell in love with the romance of hardship, and, as luck or fate would have it, my story of immigrant struggle came along just at the right time.

We managed to hide the rendezvous and brief encounters for the best part of two years while I dutifully finished out med school. She loved the fact that I was, in her words, torn from my social climb by an irresistible creative urge to paint. I'd never loved a woman up till that point, and I'm still not sure if I ever loved Beth, but the clandestine thrill of it was enough to sustain us until I graduated. Then, with no real internship prospects lined up, and buoyed by the sale of a couple of my Braque-like abstractions to a private collector in Phoenix, we played out Beth's narrative of doomed love by eloping to Florida and marrying on a wet, stormy day at Miami City Hall.

We drifted around Florida for a few months, patting ourselves on the back for being so naughty, and then headed back to California, where I managed to get a surgical internship at San Francisco Public.

The marriage was a disgrace for the Cartwright family. I got phone calls from Tom every second night, at first openly hostile, threatening to break my jaw, then, eventually, conciliatory ones, offers of money if we agreed to an annulment. Beth fed off the scandal, her affection for me swelling with every failed attempt by her family to hush the marriage up, or kidnap her from my loose grip. We lived in an apartment above a block of ethnic food shops on Lower Haight Street, and she was, I think, genuinely happy for a year. She encouraged me to paint, and she seemed to revel in the meanness of our circumstances.

But week followed week, and month followed month. The simple reality of our ill-conceived life – hushed up, pushed to the corners – began to gnaw at her sensibilities. And then, inevitably, money became an issue. While she remained with me, Beth lost her trust fund entitlements, and for the first time in her life she was faced with the grim prospect of making do. My pay from the hospital was meagre at best, not much more than a stipend to cover rent and basic expenses. Plus interning as an orthopaedic surgeon meant regular fifteen-hour days busting my hump at San Francisco Public.

I don't know whether she loved me, but there was a certain, undeniable affection between us. And I think the affection could have overcome the lack of money and the harsh living, but it certainly wasn't enough to make up for the loss of her precious connections. Because the thing about me, back then and even now, is that I've always been alone. Even with a houseful of Czech relatives hanging from the rafters, I've always been alone. I don't think she properly understood this affliction at first, took it for being something romantic, a stagey, affected detachment perhaps. But it was nothing so grand. It was mundane and awkward and lonely.

Pretty soon the sheen wore off, and I think the characters in the books she had read must have started to seem damaged rather than romantic. And so once the gloss had gone, and Tuesday just became plain old Tuesday, she wanted out.

We went through the formal motions at first, sitting up all night arguing, me drinking whatever I could lay my hands on, her imagining past acts of neglect and cruelty. But the arguments lacked a central force, a lifeblood of hard emotion. Because when we got down to it, we discovered what I think we'd both always known: that there was nothing there. I was something that Beth had conceived in her dormitory at Sarah Lawrence, and she'd made me into three dimensions by the sheer force of her imagination.

But soon enough we all get tired of fiction. She started answering Tom's persistent calls, even phoning him sometimes. I voluntarily worked longer hours at the hospital, spent my off-hours in grimy corner bars, and receded into the distance, into her index of experience between romance and ruin. It didn't take long, a few weeks at most, for her to drift away with the prevailing wind back to Los Angeles, back into the family fold.

I didn't bother putting up a fight.

CHAPTER 13

The New Zealand medical community was for some reason governed by an organisation known as the British Medical Association, although as far as I could tell there wasn't one Briton on their books. The British Med held monthly meetings at the Ambassador Hotel on Nelson Street, overlooking Princes Wharf where on any given day half of General Eisenhower's Pacific Fleet was likely to be tied up with a few yards of old rope.

The meetings were theoretically designed as a forum in which to share ideas about medical developments and practices, but they invariably ended up with the Army and Marine brass brow-beating the New Zealanders about safe milk pasteurisation and food refrigeration. The locals seemed to take it in their stride, though. In all my time in Auckland, I never met a single Kiwi man who wasn't at least half-expecting to be criticised for something. Keynote speakers were also high on the agenda. At the April meeting the guest was the legendary Colonel Swanson from the Second Marines.

Swanson was in his second war, having made his mark as a gifted young cutter in the Chateau Thierry in 1917. He was a chest man, and about the best in the business. Legend had it that while the Second Marines were based in the Philippines he operated with a loaded Colt .45 in a side holster, replete with a custom-made ivory handle.

Rumour had it that he made all his surgeons spend two nights a week on his camp's watchtower so that they could get a better perspective on their nation's predicament.

His speech, which spent an inordinate amount of time on the psychology of two geckos that had lived in his tent, was followed by the now-familiar soiree in an adjacent ballroom, a little after party that included the wives and associates of the British Med fellows. I hated these gatherings with a passion, but like everything else in the Corps, they were not optional.

The waiters circulated the ballroom with glasses of Napa Valley wine happily supplied by Colonel Jacobi of the 39th, whose family had grown grapes in the region for the best part of a century. I figured that to do my duty I had to stick around for an hour, but I didn't plan on staying a minute longer than necessary.

I took a glass of wine and backed myself into the corner of the room where the wait-staff had their basis of operations. I was skilled at identifying these locations at official events – spots where there was enough activity to enable you to get lost in the human press, where you could drink yourself out of diffidence, where you could patiently bide your time.

My tactic proved quite successful at first, and I spent a happy ten minutes sipping my wine and watching Cartwright shadow Colonel Ford around the room, much the same way he used to ghost his father a few years earlier. I could have gone on this way for the remainder of my hour if one of the busboys hadn't noisily dropped a full tray of wine glasses three feet away from where I stood. Everybody in the room looked in my direction as the red-faced kid knelt on his haunches, manfully grabbing at large shards of glass. The lingering eyes eventually turned back to their conversations, but I'd attracted the attention of Ford, and, as a consequence, Cartwright too. Colonel Ford had the kind of face that betrayed a certain knowledge of elemental things, life and death, the darkness of men's hearts. It was written in the folds around his slate grey eyes, in the taut sinew below his Midwestern jaw. He looked me up and down in the dim chandelier light, a brief moment in which I assumed he was considering his options, before waving me over.

'What were you doing over there, Sokol?'

'Um, just . . .' I shrugged my shoulders.

'You've got to make like Major Cartwright here and mix in with the natives. Every Marine needs the trust of the local population.'

'Yes, sir.'

Cartwright, who was standing at Ford's shoulder with a drink in his hand, was positively beaming. He blushed a deep, glowing red and nodded gravely at me a few times.

As Ford was speaking I heard the loud voice of a woman above the general din in the background. She spoke in a high pitch with what I took to be an English accent, although a better description of it would have been stage English – the kind of thing you hear in certain parts of Boston or New Hampshire. This woman's sing-song voice drew closer and closer, and when I finally turned in the direction it was coming from it took me a few seconds to spot her, way down there, five-foot nothing, standing at Colonel Ford's waist.

'I say, Colonel?'

Ford turned and for a terrific vaudeville moment looked straight over her head, wondering where the sound was coming from.

'Down here, Colonel. Farther from God.'

Ford looked down at the woman's head. The skin on her face was powdered almost completely white and she was dressed in tweed, masculinely so, as if she had half thought she might pop out into the woods for a hunt on the way home. Her ash-coloured hair was pulled into a tight bun at the back of her head, which accentuated the Napoleonic bump of her forehead.

'Gertrude Walters,' she said, extending her dainty hand out to Ford, who took it as if it were a shovel handle.

'Ma'am.' He gave her a polite nod and let go of her hand. Ford had a charming, almost socialist way of greeting everybody in the same flippant, administrative manner, male or female, janitor or general. It was as if he'd been expecting you for hours and had grown sick of waiting.

'My husband, you know, Doctor Walters was a fellow of the British Medical. Not in this country, though. In England, you understand.'

'Is your husband here, Mrs Walters?' asked Ford.

'Oh, no. Lord no. He died two years ago.' She said this last sentence with a raised inflection, almost as if she were posing a question. Ford looked at me, for what reason I do not know, before turning back to her.

'I'm sorry to hear that, ma'am.'

'We're sorry too. But one mustn't be morbid for too long, must one? I say, you Americans aren't ones to go in for morbidity, are you?'

Ford looked at me again. He clearly had no idea how to speak to this dot of a woman. Not knowing what to say, he stiffened his posture, unintentionally exaggerating the height difference between them. I couldn't help but smile.

'I dare say you'll rule the world when all this nonsense is over,' Mrs Walters continued, a persistent fly on a horse. 'Then where will we be?'

'Where will we be?'

'I don't mean to tease, Colonel. It's just that you Americans are so delightfully literal. I simply can't help myself. But enough of that, gentlemen,' she said, including Cartwright and me for the first time. 'I would like to present my daughter. Miss Emily Walters.'

And here is where my story begins.

Mrs Walters looked behind herself and, finding nothing,

spun around another twenty or thirty degrees before plucking the young Miss Walters from the thick of the crowd. She had been hiding in that way of hers that became so familiar to me later on. She stepped towards us, from the misty black of a dream. She was tall and slender-boned with dark, chestnut hair and viridian eyes. She was utterly improbable, standing there in the atrophying light of the ballroom – something exotic and half-imagined, an undergraduate fantasy of European sophistication. We three Marines were rendered silent by her.

I felt cold and sick and incapable as I watched Mrs Walters introduce her daughter to Ford, then Cartwright, then, still watching, to me. I took the ends of her fingers in my hand and felt something close to despair as I noticed the faint curl of a smile form at the corners of her mouth. A smile that hadn't been offered to my colleagues. I had spent all of my painting life railing against sentimentality of any stripe, but as I stood there in that gaudy ballroom I was powerless to stop its saccharine tide. It may have been nothing, just a slight creasing of her milky skin at the dimples, but I saw it. Cartwright must have seen it as well, because by the time I released her pencil-thin fingers he had moved around behind me and had insinuated himself in between mother and daughter.

The move was pure Cartwright – radical, bold, presumptive. I could have murdered him on the spot. He leaned in, all Yankee chivalry.

'Do you come to the British Med meetings often, ma'am?' he asked Mrs Walters.

'Not if I can help it, Major.' The mother's tone was ironic but not dismissive. Cartwright asked another couple of nonsense questions, and it was clear that she was charmed. Cartwright was clever enough to include Ford in the questions, drawing the ruddy old bastard in with a tone right on the precipice of condescension.

'The Colonel has us all working very hard, ma'am. It's just a matter of time before we're shipped to the tropics, so we have to keep ourselves sharp.'

Ford sprung to life and proceeded to give a discourse on the threat to democracy's rightful grip on the Pacific. Mrs Walters peppered him with questions, little birdlike chirps which he shot back with no-nonsense solemnity. Her knowledge of the Pacific situation seemed to catch him off-guard, but after a while I stopped listening. Instead I watched her, and watched Cartwright watching her. This little charade of his was merely pretext. Everything Cartwright did had an endgame, and in this case it was clear enough that he was charming the mother to get at the daughter. It was reversion to type. His breeding, his Martha's Vineyard manners prevented him going straight to the source in these situations. There was a natural order of socialising that Cartwright understood as well as night and day, and the first, the cardinal rule is that the mothers of dames need first be wooed before the dames themselves are in play.

Being a low scoundrel, I knew nothing of this. I would have buried the mother in a shallow grave just to get near her. But I didn't have to go that far, as the hapless busboy provided me with a perfect opportunity. He was wielding another tray of glasses and was set on a collision course with Emily's shoulder. I could see him coming, but my arms felt heavy and useless, stripped of all instinct. I took her by her thin wrist and clumsily pulled her towards me. She moved freely with my guidance, not alarmed by the suddenness or strangeness of my hand upon her. But while her body was malleable, her eyes locked on me with a brilliant green expression somewhere between alarm and guilt. I had the sense that I'd caught her in the act of something secret, something innate.

'Sorry,' I said, reluctantly letting go of her wrist and motioning with my head at the passing busboy.

When she saw him her eyes relaxed. 'Not at all, Captain,'

87

she said, a model of detachment. 'I have a habit of running into people.'

I think she was about to smile when Cartwright boomed a few syllables at us.

'Your mother tells . . . Miss Walters?' he said, stumbling for her attention.

She had heard him as well as I did, but her eyes remained on mine for a critical pause before she turned. It was a luxurious moment, made all the better by Cartwright not seeming to detect its import.

'Your mother says you are quite the musician. A pianist, I believe.'

A soft shade of red warmed her pale skin and she swallowed once, hard, an effort at composure.

'Mother speaks too highly of my playing. I don't believe she is the best judge. I am mediocre at best, Major.'

Her voice was quiet but true. She seemed to know the effect she was having on us, the turbulence in the air her presence created. I got the distinct impression that she had seen men wilt before her more than once. I also noticed that where the mother's English accent had a touch of the stage about it, Emily's was clear and resonant.

'Nonsense,' said Mrs Walters, looking up at Cartwright defensively. 'She plays like a force of nature. Dr Walters used to say that her playing reminded him of the West Country in England. We had a house in the West Country, you know.'

Colonel Ford was slowly leaning to his left, away from the small woman at his side, his feet planted firm out of politeness. He looked like an old barge listing in a wharf.

'She plays like the West Country?' he said, all gravel and smoke.

'Yes, Colonel. Do you know it? Full of mist and gentle sunlight. The sound of water lapping over stony riverbeds.'

She waited for a response, a recognition of the accurateness of her metaphor, but it appeared that none of us had anything to say.

'Never been there,' said Ford.

'Well, I'm sure you sound swell anyways,' said Cartwright, nodding his golden head at Emily.

'Thank you,' she said, folding her hands together in front of her and smiling.

'Swell indeed, Major,' said Mrs Walters, trying to retrieve some momentum. 'And if you want to learn precisely how swell, then I cordially invite the three of you to hear Emily play in our home at Parnell.'

As Cartwright did the emphatic acceptance for all of us I rocked back on my heels and stole another glance at Miss Walters, thanking God, thanking Cartwright, for the opportunity to see her again. Colonel Ford coughed loudly into his clenched fist.

'Excuse me, ma'am,' he said, after he'd finally managed to get Cartwright to shut up. 'I thank you for the invitation. It's most gracious. But I think I'll leave it to these two young men to keep you company.'

'But Colonel, you absolutely must come. You must at least come to see Dr Walters's collection of medical journals. He—'

'Thank you once again. But my days and nights are full up. Now if you'll excuse me, I best be getting back to the ranch.'

And with that he was gone. It was a skilled exit – polite, offering neither excuse nor explanation, but leaving no room for argument. I would have liked to use it myself in the future, but think its success relied a little too much on Ford's stature, which was singular and complete.

'Such a strange man,' Mrs Walters said, her black eyes bouncing from Cartwright's to mine then back again.

'The colonel has many responsibilities, Mrs Walters,' said Cartwright magnanimously. 'It's a lot of work running a deployment like this.'

I stole another furtive glance at Emily, who was now looking at the ground. I got the feeling she was used to spending large swathes of time listening to her mother in social settings. She looked up before I had time to avert my eyes and caught me dead in the act. She smiled again, quickly, before looking back down at the ground. That same delightful curl of the lip, that same small crease in her cheek.

Mrs Walters said, 'Really? And what is it, Major, that you Americans are doing here? In New Zealand of all places.'

Cartwright fumbled, his collection of press-secretary stock responses momentarily failing him.

'Well, we're, ah, we're securing the country. From the Nips.'

'The who?' said Emily. The question caught us all off guard. I could see even her mother was surprised at its directness.

Cartwright did his best to contain a rich blush that was swimming up his neck from his starched green collar.

'I take it by "Nips",' said Mrs Walters, patting her daughter on the arm, 'you mean the Japanese. Is that right, Major?'

'Well, yes. Of course.'

'I see,' she said, adjusting the position of her head to regard him from a certain angle.

'And is it your opinion, Major, that the Japanese would be here by now if you and your friends hadn't come to . . . to save us?'

'Well,' said Cartwright, stumbling again. 'I mean . . . of course they would be.'

'How glorious of you to come, then. Defending our honour like this. And will you stay, Major? Pray, how long do you intend to keep us safe?'

He looked at me, but I had nothing to offer.

'Until we have them beat,' he said, laughing and shaking his head at the obviousness of it.

'Pardon me, Major,' said Emily, taking a small step away

from her mother's side. 'But my understanding is that the Japanese have been stopped in Darwin, and that they haven't made any further attempts to move south. If they're not moving south, isn't it better to put your resources somewhere else? Wouldn't Fiji or Samoa make more sense?'

Cartwright was on the canvas. Women didn't speak like this where he came from. They didn't speak like this where I came from, either. 'Well,' he said, slowly, deliberately, 'they're a relentless enemy. If you give them an inch—'

'Yes, yes, yes,' said Mrs Walters, waving her small arm at the cliché, 'they'll take a mile. We understand that, Major. But enough of politics. Now,' she said, turning her head to look at me for what felt like the first time. 'You, Captain. What's your story in all of this?'

'I'm a doctor. At Victoria—'

'Well, I know that. We've done the introductions, Captain. But I mean specifically. What's your area?'

'Orthopaedic, mainly. Although that involves a bit of vascular surgery from time to time.'

She seemed thoroughly disappointed. 'Oh, I don't know how you do it, breaking bones all day like a caveman. And you, Major,' she said, turning to Cartwright. 'What do you do?'

'I'm a plastic surgeon. But with Marines I'll likely—'

'You mean you do nose jobs?'

He paused before answering, his face completely red now. I thought of stoic old Mildred back home in San Francisco, writing Cartwright one of her ten-page epics on her latest polo injury, or hiking in the Sierra Nevadas with a few keen girls from the Country Club. 'Among other things,' he finally said, his voice gone quiet.

'What about Dr Walters?' I asked. 'What did he do?'

Mrs Walters seemed relieved by the question, as if she'd been trying to elicit it all along. She took a step towards me and, theatrically, cast a couple of quick glances over her shoulders before leaning in very close.

'Psychiatry,' she said discreetly. It was as if she were giving us the answer to a question that had haunted the ages.

I could see Cartwright recoil a shade, just enough to give Mrs Walters and Emily and me, and anyone else who may have been listening, a little visual demonstration of his distaste for the profession. I had encountered the Cartwrightian abhorrence for psychoanalysis before, when, in a fit of pique as our divorce papers were being signed, I suggested that Beth could do with an evaluation. The comment was flippant enough, but Tom and his father took it as an insult, not only to Beth, but to the entire family line. In spite of all of his incursions into my physical space, it was the only time when I seriously thought Tom was going to hit me. Not just hit me – thrash me within an inch of my life.

Mrs Walters was sensitive enough to spot Cartwright's instinctive aversion.

'I take it you're not enamoured of the science, either,' she said.

He looked at Emily before answering, but her eyes were firmly fixed on the patterned red and green carpeting. He was beginning to see that his charms had failed him.

'I have no opinion either way,' he said, in the manner of a deponent at a congressional hearing.

'And you?' she said, sharply turning her sparrow's face to me.

'Mother,' said Emily in a tone of mild reproach. 'Let the gentlemen be. They're just being polite.'

Mrs Walters let out a prolonged breath, or maybe a sigh, that sounded as though it had been buried in her lungs for a thousand years.

'I just think it remarkable that these people, these colonial people deny themselves the self-knowledge that's at their fingertips.' She looked up at me now, having given up on

Cartwright. 'I had thought that Americans would be different. It's not surprising they don't get it here, in this silly little country. But isn't America supposed to be the new centre of the world? Captain? Shouldn't a room full of its most educated people be receptive to new ideas? To new ways of understanding the world, or themselves for that matter?'

Emily took her mother's small hand in her own. The effect was instant, the elder Walters immediately succumbing to her daughter's touch. How I wanted those porcelain hands to reach out to me, to reassure me.

'Thank you,' said Emily, looking up at Cartwright and me. 'Mother does get excited at times. She hasn't been well since Dr Walters . . . since Father passed away.'

'Don't apologise,' I said, the words slipping out of my mouth without a shred of control. But the effect was good; it was the first coherent thing I'd managed to utter since I'd laid eyes on her. 'Your mother makes a lot of sense.'

She put her arm protectively around her now, suddenly frail, mother, and was about to lead her from the room when she stopped.

'Oh, and you must come for tea. Both of you. We would like to hear more about your camp. Perhaps we could even continue our discussion of the Japanese situation,' she said, an ironic smile bunching at the corners of her eyes.

'It would be my great pleasure,' boomed Cartwright, his confidence restored now that the old woman had faded. He made a great show of getting the address and organising the time and helping Mrs Walters down the stairs, but I was confident it was all for nothing. I may have been out of my head, but something, some feeling in the pit of my gut told me that I would have her.

I stood alone and rooted to the spot, still sensing her presence in the air around me, sick with a sudden and bitter loneliness.

CHAPTER 14

It was after two o'clock by the time I got away from the diner, and for the first ten or fifteen minutes back out on the road I was barely aware I was driving. I'd read almost to the end of the book by the time I left, and I was finding it hard to tear myself from its familiar, well-evoked world back into the present. I had suppressed these memories for so long now that the odd glimpse or flash I did occasionally get seemed antiquated and removed, as if they were the fragments of somebody else's memories, some other person's heartbreak and ruin. But Sturgis's book had cracked the prison wall, and they were all clambering to get out now – memories in sharp relief, poignant, painfully real.

But as much as I had to tear myself away, I didn't want to finish it. He had drawn his main character in sympathetic colours, but that was no guarantee he would exonerate him. I had spent the last twenty years not knowing what he thought of me. We had a reconciliation of sorts in the jungle on Cape Torokina, but I knew I couldn't rest on that. We were all delirious with shell-shock and exhaustion by then; at one point Sturgis had even been yellow-eyed with malaria. A battlefield is no place in which to be forgiven. Nothing sticks in a battlefield except bullets and shrapnel. I knew this, and that's why I was so scared of reaching the end of his book.

I forced myself to listen to the hum of the De Ville's engine in an attempt to reconnect with the present, but I couldn't seem to shake the dizzy fog of memories. The shame usually started in my head; a numb, sedated feeling like everything was happening a second or two before I could grasp its significance. But this time it was all in my chest. Unless you've tried it, no man can know the feeling of giving yourself to death. Not only giving yourself, but being its agent, forcing its hand. What is shameful about the memory is not the sorrow, or even the pitiable state that led me to fashion a noose in that dark stockade cell. It was the pure joy once I'd crossed the line, when my body decided to give up the struggle for air and just succumb. There was a freedom then that was like nothing I can put in words. I have tried, guiltily, to render an idea of it in paint, or to hear it in music, but nothing can come close. Nothing can be so pure.

The act itself was prosaic in comparison. They had banged me up in a remand cell at Camp Elliot while they figured out the charge. They'd made the mistake of locking me up with loose sheets on my mattress, just as they'd done with her in Auckland, and by the eighth day of my incarceration it seemed like the only option. I managed to tie a reasonable knot around the exposed gas pipes running along the ceiling of the cell, slipped the loop of the noose over my head and stepped off the bed. I can vaguely recall the sound of a whistle blowing before everything went dark. When I awoke twelve hours later I was drugged to the teeth and strapped to a bed in a bleached white room. And still my first thought was of her.

Missy may have sent me on this trip for my own good, but I couldn't help feeling that all this confronting the past just amounted to a further betrayal of her on my part. I lived with that betrayal every day. I consciously held something back from her – not just entry to my studio, or the fact of marriage, which I'd known she'd wanted for too many years now, but a part of my very self, the part that resided in an old tool shed day in and day out, the part that ended up in flashes of colour and abstraction on canvases I knew she couldn't understand. I betrayed her every day for the waning memory of a ghost and I hated myself for it. But I couldn't stop loving the ghost.

I'd only travelled a few miles when I rounded a bend in the road that opened up to a long stretch of asphalt which ran straight as an arrow towards the horizon, somewhere above which sat Los Angeles. Up in the distance, a hazy mile or so away, I thought I could make out the VW van that I'd seen at the diner earlier on, the get-away car that those kids had taken off in. The van was parked crookedly off the road, and as I drew closer I could see the outline of a couple of people spilling out of its side door. I took my foot off the gas and lightly touched the brake a few times, just enough to slow me down so I could get a better look. It looked as though a fight was taking place, but all I could see was the bare outline. Suddenly the van started up with a hollow, lawn-mower kind of sound, and one of the fighters was sent tumbling down into the culvert off the side of the road. The van started to move, slowly, and the other guy, the one responsible for sending his buddy down into the ditch, shouted a few obscenities at his fallen friend and cantered off up to the side of the moving van. He jumped up onto the foot ledge of the sliding side door and held onto the frame, looking back and waving his free arm as if he were Jesse James robbing a train.

I eased the De Ville up about twenty yards or so from where I thought the kid lay and spent a few seconds debating with myself about whether I should get out. I had been deregistered now for over twenty years, so the professional obligation had long since passed, but something of the ethics remained, a recurring thorn that was responsible for probably half of my human contact since I'd arrived in San Diego. I got out of the car before my reluctance got the better of me and wandered over to the lip of the culvert. The day was really starting to heat up now and I could feel a light, salty film of sweat glistening on my forehead. I looked down into the dusty brown trench.

'Hi.'

It was the kid from the diner, the one with the horn-rimmed glasses who'd said the thing about shooting up the place. He was lying on his back but had propped himself up on his elbows. A steady stream of blood flowed from his nose onto his wispy, post-adolescent beard.

'You okay?' I said.

'Never better.'

He pulled the tail of his loose, floral shirt up to his nose and gave it a gentle wipe. He winced at the touch. I walked a few steps along the road and found a manageable entrance into the culvert, my shoes sliding on the loose, dry dirt on the surface. As I approached him the kid looked up at me, letting his bloody shirt-tail drop.

'Here, let me have a look at that,' I said, easing myself down onto my haunches, taking the side of his face in my hand so that his generous nose pointed straight at me. In all the years that have gone by, even with all the active forgetting I've done, I haven't lost the physician's sense of entitlement with the damaged body.

'What are you doing, man?'

The protest was limp; I think he sensed the authority of my hand, that I wasn't just some Good Samaritan amateur.

'I'm looking at your broken nose. You have a fracture of the anterior nasal spine. It looks as though it's haemorrhaging as well. Do you want me to pack it?'

'What are you, crazy?'

He quickly backed away from me and stumbled up to his feet, one hand still clasped to his nose to staunch the flow of blood. It was damned hot in that hole. The sun was high in the sky and bore down on us. I got an uncomfortable sense of déjà vu for a moment – the heat, the dusty bunker, some human drama.

'We're a long way from a hospital. Unless we pack it now and maybe even reset it there's a good chance it'll stay that way for good.'

'What way? What's wrong with it?'

'It looks like it's trying to point you south.'

He took a moment to absorb all of this. I eased myself up, the brittle cartilage in my knees hanging on for dear life.

'Hey,' he said, pointing his free hand at me. 'You're that guy from the diner.'

'That's right.'

'No kidding?'

'No kidding.'

He gave me a goofy smile. He kept his shirt-tail up to his face and took a moment to inspect the damage done to his glasses.

'Are you a doctor?' he asked.

'No.'

He rocked his head back and laughed, a kind of sinister movie laugh. 'Well then there's no fucking way I'm going to let you pack and – what is it? – reset my nose.'

'Okay. Fine.' I shrugged my shoulders and hitched my pants, readying myself for the unpleasant task of trying to haul my ass out of the ditch and back up to the road. It took a couple of goes, but I eventually made it up. I walked along the side of the road a few steps so that my feet were level with the kid's head. The heat coming off the asphalt was thick and stifling.

'Make sure you get that checked out as soon as you can,' I said. 'I'd say you've got ten or fifteen minutes before you pass out.'

Looking down on him he seemed a lot smaller, in size and effect. Through the horn-rimmed glasses and the straggly facial hair he was nothing more than a skinny kid, the kind of kid that attended my freshman painting classes, all bravado and image, tremendously burdened by having to live up to a meticulously crafted identity. I turned away from him, feeling a pool of sweat come to life at the small of my back.

'Wait.'

I didn't bother turning around. He hurled himself out of the ditch and sprang to my side, as loose and free as a gazelle. A gazelle with a broken nose.

'Wait up,' he said, breathing deeply through his mouth. His eyes were starting to turn black and his nose, swollen like a profiterole, was trending purple. The trickle of blood kept dropping into his stinky shirt. He looked up and down the highway at the stark emptiness before casting an anxious glance at the burning sky.

'Where are you heading?' he said.

'Los Angeles.'

'Huh.' He looked at me expectantly, the prospect of having to ask the question clearly chewing him up inside.

'You need a ride somewhere?'

'Well, I mean . . . So you're heading to L.A.?'

'Like I said.'

'Sure, sure.' He waved a big, bony hand in the air in concession. He was getting younger by the second. I could see him now with his frizzy hair cut and washed, his face shaved, donning a freshly pressed button-down shirt, captain of the school debating team. 'I'm Eddie, by the way. Eddie Schuler.'

'Peter.'

'So, um, perhaps I could just, you know, drive along for a while and . . . you know, just jump out wherever.'

'On one condition.'

'What?' A quick flash of terror went through his eyes, and

I think he must have recalled one of the thousand stories he'd probably heard about kindly gentlemen picking up young men on the side of the road.

'You let me at least pack that nose of yours.'

He let a stream of hot, damp air out of his gaping mouth. 'Here?'

'There's a truck-stop a few miles up. We'll get some ice and swabs and do it there.'

He looked up and down the road again.

'All right.'

CHAPTER 15

In the days following the British Med conference I developed a cold that laid me out flat. It was getting into April and the raw umber and bruised red colours of fall had taken a hold over Auckland. The Victoria Park camp was slowly turning into a sea of waxy gold leaves, and the rain was coming even more frequently. As the nights drew in and the air got thicker, the daily stench pouring out of Perfectus became almost too much to bear. A few of the nurses even started to develop bronchial problems with all the smoke in the air. None of which, I should say, helped me any with my cold.

But as I lay on my cot listening to the improbably short torrents of rain splat on the canvas roof of my tent, all I could think of was Emily. I replayed the encounter over and over in my head, dwelling on every word said, every movement of her willowy body, every frame of every single look she happened to give me. At the time I felt confident that there had been some sort of connection between us, however fleeting, but after days of angsty forensic analysis with a head full of mucous I wasn't so sure.

As the day approached for the scheduled tea my cold started to turn into the 'flu, and my 'flu into despair. I roused myself from my cot and had Sturgis walk me around the perimeter of the camp three times a day, my eyes red and weeping, the mucous turning hard and waxy. When it became clear that exercise wasn't going to cut it I broke into the hospital late one night and wired myself up to a glucose drip. I was so weak that it took me three attempts to hit the vein, but I got there in the end and within two or three hours I started to come round.

On the morning we were due up at the Walterses' house I got a message to report to Colonel Ford's office on the double. As I walked through the rain-soaked, khaki camp I considered, in a mild panic, the possible reason for the summons. I knew he hadn't taken well to Mrs Walters, and I had a bad feeling that he was going to can the whole visit on account of the woman's terrible metaphors. Another thought occurred to me as well. He knew that there'd been tension between Cartwright and me over the San Francisco incident. He must have also seen how we were both struck by the young Miss Walters. The old bastard was wily enough to get a read on such things, and it wouldn't have surprised me if he had thought to pre-empt a run-in between two of his surgeons. When I opened the door to his office and saw Cartwright, the thought looked like a winner.

'You wanted to see me, sir?'

Ford had his big feet up on the corner of his desk, and he was chewing the end of a wet, rancid cigar.

'Siddown, Sokol.'

I did as he said. I looked at Cartwright, who had taken a seat to the side of Ford's desk rather than in front of it, all the better to give him a degree of control over the proceedings. He had an astute tactical eye in such matters, and I could see that I was at a disadvantage positioned where I was, three feet away from the muddy soles of Ford's boondockers.

'Major,' I said, willing myself to look him up and down.

'Captain.'

Ford swung his feet off the desk and sat up straight in his chair. He looked old and tired in the weak morning sun coming in through the window above his head.

'Let's cut the crap, shall we,' he said. 'Corporal Barnes

102

has put it in my schedule that you two are on day leave this afternoon at Mrs Gertrude Walters's house in Parnell.'

He looked at me questioningly. I shot a glance over at Cartwright who looked back at me smugly, as if he already knew the answer to whatever it was Ford was driving at and just wanted to see me squirm.

'Um. Yes, sir,' I said.

'The woman is a dingbat. I'm here to tell you that, Sokol. Whole family, dead and alive, all of them strange birds. Colonel Venning up at the 39th told me so. They've got a bunch of local doctors working up there at Cornwall Park. They say the husband was a real quack back in England. Total fucking nut-job, Sokol.' He looked over at Cartwright gravely, then back at me. 'A psychiatrist.'

I didn't know what to say. He said the word cautiously, as if its mere utterance might give him a disease. Cartwright looked at me and nodded solemnly.

'Excuse me, sir,' I said. 'But don't we have psychiatrists in the Marines as well?'

'Are you busting my chops, Sokol?'

'No, sir.'

He pointed his index finger at me, thumb up, a child's imitation of a hand gun.

'You better not be busting my chops, kiddo.'

'I'm, ah, I'm not, sir.'

'Listen to me,' he said, leaning forward a little, placing his hands flat on the desk in front of him. 'This guy was a first class fruitcake. We're not talking about a few pills for shell-shock here. Are we, Major?'

'No, sir,' said Cartwright.

'This guy, he was . . . I mean he, he wrote about . . . you know. Things.'

'Things, sir?'

He was struggling with some deep, innate awkwardness for

103

some reason. He kept looking at me and raising his eyebrows, like I was supposed to pick up on some obvious sub-text.

'I'm not sure I follow, Colonel.'

'Ah, Christ,' he said, waving his hand in the air. The gold signet on his pinkie caught the sunlight coming in behind him and flashed it in my eyes. 'The hell with it. Go up there and do your goddamn thing. All I'm saying is, keep your guard up. Both of you.'

'Yes, sir,' said Cartwright, a trifle too loud.

'Yes, sir,' I said.

We had Sturgis drive us up to Parnell in a jeep. Cartwright was in the back trimming his nose hair with a small pair of scissors and a pocket mirror held up to his immaculate face. I rode shotgun with Sturgis, uncomfortable in my stiff, neatly pressed number one uniform. We were making our way along the waterfront down Tamaki Drive, an ugly scene of reclaimed land that had been turned into a sprawling port. The *Mount Vernon* was still berthed there, along with a couple of other Navy vessels that couldn't fit into the dock across the harbour in Devonport. Like everything else in the city, our presence had coloured the waterfront khaki green. Sturgis had started talking but it took me a moment to detach myself from the grim scene flashing by us.

'. . . and she brings one every time,' he said, having to strain his voice over the sound of the wind whistling over the two-foot windshield and the honest percussion of the engine.

'What?'

As I turned to him a small gust of wind caught the brim of my hat, which was only loosely sitting atop of my head, and sent it flying back behind me. I uselessly flailed my arms in the air before turning around to see that the hat had crashed straight into Cartwright's pocket mirror, causing him a painful moment with the scissors which were still scouring the inside of his nose.

'Jesus Christ, Sokol.'

'What? Come on, it was an accident.'

He handed me my hat back and resumed his follicle examination. He was determined to be ready, come whatever.

'Lucky,' said Sturgis, a stupid look on his face.

'Lucky.'

I fitted the hat back on my head, pulling the brim down tight so that I had to cock my chin slightly in order to see straight. I was anxious, nervous. There was a terrible sick feeling swirling around in my stomach and I felt as though I could have thrown up.

'What were you saying?' I said to Sturgis, trying to take my mind off her.

'Your hat. It was lucky it didn't—'

'No. Before that,' I yelled into the wind.

'Oh. She brings a cake. Like, every day. And believe me, they're not good. I mean, at all.' We rounded a bend and came on to Parnell Road. 'Timmins used one as a discus the other day and I swear to God it didn't break. He got some good distance on it too.'

'Who brings the cakes?'

He shot me a confused look. 'I just got through telling you.'

'Sorry. The wind.'

He shook his head. 'The old lady. You must have seen her. She lives up in Ponsonby somewheres. She's been coming to the camp almost every day now for over a week.'

He looked at me questioningly, his mouth open, totally focused on the moment. I spent four-fifths of my life somewhere out of the present tense, and I envied his dumb good fortune to be so interested, so connected to the here and now. Even at that moment, on my way to see the woman who had haunted my mind for the past eight days, I felt only a tangential association with the clump of flesh and bones wearing my pants. I was always someplace else.

'Never seen her,' I said.

Sturgis shook his head again. 'Well, she's a strange one.'

We drove on in gusty silence for a moment before Sturgis pointed out that we were in the main part of Parnell Village, a cutesy area with big, wooden villas, large swathes of green lawn, and a smattering of quaint, whitewashed shops. It could have passed for one of those persistently nameless New England towns the Cartwrights liked to spend their summers in. Sturgis drove slowly, one hand on the wheel, the other negotiating a street map that refused to bend to his command. It felt great to be out of the camp and away from Ponsonby. Up here there were very few signs that a war was in progress. The docile streets seemed to render the prospect of bombs and guns and submarines faintly absurd. I could see Cartwright behind me in the reflection of the wing mirror, tending to the hair on his head now.

Sturgis had figured out the direction we needed to take and was busy stuffing the map down the side of his seat.

'Did Timmins and O'Keefe ever make it to that cathouse?' I asked.

Sturgis, keeping his sights on the road ahead of him, furrowed his brow and dug his chin into his chest.

'You'll have to be more specific, sir. It's not an uncommon occurrence.'

'The Oriental one. Remember the other week, after we saw that giant in Western Park. They said—'

'Oh yeah,' he said, a wicked smile lighting up every inch of his face.

'So they've been.'

'The whole fucking battalion's been, if you'll pardon my French.'

I looked in the wing mirror and could see Cartwright look

up at the back of Sturgis's head. I waited a few seconds until he resumed his preening.

'And was he there?'

'Who?'

'The giant. The Chinaman or whatever he is.'

'Oh. You bet. He's always there. He's the goddamn lord of that do-main.'

I nodded my head and looked back out at the houses slipping by us. We were getting close now. It was a pretty area, streets all tree-lined, picket fences, quiet as all hell. Ever since we'd turned off Parnell Road the jeep had been the only detectable sign of life around.

'I'll tell you who else is known to visit there,' Sturgis said, changing down gears with a jumpy clutch.

'Who?' I wasn't in the mood to talk now. My stomach was starting to cramp up.

'Oscar Walters.'

'Who?'

'That guy who made the speech about chess. You know. At Western Park. The English—'

All of a sudden the jeep ground to an ungainly halt, and as I rocked back and forth on my seat Sturgis slapped me on the back and said, '—guy. Well, here we are, sirs. Don't do anything I wouldn't do.'

'That's enough, Corporal,' said Cartwright, leaping out of the back and onto the road like he was Jesse Owens. Cartwright detested freshness in anyone below the rank of colonel. He smoothed his uniform out with his hands and drew in a deep breath of damp air. He was primed for this and he was determined to let me know it.

I got out of the jeep and stepped on to the sidewalk, my legs starting to feel a little weak. As soon as I closed the door Sturgis roared off in a storm of noise, and before I had gathered my senses, I turned to see Cartwright marching up the path to the front door. The house was much like its neighbours, a grand two-storey wooden affair painted white with dark green trim at the sills and eves. The Marseille-tiled roof was punctured by no less than six chimneys, only one of which looked to be smoking. The front lawn rose gently up from the street to the front porch. On either side of the path leading to the front door was a twin set of matching lemon trees, which accentuated the overall symmetry of the place – a door smack in the middle, an even number of windows on either side, each half of the front a mirror image of the other. I drew in a deep breath as Cartwright had done, mine not so confident, and wondered whether the symmetry and balance that existed on the outside of the house had any relative on the inside. From what I had been told about the Walters family so far, I assumed not.

CHAPTER 16

We were shown in by a broad old man dressed in black. He must have had something wrong with his eyes as he wore dark glasses in thin wire frames. He bowed with a stiff, almost imperceptible nod of his head and held the door open for us without saying a word. It took me a moment or two to figure out he was a butler. I gave him a look of thanks as I passed over the threshold, but his expression didn't register anything in return. The skin had long since dropped from what must have been a full face, so that he now had the appearance of an old Shar Pei, his melancholy jowls sagging below the invisible line of his jaw. The area just above the side of his mouth, though, seemed to be twisted and slightly paralysed, as if he'd had a stroke.

He led us sullenly down a wide, dark, wainscoted hallway that was lined with framed portraits of what must have been earlier editions of the Walters clan. We were then shown into a room running off to the right of the hallway, but not before the old butler spent an awkward few moments trying to negotiate the latch on the heavy oak doors that led into the room. I was standing close enough to him to see that the joints of his fingers were badly knotted with arthritis. He eventually sprung the latch and pushed one of the doors open. His black uniform was worn at the elbows and cuffs, and the stitching had popped around the top of both shoulders. I watched myself nod at him in the reflection of his dark glasses, but his twisted face didn't show anything in response.

'Inside,' he said in a strange, harsh accent that I couldn't pick.

We were shown into a largish room that was lined with books on every wall – a library, in fact. The shelving went from floor to ceiling and ran around the entire perimeter of the room save for the space taken up by a deep fireplace and tasteful marble mantelpiece. Although the room was freezing the fireplace was clean, and didn't look as though it had staged a fire in some time. The mantelpiece was cluttered with framed photographs and ceramic ornaments bearing simple watercolour scenes of village and market life. I had seen something like these pieces in a book once, and faintly remembered they were from Belgium or Holland or someplace. Germany, maybe.

It was difficult to focus on the ornaments, though, as they, like everything else in the room, were overshadowed by an immense oil painting that was hung on the chimney above the mantelpiece. It was a portrait of an age-ravaged man, his head only, and it looked to me as though it was based on one of the later Rembrandt self-portraits, the beret and turned-up collar ones. The brushwork was a thick and heavy-handed impasto, building up solemn earth tones of burnt sienna, yellow ochre and warm sepia to present the mottled face, which emerged out of a background of coal black. The face was so close to the picture plane you had the feeling that it was going to tip out of the frame. I was so taken by the proficiency of the artist's technique that it took me a few moments to notice the eyes of the subject, burning out of that formidable head. I had never seen painted eyes like that before, not even in New York. It took every ounce of my will to maintain eye contact with them. They were alive with something, some knowledge or sorcery that I didn't care to understand. I took a couple of steps back and to the left, but they followed me, they watched me, looking straight into the blackest corner of my heart.

I was about to move towards the picture again when the old butler finally decided to speak. I had totally forgotten he was in the room.

'Sit,' he said, pointing Cartwright and me to a pair of wing-backed reading chairs that were positioned in the middle of the room around a low, cherrywood coffee table. Again the word was too short to determine the provenance of the accent, but whatever it was it certainly wasn't English.

We did as he bade, and once he was confident our asses had hit the leather cushions, he disappeared out of the room. I looked over at Cartwright, who was now staring up at the painting. The room was dark, with only a narrow beam of light coming in through the windows. The rest was obscured by a set of almost completely drawn wine-red velvet curtains.

'Sokol,' said Cartwright in a low, conspiratorial tone. He looked over his shoulder to make sure the butler had gone.

'What?'

'Do you . . .' He nodded back over his shoulder again.

'What?'

'Do you think he's German?'

Just as he said this we heard some low mumbling coming from another room, as though the speakers were trying to suppress an argument. Then a door slammed.

'I don't know,' I said as Cartwright turned back round to face me. 'What I do know is that this room is like an ice-box.'

Cartwright grunted something and cast another wary look back up at the painting looming down on us.

'This place gives me the creeps,' he said.

The book collection was impressive. I recalled Mrs Walters at the British Med soiree telling Colonel Ford that he must see her husband's collection of medical journals. I did a scan of the shelves to see if I could spot them, my nose starting to run a little from the cold. From what I could tell, the collection was divided into subjects, and those subjects had been arranged alphabetically. I hit upon the 'M' section and was working my way past mathematics when I heard the butler fumbling with the latch on the doors again. We both looked at him through the glass panes as he eventually managed to push one of the doors open.

'You are to come,' he said, a chastened edge in his tone. 'I was mistake.'

He stood firm at the double doors waiting for us to obey his command. Cartwright gave me a little look as we stood up and followed him out of the room. He led us farther down the long hallway until we came to a closed door right at the end. The butler lightly knocked on the door, three apologetic taps with his twisted knuckles. He had a perfect ring of dandruff running around the base of the collar on his black tunic. There was some rustling on the other side of the door and a few quick, clicking footsteps. My stomach rose into my throat and I felt, in spite of the bracing chill in the hallway, a few beads of sweat push through the pores of my forehead.

A voice on the other side of the door said, 'Show the gentlemen in now, Winston.'

The old butler shook his head and clucked his tongue a couple of times. I got the impression that whoever he was and wherever he came from, his name was certainly not Winston.

He opened the door onto a small, bright sitting room, which was like an addendum to a more formal dining room that ran off to the left. The brilliance of the light was so intense, and so distinct from the gloomy library and hallway, that it was like stepping into a different house entirely. A flood of streaky light poured in through two large sash windows, and a small fire burned in a wrought-iron fireplace that was positioned on the threshold of the dining room.

Mrs Walters was on her feet to greet us as we stepped into

the mercifully warm room. Emily was nowhere to be seen.

'Gentlemen,' she said, proffering her hand in mid-air first to Cartwright and then to me to take. 'I do apologise for Winston. He is, well, old, you see, and has trouble remembering certain things. He's a dear, though.'

She spoke as if she were referring to a loveable, but bothersome old family dog whose bowels had gone to seed. Winston stood at the door awaiting his next instruction, his twisted, jowly face expressionless behind those dark glasses. Mrs Walters looked exactly the same as she had at the British Med meeting. I think she was even wearing the same grey woollen suit.

'Please sit down, gentlemen,' she said, showing us to a beautiful but rather uncomfortable looking chaise longue that faced the windows. 'Winston. Please fetch Miss Walters now.'

Cartwright and I both reacted to the mention of her name – a fleeting tremor of the limbs, a spasm of molecules. It was uncomfortable sitting so close to Cartwright. I could feel his presence exuding from him, the generous dominion of air-space that followed him around wherever he went, sucking the life out of anybody who came too close and professed not to be enchanted by him. I felt I could murder him on the spot, stick a knife in his chest and not think twice about it. I could see him clenching and unclenching his fist, a little Cartwrightian tic I'd seen many times over the years. Mrs Walters sat down opposite us in a long, low-backed couch that ran beneath the windowsills.

'We brought Winston over from England, you know,' Mrs Walters said. The sun pouring in behind her gave her ash-coloured head a perfect halo. 'He does miss it so, our country house in Tewksbury especially. Have you ever been to Tewksbury, Captain?'

'I've never been to England, ma'am,' I said, a little surprised she'd addressed me instead of Cartwright.

'Of course. Americans are not renowned for their travel, are they? Unless there's a war to fight.' She looked into the gap directly between us, her eyes glassy. 'The English countryside is a wonderful place, Captain. It's as though the air, the very soil beneath your feet is full of words. Old words too. Words from dead languages, words we can no longer say, or even spell.' She looked at me now, a withering hawkish look that rose and fell as quick as a trill. 'Of course, in New Zealand there's nothing but silence. You will not be bothered by words in this country, gentlemen.'

She sat back and waited for one of us to pick up the thread. There was nothing in my head at that moment, nothing but the echo of the blood pulsing in my ears. I could see that Cartwright desperately wanted to say something, wanted to get on the front foot and lead with something impressive, something expansive, but nothing was coming. He leaned forward and clapped his hands together, but still nothing.

'Still,' said Mrs Walters, throwing him a line, 'we've all had to make sacrifices, haven't we?'

'Yes, ma'am,' said Cartwright, almost leaping off the edge of the chaise longue. 'The world's in a perilous state. Folks everywhere need to do their bit to make sure we pull through it.'

'You don't half cut to the quick, do you, Major?'

For some reason Cartwright saw this as a compliment.

'You'll have to excuse me, ma'am. My people raised me to speak my intentions plain and clear.'

'Admirable, I'm sure. Something of an American fetish, isn't it? Speaking plainly? And your people, Major. Tell me of them.'

'Well,' he said, steadying his big frame on the dainty antique, 'my mother's side is from Virginia. We can trace the line back to the *Mayflower*, I believe. And my great-granddaddy on my father's side was the first Cartwright doctor. He came over from your ways and set up camp in Massachusetts originally, but after the war with the spics he saw the potential in California. The rest of us have been out there ever since.'

'And what do they do in California, Major?' said Mrs Walters, clearly taken with the Yankee bullshit he was so assiduously feeding her.

'Practise medicine, mainly. My granddaddy had a big hand in Los Angeles early on, so a few of us are still connected to that.'

Mrs Walters smiled and nodded as one might nod at a stock agent rattling off the credentials of a young colt. I was looking forward to the bit where Cartwright told her he was married, but I noticed that his ring finger was conspicuously naked. Perhaps he would keep this little piece of information to himself for the time being. I was familiar with his Wasp routine, but the plain speaking bit was new. In my experience Cartwright's diction shaded to purple if anything. The plain talking was a recent development, and could only have come from his desire to please Ford and Green, plain speakers to beat the band.

'And if one were to travel to America,' Mrs Walters said, 'where do you think one should visit? I mean, for a person in my position. I'd always imagined the east coast would be my preference.'

'Of course there's more society back east, but in my humble opinion the west—'

There was a sharp tap on the door which made the three of us jump.

'Miss Walters,' Winston's disembodied voice announced from behind the door.

'Come, Winston,' called Mrs Walters.

I corrected my posture and sat up as straight as possible. I could see that Mrs Walters was nervous too, smoothing her charcoal skirt and steadying her tiny frame, a queer-looking smile stretched across her taut, refined face. She caught me looking at her and for a brief instant, no longer than a frame in the reel, I think she realised that I knew her game. And maybe I did too, because in that moment I saw something in her eyes I hadn't seen before. Something like desperation. She twisted her chin, pointedly looking over my shoulder and at the door, behind which Winston was once again having trouble springing the latch. The three of us watched the brass handle do a ghost rattle as the absurd racket went on interminably on the other side. I could sense that Cartwright was about to spring to his feet, but just then we heard her voice, low and coded, coming through the solid oak door.

'It's all right, Winston. I've got it.'

The door swung open silently. Although she would have been closest to the entrance she had the grace to stand aside so Winston could enter first and introduce her. He took two steps into the room, came to a parade-ground halt, and addressed us by looking at a spot three feet above the level of our heads.

'Miss Emily Wasser . . . Walters.'

There was a sudden compression of air in the room. The colour ran from Winston's face, and he looked ashen. I looked over at Mrs Walters, who had brought her hand to her mouth. It felt as though the room was about to turn in on itself, when the chaise longue creaked and Cartwright's leather-soled shoes hit the floorboards with a hard slap.

'Enchanted, Miss Walters,' he said, careening across the room towards Emily with his hand outstretched, as if he were a believer running to the light.

Emily, on a spur of involuntary instinct, backed away. Cartwright stopped abruptly at the sight of her recoiling and managed a pretty good recovery.

'Delighted to see you,' he said, extending his hand again, but this time with a cocked elbow and an upturned palm.

'And you, Major,' she said, taking his hand. 'You'll have to excuse me. I'm a little on edge today.'

I'd got to my feet and had moved around the chaise longue so that I stood on the other side of Winston, who had recovered something of his former colour.

'Miss Walters,' I said, offering her my hand across the great expanse of Winston's chest.

She took it with a firm grasp this time and looked me knowingly in the eyes. She had that same air of detached self-possession about her, as if she had simply come in to observe us rather than participate. I held her hand for a fraction longer than necessary, reluctant to let go.

'Captain.'

She was dressed in a full-length cream dress with a matching satin jacket draped over her shoulders. Over the past eight days I had worked so hard to preserve the memory of her face that it had become distorted and vague, a memory of a feeling rather than an image. But now she was real again. Loose curls of her chocolate hair draped across her collarbone, and her milky cheeks, elegant flat planes slightly sunken under the bone, were warmed with the faintest suggestion of pink. Her eyes, which shone to a harlequin sea green within the frame of her dark hair, seemed to soak up all the brilliant yellow light of the room.

We all took our seats again, with Emily sitting on some uncomfortable Edwardian-looking thing just off to the side of the couch her mother sat on. Mrs Walters was not unaware that both Cartwright and I admired the way her daughter took her seat and smoothed her dress across her knees.

'We'll take tea now, Winston,' Mrs Walters said.

Winston took a moment to react to this; he seemed to be doing something with his fingers, counting off sums perhaps, or some sort of exercise to relieve the pain of his arthritis. The room was silent for a moment before he looked up at

Mrs Walters with a clouded expression.

'Tea,' he said, loudly, snapping himself out of the sprawling plains of his mind. He bowed his head and left the room, closing the door behind him.

'Major Cartwright was just extolling the virtues of America's west coast, dear,' said Mrs Walters, beaming at Cartwright. 'It seems as if it's not entirely without good society.'

'Is that true, Major?' said Emily. 'I've often read that California is, well, rather coarse.'

'Emily! Excuse her, Major. Miss Walters has a . . . directness about her, at times.' She looked sideways at her daughter, tapping her affectionately on the knee. 'But I suppose the point stands. I too have heard that the American West lacks the refinement of New England. Pray, is it coarse, Major?'

'Not at all,' said Cartwright, his tone betraying a hint of defensiveness in spite of himself. 'I would think Miss Walters, and indeed you, ma'am, would be pleasantly surprised if you were to visit us in San Francisco.'

'What a capital idea,' Mrs Walters said, clapping her hands together in delight.

'Have either of you ever been to the States?' asked Cartwright, addressing Emily.

'I'm afraid not,' said Emily. 'Until we came here I'd never left England.'

She appeared to regret saying this as soon as the words left her mouth. Her expression clouded over, and her body slumped a little in its chair. For the briefest moment I thought I saw her studied austerity collapse. Mrs Walters seemed affected by the words as well, making a sudden movement forward so that she sat on the very edge of the couch.

'And what about you, Captain,' she said. 'Are you a society man, or one of these rough and tumble American types? Out in the woods with a shotgun and a book of, who is it, Walt Whitman?'

118

'I don't think I'm either.'

She seemed relieved by my answer as it gave her an opportunity to change the direction and tone of the proceedings.

'What on earth do you do, then?' she said teasingly.

'I keep to myself where I can.'

'And how is that working out for you?'

I nodded and smiled.

Mrs Walters felt comfortable enough to sit back in the couch again, but her eagle eyes never left me for a moment. She seemed to be regarding me with something like mirth or playful derision.

'Sokol,' she said inquisitively, cocking her jaw to regard me down the furiously straight line of her thin nose. 'Is that a . . . a Jewish name, Captain?'

I felt Cartwright squirm, heard the pop of his dry lips parting, but for some reason the question didn't surprise me. It seemed right that she would ask.

'Not for a long time,' I said and left it at that. It was the truth after all. The Sokols I knew had left religion and its attendant troubles on the fraught shores of Europe. Either there or in the cold delousing showers of Ellis Island. Like many new Americans at that time, the only tenet they bothered worrying about was survival. But the fact of my not being Jewish was not my father's doing alone. If I had wanted to, nobody would have stopped me going to temple. I know my mother would have gladly taken me if I'd shown an interest. But, being my father's son, it had always been my peculiar disposition to want to rid myself of encumbrances, anything that told me I belonged to something, anything that said I was part of something. My discovery of art, my discovery of painting only served to narrow me further. Where before it had only been an awkward instinct, now I had a reason to stand outside the frame, to reject and spurn. An unscientific love of colour and light was as close as I got to God.

'So,' said Emily, leaning towards me slightly. 'So, you're not Jewish?'

'No.'

A short pause followed while the particles in the room sparked and crackled. I couldn't help feeling as though I'd said the wrong thing. Mrs Walters still eyed me down the ridge of her nose. She seemed unconvinced. Finally she looked at Cartwright and smiled.

'Were you aware, Major, that there is a Japanese internment camp in Auckland?' She said this as though she were referring to a restaurant or an interesting theatre.

'Ah, no. I wasn't aware of that,' he said, struggling as I was to adapt to the sudden change in tack.

'In Papakura,' Emily said gravely. 'South of here.'

We both looked at her and nodded.

'My daughter and I volunteer at the women's camp,' Mrs Walters said. She was speaking to Cartwright, but I couldn't help feeling she was addressing me for some reason. She suddenly threw her head back in laughter. 'We do all sorts,' she said, amused at herself. 'We cook and clean, teach the poor things English and civil manners. You wouldn't believe it, but most of them have never eaten with a knife and fork in their lives. It's quite incredible.' She looked at Emily affectionately. 'My daughter has even scrubbed the floors these people walk on.'

'We work with the nuns from a local convent,' said Emily, almost challengingly. 'We're the only local civilians who would agree to help.'

'Yes,' said Mrs Walters in a slow, musing manner. 'I understand the men can be quite – well, nasty, if given half the chance. But the women are angels. So sweet and industrious. They let the odd few out, you know, to help out in the factories and so on.' She smiled knowingly. 'We try to do our best, Major. In the circumstances.'

120

Cartwright cleared his throat. 'I guess it can't hurt,' he said gallantly. 'They're the enemy, but it pays to be Christian all the same.'

Mrs Walters smiled and lowered the point of her chin into her delicate chest.

'Quite, Major. You see, my daughter and I . . .,' she said, twirling her hand playfully in the air, 'we're people who know a thing or two about persecution. Did you know that, Captain?' she asked, turning sharply towards me.

The question felt like an accusation, and my mind went blank as I fumbled for a response. Fortunately, I was saved from answering by a loud rattling at the door. We all turned to listen to another one of Winston's epic battles with the doorknob. This time the stakes were higher though, because by the sounds of things he was trying to balance a tray of teacups at the same time. It went on for four or five seconds before the twitching in Cartwright's leg got the better of him and he leapt to his feet to relieve Winston of his struggle. Just as Cartwright was about to spring the door the thing flew open and the old man came lunging into the room, off-balance and wielding his silver tray of tea things, forcing Cartwright into the ungainly position of trying to break Winston's fall without unsettling the laden tray in his arms. Somehow Winston managed to recover, and we were all able to breathe again. I turned back around to see Emily looking flush at me, a sly, almost mischievous expression playing at the corners of her mouth and eyes.

The tea was served in Royal Copenhagen china cups. As Winston placed my cup on the small mahogany table before me I noticed thick lines of black dirt encased underneath the tips of his fingernails, as if he'd just been digging a hole in the ground with his bare hands rather than brewing a pot of tea.

'I expect we should like to travel to America, Major,' Mrs Walters said, taking a cucumber sandwich from the small stack piled on the silver tray, pointedly moving us on to a less challenging topic. 'I mean, once this nonsense is all over.' She made another circular motion with her hand.

Cartwright and I made pitiful attempts to nibble our way through the sandwiches we'd picked up. The bread was stale and hadn't been buttered, and the cucumber was old as well, its thin slices quivering like bad oysters on the tongue before they went down. In spite of this, Mrs Walters and Emily ate with great, purposeful gusto, helping themselves to one sandwich after another in silence. Pretty soon the tray was emptied, well before Cartwright and I had managed to negotiate a half each. I couldn't help noticing the way the women ate – without reserve, without a shred of the self-consciousness they seemed to approach everything else with.

'Yes,' said Mrs Walters, leaning back in her seat, her eyes glazing as the stale bread expanded in her tiny stomach. 'I think one would jump at the chance to go to America.'

This comment lingered in the sad air for a moment. The only other sound came from the crackle and fizz of burning coal in the fireplace, and the metronome tick of a grandfather clock located somewhere in the adjacent dining room.

'Mother,' said Emily. 'Shall we show the gentlemen around the grounds?'

Cartwright sprang off the chaise longue at this. 'Well, that sounds like a swell idea,' he said, taking Emily's hand and helping her out of her chair.

'If we must, if we must,' said Mrs Walters, looking un-enthused, but nevertheless holding out a wizened, bluish hand for me to take.

It was great to be outside again. What remained of the after-noon sunlight was watery and limp. The back yard, or what Emily had referred to as the 'grounds', was a vast block of unkempt lawn overrun by crab weed and fenced in by a grim block wall that reminded me of the mausoleums in all those forgotten New England cemeteries. Three enormous walnut trees broke up the section at various intervals, and were all one good gust of wind away from shedding their papery brown leaves. From where we stood on the back porch the block wall running across the back of the section would have been a good two football fields away. Off to the right was a faded white clapboard garden shed that backed on to a sizeable vegetable plot. We heard a sound coming from that direction and turned to see Winston, still in his black uniform, but now donning an oversized pair of tattered work boots, emerge from the shed, a shovel and a hoe slung over either shoulder.

'Quite the factotum, isn't he?' I said without thinking.

'Times are lean, Captain,' said Mrs Walters without looking at me. Her tone suggested a hint of insult, even reproach. 'When Doctor Walters was alive we had a gardener and a cook. The children had tutors for their instruction.'

I watched as Winston manfully drove his shovel into the rich, dark earth. I imagined the grimace, the wince of pain as his crippled paws absorbed the jar.

'Both of my children had tutors, Captain. Several tutors, in fact. My son, Oscar, was accepted into Cambridge, you know. To read for a degree.'

'Terrific school,' said Cartwright, taking a step down off the porch. The step groaned beneath his weight. Cartwright sucked in a big gulp of air and beat his fists on his chest with a single resounding thud. He turned around and smiled up at us. 'The air in this country is truly exceptional. I wonder if you two ladies would care to join me on a wander round the yard. Or should I say a turn?'

Mrs Walters cocked her head back and laughed, almost leaping into Cartwright's arms. Emily looked sideways at me before dutifully following her mother down the steps.

'I'll catch up with you soon,' I said. 'I just want to freshen up.'

'Do your best, Captain,' said Emily, her face radiant in the buttery light. 'But don't expect miracles.'

I took a leak in the bathroom situated on the opposite side of the hallway from the library. I'd fully intended on heading back outside to meet the others, but the rogues' gallery of portraits lining the hallway was too intriguing to pass by. There was everything from professional photographs of children in white frocks and bonnets to stern oil colours of even sterner cavalry officers and gentlemen. The pictures showing what I took to be the patriarchal line all bore some kind of resemblance to the looming subject in the library. I wandered all the way down to the front entrance, where, on the right-hand wall was a framed photograph of five prim, genteel looking men with their hair immaculately combed and oiled, their beards neatly trimmed around their lean faces. The inscription at the bottom of the picture read 'Royal College of Psychiatrists: London, 1934'. I took a step closer to the picture and ran the palm of my hand across the dusty, greasy flat plane of glass. And there he was, one from the left: Dr Michael Walters. I studied his features closely – the black hair, the proud, opaque face, those interrogating eyes – trying to get an imprint of them on my mind, something to compare against the painting in the library. I padded my way back up the hallway trying to think what it was about those eyes that was so unsettling. Looking at them was like catching a glimpse of something you weren't supposed to see – a married woman with her lover, an act of secret violence or deceit. They seemed to laden me with a burden that I couldn't understand.

I unhooked the latch on the double-doors to the library feeling the hollow-stomach excitement of guilt and nerves, charged with an adrenaline that had been absent from my life for a long time. The chill of the air pinched the skin on my face and brought my heart up an inch closer to my mouth. I couldn't say why I felt so bad about coming into the room, why it felt like such an invasion, why I seemed to know somehow that my presence wasn't welcomed. I went straight over to the marble mantelpiece and looked up at the picture. There was no mistaking the resemblance to the Dr Walters in the photograph, but the painter appeared to have taken a couple of liberties with the face. The nose, one half of a protractor in the photograph, had been levelled off some and given a wider bridge. The effect was to bring the eyes into greater prominence. It didn't escape me that that giving him a slightly bulbous, Dutch Golden Age nose may also have been an attempt to obscure something more elemental in Dr Walters.

For all of that it was a damned good picture. I imagined Dr Walters had carried a notion of himself as some kind of shaman, an intellectual, classically trained sage who held the minds and souls of lesser men in the palm of his hand. I let the fantasy spin out a little further as I stepped back from the painting's dominion, picturing the doctor negotiating with the artist over the effect he was after. Here is a man who can see, I imagined him saying. While the rest of you are looking, here is a man who can actually see.

I finally turned my back on the painting and started making my way around the book shelves. To the left of where I stood there was a chunk of shelving devoted to the Judicial Reports of the House of Lords, a serious block of navy blue volumes dating back to 1900. My attention, however, was squarely focused on the M section, and in particular medicine, a category Dr Walters had seen as encompassing psychiatry. As a fellow doctor I respected this. He wasn't so sure of himself to consider his controversial field as something distinct from blood and bones, yet he had the earnest confidence to say that what he did was indeed medicine, and not some back alley, leaf-rubbing voodooism.

125

I crouched down on my haunches and scanned the rows, looking for the journals Mrs Walters had mentioned. I ran my index finger along the dusty spines of the books, still feeling apprehensive. The room was so cold that I could see a faint trace of my warm breath in the air. The tingling sensation in my finger put me in a kind of trance, so that I was no longer properly reading the inscriptions on the books. I could have done this for hours, crouched down in this icy room, scanning the hills and dales of the volumes with the tip of my finger. But for some reason I stopped on one in particular, a thin volume with a cover of tight blue leather.

I plucked the book off the shelf in front of me and held it tightly in my hands. I stood up and looked up at the painting again, at the eyes and the face of the man who seemed to be alive in his frame. I hefted the volume in my hand so I could read the spine: *The London Review of Medicine* (1936) Vol. IX. For some reason I had a prescient feeling about the book, as if somebody had guided my hand, as if somebody or something had willed me to pluck it out from the shelf. I opened it up to the contents page, and there, the third article in at page 97, was Dr Michael Walters, author of *Treatment of Fixated Latency Period: A Case Study of a German Boy*.

'I see you've taken up Mother's offer.'

'What?'

I turned, jumped, to see Emily standing in the doorway. I didn't know how she managed to come in, to walk across the bare floorboards of the hallway without me hearing. She didn't seem real, standing there with her dark, touseled hair and flushed, apple-red cheeks on the threshold of the bleak library.

'Although I'm not sure those are the journals she was referring to. There's another, less controversial set in the study.'

'Excuse me?'

It was taking me a while to recover from the fright. She laughed gently, the way one laughs at a child trying to participate in an adult conversation, but I sensed that her detachment wasn't as complete as she would have liked it to have been. Or appeared to have been. She looked at the book in my hand for a moment before taking a few steps into the room, stopping by the edge of the mantelpiece. She looked up at the painting.

'I take it you've worked out who that is,' she said.

'Dr Walters, I assume.' My tongue felt like it had been shot with novocaine. 'Your father.'

She looked at me for a long moment, her lovely green eyes glassy.

'Yes,' she said finally, a little mysteriously, as if she were talking to herself, thinking aloud. Her lips didn't quite close on the hiss of the s. She looked at me for a moment without seeming to see me. And then, coming to again, she calmly averted her eyes.

I didn't know what to say so I said, 'I was just taking a look at this article your father wrote.'

'Which one is that?' she asked, the flush rising in her cheeks again.

'Ah. I believe it's called "Latency Period in a German—"'

'Treatment of Fixated Latency Period,' she said, the words like ice on her tongue. 'I know the one, Captain.' She looked at me boldly, the sides of her eyes bunching together slightly, sharpening her open, forensic stare. I guess I had, in the past, prided myself on having a certain intuitive talent for reading people's characters, for stripping back the layers of presentation to see the little insecurities, the little lies people tell themselves. As a painter it is necessary to look at the world this way, to not accept what your eyes are actually seeing. But at that moment I had absolutely no idea what was happening in Emily's head. In the two minutes she'd been in the library

127

with me she seemed to have run a gamut of emotions and attitudes, but had never settled on one long enough to allow me to get a read.

'You have a reassuring face, Captain.'

Her words hung in the cool air.

'Reassuring?'

'Yes.'

I raised my eyebrows and handed her the book; it seemed like the right thing to do, as if I were handing over a weapon to a cop. She took it and placed it back on the shelf with the minimum of fuss. When she turned back around to face me she was wearing the smile I'd seen in the sitting room earlier, when Winston and Cartwright were doing their avant-garde dance with the tea tray.

'That's a very bold thing to say.'

'I guess it depends on who you say it to,' she said.

'That's probably right.'

And then a great thing happened: we looked at each other and laughed, simply, innocently, just for a few seconds, at nothing at all.

'You're very beautiful,' I said when the laughing had stopped.

'Speaking of bold.'

But it worked, goddamn it. She tried to hold my gaze in the spirit of banter or repartee, but what I'd said had stunned her, wobbling her natural poise. She laughed, but this time I didn't join in. She looked down at her feet, her thick chestnut hair falling over her forehead. I was sick with wanting to touch her.

'There you are!' cried Mrs Walters.

She stood in the hallway looking in, Cartwright at her flank. I couldn't say how long they'd been there – they may have even heard my declaration. The quizzical look on the old woman's face, and the famous scowl on Cartwright's, suggested that even if they hadn't heard it, our demeanour, the

128

way our bodies were hanging in the queer space of the library, probably betrayed us. Not that I gave a damn. I had shown her my cards, and she had been good enough not to slap my face or pity me. It was only a start, but it was enough for now.

'What on earth are you two doing in there? Major Cartwright and I did three whole laps of the grounds. I was beginning to feel like a racehorse.'

'Captain Sokol was interested in the painting,' said Emily, flatly.

Something in her manner had changed again. Her slender shoulders hunched slightly and she seemed, almost imperceptibly, to cave in on herself. It occurred to me for the first time that she looked nothing like her mother.

'We had an artist from the Continent paint that,' said Mrs Walters, finally coming into the room. Her usual swagger had left her, and she looked a little nervous, a little timid even. She only took a few steps over the threshold before stopping and looking up at her late husband. 'It is tremendously difficult to get good artists in England, Captain.'

'Really?' I smiled at Cartwright as he walked in, taking long, purposeful strides beyond Mrs Walters and into the centre of the room. He tried to ignore me by looking up at the painting. His jaw was set in his characteristic boyish demonstration of displeasure or dissatisfaction. I could see that he was itching to lay into me about something. I turned back to Mrs Walters. 'Why's that?'

'No passion,' she said, as if she were giving the answer to a simple equation.

'Where was the painter from?' asked Cartwright. He stood square on with the picture, his feet set wide apart, his head cocked back. He asked his question without moving, without looking at Mrs Walters. I could see he'd had enough of her now.

'I don't recall,' said Mrs Walters, unconvincingly. 'It was done so long ago.'

'No it wasn't,' said Cartwright. 'The artist signed it off there in the corner. 1935.' He pointed at the bottom left corner of the picture, labouring his point, at his vindictive best. 'G.T.R. 1935. It's not that long ago.'

'I believe he was Swiss,' Emily said, stepping away from me and towards her mother, her green eyes almost gone black with dilation.

Cartwright said, 'Swiss?' without taking his eyes off the picture, his brow creased, as if he'd never heard of the word.

'Yes, Major. Isn't that right mother? You remember the gentleman.'

'Swiss. Yes. You're absolutely right, dear.' She laughed, a single hoot, but it was brittle and forced. 'All this clean air, Major. I must be losing my marbles.'

Cartwright cast a wry, derisive look at me, but he was unable to do malice properly. He was too well-fed for malice – had spent too many afternoons on his father's yacht, danced with too many debutantes in spring to form the hard core necessary for malice. The best he could muster was petty cynicism and campus point-scoring. Or so I thought.

'Since when have the Swiss been passionate?' he said, rocking back on his heels and digging his hands into his hip pockets. He looked immensely pleased with himself.

Nobody said anything for a moment. Somewhere in the vast house we heard Winston battling with another doorknob, but nobody was in the mood any more.

'Emily, dear,' said Mrs Walters in a hollow, deflated tone. 'Will you play for the gentlemen?'

Emily looked horrified at the suggestion, but I think she sensed as I did that we all needed to get the hell out of the library. She nodded, which had the effect of immediately flicking Mrs Walters's light back on. The old woman's face beamed and she clapped her hands together loudly.

'Lovely,' she said. 'This way, gentlemen.'

She beckoned us to follow her out the door as she shot out herself in excitement. I was about to follow Emily when Cartwright grabbed me forcefully by the arm. He waited until Emily had left the room before he leant in close to my ear. I could feel his warm breath on my neck.

'You told her I was married, didn't you?' he said aggressively.

'Who?'

'The mother.'

'No,' I said with raised inflection.

'Don't bullshit me, Sokol. I know what you're like.'

'What's that supposed to mean?'

'How did she know then, huh? I'm not wearing a goddamn ring. I certainly didn't tell her. How'd she know, Sokol?'

He tightened his grip on my arm, so I pushed him away with my free hand.

'Get your hands off of me!' I said. He stepped back, but his face had turned scarlet with anger. 'I've only seen her in your presence, you idiot. What do you think, I slipped her a note?'

He wanted to bark back, but was stumped by my logic.

'Well,' he said, searching, 'you told Miss Walters just then, didn't you? Didn't you?'

'No. And . . . Jesus, Cartwright. What are you talking about? You *are* married.'

'Gentlemen,' cried Mrs Walters. She stood in the doorway and clapped her hands like a school matron. 'This way please.'

We listened to Emily play one of Debussy's *Arabesques* in a bright, spacious living room at the front of the house. The air in the room was so cold that my toes began to tingle inside my boots and woollen socks. I wondered whether the temperature was having an effect on Emily's playing, because it didn't sound too good. Her timing was erratic, and she didn't seem to have any feel for dynamics or articulation. It didn't help that the antique grand was badly out of tune. Like everything else in the house, like Winston and the marble coffee tables, the library and the sterling silver tea tray, the piano seemed to belong to a distant memory of a former life, to a different continent, perhaps even to a different language.

The poverty of Emily's playing, however, was lost on Mrs Walters. She stood at the end of the piano's belly, a wistful smile pasted across her narrow face, one hand resting on the closed lid in the style of a parlour singer. Cartwright and I sat at opposite ends of a long couch watching the performance. Occasionally Mrs Walters would hum the melody, eerily harmonising with the out-of-tune piano, and say 'The West Country, gentleman. It sounds like the West Country.'

I assumed this referred to some idyllic fantasy she had of the English countryside, but it occurred to me that nobody from England would say such an absurd thing. It was almost as if she were trying to convince us of something; that the whole afternoon had been dedicated to convincing us of something, but like Emily's playing it simply didn't ring true.

Cartwright's patience was shot, and during the entire performance he maintained a brooding glare over the piano at the top of Emily's head, his left leg shaking furiously. He made a show of wincing at every false note as if he were in physical pain, and when Mrs Walters looked at him and voiced one of her stupid metaphors he made an even greater show of pretending not to hear her.

Cartwright obviously knew the piece because the moment Emily fingered the last chord he was on his feet.

'You play very . . . well, Miss Walters,' he said.

I was relieved to hear that he'd finally dropped the false Yankee act and was back to his mildly bitter, churlish self. Emily stood up from behind the piano and closed the lid over the keyboard, loudly, as if it were an act of contrition. She smiled blandly at Cartwright, but it came across more as a grimace.

'I think we both know you're being too kind,' she said.

He nodded at her and tucked his hat under his arm, a little regimental flourish.

'I thank you for your hospitality, Mrs Walters, but now it's—'

'But you're not leaving, Major?' Mrs Walters protested. 'Why, Emily has just started. And, and you haven't even had a chance to—'

'Thank you,' he said flatly. 'All the same. But I don't need to remind you, ma'am, that there's a war on and the Captain and I are required back at base. There are wounded men we have to attend to.'

'Do you have many wounded in the hospital?' asked Emily in a plain tone, the embarrassment of her recital already well behind her.

'Yes we do,' Cartwright said gravely. 'Men, American men, injured in battle.'

'Where were they injured, Major?' asked Mrs Walters, her eyes alive with interest.

'The Solomons, of course. The fighting is especially heavy there at the moment. The Nips . . . I mean, the Japanese are digging their heels in.'

Mrs Walters laughed in an affected manner that was, I think, supposed to demonstrate her female silliness. 'Why on earth must you attack each other over these tiny islands? I've never understood it.'

Cartwright smiled and relaxed his shoulders. This was the kind of question one of his aunts might ask at the dinner table, endearingly earnest, a patsy question designed to let one of the men hold forth.

'It's vital that we secure the islands, ma'am,' he said solemnly. 'If we can build an airfield there we can secure the whole basin in—'

'An airfield?' asked Mrs Walters musingly.

'Correct.' He was the Secretary of the Navy giving the press pool a briefing. 'An airfield would allow supplies to be flown in. It's vital for the region's security.'

'But surely, Major,' said Mrs Walters provocatively, 'that sort of thing would take months. Airfields don't just pop up overnight.'

He laughed gently again, enjoying himself now. 'I assure you, ma'am, our boys work fast. I operated on an engineer yesterday who informed me that things were already underway. But,' he said, cocking out his wrist and looking at his watch, all folksy and good-natured, 'as I was saying, the Captain and I have our duties to be getting back to.'

I stood up from the couch. I'd noticed Emily's quick looks in my direction as this exchange had been going on. I thought, I hoped, she was trying to signal something to me; something like, 'don't go'.

'Cart . . . I mean, Major,' I stumblingly said. 'We don't have a ride. We have to call Sturgis to pick us up.'

Cartwright took this like a blow to the head – it dazed him, and he needed a woozy moment to gather himself. Although he was arrogant and vain, he certainly was a man who was conscious, and even skilled in the art of social graces. His abrupt declaration that we were leaving, coming as it did out of the blue, would not have come naturally to him. I assumed he'd done it on the theory that he could just slip out the door, pile into the jeep and speed away from the Walters family for good. But now he was trapped and he looked genuinely confused, a little helpless even.

'I'll give him a call,' I said. 'Could you show me to the telephone, Miss Walters?'

'Certainly, Captain.'

She led me back up the long hallway and into a small office off to the right. It wasn't much bigger than a wardrobe, having just enough room for a roll-top desk and chair, a small bookshelf containing a few reference books, and the telephone. She stepped inside the small room with me, unnecessarily pointing out the telephone on the wall above the desk. She was a matter of inches away, and I could smell the lavender sting of soap on her arms. I could feel the heat of her body, could feel the tension in the complicated airspace between us.

'The telephone, Captain.'

'Thank you.'

We looked at each other for a long, drawn-out moment. A bolder man would have grabbed her lithe body without hesitation, but I wasn't made of that mould. Back down the hallway an awful, clanging sound started up, followed by a few short notes of Mrs Walters's pitchy voice. I couldn't help but smile at the thought of Cartwright down in that room, alone with the mad woman, his jaw set tight as he listened to the racket.

'Mother,' Emily said, her eyes glinting.

'Cartwright,' I said.

We both laughed, lightly at first, then harder, louder. I couldn't stop. I laughed at everything and nothing. I laughed as though I wasn't in my body, as though I had no connection to anyone or anything. I laughed without a single thought in my head. And then we stopped, and the bubbly silence that followed felt enormous. I took a step forward, put my hand to her face, and kissed her deeply, without restraint.

It was over fast. As we disengaged I instinctively took a jerky step back and crashed into the desk behind me. She did the same thing herself, banging into the bookshelf on the opposite wall. It was an awkwardness befitting the spontaneity that preceded it. I made a show of having to use the telephone and she went through a few pointless and jaunty instructions before straightening herself up and shuffling past me. She was almost out the door when I said, 'Emily.'

'Yes.'

'My name is Peter.'

She smiled as she watched me dial the number, her absinthe green eyes glowing in the dim light, seeing me whole.

We didn't have to wait long for Sturgis to show up. Apparently he hadn't made it back to camp, so I had Diddle radio him for me. After a few unsuccessful attempts he finally managed to track him down in one of the Parnell Village bars, not two minutes' drive from the house, where he'd been playing poker and drinking since he'd left us.

We were all sitting in the front living room when we heard the jeep rattle up the quiet, sleepy street. Cartwright was on his feet in a heartbeat and doing a second round of goodbyes when we all heard a key turning in the lock in the front door. This was followed by a few hard, slow footsteps.

'Winston,' said the owner of the footsteps. The sound of his voice echoed up the long hallway.

I noticed that Emily and Mrs Walters had both returned to their chairs at the far end of the room. Cartwright and I remained standing, looking at the closed living room door, waiting. Just then a loud horn sounded out on the street, and it took me a moment to realise that the jeep had come to a stop and that Sturgis was waiting outside. We listened as the man in the hallway had a brief, hushed conversation with Winston. The women were completely silent; neither one of them would look at us.

The doorknob rattled as Winston fumbled with it on the other side for a few seconds. Finally it sprung open, and the old man took a shaky step inside.

'Mr Walters,' he said.

Winston stood back as a tall, thin man in glasses entered the room. It was Oscar Walters – the chess guy. I almost laughed at the sight of him; I couldn't believe I had been so dense as to not make the connection. He looked uneasy at the sight of two uniformed Marines standing in the middle of his living room. His small round spectacles were slightly fogged, and his face was the very image of his mother's – pale, withdrawn, sharp little eyes deeply set in his head. He also had the same angular cheekbones and protruding forehead. He appeared to have an old bruise under his right eye and a few scratches on his hands. As always, he was dressed entirely in black. He was carrying an old, worn-looking leather attaché case that was brimming with books and papers.

He stared at Cartwright and me for a few stunned moments before he was able to compose himself and turn the surprise into contempt. He looked over at Emily and Mrs Walters, both of whom were looking at the ground.

'Who are they?' he said, addressing either one of them.

Mrs Walters sprang to her feet but didn't take any steps towards either him or us. She was clearly very nervous.

'They are doctors, Oscar,' she said. 'From the Victoria Park camp. We met them at the British Medical Society conference.'

'From Victoria Park?' said Oscar, looking me up and down. 'I recognise you.' He said this as though I should be embarrassed by the fact.

'I saw you speak at Western Park,' I said. 'Quite a performance. I'd never been interested in chess before, but after hearing you speak . . .'

'What's this?' said Cartwright, turning to me.

Mrs Walters laughed loudly. 'This is Captain Sokol and Major Cartwright. They're doctors, Oscar. From the Vic—'

'Captain Smokol,' he said, his inflection falling at the end to indicate what I took to be reproach, distaste.

'It's Sokol.'

'I'm sure it is,' he said queerly, briefly eyeing his mother. 'I see you in Ponsonby often, that pack of goons following you around.' He ran his hand down the line of his jaw and looked up at the ceiling. 'Surprising. I thought a doctor, a man of medicine would have known better.'

'Oscar!' cried Mrs Walters, taking a few stunted steps towards him before stopping abruptly.

Emily had got to her feet and, I believe, was about to come to my side when Sturgis sounded the horn again with a long, sustained blast.

'That's one of them out there now,' said Oscar with a derisive grin. 'He must be in a rush to get back to the whorehouse. In need of a pipe, I should imagine. You shouldn't keep him waiting.'

Cartwright took a very deliberate, very choreographed step towards him. 'Now listen here, buddy. That's a Marine you're talking about.'

'Yes,' said Oscar slowly, unperturbed by Cartwright's advance. 'I take it you are in the Third Division. Is that right, Major?'

The question, the casual, knowledgeable tone in which it was spoken, seemed to surprise Cartwright. 'That's correct,' he said.

'I have colleagues who work down on the wharf. They tell me that your men are not even training like the other divisions that have graced us with their presence. Is New Zealand a vacation for the Third, Major, or have you all decided that you like it so much you can't leave?'

'Oscar,' said Mrs Walters in the chiding tone of an embarrassed mother. 'There's no need to be so . . . sarcastic all the time.'

Cartwright rocked back on his heels and hunched his shoulders magnanimously. He was prepared to let the young Mr Walters's impudence go by – he was just a kid after all. 'I can assure you that our boys are training hard.' He laughed good-naturedly again and hitched his pants. 'Just yesterday one of the men broke his leg in three places in an exercise down on Shelly Beach. It was a helluva thing to get into a cast, as the Captain will tell you.' He looked expansively round the room, paying particular attention to Emily. 'I can assure you, son, the Third won't be here for long. We're a fighting operation.'

The horn rang out again. I placed my hand on Cartwright's shoulder, which was hard and knotted with tension.

'We better go,' I said. I thanked Mrs Walters and took Emily's hand, as nonchalantly as possible. 'It was lovely to see you,' I said, feeling like an idiot.

Oscar watched us all the way out of the house, openly bristling at his mother's suggestion that we return sometime soon to 'break bread'. I tried not to look at Emily out of concern that I might get her in to some sort of trouble, but as I took my seat in the back of the jeep I couldn't resist one last look. Mrs Walters was chasing her son up the dark hallway, but Emily stood on the wide front porch, her arms crossed over her chest, swaying gently from side to side. Cartwright moodily ordered Sturgis to drive. As we started to move I offered her a small wave, which she returned with a sad smile and a raised open hand, almost as if she were asking me to stop.

CHAPTER 17

Young Eddie had gone quiet since we'd got back into the De Ville. The resetting and packing of his beak hadn't been a pleasant experience for him. To make matters worse, he'd been forced to go through with it in front of an audience of hicks who thought that a bit of pain was just what the kid needed, seeing how he was dressed and all. When I asked for a bag of ice and some cotton buds the truck-stop owner got interested, or suspicious, and wanted to know more. One thing led to another and eventually Eddie and I found ourselves in the dirty, greasy truck-stop bathroom, executing the procedure with a crowd of the owner's family and a few of his sweaty trucker colleagues in tow.

In spite of the embarrassment it must have caused him (one of the truckers had pointed out that a big Jew nose like the one Eddie possessed might require an extra pair of hands to get it straight), his nose was pointing north again and the bleeding had stopped. He sat slouched in the passenger seat as we ambled our way towards L.A., holding a few cubes of ice wrapped in a handkerchief to his face, his big round mop of frizzy black hair pressed against the side window.

'I'm sorry you had to hear that,' I said. 'Back there. About your nose.'

He looked at me and took the bundle of ice away from his face. He touched his nose delicately and winced.

140

'My nose?' he said.

'Yeah. You know. The trucker guy.'

'Oh.' He seemed surprised at my having brought it up. 'I thought it was funny. Given its provenance and all.'

'You mean the fact that he was a hairy-knuckled ... whatever.'

'Exactly. Good line for a guy who's no Lenny Bruce.'

He brought the ice back to his face and rested his frizzy head against the window again. He had a kind of slouching amiableness that I liked. We drove on for a while through the fiery orange afternoon. Pretty soon the ice in the handkerchief had lost its status as solid matter and had turned the rag in his hand into a sodden wet, bloody mess. He wound down the window and looked over at me, seeking permission. I nodded my head and he screwed the handkerchief up into a tight ball and hoisted it out the back of his hand in a long arc to the side of the road. Having dispensed with the rag, he flipped down the sun visor and checked himself out in the cracked, rectangular mirror, cautiously touching the purple mountain on his bony face. He looked at it from various angles, and seemed to be enormously proud of the result.

'You going to ask what happened? How I ended up looking like Sonny Liston?'

'Not if you don't want me to,' I said.

I think I'd managed to snooker him; he had a story to tell with a nose to prove it and he was dying to let it out, but at the same time he had enough self-awareness to not volunteer anything too dramatic to a stranger. I laughed for some reason.

'So how do you know how to fix noses anyway?'

'I'm an old salt. You live as long as I have and you'll learn a few things too.'

'Good answer,' he said, laughing along with me and nodding his head at I'm not sure what.

We were passing through Oceanside, where I'd spent

a couple of months painting back in '46. If I didn't have a passenger I might have turned off on the beach exit and taken a wander along the pier. But I was glad Eddie was with me now. I didn't want to have to think about the past or where I was now heading. As long as Eddie was with me, the car would eventually end up where it would. If I happened to see Sturgis, so be it. If not, so be that. This arc that I was riding, the thing that actually got me out on the road this morning, was not about Sturgis anyway. I realised that now. In a way, it wasn't even about Emily any more. I think it hadn't been about her for a long time, but I'd been too caught up in my own story to know it. Only one person mattered to me now, and I had to find a way to make it back to her so I could see her anew, away from the tawdry reflection of history.

'Mind if I smoke?' said Eddie, holding up a pack of Camels in his hand.

'If you must. The smoke may hurt your nose, though.'

'I take it you don't want one.'

I shook my head. 'They'll kill you, Eddie.'

'So will a lot of things.'

'That's true.'

He lit his cigarette and exhaled a gassy blue plume of smoke at the windscreen.

'Jeez,' he said, holding the cigarette up to his eyes for inspection. 'Weird. I can't taste a thing.'

'That's because your nasal passages have cement in them. I really wouldn't do that if I were you.'

He shrugged and kept smoking, clearly amused by the mysterious workings of his damaged body.

'So,' he said, turning to look at me, 'you're married with kids and all the rest? Grandkids even, if that's not impolite.'

I waited a moment before answering. I felt as though I had been caught out, and wanted to get my story straight. In the end all I could manage was a lousy, 'Nope.'

142

'Huh. No kidding?'

'No kidding.'

I looked at my watch: a quarter to three. She would be in her big leather chair in the piano room now, curled up in a ball with a dry, footnoted-to-hell journal article, underlining the salient bits with her tradesman's pencil, puffing away on one of those stinky black-tobacco cigarettes she buys from the Thai grocer. She would be utterly silent, lost in a swathe of implacable courier font, as serene and dignified as any queen that ever lived.

'Why not?' said Eddie with the trademark brusqueness of youth.

Again I paused, partly to emerge out of my reverie, partly to acknowledge that the question pissed me off for some reason. I zeroed in on the road slipping underneath us and wondered for a moment how this ever happened, how my life had led me to this point, to this car on this day. I wanted to go home to Missy.

'Listen, Eddie. Where are you headed? I'm not sure I need to go to L.A. any more. I—'

'Hey,' he said excitedly. 'Are you reading this book?'

I looked over at him and saw that he was holding up Sturgis's book.

'Um. Yeah.'

'No kidding. I love this book, man. Sturgis is like one of my heroes.'

It took me a dizzy minute to come to grips with all of this. I could almost feel the neurons firing helter-skelter in my head. The De Ville started to drift across the centre line and I only just came to in time to pull it back, narrowly avoiding an oncoming motorcyclist.

'Whoa,' screamed Eddie. 'That was like, really fucking close, man. You okay?' He looked around at the motorcyclist, who, I could see in the rear-view mirror, had stopped in the middle of the road and was waving his arm at us.

'You've read that book? I thought it had only just come out the other day.'

He turned back round with a big, toothy grin on his smashed-up face. 'I'm in Professor Sturgis's sophomore writing class. He showed us an advance copy a couple of months ago. It's great, isn't it? Man, some of those scenes in the Pacific, in Bougainville are just—'

I pulled over to the side of the road, stopping abruptly on a patch of loose gravel so that the car did a wobbly little fishtail before coming to a halt. My chest felt constricted and I was having trouble breathing. I kicked the door open and tumbled out. The heat hit me instantly, sucking what little air I was managing on out of my lungs. I walked around to the back of the car and leaned on the trunk, legs spread as if I were being arrested. After a moment or two Eddie's door creaked open, slowly, tentatively. I heard him step out.

'Are you okay, Peter? What's the problem?'

He had come round to the back and stood by me at a safe, cautious distance. I could sense he was a little afraid of me, but still had the decency to be concerned for my well-being. I could tell he was a well-bred kid; that for all the anarchistic nonsense he'd been spouting in the diner, he was essentially a nice, well-mannered boy. I leant on the trunk trying to get some ownership back over my body. I sucked in some deep breaths and stood up straight, looking up at the flaming red sky. Eddie stood patiently at my side, waiting for an explanation.

'You go to U.C.L.A.?' I asked, squinting in the sunlight.

He was surprised by the question. He tried to screw his face up, but the swollen edifice in the middle of it wouldn't budge.

'Yeah,' he said eventually. 'I mean, I'm enrolled. I try to make it to Professor Sturgis's classes when I can.'

My heart rate was coming back to normal, but I still felt

light and giddy, strangely elated even. For a short moment I felt as though I could hear and see everything in the current frame – the birds in the wattles off the roadside, the sound of crickets in the long grass, the wavy heat-ripple shimmering on the asphalt horizon.

I said, 'When you're not shooting up diners.'

'Right,' said Eddie with an open, unembarrassed chuckle.

I knelt down and picked up a rough chunk of gravel from the road. It felt warm in my hand, full of history and essence.

'So you're a writer?'

He dug his hands into his hip pockets and looked away from me, first at the car, then back down the vacant highway.

'Nah. I mean, not really. You know, I've written a few stories and all, but . . .' He shrugged his narrow shoulders and kicked a few loose stones into the long, tinder-dry grass at the side of the road.

'And Sturgis. He's your teacher?'

'Yeah.'

I looked at him without focusing properly. In the haze he had the appearance of a carnival freak – a perfectly round frizz of dark hair, a clownish purple nose and bruised eyes, a pair of oversized black-framed glasses. He kicked another stone into the grass.

'Why?' he said. 'Do you know him?'

CHAPTER 18

It rained for five days straight following our visit to the Walterses' house. The weather in Auckland had turned for the worse once and for all, and so I was in the unusual position of having to steel myself for a winter in May. The dreamy yellow and dark cherry colours of fall had disappeared, leaving the camp choked in a swamp of soggy leaves and mud.

At the same time the incoming wounded started to pile up fast. The word 'Guadalcanal' seemed to be on everybody's lips, from the Birdcage to the mess hall. I tried to ignore it as best I could, and, in a strange way, the increase in surgery helped. It also got my mind off Emily and how in the hell I was going to see her again.

The extra work came just at the right time for Sturgis and his crew as well. They'd had over two months on their cans and were fast unlearning everything about Marine life they'd been drilled on at Elliot. I'd quizzed Sturgis on Oscar Walters's insinuation about opium, but he'd brushed me off with uncharacteristic reticence. Timmins and O'Keefe didn't say boo about opium, but were garrulous on the virtues of the Oriental whores, whom they visited as often as they could. I would have given them a lecture on V.D., a lecture they'd already heard many times, but whoring was as much a part of Marine life for the enlisted men as saluting the flag at dawn and getting your chops busted by drill sergeants. It came with the territory. All I could do was hand out the prophylactics and, if they didn't work, administer the penicillin.

But whoring was only half of the problem. The real issue was the prizefights some of the Army boys had been organising with the local men up in Ponsonby. From what I could distil from O'Keefe's account of it, the leathernecks hated the doughboys, the doughboys hated the leathernecks, and the local men hated anybody American (doughboy, leatherneck or otherwise). The first few weeks had been anarchy, a state of nature. But American men have a famous distaste for anarchy, and pretty soon the more enterprising among them saw fit to bend the chaos to the altogether more meaningful frame of commerce.

And so the prizefights began, mostly staged in one of the densely wooded corners of Western Park, but also, where need required, in public bars, on sidewalks, and in the many and varied local cathouses. They would have gone on earning Sturgis a nice little sideline if O'Keefe hadn't decided to stage an impromptu match with a sailor at the Red Cross one night while Artie Shaw and his orchestra were winding down from a three-hour set. He got his ass kicked bad, the sailor unceremoniously gifting O'Keefe a better-than-average concussion, three broken ribs and a fractured clavicle. All this just as a fresh shipment of wounded rolled in from the Pacific.

Colonel Ford got wind of the prizefights and summoned all medical personnel to an urgent meeting in the mess hall one soggy morning. With everybody seated around the trestle tables, Ford stood wearily at the food service area, leaning on one of the shiny aluminium trays that would soon be housing our daily feed of barely edible meat in three shades of grey. Cartwright stood solemnly next to him, the nasty deputy to Ford's grizzled, but fair, sheriff.

Ford opened by telling us that the situation with the locals was unacceptable, and that we were a disgrace not only to the Corps, but to the President and to God himself. Cartwright nodded at this and closed his eyes tightly.

'And, as far as I see it,' Ford said, 'this speech is long overdue. There's been a plague over this unit from the very start. The discipline is poor, always has been. You're Marines, for chrissake. This ain't your daddy's goddamn country club. Take a look at the faces of the men in pre-op, the busted-up kids in the O.R. Take a look at their eyes. They're war eyes. Nothing like them. I had 'em in '17 in France. Pretty soon that'll be you. Shit scared and loving it. Doing a man's fucking job for your country.'

I took a look around the mess hall, at Sturgis who was rubbing his hand up and down Nurse Muller's leg while she tried not to smile, at O'Keefe who kept staring into the kitchen area, his arm in a sling, dumbly waiting for the food to magically arrive. Timmins was watching a fly spin out a crazy dance on the chair in front of him. I'd seen the eyes that Ford spoke of. The kids certainly looked shit-scared to me, but I'm not so sure they were loving anything. In any event, I doubted whether Sturgis and his buddies had properly looked at them. They were too young to notice fear – intrinsic, marrow-of-the-bone fear. They weren't old enough to appreciate what it was to die, or, in a not so inexplicable way, that death was even possible.

'As far as I can tell,' Ford continued, 'the problem started in San Francisco, when Sergeant Kazanski was arrested.'

Suddenly everybody was listening. Kazanski had been a popular man at Elliot, and I knew first hand that what happened that night still rankled with the enlisted men. It was why they resented Cartwright, and probably why Ford was having to give this speech. I looked down at the uneven canvas floor in front of me, but I could still feel the air thickening with tension. I could see that Sturgis was looking at me from across the room, but I decided not to return his look.

'That set the whole goddamn scene. I know that. But I don't blame you,' Ford said, alive to the aggravation. 'The problem is a lack of leadership.' He stopped and looked directly at me for an almost imperceptible moment, the tiniest of pauses, before turning back to the centre of the crowd. He'd made his point. 'We're in a foreign country and we need these people on our side if we're to do our jobs. And so what I'm about to announce to you all now is going to address that problem once and for all.' He paused again, but this time to turn to Cartwright, who was as stiff as a board next to him. He placed an avuncular hand on Cartwright's shoulder and pushed him forward a little. 'And so,' said Ford, looking back at us with a forced smile, 'it is my honour to announce that Major Cartwright will be promoted to the rank of lieutenant colonel, effective today at thirteen hundred hours.'

Silence. Heavy, pregnant, nasty silence. Nothing happened for five, six, seven seconds until Ford started clapping, alone and without any rhythm, the flat reports issuing from his old-man hands and hanging in the stunned air like birds shot in mid-flight. Eventually everybody followed the colonel's lead, but the pause was telling and recognisable enough to warrant another serve about our inadequacy for the title of United States Marines.

'On top of your regular duties,' said Ford when he'd calmed down a shade, 'you'll all report to Colonel Cartwright for P.R. detail. Colonel Cartwright will assign you daily tasks, which you'll perform like soldiers, not men without dicks.' He stopped mid-stride, and I think for the first time recognised that he had nurses, actual female ones, under his command. 'And ladies . . . And . . .' He rubbed his hand across his face. 'You'll all do it or you'll be coming to me for the ass-kicking of a lifetime.'

CHAPTER 19

My first P.R. detail was to the house of the strange woman who'd been bringing cakes to the camp every day. Sturgis had told me about her, but I'd never seen her myself. Legend had it that she would come to the camp's gates every morning at nine where she would be duly blocked by one of the M.P.s. She would then stand there, cake in hand, for however long it took for one of the guards to retrieve somebody from inside the camp to relieve her of the cake and thank her. Sturgis had developed a fascination with the woman and made sure he was always available every morning to meet this strange lady. She rarely said anything; just nodded and smiled, handing over the thing she identified as a pound cake before trudging back up the hill to Ponsonby.

Nobody ate the cakes. Diddle had tried biting into a slice once, but had just about lost a tooth in the process. They were dense, solid affairs resembling a type of timber more than anything you would call food. Their density and resilience, however, made them ideal discuses that the men used in the yard for recreation. It wasn't until Cartwright was walking through the camp one watery yellow afternoon with Colonel Ford that the cakes became the subject of officer scrutiny.

A small crowd had gathered in the yard for O'Keefe's throw, which was an attempt to regain the record that Private Byrd had taken from him the previous day. O'Keefe was serious about the title, and had developed a pretty nice throwing technique. He stood with his back to the crowd, which had lined up along two sides of a narrow tunnel of grass for the cake to land in. O'Keefe slowly, meditatively, swung the cake from side to side, trying to get a comfortable, lucid, pendulum rhythm going in the swing of his arm. He wound up and pirouetted on his left foot, springing his lumbering frame around on the tip of his black boondocker for three complete revolutions before letting the thing go – not straight up the centre of the tunnel, but high and wide over the left-hand row of spectators, handsomely arcing all the way to the latrine tent at the yard's edge, where Colonel Ford was emerging from behind a door with a complacent, satisfied look on his face.

The cake landed flat on its base in between Ford and the waiting Cartwright, making a loud slap on the hard, well-trodden piece of ground in front of the john. Ford barely flinched but Cartwright dove headfirst into the bed of chrysanthemums that Nurse Anderson had planted along the latrine's edge. The sight of rugged old Ford shaking his head over Cartwright, who was rolling around in the flowerbed with his head in his hands, was just too much for the assembled spectators to handle, sending them falling over one another in laughter.

Ford had the grace and experience to let the men have their fun and simply walked away. Cartwright, however, launched a full-scale senate inquiry. O'Keefe was stripped of all leave for a month (presumably for having a wayward aim) and Sturgis was ordered to visit the lady who'd been bringing the cakes to camp every day. When I volunteered to chaperone Sturgis on this delicate mission, Cartwright's punishment collapsed in on itself, and he insisted on accompanying us.

The woman, whose name was Mrs Doreen Taylor, lived on Scanlan Street in Ponsonby, just fifteen minutes' walk from the camp. The morning we were to visit Mrs Taylor was bitingly cold, and a low, soupy fog had set in so wet and thick it clung to your skin. The three of us walked up Franklin Road, kicking our way through the crisp, crunchy leaves that had fallen from the plane trees lining either side of the road. It was a Monday morning and the street was bustling with people out and about, all wrapped up in thick woollen coats and scarves. They generally avoided our gazes and gave us a wide berth on the sidewalk. New Zealanders, unless they were drunk, weren't given to outright resentment; it had to be inferred from the downcast eyes, the raised eyebrows, the guarded, suspicious tone in their voices. Ford had been right – the honeymoon period was over, and these people wanted their lives (and their country) back.

I was admiring the play of colour as the weak morning sun tried to penetrate the blanket of slowly dissolving fog when Cartwright put his hand on my arm and stopped me.

'Walk ahead, Corporal,' he said to Sturgis, waiting until he'd gone on a few paces before he turned to face me, his proprietary hand still on my arm. 'I need to talk to you.'

I looked down at his hand and waited for him to remove it. 'What can I do for you, Colonel?' I said, starting to walk again. Sturgis was a good twenty yards ahead now and clearly out of earshot, but Cartwright made me wait another few seconds.

'I need to talk to you.'

'So you've said.'

He came up to my side, so close our shoulders were almost bumping, and slowed the pace down to a crawl. His hands were cutting the air in front of him as he tried to compose himself for what he had to say. I'd expected him to mention the Kazanski thing. Ever since he got the promotion he'd studiously avoided me around camp. He had a politician's vulgar sense for the power of information, and assumed that people in general must be scurrilous and relish having dirt on others. Because dirt to somebody like Cartwright bought a lot of things – obligation, favour, something like loyalty. I was well acquainted with his need for control, and how unpredictable he was without it. Having me and the rest of the unit know that he was the one responsible for getting Kazanski busted must have kept him awake at night. It made him vulnerable. What made it worse was that I had taken the rap. I had done it because it was easier that way. I knew the brass didn't expect anything from me and I didn't want anything from them. Plus, I did feel responsible for what had happened. I had known for a long time what Cartwright was like when he was tight, and I hadn't done enough to stop a situation I should have known was coming. But Cartwright had misinterpreted it as some kind of heroic gesture designed to win the men over.

But it wasn't Kazanski that was bugging him.

'I know you told her that I'm married. I don't care, Sokol. But just don't deny it.'

His words brought me to an abrupt halt. I looked at his chiselled, classically handsome face. The chill morning air had given his cheeks a faint, pinkish glow, and what with the thick golden blond hair running around the bottom of his hat he could have easily passed for a character in one of those twisted Nazi film reels of outrageously healthy, milk-fed specimens doing naked callisthenics in clover fields.

I said, 'What?'

'It's not important now, anyway,' he said, waving his gloved hand in the air as if he were swatting a fly.

The air was cold enough for his breath to steam as it left his mouth. He walked slowly beside me, hands behind his back, shoulders bent slightly forward.

'I've spoken to the mother,' he continued, 'and she has given her consent.'

'Mrs Walters?'

'That's right.' He looked at me with a grim, determined

expression, almost as if he were expecting an onslaught.

'I might be missing something here, but, um, you are married. Aren't you?'

He pulled me by the arm again to make me stop. Sturgis was so far ahead now as to be almost out of sight.

'There's something I think I should tell you,' Cartwright said, his eyes dancing around various points on my face, unable to settle anywhere. 'I'm not telling you this because you have any right to the information. But we are . . . connected. In a manner of speaking. And, well, I know that you were quite taken by her, as any man would be.'

I removed his hand from my wrist. 'What are you telling me, Cartwright?'

'That's Colonel, you ass.'

I smiled at him. He wanted to bite, but I could see the cogs of his mind turning over, telling him to let it slide, that he had a higher purpose that needed to be addressed. I had an instinct for what it was and could feel a tight knot quickly binding in the pit of my gut.

'Okay, then. What is it, Colonel?'

He didn't hesitate. 'I've spoken to the mother and it has all been agreed. I'm going to go up there on Wednesday morning, when I will . . . when I'll make my offer to Miss Walters.'

We were standing in the middle of the sidewalk facing off against each other, forcing the other pedestrians to have to dirty their shoes on the grass edges to get around us. I was faintly aware of their hushed insults and curses as they passed.

'What offer?' I said through gritted teeth. The knot in my gut tightened.

'I'm going to ask Miss Walters, and her mother, of course, to, ah, to come back with me to California.'

'And do what?'

He furrowed his brow in response, as if the answer were obvious.

154

'But what about Mildred? There's no way she'll give you a divorce. You know—'

Cartwright raised his hand in the air. He was working his jaw slowly, trying to harden his expression, or contain something that wanted to get out. Either way the look demanded that I stop.

'I'll tell you this,' he said deliberately, 'so that there's no misunderstanding, and out of respect for the fact that you have a . . . an affection for Miss Walters. Mildred and I haven't . . . I mean, our marriage has been dead for a long time. I wrote her last week, as soon as we got back from Parnell, and agreed to the divorce she's wanted for years.'

I felt time close in around me. I couldn't see anything other than the steam of my breath coming out of my open mouth in a series of small clouds, each one the dead current of so many unspoken syllables.

'It's done, Sokol. I just have to see my attorney in San Francisco when I get back. Mrs Walters has agreed to bring Miss Walters over once I'm back home and the papers have been filed.'

'Have you even talked to Emily? I mean, have you asked her anything at all?'

My words sounded whiny and ridiculous. Cartwright shook his head and laughed.

'You've got no idea, have you?' he said, still laughing. 'You've seen them. You've been to their house, for Christ's sake.' He tightened his lips and bent in towards me, almost menacingly. 'They're starving, Sokol. They've got nothing. They're desperate as hell.'

'And so, what, you get her that way? You buy her from her mother?'

'Don't be an ass all your life, man.' He was angry now. 'There's a real world happening while you paint your god-damn pictures. You know it's the best offer she'll ever get.

It's locked, Sokol. It's done.'

He turned away from me and marched up the road, his posture straight as a ramrod, his arms swinging jauntily, out of time with the anxious step of his legs. I stood rooted to the spot, all heavy and numb, and watched with flat eyes as he dissolved into the thick of the morning fog. A few crisp, auburn leaves fell from the canopy of trees overhanging the road, spinning haphazardly until they hit the ground. I was an observer, a passenger, and this sort of thing would always be my fate. I would always be standing rooted to the spot, stunned by brutal simplicity, by direct action. He was right, after all. They were desperate. Maybe they were even starving. I'd just been too wrapped up in Emily to notice.

And now she was gone.

Mrs Taylor's house was small and dark, with a low-slung ceiling that seemed to squeeze the air out of the place so that it was almost hard to breathe. What air was left seemed atrophied, a hundred years old. We spent an uncomfortable hour at her kitchen table sipping weak tea and politely chewing on broken biscuits from a tin bearing the image of a youthful Queen Victoria. We'd come expecting to confront one of her famous cakes, but our visit had caught her on the hop, and she seemed mortified at having nothing home-baked to offer. She was short and slightly frumpy, and had a thick helmet of bronze hair perched atop her head like a bowl. She didn't seem particularly interested in Cartwright and me, but doted on Sturgis, who dutifully relented to her insistent offers to make him a cheese and pickle sandwich. I couldn't bring myself to look at Cartwright, and it was almost intolerable to be sitting so close to him, to have to hear the faint whistle of his breath, the rustle of his jacket as he shifted in his seat. The whole event would have been entirely unmemorable had she not caught me looking at a framed picture on the wall as we got up to leave. It was of a doughy young man in uniform. His round chin was jutted out and his face was set in a tough expression, but his pale eyes betrayed him, revealing the natural timidity of his age. He couldn't have been a day older than eighteen. Even his uniform, in its standard-size bulkiness, seemed to mock him. For all that he was a parody of a soldier, of a hapless modern-age warrior, I knew the picture was no joke.

'My son, Captain,' Mrs Taylor said, looking at me with watery eyes.

Cartwright and Sturgis turned to look at the picture. The stifled air was suddenly thick with an unspeakable gloom so real it caught my breath and constricted my chest. I could see her eyes beginning to moisten, and it was all I could do to look at the ground. But before I was able to avert my eyes I saw her take Sturgis's hand, an action so plain and involuntary that it seemed to stun her as she did it. Sturgis held her hand as if it were a precious stone, tensely, unnaturally. He looked at me for support but all I could offer him was a shrug of my shoulders.

There was nothing to say, so Cartwright said, 'How old is your son, ma'am?' His words hung in the air, separate from everything, refusing to land. She squeezed Sturgis's hand, hard, till the whites of her knuckles shone through. 'I suppose he's in North Africa fighting the Jerrys,' Cartwright continued. His obtuseness was confounding, even to me, who'd known him all these years. 'The New Zealand boys have done a wonderful job up there. You should be proud, ma'am. It's—'

'He was eighteen,' she said, in a voice barely louder than a whisper. 'He was only eighteen.'

At this she started crying. She hunched forward and into the cave of Sturgis's chest. He placed his hand on her rounded back and tried to calm her, but with each cooing word he uttered, her sobs became more powerful, more wrenching. Sturgis had to dance around the room with her to keep on his feet. Pretty soon the sobbing gave way to a horrid, primitive wailing that scared the daylights out of me. Cartwright had jumped back against the wall as if he'd just seen a ghost. I helped Sturgis steer her into a seat and grabbed a brown paper bag from the kitchen for her to breathe into. After a couple of minutes the choking sound began to give way until there was nothing but a silent, steady stream of tears rolling down her splotchy face.

'I'm sorry,' she said. 'I'm so sorry. I don't mean to scare you away.'

'It's all right,' Sturgis said, laughing, at what I don't know. But it seemed to work. She squeezed his hand again and began to laugh with him, looking into his face as if she were trying to find something.

When she had finally come round, and it seemed safe to leave, we made our way from the kitchen into a short hallway that led to the front door, Mrs Taylor coming up behind us. Cartwright declared that he had to use the bathroom and, not getting a response, took a guess and put his hand on the first of three closed doors in the hall. He twisted the knob and the latch snapped loudly, as if it hadn't been opened in some time. He was just about to push the door open when I heard a loud scream coming from behind us. The sound was unnatural, inorganic, lacking a source in nature. Cartwright froze, his hand still wrapped around the doorknob.

'Don't go in there!' Mrs Taylor screamed. 'Stop! Stop!'

Sturgis and I had both crouched down in the crossfire of her screeching, almost as if we were dodging bullets. She was frenzied and out of control.

'Don't go in there! Stop it! Stop it!'

These last words violently tore themselves from her throat. She hugged the open door frame at the intersection of the hallway and the kitchen, clinging to it as if it were a lamppost in a storm. I finally gathered my wits and tried to prise her away from the frame and back to her seat, but she didn't come easily. When I finally got her down I administered more water and made her take another pull on the brown paper bag. After a few shocked moments Cartwright and Sturgis tentatively poked their heads through the open door to see what was happening. I took her heart rate, which was within a normal range, and made her drink more water until her chest-heaving abated. When she'd finally calmed I could sense her deep shame as she leaned over the kitchen table and buried her head in her thick arms.

I looked up at Sturgis and Cartwright, who were nothing more than a pair of disembodied heads in the darkness of the door opening. They were both making jerking motions behind them with their eyes and heads, jerking motions directed at the door. I hardly needed the hint.

I stood slowly and patted Mrs Taylor gently on the back. I took one last look at the boy on the wall and stepped quietly from the room.

CHAPTER 20

The three of us walked back to camp through the Ponsonby district in silence. The fog had lifted, revealing a clear, sparkling day. It was still early, just past eleven o'clock, and Ponsonby Road had a sleepy, hung-over look to it. Barkeepers had their doors and windows wide open trying to clear the rank air from the night before; the brothels were boarded up and temporarily closed for business. We stepped over an Army bum asleep on the sidewalk, hugging an empty quart bottle of beer, a puddle of drool beside his open mouth. I made to roll him over but Cartwright pushed me on. He was Army, after all.

I was still too overwhelmed by Mrs Taylor's breakdown to think properly about what Cartwright had said on the way up. He was calling me out, I knew that much. And I guess that what he knew of me, the kind of person I had presented to him over the past few years, would have given him cause for confidence. I'd never been famous for manning up to the kind of confrontations that Cartwright and his line prided themselves on. But ever since Beth, my retreat had got worse. Everything that was essential in me, that was either detached and European, or vital and American, I'd bleed onto canvas, alone, with my back to the world, like a madman smearing shit on his walls in the middle of the night. Cartwright knew what I felt for her; any fool could have seen it. But that wasn't the issue here. The issue was whether I would do anything about it. Cartwright had done the math as he always did it – pre-emptively. It wasn't a challenge he was presenting me with; it was an answer.

As we rounded the corner to Franklin Road our silent progress was halted by a crowd of people who had formed a ring four or five deep around what I took to be a scuffle. The crowd had spilled out onto the road so that the passing cars had to swing out wide into the other lane to get by. Before I knew what was happening, Sturgis had threaded his nimble frame through the web of legs and arms and was calling to me above the shouts and cheers. I'd assumed it was just another prizefight, but Sturgis's tone was urgent, almost pleading. I looked around for Cartwright but couldn't see him anywhere. I pushed my way through the crowd, loudly declaring I was a doctor. In the tussle to get to the front it occurred to me that the scrap, whoever it was between, was taking place right out in front of the Ponsonby International Chess Club and Philosophical Society.

I had to prise my way through a ring of local toughs at the front who were enjoying the sight of American blood being spilled; O'Keefe's American blood, to be exact. He and Private Diddle were being dealt to by two guys in black suits and a squat little Oriental, the one I'd seen hiding behind the giant at Western Park, I think. Sturgis had tried to insinuate himself into the melee, but his fighting instincts weren't as good as his loving ones. I arrived on the scene just in time to see him being dispatched over the chess club's waist-high wire fence into a cropped hedgerow.

'I'm a doctor,' I shouted at the wrestling bodies, to absolutely no avail. I kept shouting it because I didn't know what else to do, and it didn't take long for me to become just another source of amusement to the rowdy crowd. I looked around for Cartwright, but I couldn't see him through the throng. I had hoped that a colonel might have had the authority, objective if not moral, to bring people to their senses. The guys in black were strong and tough – the toughest philosophers and chess players I'd ever seen. One of them had O'Keefe in a tight headlock and was about to bring his mallet of a fist down on the crown of his head. I couldn't wait any longer. I pushed my way through the flying fists, hunched like a stalking cat, and jumped on the back of the guy holding O'Keefe. In spite of all my dead weight on his back, I couldn't bring him down. He held onto O'Keefe for all he was worth while I rode him like a mule. I was totally useless. I put my arm around the front of him so that my hand was on the back of O'Keefe's head and pushed hard, trying to free him from the vice-like grip. I just started to feel the guy's hold loosening when a sharp, burning pain ran up my arm and momentarily blinded me. When I managed to focus my eyes on the source of the pain I could see the philosopher's mouth wrapped around my forearm, his teeth locked onto my wrist as if he were a dog with a fresh bone. I shrieked like a baby, as much from the surprise as from the pain, and released my grip, falling to the ground like a third-rate cowboy. I hit the pavement with a thud, face down, my elbows crashing uncontested into the concrete, absorbing all my weight. Out of pure survival instinct I flipped onto my back and saw the black-suited ogre standing over me, a vision of death itself. The sky was beautiful behind him, a washed-out yellowy blue burnished with white light. He clenched his right fist and with the other hand grabbed me by the shirtfront, pulling me up off the ground to meet the full force of his looming blow. I closed my eyes and waited.

But somewhere in the thoughtless pause, in that numb second while I hovered a foot above the ground, two loud voices called out clear above the cheering crowd, the first unmistakably in English, the second in something incomprehensible. I opened my eyes, just barely, while the philosopher held me up off the ground. He still had his fist cocked, but was looking over at the small white house to his left, his organisation's headquarters, where at least one of the voices had come from. The crowd had gone quiet, watching him go through his slow-witted thought process. It was alarmingly clear to me that this guy, whoever he was, was new to the game of taking orders. The English voice rang out again, authoritative and familiar.

'Put him down,' it said.

I tried to crane my neck in the direction of the house, but it was too sore with the strain of supporting the weight of my head to turn properly. I needn't have worried as the philosopher decided to obey, and with a simple unclenching of his fist, sent me crashing to the ground again. I had to force myself to breathe, sucking the stinging air into my lungs, my head dizzy. When I was sure he'd gone I sat up, just in time to see the squat Oriental dart off up a narrow alleyway that ran alongside the chess club house. I couldn't be sure, but I think I caught a glimpse of the giant that I'd seen before, on the hood of that parked car, and in Western Park the other week. I unsteadily got to my feet, but by the time I was up they were both gone.

As the crowd began to disperse I saw Sturgis materialise from the other side of the hedgerow, a sheepish look on his face. I assumed that after his initial sortie into the thick of the action he had watched the rest from deep cover. He was still on the wrong side of the fence, and as the two black-suited philosophers retreated back up the path towards their sanctuary, the one who'd wanted to crush my face into a Spanish omelette gave him a stiff, hard push in the chest, toppling him back into the hedgerow.

'Fucking Yank,' he said.

'Go home, you Yankee pig,' said his buddy, hoiking a well-aimed spit at Sturgis, which landed on the epaulette on his left shoulder.

They had both spoken, for what it was worth, in Kiwi accents. I watched as they walked up the front steps and in through the front door of the house, which was held open by Oscar Walters. He held my gaze for a few moments while his thugs disappeared into the darkness of the house. His face registered no discernible expression. He stepped inside and closed the door behind him.

'You okay, sir?'

It was O'Keefe. He had bloody lips, a bloody mouth, and wore a stupid, shit-kicking grin. He could have been a kid at the carnie, slightly ruffled by all the wild rides, a little nauseous from a half dozen raspberry popsicles. I looked at him and shook my head.

'Yeah. Whatever. You better let me take a look at that.'

He took a step back, still grinning. 'It's nothin',' he said, wiping his mouth with the open cuff of his khaki shirt. 'Good thing you came along though, sir. Me and Diddle were about to take a good beating.' He wiped his mouth again and let out a deep breath, chest puffed out, as if he were a hiker having just made it to his hut. 'These locals do love a bit of the rough stuff,' he said, laughing. 'Yes, sir.'

'Where is Diddle, anyway?'

We both looked around. Sturgis, having negotiated his way out of the hedge, wandered over to us. I couldn't see Diddle anywhere.

'That chink,' Sturgis said, smiling and pointing his thumb back behind him, 'that chink was one strong son-of-a-bitch.'

'Over here,' said a nearby voice.

We all looked to the left, to the house neighbouring the chess club. The sound had come from behind a six-foot paling fence. We all had to take a step closer to it before we could see Diddle, his eyes just peering at us above the line of the fence, his bright orange mop of hair like a slowly rising sun.

'Is it all clear?' he asked.

'Come out here, you pussy piece of shit,' yelled O'Keefe, laughing his ass off.

The three of them were having the time of their lives. With a bang and a series of crashes, Diddle hauled his pudding of a body over the rickety fence. I couldn't suppress a smile myself. These guys were medical corpsmen; they bore no relation to the fabled Marine infantrymen, the guys we heard so much of, the ones in Italy and Africa, storming beaches, taking cities. These medical guys could barely pick their noses. They weren't real Marines; not yet, anyway.

'That chink was a strong son-of-a-bitch,' Diddle said.

'Don't I know it,' said Sturgis, giving me a wink.

'You ticked off at us, sir?' asked Diddle, looking up at me as if I were a schoolmaster.

'Why were you fighting these guys?' I said, trying to sound neutral and responsible.

O'Keefe put his hand on Diddle's chest to stop him from answering. It wasn't often that O'Keefe got to feel superior, and he seemed determined to take his opportunity.

'If you don't mind, sir,' he said, looking at me earnestly, his big red mouth agape. 'Diddle and me were, were . . . I mean, sir, I can tell you this because you're a man of the world and all. Well, me and Diddle here were in the celestial cathouse down yonder when that big, tall chink son-of-a-bitch kicked us out.' He looked around, cautiously, and took a step closer to me – he could have been giving me the Luftwaffe's latest flight plans. 'Well, one thing kinda led to another, which led to that fat little chink asshole and those two beatniks beating the crap out of us. Totally un-fucking-provoked, I might add. Like they were just out to get us for some reason.'

'I thought Marines didn't take beatings,' I said.

'So did I,' Diddle said. 'That's why I signed up.'

Sturgis groaned; he wasn't buying the story. 'What were you doing at the cathouse at eleven in the morning?'

'What are you, teacher's pet?' O'Keefe said. He tried to look disdainful, but the baby fat on his cheeks conspired against him, turning it into a look more reminiscent of constipation. 'You goddamn know as well as I do that morning's the best time for the going good.'

'All right, all right,' I said, waving a hand in the air. 'Come on O'Keefe. I better get you back to camp and have a look at that mouth.'

We headed off down the hill, the four of us crunching our way through the brittle fallen leaves covering the sidewalk. As we were nearing camp, Sturgis came up beside me and whispered, 'Where's Colonel Cartwright?'

'No idea,' I said, looking straight ahead.

CHAPTER 21

I considered Eddie's question for a moment. We were still on the side of the empty highway, the mid-afternoon Southern Californian sun beating down on us relentlessly. I put my hand on the trunk of the De Ville. The metal was blisteringly hot, and I whipped my hand away immediately, bringing it up to my face, my palm open and quivering.

Did I know Sturgis? The question seemed so difficult to answer. I knew him once, but not the version Eddie was referring to; the P. Anthony Sturgis, author of a fine novel, successful literature professor, the man I had been either consciously or unconsciously running from these past decades.

Eddie kept looking at me, his shock of frizzy hair completely immobile in the gentle wind swirling around us, the purple Fuji on his face swelling up larger by the second. I guess he didn't care one way or another about the answer; it was me who cared. The question was entirely innocent. I'd spent twenty-odd years scrupulously avoiding situations like this – chance encounters that wanted to blossom into something bigger, people who wanted to connect, bridge distances. It had gone on so long I was no longer sure exactly what it was I was running from any more, what I was hiding from. I knew it started with old-fashioned guilt and a broken heart, but it had grown out from there, this inertia, this paralysis. It had kept me from everything except my art, which was

167

possible because it was personal and silent.

It kept me, no matter how badly I wanted to do it, from calling Missy my wife.

And so I looked at Eddie on the sun-drenched highway and said, 'Yeah, I knew him once.'

'No kidding?'

'No kidding.'

We got back in the car and headed slowly and silently north. I felt strangely light, loose-limbed. Eddie hadn't said anything else, but I got the feeling he was interested and was waiting for me to make the next move, to say something by way of explanation. I checked my watch: ten to three. We were still a good hour away from Westwood, but there was no rush, as the lecture didn't start until six. Not that I was sure I was actually heading there.

We passed a truck heading south that was so big and moving so fast that it wobbled my rusty old De Ville like a drunkard trying to walk a straight line. Eddie looked at me and smiled. Sun on the grimy windscreen. I had nothing in my head for what seemed like the first time in years. I felt entirely within the present, without the usual rambling inner monologue, the deflating half-formed thoughts. I was conscious of the sounds of the car, of the acres of road we swallowed up as we ploughed forward, of the queer dynamic sitting in the space between us. And then without context or a trace of forethought, I said something that deeply surprised me.

'I knew Sturgis during the war. We were in the same unit.'

I kept looking straight ahead at the blurry horizon, resisting the temptation to catch his reaction. I could feel his bespectacled eyes on me.

'I knew it,' he said, leaning back in his seat, pleased with himself. I resented the rich tone, the satisfaction in it.

'You knew, huh? How did you know?'

He shrugged and looked out the window. 'I don't know.

168

The book. The way you ran off the road back there.' He paused for a moment, as if he'd just taken a false step. I think he'd been caught by my tone and wasn't sure what to make of it. I could sense him backtracking. 'I don't mean to be, you know, presumptuous or whatever. I just got a feeling is all.'

We were passing through Niguel where the earth is blood red and the sky is enormous and forbidding. The kind of place people like to die in – under the hot sun, alone, humbled.

'He would have been about your age back then,' I said.

'That's pretty young to be in a war.'

There was a suggestion of resignation or fear, something complex in his voice that I couldn't quite grasp. I was about to say something to him, but at the point of delivery nothing came. I looked across to see that he had picked up the book again. He was thumbing through the pages absent-mindedly, closing it and opening it at random points.

'So, are you in this book?' he asked, his brow furrowed, looking at me now.

'I don't know. I haven't read it.'

'Huh,' he said, scrunching up his face, which must have stung his aching nose. He winced with the pain and looked shocked, as if he'd completely forgotten about it. He pulled down the sun visor and examined himself in the mirror again.

I was glad of the distraction. I wanted to know what he thought of the book, of the story, without the inhibiting knowledge that he was riding with the principal player. My old protective instincts reared themselves again, and I found myself slipping back into the old familiar lie.

'I was an orderly in the Third. With Sturgis.'

Eddie looked around at me again, eyebrows raised over his glasses, his fingers lightly pinching the bridge of his nose.

'No kidding?'

'No kidding.'

It worked; he took the line. Mind you, the likelihood of

me being the souped-up doctor as rendered in Sturgis's book wasn't too difficult to dismiss. I am a tired-looking sixty, a man in plain chino pants and a pale blue short-sleeve shirt. I had even cut myself shaving that morning so that there was a thin red scab running down the cleft of my chin. I just didn't look like the kind of guy who gets mixed up in the eye of a storm.

'Are you on your way to see him?' said Eddie, running his long, bony index finger over the two lonely characters on the cover of the book.

A cool bead of sweat loosened itself from my armpit and ran icily down my side.

'Maybe.' The loose-limbed feeling had gone now, replaced by the familiar tightness. The heat was making it hard to breathe, and I had to consciously think to inhale for a moment. 'I mean, I'm not sure. I'm supposed to be going to the official launch of that book you're holding.'

'Did he invite you?'

'No, my . . . my companion is making me go. I'm doing it for her, really.'

'Companion? What the hell's a companion?'

It was a damned good question, and my inability to find a ready answer made me feel foolish. Perhaps in the way I'd made Missy feel foolish all these years. I looked straight at the road ahead of me as my eyes quickly, inexplicably, filled with tears. I had to pull an assortment of faces to prevent the salty liquid falling from my eyes and running down my craggy cheeks. I think I'd always known what my stupid pain and silence had done to Missy, but I'd never before been gripped with so keen an awareness of it. My pathetic self-loathing had always stood between us; I had indulged it and coddled it in my painting and in my ridiculous sensibility to the point where it wasn't even real any more, to the point where it was little more than indulgent mythology, the flatulent stuff of legend.

Somehow I had managed to make art out of it, build a career and a middling reputation on its sandy ground. But it had prevented me from marrying Missy, and I was starting to see now that the rest didn't amount to a hill of shit.

I'd managed to staunch the tears before they burst their dams, but I was unable to contain the realisation, or maybe the dread, that I'd made a mockery out of the woman who loved me. I'd spent twenty years being a complete ass, but for some reason she had stayed with me. So I didn't answer Eddie's question because I couldn't. I couldn't insult her any longer.

'Anyways,' I said, trying to sound upbeat, 'I'm not sure if I'll go to the lecture. I guess I'm just driving.'

'I know the feeling,' he said miserably.

I turned to look at him. He'd put the book down and was resting his frizzy head on the side window again, watching the barren landscape slip by. He looked as solemn as a monk.

'Where am I taking you, Eddie?'

The question hung in the dank air of the car. His body slumped a little further into itself.

'Ah, just anywhere near Los Angeles,' he said, waving a hand indeterminately.

'No particular place?'

'No particular place.'

We passed a green road sign shimmering in the sun, which pointed us towards L.A., and told us there were fifty miles to go. Fifty miles for the two of us to figure out where we were going.

'Were they your friends back there?' I asked.

'Nah.' He still had his head planted against the side window, his concert-pianist fingers gripping the book tightly. 'I mean, I guess I know them, but . . .' He trailed off with a measure of ambiguity. I got the strong impression that he wanted to talk, but, perhaps because his vanity required it, he needed a degree of coaxing. I was more than willing to oblige as it took my mind off Missy and the cancerous little knot in my stomach the thought of her produced.

'Why were you running with them? If you didn't know them?'

'I just needed to get out of L.A. Away from school and . . .' He paused and I looked across at him. 'And my dad.'

'What's the problem?'

He straightened up in his seat and searched my face for any latent condescension or sarcasm. I noticed this look often with my painting students – a kind of wide-eyed confusion somewhere between the real and the unreal, between honest sincerity and instinctive irony. I may have been a surgeon once, and a captain in the United States Marines, but I still have the look of a regular, toiling schmo who has neither the energy nor the inclination to fuck with anyone. I believe that Eddie saw this after a moment or two, as most of my students did as well, and felt reassured enough to speak.

'He wants me to enlist. Go to Vietnam.'

'You're kidding?' I said, a little taken aback. I hadn't seen this coming at all. 'Jesus.'

'He doesn't get a lot of air-time with my dad'.

'Oh,' I said, having to check him for the sarcasm now. 'Right.'

The road was flat and wide and the De Ville purred smoothly along it. I felt a certain weightlessness I often experience when driving on freeways, as if I'm being sucked up in the relentless pull of a slipstream, as if I could take my hands off the wheel and my foot off the gas and nothing would change; I'd just keep moving along in a steady rhythm, stately and graceful.

'Well,' I said, 'it's not like you have to go. You've got college deferment, right?'

'I did. Until my dad suspended my tuition last semester.' He waved the book in the air. 'He's not going to pay any more.'

I thought he was going to cry – there was static in the air around him, molecules colliding everywhere, and I could feel the sadness radiating off his chest. It took me a long moment to think of what to say.

'Tell your dad to go fuck himself,' I managed, but it was dumb thing to say. I got the impression Eddie wasn't in the business of telling old man Schuler to fuck anything.

He pushed his hand through his thick, steel-wool hair and roused himself by clapping the hardback book against his thigh. I could tell it had cost him a lot to reveal this dark problem to me.

'I guess I've been out here with Sam and them all,' he said, hitching his thumb back over his shoulder, 'just not thinking about it. I haven't been home since he told me he'd cut the tuition.'

I nodded, keeping my eyes on the road. He sighed a couple of times and slapped the book against his leg again.

'So you haven't read this, huh?' he said, trying to sound cheerful, but his voice was tinny and hollow.

'Nope.'

'So you don't even know if you're in it then.'

I laughed. 'I guess not. Although I can't imagine why he would want to write about me.'

'Do you think you'll read it?'

'I don't know,' I said. 'I'm not much of a reader.'

He whistled theatrically, a little, comic 'Well, doctor!' I liked this. He struck me as the kind of kid who could rattle off imitations for hours on end, doing shtick with his gawky buddies while the football players were off getting laid.

'Not a reader, huh?'

'Not much of one,' I said. 'These days, at least.'

'Mind if I tell you about it, then?'

We couldn't have been any more than thirty-five miles away now. It occurred to me that if he went ahead and told me the story I would find out whether Sturgis had forgiven me. I would find out without having to see him, without even having to endure the pain of reading it myself. I'd learn it second-hand. I'd learn it without any emphasis being placed on its fact; it would simply be one small part of a much bigger story, little more than an incidental reflection, an authorial aside.

'Sure,' I said. 'Why not?'

CHAPTER 22

The day after O'Keefe and Diddle's fight outside the chess club, another boatload of wounded arrived from Guadalcanal requiring secondary surgery and rehabilitation. They were mostly from the First Division, which had been formed well before the Third, and had been in active battle for over a year now, starting in the Philippines with MacArthur, then moving slowly west through the islands and atolls whose strange names now had as much resonance as the great cities of Europe.

There were also another half-dozen men from the Third who required surgery. They had been injured during a training accident at Shelly Beach, just a few miles from the camp. Apparently one of the piers that they had used to land on had inexplicably collapsed, sending scores of men armed with heavy weapons and equipment crashing to the rocks on the shallow foreshore below.

The stretch lasted over twenty hours, and was our first real taste of things to come. Most of the injured had at least one fracture on them, and so we were up to our knees in Plaster-of-Paris, splints and Kirchner wire. I spent five hours in the O.R. working on the radial head of a private's elbow, which had suffered severe damage to the articular cartilage. It was a finicky procedure, but one whose artistry I enjoyed, using a bone saw to get deep into the joint at the intersection of the radius and the ulna, cleaning out the tiny bone fragments and doing what I could with the wasted cartilage over the capitellum. Cartwright watched silently as I went through the delicate process of closing the wound, first over the articular capsule, then the ropey network of tendons, before finishing with a clean suture along the waxy skin. I could see in his blue eyes that he was impressed, in spite of himself. But a military O.R. is not the kind of place where you're likely to get a pat on the back.

Although I was an orthopaedic surgeon, I found myself doing more and more vascular work, assisting Colonel Ford wherever I could. The nature of battlefield injuries meant that for any given hurt kid you were usually dealing with at least two or three body systems. Where there was a compound fracture, vascular and nerve damage usually followed. Ford, a diplomate of the American Board of Surgery, was a master of the vascular system, and it was a pleasure to watch him work.

We stood at the same table for eight hours straight as the orderlies slapped down one patient after another in front of us. The last kid was tricky, a corporal from Albuquerque who'd suffered invasive fragment wounds of the left knee and upper thigh. The wounds had been debrided by a field surgeon, and he'd had definitive surgery on the ship somewhere between the Solomons and Auckland. But while recovering from the surgery, and still en route to New Zealand, the knee continued to haemorrhage, dangerously lowering his blood protein levels. I assisted Ford in removing a nasty, coagulated clot from the popliteal. It was only after doing this that we could see the smoking gun, an angry gash in the wall of the artery. With a steady pair of pickups, while I retracted the quivering tissue around the cartilage, Ford removed the tiny fragment splinter that the ship surgeon had missed, pruned the shredded half-inch of the popliteal, and wound a delicate, almost beautiful ligature around the artery with standard-issue supply catgut.

He did all of this while whistling the theme from 'Flight of the Bumble Bee', badly out of tune, over and over. When he'd finished he told me to close the kid up and turned to Sturgis, who was waiting in the triage room, and yelled 'next', as if he were a butcher in Queens, calling up the next little lady in line for her pound of lamb chops.

I was dead on my feet by the time we were finished, but I couldn't help thinking that this was only the beginning. By the time I'd managed to shower, drink a half bottle of scotch at the Birdcage and sleep for a fitful seven hours, it was Tuesday afternoon. The plain fact of it sent me into something like a panic attack. In the blood and guts of the O.R. I'd somehow managed to forget that Cartwright was going up to the Walterses' place on Wednesday morning to deliver his proposal, or offer, or whatever the hell it was, to Emily. I lay on my cot, my back and neck stiff and knotty, every bone in my body like lead, and listened as a light drizzle of rain tickled my canvas roof. If I was going to do anything I had to do it now. I'd only got halfway through the thought when I found my legs swinging out of the cot. I was on my feet and dressed before my mind had had a chance to catch up.

I found Sturgis alone in the mess tent nursing a cup of coffee, his face a little red and puffy underneath his woollen cap. It was cold, and he had the collars of his coat turned up so they were covering his neck. I poured myself a coffee and sat down opposite him.

'Rough night?' I asked. At one point or another I'd seen him in the Birdcage last night, following Nurse Muller around like a khaki shadow, but I was enjoying drinking alone so hadn't paid him much notice.

He looked up at me, his eyes bleary, the spirit sucked out of him. 'Rough week,' he said.

'How are you and Nurse Muller getting along?'

'You mean last night?'

'I thought you were going to recite the Gettysburg address there at one point. She takes a while to come around, huh?'

'Goddamn that broad,' he said, slapping his hand down onto the table. 'I just about closed it too. I told her I had a surprise waiting for her in my tent. Bad line, I know, but the point is she actually wanted to come.'

'So what happened?'

'Take a guess.'

'Let me see. Timmins? O'Keefe? Or maybe Diddle this time.'

'You were right first time. The dumb asshole decided it'd be a good idea to break a pool cue over some local's head.'

'Why'd he do that?'

'The local had broken one over his head first.'

'Figures.'

The coffee had the consistency and taste of watered-down boot polish. I drank it anyway just to warm up.

'So,' I said, a little sheepishly, 'want to drive me up to Parnell?'

'What, are you kidding? In this weather?'

'I'll make it worth your while.'

'How much?'

'Five bucks.'

He grinned; the kid was a poker player, and a much better one than me.

'Eight bucks,' I said.

'Eight bucks and—'

'Or I could just order you to do it for nothing.'

'Sold at eight dollars.'

After the marathon surgical effort it wasn't difficult getting a leave pass from Ford. I went to Ford because I didn't want to rouse Cartwright's suspicious mind. If he knew where I was going he would have cabled Washington for an execution order on the spot. As we drove out of the camp I pointed

178

Sturgis in the direction of Franklin Road rather than the waterfront.

'Where are we going?' he yelled above the wind and the engine. He was hung-over and still a little jittery.

'Take me up to the chess club. I want to check something out first.'

We pulled up alongside the innocuous-looking white cottage. The curtains were drawn in all the front windows. I got Sturgis to edge up a little farther so that I could look up the narrow path the Orientals had gone down the other day. It was long and dark, overhung with tree branches from the neighbouring property. I couldn't tell where it led.

'What are we looking for?' Sturgis asked.

'Oscar Walters. It would be better for me if he wasn't up at the house today.'

Sturgis laughed, a single derisive snort. 'You're not going to find him here, Captain.'

'What do you mean?'

'He'll be at the chink cathouse is what I mean.' He said this as though it were self-evident.

'At the cathouse?' The idea of Oscar Walters I had in my head did not involve mid-afternoon whoring. I took another look at the curtained windows. 'He's an intellectual, Sturgis. He's not going to be at any brothel.'

'Um, he may be an intellectual, sir, but, ah, he's also one hell of a dope fiend. Everybody knows about it.'

'Opium?' I said redundantly.

'Lots of it, sir.'

I was surprised by this, but the notion wasn't entirely unbelievable. In New York I'd known many people who'd fallen victim to the dragon's charms, people from all over the place. Oscar Walters fit the profile as well – pale, thin, the arrogant possessor of a miserable knowledge.

'Where is this cathouse, anyway?'

Sturgis pointed up the long, narrow path. 'I imagine you could get to it thataway, if discreetness was your object, but the rest of us take the front entrance.' He put the jeep into gear and revved the idling engine a couple of times. 'Hang on, I'll show you.'

We drove up to the end of Franklin Road, swung a left and headed down Ponsonby until we were at the corner of Collingwood. Sturgis pulled the jeep into a gravel driveway that was cut into a row of two-storey redbrick shops that ran almost the length of the block from Franklin to Collingwood. We stopped halfway up, the second storey of one of the shops suspended above us.

'I don't think I should take the jeep right up,' he said, looking at me for some sort of guidance.

'Right,' I said, nodding vigorously. 'Better not.'

We got out and walked up the remainder of the driveway, which, with the second storey above us, was more like a long tunnel. I could hear pigeons cooing in the steel beams directly above our heads. The driveway opened out onto a small courtyard that was littered with junk – boxes of old books, crates of empty beer bottles, scrap metal, and randomly strewn car parts. A couple of old, rusted Model T Fords were dying a slow death in the far corner, one of them with all its wheels missing.

'What is this place?'

'Up there,' said Sturgis, pointing up to his left at the back of the building. A weather-beaten wooden staircase ran diagonally up the redbrick wall to a rickety, precarious landing that was badly sunken in one corner. The landing led on to a windowless steel door, which was closed. It was the kind of door that looked as though it would take some opening.

'That's it?' I said, a little disappointed. My imagination had been busily working away on this scene over the past few weeks to produce a gauzy, shady black and brown image. The components – opium, Oriental whores, queer philosophy – demanded something exotic. Instead I got a nondescript junkyard and a sealed factory door.

'That's it,' said Sturgis.

There were no windows around the door, no windows at the back of any of the shops in the row, so it didn't seem necessary to mask our presence.

'I take it you've been up there?' I said.

'Just a couple of times. Not for the whores, mind.'

I turned to face Sturgis, my feet making a loud crunching noise on the gravel.

'Opium?'

He nodded once.

'What's it like?'

'I don't know,' he said, still looking up at the imposing steel door. 'Scary.'

'Why?'

'It's hard to say. It's like everything becomes, I don't know, obvious.'

He fell silent for a moment after this, but it was a laden silence, heavy and ripe. I caught a whiff of it in the cool air.

'What is it?' I asked, sensing he had something he wanted to tell me, to reveal to me.

He took his cap off and scratched his head. 'Ah, I'm, um, I'm not sure I should be telling you this, Captain, but . . .'

'What?'

'The whores in there,' he said, nodding in the direction of the steel door, 'I don't think they're Chinese.'

'So?'

'Well, I think they might be Nips, sir.'

I laughed. He looked so earnest and sincere, so alive with the prospect of scandal, that I just couldn't help myself. He was on the make for stories, and he was determined to find them wherever he went. I could see he was offended by my response.

'I don't think so, Sturgis,' I said, patting him on the shoulder. He wriggled free from my condescending hand.

'It's true, sir. I'm sure they're Nips. I spent some time fruit picking out West, out in Oregon. I know how the Nips talk.'

'And do you know how Chinese sounds?'

'Well . . . I mean, no, but . . .'

'Are you telling me that giant son-of-a-bitch is Japanese also?'

He hunched his shoulders. He looked deflated, his punch line ruined. 'No, he ain't. He's a chink through-and-through. But the whores seem different. A few of them know English as well. Pidgin English, like about Oki's level.'

I laughed.

'I could swear they're Nips, Captain.'

'Listen, Sturgis. I'm an officer. I've been to the security briefings. If they were Japanese, they'd be interned. There's just no doubt about it. The Government here's rounded up every last one of them.'

Just then we heard some muffled voices coming from behind the tall wooden fence opposite the row of buildings. Sturgis, alive and frisky again, took me lightly by the arm and steered me to a corner of the courtyard where, on his instruction, we crouched down behind a pile of rusty old oil drums.

'What are we doing?' I whispered, feeling like a complete innocent.

'I think that's your man,' Sturgis said, pointing between the drums to the fence.

About halfway along the line of palings a gate swung open out of nowhere. I hadn't seen the hinges in the fence at all. Oscar Walters suddenly stepped through the opening. He was dressed in his usual stark black outfit, and was busy talking over his shoulder to somebody behind him. It was the giant Chinaman who, on passing through the gate, had to crouch to duck under a hanging tree branch. He must have been close to seven feet and was at least half a head taller than the top of the fence. They walked across the courtyard, both of them with the same emaciated, haunted look. Oscar was saying something to the Chinaman, but I couldn't make out the words. It sounded like English, though.

They climbed the staircase, which sagged and creaked under their weight. When they got to the landing, Oscar stood aside and let the Chinaman knock what I took to be a coded pattern on the door, four quick quavers followed by a full value minim. He then said something to the door, which had the guttural, bouncy sound of Chinese about it. He was certainly no Nip. The door opened just enough to let them in before closing again.

Sturgis looked at me and smiled, his eyes full of intrigue.

'It's not all stale beer and bar fights in this country, you know.'

'I guess not,' I said.

We stood up and threaded our way through the drums back to the mouth of the driveway. I looked back at the fence, trying to find the invisible gate, but couldn't make it out in the monotony of the palings.

'You don't suppose that's where the chess club's path comes out, do you?'

'I think that's a fair assumption, sir.'

'Wiseass,' I said, climbing back into the jeep.

CHAPTER 23

I had Sturgis drop me at the bottom of the Walterses'
street. He'd had the talking bug on the drive up – something about a Nigerian alto player he'd seen in the Village
– and I hadn't had the chance to compose myself. Ever since
I'd woken up earlier that afternoon, the sugary taste of sleep
on my lips, a noxious cloud of scotch-breath trapped in my
small canvas tent, I'd known that I had to see Emily. I also
knew that I had to do something about Cartwright, but just
what I wasn't sure. And then all of a sudden I was in Parnell,
thirty yards from her house, and I hadn't the faintest notion
what I was going to do when I got there.

As I slowly made my way towards the house, the drizzly
film of rain that had been around all day started to come
down in harder, bigger drops. I looked up to see the pale,
ash-coloured sky rapidly darkening. I walked up the path
and rang the doorbell, my stomach twisted with nerves, not a
single coherent thought in my head.

There was a rattling sound on the other side of the thick
oak door. I could vaguely see Winston's silhouette through
the stained-glass windows to the side. He was bent in towards
the doorknob as if he were squaring up to a mortal enemy. It
went on for a few anxious moments, in which time I heard him
spit out a few expletives. Again I couldn't catch the language,
but, whatever it was, it wasn't English. Eventually the door

sprung open.

'Hi there, Winston,' I said, my heart skipping whole beats now that I was a step closer to her.

Winston's hulking, forlorn frame took up most of the doorway. His expression was impassive behind his dark, square glasses. In the bleached daylight I could see clearly the gnarled, twisted patch of muscle and skin on his left cheek, an absurdly frozen spot on an otherwise hangdog, saggy face. I don't think he had any idea who I was.

'What?' he said, curt and abrupt. The small paralysis didn't seem to affect the necessary movements of his mouth required for speech.

'It's me,' I said, a little dimly, looking at myself in the reflection of his coal-black lenses. 'Captain Sokol. I was up here a couple of weeks—'

'Ach!' He waved his big, meaty paw in the short space between us and nodded his head. 'Yes, yes, yes.'

He continued nodding for some time, but remained un-moving in the doorway. Clearly the memory of me alone was not enough to secure entry.

'I'm, um, I'm here to see Miss Walters. Is she at home?'

He kept glaring at me, but without seeing his eyes it was impossible to tell what he was thinking, if anything. In spite of that, I had the distinct impression that at that time, in those very few seconds, he did not know who Miss Walters was. I would have patted him on the shoulder and brushed past him if he had been a smaller man, but his sheer largeness seemed to counsel against such a course. It was starting to look impossible when, fortunately, a woman's voice trickled down the hallway towards us.

'Who's there, Winston?'

He remained unmoved. I bounced up on my tiptoes, trying to see over his shoulder, but the hallway was too dark to make anything out. Not knowing what else to do, I took the liberty of calling out down the hallway.

'It's Captain Sokol. From the Third Marine Division.' I waited for a couple of seconds, but no response. 'Victoria Park camp.'

The ominous silence continued for a few beats, followed by the clanging sound of hurried footsteps on the floorboards. After an unreasonable delay, in which time Winston's dark-glassed gaze never once left me, Mrs Walters marched up the hallway like an actress emerging out of a blackened set. She laid a hand on Winston's tree trunk of an arm and gently dislodged him from the doorframe with a few soothing, muted words.

'Winston. Tell Miss Walters that Captain Sokol is here. And prepare some tea, please.'

She spun on her heel and beamed a radiant smile at me, creasing the papery skin on her face into a roadmap of fine and furrowed lines. She appeared thinner than when I last saw her, small and frail, not a shadow of the formidable woman she had presented at the British Med function. I felt a strange sense of guilt just for standing there and looking at her. Her eyes seemed to acknowledge my embarrassment.

'Captain Sokol. What a wonderful surprise. Do come in.'

She led me to the sitting room at the end of the hallway where we'd eaten our sandwiches last time. The house was freezing, but once again there was a small fire burning in the sitting-room fireplace. She pointed to the beautiful, un-comfortable chaise longue and sat herself down on the long couch opposite me. I noticed a small chess set to the side of the couch, complete with its pieces scattered at various points across the board. Beside this was a writing pad and pen. She caught me looking at the arrangement, which I assumed she had just put aside for my benefit.

'Do you play chess, Captain?' she asked, her face taut and defensive.

'I'm afraid not. I don't have much of a knack for it.'

'Why would that be? You're a doctor, a scientist; surely you could perform the necessary calculations.'

'It's not that,' I said, leaning back on the dainty arm of the chaise longue. 'I guess I just have trouble anticipating things in advance.'

'Quite,' she said, allowing herself a small smile.

'Were you keeping track of the pieces?' I asked, nodding down at the writing pad and pen.

'Oh, no. No. I . . . we belong to an international chess association. I believe you heard my son speak of it?'

'Right. In Western Park. He made it sound as though the game could end the war. Save humanity.'

She bowed her head and smoothed out her tweed skirt. 'My son is given to a certain loftiness of tone,' she said affectionately. 'It's just his style.'

'I understand,' I said, still looking at the writing pad. The page was almost completely written over, but the text contained many deletions – big, striking black lines slashed through whole sentences and paragraphs. Mrs Walters cleared her throat.

'As I was saying, we belong to an international chess affiliation. We correspond with other members, share anecdotes and stories, and play long, drawn-out games across the world, writing each other our moves one at a time.' She looked at me sharply. 'We can't control the war, Captain. The separation it entails, the distance from one's people. But we can stay in touch, and remember who we are.'

I paused, feeling the heat of her insinuation in the air, and searched for something to say. In the end all I could manage was a simple, 'Yes.'

She smiled knowingly and clapped her hands, making a point of changing the subject. 'So. To what do we owe this honour, Captain?'

A glint had returned to her eye after the initial awkwardness, and I got the feeling that she knew my intent, or some notion of it at least. In fact, I got the distinct impression she had been waiting for me.

'I just happened to be in Parnell and, ah, thought I'd call in.'

'Charming. It's been so long since we've had callers. In London our townhouse was like a saloon, you know.' Her eyes smiled miserably. She looked up into the middle distance and raised her hands wistfully. 'So many people,' she said, her voice soft and croaky.

'I was hoping to see Miss Walters,' I said after a respectful pause. 'I mean, as well.'

'Of course you were,' she said knowingly.

In the window above Mrs Walters's head I could see the dark clouds thickening. The wind had picked up, making a whistling sound in the chimney and causing the odd puff of smoke to mushroom out from the flames in the fireplace. Sheets of fine, filmy rain flew across the frame of the window. I waited for her to say something.

'Captain?'

'Yes.'

'Will Major Cartwright be joining you today?'

The question was delicately put. As she said the words it finally dawned on me why she was acting so queerly. Cartwright had spoken to her; he had told her of his intentions, had struck an agreement or some sort of an arrangement with her. I had been so fixed on Cartwright that it hadn't occurred to me that Mrs Walters had, at the very least, co-authored the plan. It was in my nature to fail to appreciate such a thing.

'It's Colonel Cartwright now,' I said.

'Oh.'

I could have chided myself, but there was no point. I would spend the rest of my life making such naïve errors; it was simply a matter of wiring. I had no nose for politics and never would. I watched her shift in her seat, her face taut with concentration. I could see that she was treading delicately, wondering how much Cartwright had told me, whether I was aware she'd entered into a bargain to sell her daughter.

'And how are things at the camp, Captain?'

'Busy,' I said, unable to hide the irritation in my tone. My traffic was with Emily and I was impatient to see her, but there was little I could do to force the issue. 'We've had a lot of wounded in from the Pacific lately. Things seem to be heating up over there at the moment.'

'You'll have to help me out, Captain, as I don't quite understand. If these American soldiers are injured all the way up there in the tropics, why on earth are they being sent to New Zealand for treatment.'

'We only take the ones who need long-term care or secondary surgery.'

'I see,' she said. 'And will they go back to battle, these men you treat?'

'That's the idea. If they're hurt bad enough, they get sent straight home from the Pacific. They only come to us if there's a chance they can rebound again.'

'I see,' she said again, running her fingers down the narrow point of her chin like a wily old reporter. 'I'm interested in medicine. I guess that's what comes from being married to a physician for so long. As you know, I have a certain acquaintance with the fellows of the British Medical Society. Tell me, Captain, do you use any of the local doctors in your hospital? I only ask because I understand some of them work with the Army up in Cornwall Park.'

I had the distinct feeling that she was giving me the filibuster treatment, knowing that I was powerless to do anything about it. I tried to listen out for movements within the house, but the place was silent.

'No,' I said a little coolly. 'We do it all ourselves.'

'It's staggering, isn't it,' she said, as much to herself as to me. 'All that money. I suppose all of your supplies – the drugs, the penicillin, the beds, the scalpels – I imagine it all comes from America?'

I nodded. 'They ship it all in once a month,' I said, wondering what she was driving at.

She laughed derisively, but it wasn't hard to hear an undertone of something – rueful irony perhaps, or just plain old sorrow.

'Forgive me, Captain, but I just can't help thinking that the whole thing is designed to make a very few people a lot of money. That at the end of all this pain and suffering we'll discover that that's what it has all been about.' She let me absorb this for a moment. 'It's a terrible thought, isn't it?'

'I'm not sure I follow,' I said, slowly, cautiously.

She smiled thinly, a little condescendingly. She seemed tired and withdrawn all of a sudden. She couldn't be bothered with the challenge.

'Oh, I don't know anything,' she said, waving her blue hand in the air carelessly. 'I'm old, Captain, and it is impolite of you to listen to me so carefully. Still. People will say what they will, but certain things simply are as they are.'

I was trying to unpack this thought when the door behind me started rattling. I assumed it was Winston with the tea, so I saved myself the effort of turning around. When the door finally did spring open I got a shock to see Mrs Walters bolt out of her seat, a startled look on her face. As I turned I could feel my face blush a deep, burning red. It was Emily, and she was wielding a silver tray with a teapot and a collection of cups and saucers. I stumbled my way to my feet as she placed the tray on the mahogany table between the couch and the chaise longue.

'What on earth are you doing?' cried Mrs Walters, looking pale and stricken. 'But where is Winston?'

Emily looked at me quickly, her face almost completely expressionless, before turning to her mother.

'He's ill,' she said plainly. 'I've put him to bed upstairs.'

'He's ill? And, and you made the tea . . . yourself?'

Emily looked at me again, this time with a harried smile. I couldn't figure out whether she knew anything of Cartwright's proposal.

'How do you do, Captain?' she asked, appearing not at all surprised to see me, as if my coming to the house was the most natural thing in the world.

'I'm well. Thank you, Miss Walters,' I said, hoping her unnerving detachment wasn't just simple indifference.

She nodded before taking her seat on the Edwardian chair beside the couch. Mrs Walters and I followed her lead and resumed our seats. She was wearing the same cream-coloured dress as last time; the same cream-coloured dress she'd also worn to the British Med soiree. The only difference was that instead of the satin jacket, she now had a beige woollen shawl draped across her shoulders to combat the cold. In the gloom of that small room, its windows painted gunmetal by the storm outside, the reddy tinge in her dark, chestnut hair shone like a beacon of light and illuminated her pale, almost translucent skin. I could see her breast moving underneath the shawl, gently rising and falling with each breath, but she still didn't seem real to me. She was like a beautiful abstraction, not textbook at all, but peculiar and unknowable. I felt as though I was the only one who could see her.

For a moment nobody knew what to say. So as not to gape I looked at the tea things sitting on the gleaming silver tray. The milk was in a tall Royal Copenhagen jug, and had a rancid, almost vinegary smell.

'I'm afraid,' Mrs Walters said, 'that simply making the tea is not enough. It has to be poured as well.'

'Quite,' said Emily, smiling to herself.

I watched on wretchedly as Emily poured the tea. As long as Mrs Walters stayed in the room my plan, if it could be called that, was for nothing. I needed to see Emily alone. I made no bones about looking directly at her, but she coyly avoided looking back. She had to know of Cartwright's proposal. And if she did, what must she be thinking of me, here in her house, showing up unannounced? Pity? I couldn't bear the thought.

Mrs Cartwright broke the silence by saying, 'And so do you also come from a long line of doctors, Captain? As Colonel Cartwright does.'

'No, ma'am.'

'So, pray, what do your people do then? Out there in California.'

'My father died a few years ago. He wrote signs for a living, among other things. My mother passed away when I was young.'

Mrs Walters swallowed her tea and replaced the cup back on its saucer with a tinny clink. I could feel Emily looking at me now, but I kept my eyes closely on the old lady, who moved slightly in her seat.

'I see,' she said. 'That's the curious thing about America, isn't it? I dare say one would go a long way in England or Europe before finding a doctor whose father, how did you put it, wrote signs.'

I shrugged; in America you had to go a long way too. There was another long interval of the clinking of teacups and saucers, polite slurps, and the sound of rain, which was now lashing the windows behind Mrs Walters's head with a good deal of feeling. The room was sunk in day-darkness.

'I painted a lot of pictures,' I was surprised to hear myself say, 'when I was younger. And still do.' I looked at the Marine-Officer hat in my lap and ran my finger across the stiff brim. 'Although, not at the moment, of course.'

'A painter?' Mrs Walters said, the surprise in her tone bordering on umbrage. 'Really?'

'What do you paint?' said Emily in that quiet, level voice of hers. I could see that I had clearly piqued her interest.

'Shapes, mainly. Shapes and colours.'

'Shapes!' Mrs Walters said, clucking her tongue. 'Come now, Captain, do spare us the bohemian nonsense. You must have a speciality. Portraiture, landscapes, that sort of thing?'

'I guess, I mean, at a certain level, I do all of those things. A landscape is just a collection of shapes and colours. Same as an eye or a mouth. It's just a matter of seeing them.' I looked over at Emily, who was smiling at me faintly. Mrs Walters caught the shared look, and cleared her throat declaratively.

'If you'll forgive me, Captain,' she said, her tiny body poised on the edge of the long couch, her feet pressed firmly together, 'but why have you come here today?'

'Mother!' Emily said, her porcelain face flushing a lovely pink. 'How incredibly rude of you.'

'It's a simple question. The Captain can choose to answer it or not.'

'He's a guest in your house,' Emily said. Even though her tone was reproachful, I thought I heard in it a hint of anticipation, as though she was glad the question had been asked.

'You'll have to excuse me, Captain,' Mrs Walters said, 'but we have become very coarse since we've been in New Zealand. There's no society here, you see. One loses the touch. But all the same, I should like an answer if you don't terribly mind. I take it you know that Colonel Cartwright has called? Or telephoned, rather.'

Here we go, I thought. I desperately wanted to reach out and touch Emily, to touch her skin, to feel the heat of her mouth and tongue again. Her eyes had dilated to the point where they were almost black. She sat in her chair completely wrapped. I think she wanted this thing to play out as much as her mother did, although for what reason I still couldn't be sure.

'Um, yes. He mentioned it.'

'And you know, then, what he has proposed?'

'I know something of it.'

'And yet,' Mrs Walters said, almost hovering above the edge of the couch now, 'and yet you decided to call on us. Completely unannounced. As if you were, what, simply passing by? Tell me, Captain, what are we to make of this?'

She wasn't English. Her accent began to take on a harsh resonance the more excited she got, betraying an underlay of something jaunty and precise.

'Mother, please!' Emily said, although the interjection, I felt, was not intended to stop the cross-examination. Maybe it was a show of support, an indication of sides. 'You're being cruel.'

'Nonsense!' Mrs Walters glared at her daughter and stomped one of her tiny feet on the ground. Her eyes were wild, her mouth compressed into a hard little knot. 'The only cruel person here is . . .' She stopped herself with a sudden, jerky spasm of her body and arms. Her coiled intensity seemed so out of place in the sullen gloom of the setting – the small fireplace, the teacups, the weak grey light. She took a short moment to steady herself before shooting her fiery eyes back at me. 'I take it you know our position, Captain. Since Dr Walters passed away. You've been here, you've seen us. You must know by now.'

I nodded cautiously, not wanting to overstep my mark.

'So then you'll understand what an offer like Colonel Cartwright's means. To us. To this family.'

I nodded again.

'We are proud people, Captain. We come from . . .' She caught herself again and squeezed her eyes shut for a long, agonised moment.

'Mother,' Emily said coldly, whatever interest she had had in the outcome of the questioning gone. 'That's enough. I think you should apologise to—'

'You're determined to see this family starve, aren't you?' Mrs Walters screeched, on her feet now, standing above Emily. 'After all we've done for you, this is how you treat us!'

Emily refused to look at her and stared down at the tea things, her jaw set tight, her mouth pursed. I was amazed, even thrilled by the steadfastness of her resistance. She was an island, a castle with an enormous moat. The old woman looked from her daughter to me and back again, her small stature, her upright five-foot-nothing undermining the demonstration she was trying to make. She looked desperate to say something, to round out her argument with a logical absolute, but nothing came. I couldn't bring myself to look at her as she stomped another one of her tiny feet on the hard floorboards and left through the darkness of the adjacent dining room. After a stunned moment I could hear her leather-soled feet click-clack up a flight of stairs somewhere in the bowels of the house.

On cue, a bolt of lightning flashed outside, sending its electric light and charge through the house, its blunt pulse stunning me in the chest. The shock of it made Emily scream a solitary note of pure fright from her lungs. We had both taken a half-step out of our seats towards each other, but all at once the fright seemed to pass, and we were left stranded, crouched in uncomfortable attitudes of readiness. I didn't know what to do, whether to make the lunge towards her or to retreat back to the chaise longue. I studied her face for an indication, but she was a blank canvas again and gave me nothing. Eventually my legs gave out and I flopped back into my seat. She stood up properly then and wrapped the shawl tightly around her chiselled shoulders. She seemed on the cusp of an enormous decision, one whose opposing variables I could not even begin to understand.

'Excuse me for one moment, Captain.'

'Call me Peter.'

She blushed and looked down at her hands, quickly, then back up at me.

'Don't go,' I said. 'I need to tell you something.'

'I will come back. Just, excuse me for one moment, please?'

'Say my name.'

She knew what it meant and refused to oblige.

'Just, please, don't go,' she said, turning her back on me and marching from the room, a cumbersome step that threatened to break out into a run. I listened to her arrhythmic footsteps echoing throughout the mysterious corridors of the house.

The room was almost completely dark.

It had been over twenty minutes, and Emily still hadn't returned. I got up from the chaise longue and went over to the windows by the couch. The branches of the walnut trees were bending furiously in the wind, and sheets of rain flew across the deep, sloping yard. The joists of the house were creaking something terrible, absorbing each gust of wind with grim determination. I closed my eyes and imagined I was on a ship, some seventeenth-century wooden schooner, bound from the heart of civilisation to somewhere distant and remote and unknowable – somewhere like New Zealand.

I didn't expect her to come down. I had read her injunction to wait as a final act of politeness, or at the very best a hedging of her bets. It even occurred to me that the two of them were holed-up upstairs, waiting until I left. That they couldn't bear the thought of having to come down the stairs to tell the signwriter's boy to run along home, so they had simply decided to wait it out until I got the hint.

There was another bolt of lightning in the sky, a single artery with a patchwork of veins around it, but my eyes were barely in focus any more. I was thirty-three years old. I had been twenty-two for years, and then out of nowhere I was thirty-three. If the Japs didn't hit me in the Pacific I would be dead in thirty years, thirty-five tops. The Sokols have never been robust; we breed, we endure, then we die. I had made a point of hating the word love, with its squeamish v wedged between those sentimental vowels, but I hadn't expected to live thirty-three years without it, without experiencing something that could at least help me define it. But then again, who was I kidding? I think I'd always known in myself, in the curious alchemy of daily self-loathing and unwanted detachment, that I'd spent too much time in my own head to really love another person. I had thought myself into a marginal state – was riddled with my own marginality. The only women I seemed to meet in California, the women I occasionally slept with, were such specimens of crude good health and optimism that I couldn't bring myself to rain on them. And so I invariably left them alone.

But Emily was no Californian. She was a creature of the margins as well; I'd known it from the moment I saw her in the ballroom of the Ambassador Hotel. It was in the elusive timbre of her voice, the way her eyes would drop to the ground, fleetingly, before she willed them to readjust. It was a certain type of fatalism, as if she knew all the horrors and pleasures of the world but had learned to outgrow them, to detach herself from them. I couldn't imagine there was another person in the world like this, but there she was – cold and hungry and beautiful at the bottom of the world. It wasn't so much losing her to Cartwright that bothered me; it was what he would do to her. He would throw his stinking money at her until she couldn't resist any more; he would buy her dresses and feed her ice creams and knock her up like a Catholic with a noisy brood of Johnnys and Mary Janes – all impossibly healthy children who would grow up to be dazzling debutantes and star quarterbacks. He would overwhelm her with things and draw the delicate fatalism out like a boil, lancing it for good, and leave her just another powdered, fat-assed American matron.

I retrieved my hat from the chaise longue and opened the door to the hallway, which was almost pitch black. I groped the walls around the door but couldn't find a light switch. My cheeks, which had been rosy with the warmth of the fireplace in the sitting room, now tingled in the stark cold. I guided myself down the side of the hallway by running my hand along the wall as I went, every now and then negotiating the picture frames of the various portraits. When I reached the office the door was shut. I tried the handle but it wouldn't give at first. I had to shake it a couple of times before the latch sprung open in a loud, twanging snap. Perhaps Winston wasn't so crippled after all.

I stepped in and closed the door behind me. It took me a long time to find the light switch, my arms stretched out in front of me like Dr Frankenstein's creature, pawing at the dark with open palms. The room was as I remembered it, although it now appeared a little larger without Emily's presence. I had thought about this office and that kiss almost constantly for two weeks, and in my mind I had compressed the location, the setting of my cherished moment, into a space about the size of a nutshell. The rain was still pelting down on the windows and roof, and I knew that Sturgis would be none too pleased about having to come out in it. As I lifted the telephone receiver from its hanging cradle, the black window above the desk suddenly flashed bright white. This was followed, about a quarter beat later, by a sharp exploding sound so fundamental it made me drop the phone handle. Just as I recovered my wits a groaning sound resounded throughout the house and the light bulb above my head was slowly drained of its colour, so that once again I was standing in complete darkness. Power outage. I fumbled for the telephone receiver, knocking a small globe and a stack of papers off the desk in the process. But it was no good; the line was dead.

The wind continued to buffet the house from all angles, and the rain was so heavy that it sounded as though steel nails were falling from the sky. But I didn't care; I wanted out of the place, and fast. If the power was out down here, it would be the same upstairs. I didn't want them to come down. I didn't want to have to go through the agony of talking about fuse switches and gas lamps while my heart slowly broke. I stumbled my way to the door and was searching for the handle when, with a sound like a gramophone record coming to an abrupt halt, the power rang back on again and the dim, waxy yellow bulb above my head limped back to attention.

I tried the phone again, but the line was still dead. I figured if the weather was too rough to walk all the way back to camp, I'd take refuge in the Parnell Red Cross, which was only ten minutes' walk away. I was pulling my hat on when I heard a light tap on the door.

'Peter,' she said, her quiet voice barely audible over the wind and creaking joists. 'It's me, Emily. May I come in?'

I hesitated for some reason before answering. Maybe it was just the sound of her voice saying my name.

'Yes. Of course.'

She gently pushed the door open about a quarter way and poked her head through the gap.

'Are you all right?' she said, a queer smile on her face.

'Yes. I was just trying the phone. I need a ride back to camp and . . .'

She slipped her thin, willowy frame through the door without opening it any further and closed it behind her, gently, her back pressed against it.

'Are you leaving?'

'I, ah . . . yes.' Once again I couldn't get a read on the

undertone, the nuance. Even the meaning of the smile plastered across her face escaped me.

'We were hoping you would stay for supper.'

'We? Are you sure about that?'

She took a step towards me, away from the protection of the door, and stopped.

'Please,' she said. 'We both want you to stay.'

'Listen, Emily, I know about Cartwright, and I take it you do too. I just—'

She took another couple of steps towards me so that we were barely two feet apart. She put her finger to my lips, and the strange gesture, the thrill of her touch, just about brought me to my knees.

'Don't mind mother. She gets irrational at times.' She removed the finger from my mouth and delicately placed her hand on my shoulder. 'You don't have to worry about Colonel Cartwright either.' She paused. 'Now, will you do the honourable thing and join us for supper?'

It was all I could do to nod my head.

Supper was served in the dining room on a large walnut table that could have seated at least a dozen people. The three of us sat at the end closest to the fireplace in the nearby sitting room, but the dining room itself was so large that the heat coming from the fire was severely diluted. The silver on the table was cold to the touch. Winston had roused himself from whatever malady had earlier afflicted him, and was serving us with great circumstance.

The food was atrocious – more stale bread, geriatric-smelling eggs, and thinly sliced, chewy mutton from a very old sheep. But I had no appetite anyway. Instead I sipped cup after cup of black tea and listened to Mrs Walters chirp on about the pre-war theatre scene in London. It was as if her argument with Emily had never happened, and that I was a familiar old friend of the family.

'And tell me, Captain, is there a lively artistic scene in San Francisco?' Mrs Walters asked, politely but determinedly working her way through every morsel of food on the table.

'I guess there is. Nothing like New York, though.'

'You've been to New York?' said Emily, who was sitting opposite me.

'I did some locum work there a while back. On the Lower East Side.'

'Lower East Side,' Mrs Walters said. 'You see, so literal-minded, you Americans.' She looked at me wryly and nodded her head. 'Dr Walters was aware of this, you know. The English have never really understood that American sense of directness, that, I don't know, peculiarly guileless devotion to the task at hand. I certainly know I wouldn't like to be fighting against you.'

'I imagine the English are just as determined,' I said, feeling strangely out of my depth.

'Yes, yes, yes. Of course they're . . . I should say, we're determined. But it's more than that. I believe what Dr Walters was referring to was the American sense of grandness. You think in bigger scales. You have a flair for logistics. Did you know, Emily,' she said, pausing for a moment to chew and leaning towards her daughter, 'that the Victoria Park hospital, the Captain's hospital, doesn't use any local personnel. No local doctors, nurses, medics – nothing. Isn't that right, Captain?'

I looked at Emily, then back at Mrs Walters. 'Um. Well, yes.'

'And,' said Mrs Walters, raising her forefinger in the air to punctuate the point, 'a ship arrives every month, right on schedule, to deliver all their supplies. Right down to the beds and sheets. Isn't that what you said, Captain?'

'Yes, but . . . I fail to see why that's so extraordinary.'

Mrs Walters laughed and patted her daughter on the arm. 'Then you don't know much about British history, do you? We like to plunder the place we're in before we call home. We suck places dry. We make their people dress like us, work for us, serve us, clean us. We pillage their crops and their jewels, rename their cities, remake their gods. It's the English way. But you Americans are a different story. Sooner or later you'll leave and no one will know you've been here. Until then your supply boat will come every fourth Tuesday.'

'Thursday,' I said, at my own expense, raising my teacup at her and smiling.

Emily was looking at me with that peculiar, unreadable expression again. She had finished eating and was leaning back in her chair. It struck me that for all the harshness of her family's circumstances, she had a remarkable sense of autonomy or ownership of herself, as if she were observing her situation rather than living it. I'd felt that way my whole life, and it was intriguing to recognise it in another person.

'Will you return to San Francisco after the war?' Emily asked after a long pause.

'I assume so. That's where my life is.' I regretted the words as soon as they left my mouth, for they weren't true. Since Beth and I'd divorced I had been skimming the surface at best. There was no life to speak of in San Francisco.

Mrs Walters cleared her throat. 'And will you return to your hospital, Captain?'

I shrugged my shoulders. When I had resigned from San Francisco Public I honestly hadn't thought of what would happen if I made it back. It was not that I expected to get killed. I guess I had just never thought of the war ending.

So I said, 'Yeah, most likely,' because I knew it was the answer she wanted to hear.

'I would love to see San Francisco, Captain,' Mrs Walters said thoughtfully.

202

'I think you would like it,' I said. 'You could see our grandness first-hand. Our flair for logistics.'

'Touché, Captain. Touché.'

There was a noise from the other end of the house, like a door slamming shut. Mrs Walters and Emily's expressions froze as they glanced at each other. The cold air felt ominous all of a sudden. I could just make out Winston's voice down the other end of the long hallway. This was followed by the sound of syncopated footsteps and Winston's familiar rap at the door.

'Come,' said Mrs Walters, her voice suddenly brittle.

The door opened. Winston took a couple of steps into the room and stood aside, his back to the wall.

'Mr Walters,' he said.

Oscar emerged through the door and stood beside Winston. He was sodden wet from the rain outside. The water was dripping off his clothes and hair and face in a small torrent, forming a puddle at his feet. His gaunt, emaciated face was startlingly pale against the relentless black of his drenched clothes. His thin hair was plastered to his forehead and his round wire-rimmed glasses were slightly fogged. He was a sensational sight – all ascetic starkness and denial. I was so taken by his appearance that it took me a moment to register the fact that he was glaring at me. I pushed back my chair and got to my feet.

'For goodness' sake,' cried Mrs Walters, jumping out of her chair and stepping towards her son. 'You're positively drowned. Winston, get him a towel, would you?'

She hovered around him, but at the same time maintained a certain distance. Oscar completely ignored her and kept his cold-eyed glare on me.

'Don't move,' he said as Winston made for the door to get the towel. Winston stopped abruptly, did a kind of military kick on the floor, and stood to attention.

'So,' said Oscar, a nasty smile creasing his face. 'The pro-digal Marine returns.'

I nodded at him but could not help turning to Emily, for what I don't know. She remained in her seat, her head bowed over her empty plate. Oscar coolly acknowledged the exchange with another caustic little smile.

'Captain Smokol, isn't it?'

'Sokol.'

'Whatever.'

He made towards the table, his patent leather shoes squelching as he did so, and took a seat next to Emily. She stiffened her posture as he dragged his chair across the floor-boards. She looked vulnerable and fragile in a way that I hadn't noticed before. Oscar sat down in his wet clothes. Mrs Walters winced, but couldn't bring herself to voice a protest. She took her seat back at the table and motioned for me to do the same.

'Oscar, dear,' Mrs Walters said while Winston poured a fresh round of tea for everyone, 'you'll catch your death, you know. You need to dry off, for heaven's sake.'

He held up a hand in her direction without taking his eyes off me. He had a very efficient, clinical way of silencing people that I could see was particularly effective on his mother.

'Why don't we see what the good doctor says, hmm? Will I, Captain? Will I catch my death, do you think?'

I leaned back in my chair slowly, deliberately. 'I think you're aware of the risks,' I said.

He laughed bitterly and slurped his tea, draining the dainty little cup in one go. He snapped his fingers at Winston for a refill.

'Well said, old man. You're no slug, are you, Captain?'

For a brief interval nobody said a word. I listened as drips of water fell from the hem of Oscar's pants and the cuffs of his jacket to the floor. Water was still running from his hair down the bony topography of his face. In spite of it, he seemed calm and unperturbed, as though he were relaxing on a beach chair in the blazing sun. I recalled what Sturgis had said about opium – how it makes everything seem obvious – and wondered whether Oscar was currently acting under the influence of its mysterious charms.

'Quite a spread, mother,' he said, his black little eyes still locked on me. 'Although, I suppose no expense can be spared when the Yanks are involved.'

'It's just some leftovers,' Mrs Walters said, trying to maintain an air of dignity.

I couldn't help looking at Emily, and in doing so I believe Oscar felt as though he had won a certain victory. She was still looking down at her empty plate; in fact, she had barely moved a muscle since he had entered the room.

'Best not to make a habit of it, mother,' Oscar continued. 'These Americans have rapacious appetites. They'll eat us all out of our homes if we're not careful.'

I'm not one who is drawn to violence as a reflex, like many other men I have known. That doesn't make me a philosopher, either. I've just never had an idea of myself that I wanted to protect or enlist others into seeing. But sitting at that table, in that cold, dark room, I wanted nothing more than to reach across the wide expanse of polished walnut and smack the son-of-a-bitch on the mouth. But it was impossible; he had me trapped and he knew it. I was totally reliant on Mrs Walters and Emily to extract me from the situation. If the man of their house was a prick, who was I to declare it?

'Winston,' said Oscar, scanning the paltry offering of food laid out on the table.

'Sir?' Winston said, moving one step towards the table from his position at the door. His dark glasses had slipped down the ridge of his nose slightly and he pushed them back up.

'Where are the potatoes? They're ready, aren't they?'

'Sir. I . . . I have not dig them, sir.'

'Well, why on earth not? What the bloody hell are we supposed to eat, old man?'

Winston was crestfallen by the criticism. His tremendous shoulders slumped and his lips began to stammer but no words came out.

'Leave him,' Mrs Walters said crossly.

Oscar leaned theatrically across the table towards his mother and whispered, in a voice loud enough for everyone, including Winston, to hear, 'We cannot support him any longer. If he's going to—'

'Leave him!' snapped Emily. She remained unmoved, but I could see that her downturned face was glowing red across its cheekbones. 'He's unwell. He needs to rest.'

Oscar looked from Emily to Mrs Walters and then to me. He raised his eyebrows at me in mock astonishment and flopped back in his chair.

'Well, hello, sister. Good evening to you, too. I hadn't realised you were there.' He continued aiming his words at her long after the sound of them had disappeared. And then his eyes glazed over for a moment, as if he'd just discovered something. He turned to me quickly. 'I suppose, Captain, that my mother has been busy trying to match you with my sister. The lovely Miss Walters. What do you think, then? Attractive? Good connections? I'm afraid she wouldn't come with much, though. We've fallen on hard times somewhat, and—'

'Stop it!' screamed Mrs Walters. The four of us sat in stunned silence as her words echoed around the room. It wasn't until the reverberation faded that she brought a belated hand to her mouth, almost in a parody of shock. She kept her bony fingers wrapped around her face as a few grudging seconds ticked by.

Oscar slowly looked her over and moved forward in his chair.

'Perhaps I will have a towel after all. Winston, be a good man and fetch me one, would you?'

With another regimental stomp on the floor, Winston did as he was bidden, leaving the room after only a brief struggle with the door handle.

'So, what do you think of New Zealand, Captain? Our humble home.'

Everybody looked at me, including Emily. The colour had gone from her face and her skin was back to its usual pristine hue.

'It's nice. But I'm afraid I haven't seen too much of it.'

'You Americans like to stick to your camps, don't you? Camps and bars and brothels.'

'The first maybe,' I said. 'But it seems to me all sorts of people like the last two.'

He didn't flinch a bit.

'But the locals though. The New Zealanders. What do you make of them?'

'People are people wherever you go.'

'That's just what they say in Berlin,' he said, taking a starched white towel from Winston and wiping his face and head. When he was finished he unceremoniously threw the thing back at Winston, who caught it with his face, his hands nowhere in sight. 'You see, I find them stupid as a rule. Which is why they need you. They've slumbered along down here while the rest of the world has been sharpening their knives.' He looked at me challengingly, but I remained impassive. 'Somebody smart once said that we are driven to war. That war is simply an imperative of human nature, and that only the strong will survive. Do you agree with that, Captain? As a man of science.'

'Why don't you tell me what you think.'

'I intend to,' he said bitterly. 'But you won't be able to avoid the question for long. You Americans can't be everywhere at once. Pretty soon you'll have to decide who's worth protecting and who isn't. Then where will we be, eh? Us *Kiwis*?' He took a piece of stale bread in his hand, but stopped before bringing it to his mouth. 'Don't get me wrong. I don't blame them for being stupid; there's simply nothing here for them to nourish themselves on. I think you'll find, Captain, that in New Zealand there are sheep and there are yobs, but there's little in between.'

'You could always go back to England,' I said. 'I'm sure they're desperate for smart young men like you.' In the silence that followed this I came to understand that I'd said something singularly obtuse. I just didn't know what it was.

Oscar slowly pushed his chair back across the wooden floor. There was another snap of lightning outside, the first in a while, closely followed by a drum-roll of thunder. I could sense that I had overstepped a closely guarded mark, and in doing so I'd unwittingly brought Oscar's boorish show to a sudden close. Eventually he stood up. I waited for the parting shot – an epigram about American naïvety, or colonial backwardness, but nothing came. Winston opened the door and silently followed his master out of the room, turning his dark glasses on me fleetingly before he went.

Emily's head was buried in her plate again, her hand cupping her forehead. Mrs Walters tried to smile, but she could barely convince the tight, withered muscles in her cheeks to move.

'If you don't mind,' I said, 'I think I'll call base for a ride. Excuse me, and thank you for the food.' Emily didn't look at me as I left the room.

The phone line was still dead, though. I kept trying it in the dumb hope that it would kick in, but nothing. I wearily sat in a dusty armchair in the corner of the office while I decided what to do. After a couple of minutes I finally reconciled myself to the fact of a long, wet walk to the Parnell Red Cross and an uncomfortable night's sleep in one of the sick beds they reserved for nurses and afflicted U.S.O. personnel. I was about to creep back out into the dining room to bid an awkward goodnight when there was a cough at the door. I jumped a little and looked up to see Winston's burly frame crowding the doorway.

'Captain,' he said.

'Yes.'

'Phone is broke, no?'

'Ah, yeah.'

'You are to sleep. Spare room. Follow me.'

The bedroom that Winston led me to was a small, dismal garret at the very top of the house, which poked out of the sloping slate roof. The air in the room was stagnant and all the furniture was covered in dust. The mattress on the steel-sprung bed looked flat and listless, the kind of thing prisoners sleep on in the movies. I poked around for a bit, feeling caged-in and alone. Aside from the bed and a Victorian parlour chair, the only other piece of furniture was a free-standing oak armoire.

It was barely eight o'clock, and what with the wind and rain lashing my exposed little cabin, I knew my chances at sleep were slim at best. I stared at the armoire for ten, fifteen minutes without a single thought in my head. The only thing I was aware of was the ache in my back, a hangover from the marathon surgery stretch I hadn't yet recovered from.

I got up off the bed and opened the armoire's door in the hope that I would find some reading material, a psychoanalytic study of the sexual proclivities of West Essex rats, perhaps. But I was out of luck; there was nothing but a stack of mothballed linen that smelled faintly of urine, a pair of crinkled, almost fossilised leather brogues, and a sun-bowed tennis racquet that struck me as almost unbearably sad. I gently eased the racquet out of the way, careful not to make any noise. The leather grip was tacky in my hand. Just as I extricated it from the mountain of boiled sheets, I saw the edge of a small, dark frame in the corner where the racquet had come from. I stood still for a moment and looked at the closed bedroom door. Not a sound. I reached in and, after a couple of goes, plucked the thing out. It was thick with greasy dust. I took my handkerchief out from my hip pocket and wiped the gooey mess off the glass. It wasn't a painting, and it wasn't a picture; it was some sort of diploma. The writing was German, and it had, as far as I could tell, been awarded from the University of Berlin. The lucky graduate was a certain Mykel Wasserman. Michael Wasserman. Michael Walters.

I quickly put the diploma back where I'd found it and closed the armoire door. I felt thrilled and racked with guilt. It was all so obvious now, but I consciously, actively, refrained from thinking of the logical explanation for what I'd just found. I switched the light off and lay on the bed, my heart hammering inside my chest, and forced myself to listen to the groaning of the house against the waves of wind.

I must have drifted off at some point because I didn't hear her come in. I had a sense of proximity in my dream, someone or something looming above me. When I opened my eyes she was there. Her head was perched above me, less than two feet away. I was startled and made to sit up in the bed, but she placed her hand palm down on my chest, authoritatively, like a mother consoling a baby with colic. She took my head in her hands and pressed her forehead against mine. Warm, salty tears dripped from her eyes onto my face. She kissed me lightly with her hot, wet mouth but her lips were quivering. My heart was bashing against my rib cage in a wild rhythm. I was about to say something, to ask her if she was all right, but she pressed her thumb down over my lips.

'I'm not one of them,' she whispered, her breath steaming

hot against my cold ear. 'I'm . . . I'm not one of them.' She kissed me again and stood up, quietly, stealthily. 'Promise me something,' she said, backing away to the door, her voice small and husky.

'Anything.'

'Come back for me. As soon as you can.'

She closed the door silently. I listened as she padded softly down the attic stairs, down, somewhere, into the bosom of her unknowable house.

CHAPTER 24

The road sign said twenty miles to Los Angeles. We were passing through the satellite towns now, nameless places in the landscape, houses stuck together in haphazard clusters, randomly, unnervingly.

I had maintained a loaded silence ever since Eddie had finished recounting Sturgis's book to me. He'd told the story well, identifying the key pinches in the plot and winding his narrative between them, like thread through the eyes of so many needles. Although I'd already read most of what he'd told me, his manner of explaining it seemed new and fresh. He took Sturgis's lean, spare prose and spun it with his own frizzy-haired Eddieness, identifying idiosyncrasies and moments of bitter humour that I don't think I would have picked up on.

What fascinated me, though, was that he had properly understood the forlornness lying beneath Sturgis's sentences. I'd listened to his delivery in the rapt, open-mouthed manner of a child listening to a fairytale. I listened as he sketched out the familiar arc, as he told the narrative from the hapless hero's unreliable perspective. I didn't have to ask him any questions – it was as clear as could be. Sturgis had understood; he had understood it well enough, and he'd had the literary talent to convincingly step inside my confusion. As a fellow artist I knew that that level of understanding was hard-won, and that it only came with something approaching an intimate, basic empathy for your subject. I couldn't say whether he'd forgiven me, but I knew that he understood. The question was whether this would be enough.

But strangely, as I listened to Eddie's reedy voice, my attention was only partially on the story. The coiled, gristly tension in my gut that the thought of Missy produced was now beginning to unwind, so that I was all hollowness inside. I had spent years conveniently lying to myself that our arrangement suited her. I had used her as a crutch, as a shield against the onset of middle-aged loneliness, and the darkness of the past I was trying to forget. I had locked myself away in a shed and betrayed her for a ghost. I'd defiled her self-respect with a never-ending procession of turgid paintings that had nothing to do with her, and that she knew had nothing to do with her. I had even refused to teach her the science of my colours. This was all I could think of as my judgment was being read out.

I watched the road slip underneath us and realised that the old excuses, the old justifications didn't wash any more. I was aware of the excuses and the justifications because the guilt had always been there; I'd just chosen to never acknowledge it. And yet here I was again, out in the middle of nowhere, looking for the past.

'So,' said Eddie, breaking the long silence, 'what do you think?'

'What's that?'

'The story.'

'Oh.' I slowed down for a traffic light, the first I'd encountered since leaving San Diego. 'I'm not sure.'

'Well?' He looked at me with a half-smile. His eye sockets were almost completely black now.

'Well what?'

'Are you in it?'

'The story? Ah. No. I don't think so.'

I could tell he didn't believe me, but I was in no mood to weave together a convincing cover. I decided to change the subject.

'I'm a painter, you know.'

'No kidding?'

'No kidding. I teach down at San Diego State. But mostly I just paint.'

'Huh. I don't think I've met a proper painter before,' he said, taking his glasses off and checking out his nose in the sun-visor mirror. He gently dabbed at the swollen bridge with the pad of his forefinger.

'Don't touch that,' I said. 'It will start to go down in a day or two if you just leave it.'

'You're quite the expert on broken noses, aren't you?'

The insinuation was clear, but I realised he knew that he had no right to demand an answer. We motored on in silence for a while. I could sense that with every passing road sign pointing out the proximity of L.A., with every clump of south-side urban sprawl that became visible on the radar of the windscreen, Eddie became a touch more anxious.

'So you're a painter, huh?'

I nodded, looking straight ahead. Although my life had whittled down to the point where I was, literally, nothing more than a painter, the question was still a weighty one. Perhaps it will be my epitaph.

'And I take it,' continued Eddie after a short pause, 'that you were a painter before the war. Before you were an orderly?'

'I painted. But I don't know if I was a painter before the war. Not a real one.'

'What's the difference between painting and being a painter?'

'A painter is closer to death.'

I could feel his eyes boring into the side of my face. He was breathing loudly through his mouth again.

'Was Professor Sturgis a writer? I mean, you know, before the war and all.'

'He had designs. He may have been a bit like you.'

Eddie opened the book again and looked at Sturgis's photograph on the inside flap of the dust cover.

'Did the war help your painting?' he asked. 'Like, did it give you new ideas and things?'

I nodded slowly. 'I believe it did.'

'And that's obviously the same for Professor Sturgis, right? What with this book being about his unit, he obviously got some ideas.'

He waved the book in the dank car air between us before putting it down and lighting another Camel. He touched his nose a couple of times as he exhaled the smoke.

'Maybe it will give me something to write about,' he said softly, winding the window down an inch to let the blue smoke escape. 'Vietnam. I mean, it's got to be pretty freaky over there – the culture and the heat and the colours and whatnot. Plus the fighting as well.'

His voice was beginning to crack, and I thought for a moment that he was going to cry, but he took a couple of quick gut drags on his cigarette and calmed himself.

'What do you think, Peter?'

'I don't think you need to go to war to find something to write about,' I said flatly. The kid was deeply impressionable and, I got the feeling, susceptible to romantic notions. I didn't want to be responsible in any way for leading him to believe that getting shot at in a jungle would be a useful aesthetic experience. 'I mean, pardon me for saying this, Eddie, but what in the hell is your father thinking, anyway?'

He flicked his cigarette out of the small gap in the window and sat back in his seat in a flopping manner.

'Ah, it's difficult to understand,' he said, waving his hand across his face. 'Basically he's a Type-A Zionist, you know.

215

The nation-builder kind. He and my mom left us with my grandmother while they went off to Israel to volunteer on a kibbutz. For like six whole fucking months.'

'What's that got to do with Vietnam?'

'He likes causes, is what. He sees a cause, thinks about it for like three seconds, then goes outside and screams about it from every rooftop. He's big on the domino effect at the moment. If you can believe that.' He paused for a moment, picking something out of his teeth. 'Plus it probably has something to do with convincing everybody that we're true Americans. I don't know.'

I didn't feel qualified to comment, so I let it hang for a few moments, waiting for him to invite me back into the conversation, but the offer never came. He just sat there, absent-mindedly picking at his teeth. Pretty soon we passed a sign that said 'Welcome to Los Angeles'. We drove through Long Beach for a couple of miles before I spotted a pay phone on the side of the road. I pulled the car over.

'I won't be long,' I said. 'I just need to make a quick call.'

I closed the door of the phone booth even though nobody was around. My index finger was stabbing out our number, but I had no idea what I was going to say when she picked up. I wouldn't even be able to tell her why I was calling. The phone rang. I pictured her looking up from her reading, faintly annoyed by the disruption, and getting up to walk to the telephone in the kitchen. The dappled blood-orange dusk light would be flooding in through the windows and the glass doors.

'Hello,' she said, her voice as clear as spring water.

My heart thudded for two, three, four seconds before I hung up.

216

CHAPTER 25

Wednesday afternoon. I'd come off an eight-hour shift at 1400 hours and had been trying to kill time ever since. The leave log in Diddle's office spelt it out loud and clear: 'Lieutenant Colonel Cartwright; local leave until 1600 hours; public relations with local population.' I had to see Emily again, but I needed some kind of sign first, an indication that Cartwright's tawdry overtures had not proved successful. I spent the afternoon pacing the muddy compound at Victoria Park, throwing a flat, waterlogged football around with O'Keefe and Timmins, trying not to think.

Cartwright hadn't made it back to camp by a four-fifteen, and I had no time to hang around waiting for him. An official delegation was in town, some Senator from Virginia who'd been a general in the First World War, and a couple of nondescript congressmen. I knew it was Cartwright's job to chaperone the Senator at the brass-rubbing function at the Ambassador, and so I assumed he'd gone directly there from Parnell.

It was the usual crowd, the Army and Navy brass from Cornwall Park, Pakuranga, and all the other Auckland outfits. As was customary with these things, the hand of friendship was extended to a smattering of select locals, physicians mainly, and the inevitable two or three clammy-handed local politicians and dignitaries.

I nursed a glass of flat champagne and receded into the thick mist of cigar smoke in the ballroom, which was decorated with a portrait of FDR and an enormous, ten by eighteen Old Glory flag pinned to the wall. It wasn't long before the official delegation arrived, the crowd parting like the Red Sea for the Senator, who got a rapturous hand when he assured the assembled guests that our boys were giving the slit-eyes the thrashing of a lifetime in Guadalcanal.

It took me a while to pick Cartwright out. He was gracefully shepherding the Senator around the elegant, softly lit room. I backed into a dark corner next to a coat rack and watched him circulate, introducing his charge to Green and Ford with easy aplomb. For all his callousness and obtuseness, he had beautiful, enviable manners. But there was something amiss that night; his chest looked a little sunken, his eyes were hooded and deeply set in his face. The gestures weren't as natural as they usually were – there seemed to be a concentration of effort behind them. Even the standard Cartwright over-laughter was conspicuously absent. I moved into the crowd a little, into the open where he could see me. One look would be all it would take for me to know.

'Nigel Foster's the name. Dr Nigel Foster, I should say.'

I turned to see a tallish rake of a man standing next to me, his hand extended. He would have been around sixty, and wore a wide, loose smile on his rubbery face. I shook his hand, which was like shaking a small, leathery bag of nails. 'Oh, sorry, I didn't see you there.'

'Dr Nigel Foster's the name,' he said again. He spoke with a plumb in his mouth, but the shortened vowels of his New Zealand accent were unmistakable. He was a good-looking man, all smiley and jocular. He wore a Barbour jacket with a rose-pink scarf pointing out of the breast pocket. 'Took you by surprise, did I?'

'Not at all. Peter Sokol,' I said.

'A Marine, hey? Damn fine reputation you boys have. I see you're a doctor, then. Surgeon?'

He must have been slightly hard of hearing, as every word he said was bellowed and strained. He looked slightly off to the left of my head as he spoke.

'Yes. Orthopaedic mainly.'

'Damn fine profession, medicine.'

'Do you still practise?'

'Not really. I do a spot of consulting from time to time. The stomach's my game. You're not from Cornwall Park, are you?'

'No. Victoria.'

'Damn fine hospital up there at Cornwall Park. I got to have a poke around the other day. The American Army runs a pretty tight ship, you know.'

He playfully nudged me in the ribs, as if he anticipated I would spring to the defence of the Corps. I nodded and smiled. I could see Cartwright over Dr Foster's shoulder, but he had his back turned to me.

'Have you always practised in Auckland?' I asked.

'A spell in Manchester, and a bit of time in Sheffield. Apart from that, I'm part of the furniture in this city.'

The din of voices in the room had grown quite loud, so I had to move in towards him a little. Then it occurred to me to ask.

'You don't happen to have heard of a Dr Michael Walters, have you? He was a psychiatrist in England I think. His family moved here after he died.'

His face clouded all of a sudden. 'How do you know about him?' he asked gravely.

The question seemed serious, as if my answer had the potential to incriminate me in something. I didn't want to say that I knew the family because I wanted him to speak freely, unencumbered of his old world politeness.

'I've just heard the name mentioned a few times. He seems

to be quite famous round these parts.'

He took a step towards me, and hooked a wary glance over his left shoulder. He was standing so close to me now that I could smell the perfume in his waxy-grey Brylcreemed hair. He leaned his face in towards my chest, side on, as if he were about to listen to my heart.

'He was a German, you know.'

'German?'

'Jerrys, the lot. The whole stinking family. They knock around town with ruddy Mayfair accents, but nobody's fooled. There's a whole tribe of them up in Parnell somewhere.'

He looked up at me expectantly, waiting for a response, a Marine Corps response. I punted.

'How do you know they're German?'

'We New Zealanders know a thing or two, Captain,' he said, tapping the side of his head and smiling. 'You can't fool us so easy.'

'I thought they were . . . I mean, I thought he was English. Dr Walters.'

'I believe they were there for a while.' He looked over his shoulder again. 'After they were forced to leave Germany.'

'Why did they have to leave?' I felt foolish playing out this naïve routine, but Dr Foster was so wrapped up in relaying the scandal that not giving him the prompts would have been downright rude.

'Why do most people leave Germany these days?' He flicked his eyebrows up and down a couple of times and crossed his arms over his chest tightly.

'You mean . . .'

'I mean. With a capital J. She's a royal pain in the rump by all accounts, but what good would it do to make a scene, eh? They're harmless up there by themselves.'

He seemed to be very impressed by his own magnanimity. I looked up over his stooped frame, and as fate would have it immediately picked out Cartwright's blond head shining through the smoky haze. He was less than ten feet away from me. His Senator was bent in conversation with one of the Army colonels, leaving him free to steer his daggers straight at me. I held his contemptuous gaze for a few seconds, just long enough to learn what I needed to know. I was so thrilled, I had to fight to suppress the smile that was trying to stretch itself out across my face. Eventually the Senator unfolded himself from his discussion and the pair of them moved on, disappearing somewhere into the thick of the crowd. My heart did a few trills as I realised she'd lived up to her word. Maybe this was real. Maybe this was it. I wanted to run from the room, but Dr Foster was still in full flight.

'It would just be vindictive, anyway. And I suppose we have an obligation to these people now, what with the ruddy camps and all. But, you see, the thing with the old man was that . . . it wasn't just a question of creed. There were, how should I put this, other issues that, well, concerned people.'

He waited for me to take the bait. He was having such a ball that I had no option but to oblige.

'Issues?'

He looked furtively around again. 'I have a colleague in London who heard a thing or two. Back in the mid-'30s. You see, Walters was into that psychoanalysis thing in a big way. Did some ruddy strange things by all accounts. Queer things, Captain. Experiments on people. Not just people – family members. His children. He even published the rot, expecting to be hailed a genius, no doubt. But when it all came out he landed in the soup with the Ethics Committee of the Royal College. He fell off the face of the earth after that. And then I take it the earth swallowed him up.'

I thought of the journal article I'd found in the Walterses' library on my first visit with Cartwright. I could still remember the esoteric title, 'Treatment of Fixated Latency Period', and the way that Emily had blushed as she recited the words, sneaking up on me, catching me out. There was something else to the title as well, a second clause that escaped me. I recalled that Emily had only said the first part, and that at the time it had struck me as odd that she didn't say the whole thing when she could remember half with such disarming clarity.

'Do you know what it was he published?' I asked. 'It can't have been that controversial if it made it to print.'

He waved the question away with his hand; he had had his fun and was tired of the subject now.

'I don't know the detail,' he said gruffly. 'And quite frankly I'm glad of it. It was weird stuff, though. Sexual stuff.'

I walked back to camp in the dark, exhilarated and scared to death of what was about to come, the chain of events that would follow. Cartwright's wounded look in the ballroom was like a starter's gun, but I had no idea where the finish line on this race would be. For the time being, though, I was happy enough to simply be in the race, and I skipped through the smoke-filled Ponsonby streets with a lightness I hadn't felt in years.

I assumed I would try to telephone her first; the last thing I wanted to do was show up unannounced again. As I came to the end of Franklin Road the salty tang of garbage smoke from Perfectus's gaping mouth grew stronger. I was trying to take shallow breaths as I rounded past the Birdcage, which was heaving with bodies. The sad yellow windows glowing in the dark were steamed up with condensation, and there was the muffled sound of music, Glenn Miller if I wasn't mistaken, coming through the partially open saloon doors. Just as I was about to cross over College Hill the doors crashed open, spewing the contained din and half a dozen limp bodies out into the cold night like air from a pressure valve. One of the bodies called out to me.

'Hey Cap'n. Cap'n. Wait up.'

It was Sturgis, and he was as tight as all hell. He stumbled across the road towards me, his pisscutter crooked on his head, his shirt unbuttoned to his stomach. He held a quart bottle of beer in one hand and a half-chewed cigar in the other.

'Hey Cap'n,' he yelled. He pulled up from his ungainly trot a few feet away from me, rearing like a spooked horse. There was a fearsome smell emanating from him, smoke and sugary booze and sweat.

'What is it, Sturgis? I don't have time to stand around tonight.'

'Hey, Cap'n,' he said, hiccupping, trying to catch his breath.

I could see straight into the Birdcage through the open doors. It was a dim sea of khaki green, men pressed together like sardines in a can. There seemed to be an aura about the place, a ripple of nascent violence hovering above the crowd like a heat wave on a desert road.

'Hey Cap'n,' Sturgis said again.

'We've done this bit already.'

He laughed after a slight delay, a belly laugh that seemed to catch his hiccups again.

'At's a good'n. Hey, though. Hey, Cap'n. Seriously, though.'

'What are you doing here, Sturgis?'

He held up the bottle. 'Just getting my fill of the creature.'

'Come on. Why don't you come back to camp with me?'

'No can do, sorry. I got, um, I got twenty bucks riding on old Larry from the Thirty-ninth in there. He's a sure thing; head like a goddamn basketball.'

'Prizefight?'

'You can't stop commerce, sir. No matter – (hiccup) – no matter what you do.'

I patted him on the shoulder and made to go, but he pulled me back.

'Way, way, wait a minute. I mean, um, sir. There's a . . .

what's it? . . . there was a woman here. Before. Just sorta hanging around. I mean, Cap'n, a really fucking beautiful piece of ass, if you'll French my pardon.'

'Who was she, Sturgis?'

'M.P.s wouldn't let her in. Said she was restricted.' He just about strangled himself on the last word.

'Sturgis, look at me. Who was she?'

He stuck the wet cigar into his mouth, grinned horribly, and punched me on the arm.

'You old dog, Cap'n. Hey, though. She's a good one. I mean, she's fucking beautiful. Who would have thought you—'

'Sturgis.' I grabbed him by the arms. His eyes were badly glazed, and he looked as though he could have fallen asleep where he stood. 'Sturgis, look at me. Who was this woman?'

'She was looking for you, sir. This afternoon.'

I could feel the blood pulsing in my head. 'Listen, Sturgis. Focus now. You've got to tell me what she wanted.'

'You see, that's an easy one, Cap'n. She gave me a note and I, um, I put it in your tent.'

'A note? What did it say?'

'I put it in your tent like she asked.' He gave me a bleary smile and punched me on the arm again. 'She's a knockout, Cap'n. A real looker.'

'Okay, so let's get this clear. She gave you a note to give to me, and you put it in my tent?'

'Right. And here's the note she gave me.'

He handed me a small white envelope with my Christian name written on it in a tall, sloping hand.

'I thought you put it in my tent.'

'Right. Like she asked.'

He slumped down onto his knees in front of me and released his loose grip on the bottle so that it smashed on the road. He was about to pitch forward into the gutter, but I caught him just in time. I tucked the envelope into my jacket pocket and with a bit of effort managed to get Sturgis's loose, malleable body up over my shoulder. I staggered the hundred yards back to camp with him that way, having to stop a couple of times to catch my breath. I took him into the hospital ward, which was only a quarter full, and dumped him onto an empty bed. Nurse Anderson was on duty, and she rolled her eyes affectionately at the sight of him. The letter was burning a hole in my pocket. I couldn't wait to get back to my tent to open it, so I sat down next to Sturgis, who had already started to snore, and gently tore along the top of the envelope. The note was on a clean, small piece of bond paper and was only a couple of lines long. She had beautiful handwriting, long sloping characters, consistent flourishes. There was no salutation.

Meet me at the ferry terminal at nine tomorrow morning. I want you to show me the colours and the shapes. I will understand if you cannot make it.

Emily.

CHAPTER 26

She was five minutes late. I'd been waiting outside the terminal building in the thin drizzle since half-past eight, idly watching an Army transport ship coming into the harbour from the sea lane between Takapuna and Rangitoto Island. She came up behind me and said my name, 'Peter'. Her voice in the soft morning air was so clear and bright, it was like the sound of glass shattering.

She was wearing a full-length violet cashmere coat that covered her entire body, leaving only her pump-clad feet exposed at one end and her beautiful pale face and russet-brown head at the other. She was an illusion, a mirage in the suicide-grey of the wharf. I took her hand and she kissed me lightly on the cheek, her painted lips sticking to my skin for the briefest of moments.

'Thank you for coming,' she said, her words vaporising in the cold air.

A bell rang signalling the departure of the ferry. People clamoured around us, men in woollen coats with newspapers and cigarettes, young women in charge of small children and frail mothers-in-law, all impatiently waiting for the deckhand to lower the gangplank. Emily looked anxiously at the line quickly forming.

'Do you mind if we go to Devonport?' she asked.

'Not at all.'

'It's just that . . . I don't want Oscar to see me out here. Do you mind, Peter?'

I shook my head and led her to the window of a small ticket kiosk, where I bought two returns from a sour-faced lady who didn't have any top teeth.

'What did you do to her?' asked Emily as we walked towards the ferry.

'It's not me, it's the uniform. Watch this.'

We climbed the steep staircase to the open-air top deck, where the passengers were mostly men, and walked past the rows of the sitting until we found a seat in the left-hand corner of the bow. I discreetly directed her attention to the furrowed brows, the insults quietly spoken into open newspapers, and the general sniggers my presence was attracting. I wiped a few drops of rainwater off the seat with my handkerchief and we sat down under the infinite chrome sky.

'But what on earth is their problem?' she whispered, a look of genuine confusion twisting her face.

'What, are you kidding? I'm dressed in a Marine uniform. And they're all men. The women are different; the women like the Yankees. The men are a different story.'

She still looked confused. I was about to ask her whether she'd been living under a rock when it occurred to me that, for all practical purposes, she probably had been.

'Apparently we were liked at first, long before I got here. But the novelty's worn off.'

'Did it have something to do with your arrival, Peter?'

'It's the only thing that makes sense.'

She smiled wryly, her viridian eyes glistening in the dismal light. There was a clumsy pause for a moment, which was fortunately filled by the sound of the gunning engines.

'Peter,' she said in a small voice, barely audible over the rumbling below us. 'I'm sorry I came to your camp. It was foolish of me. But I couldn't think of any other way to see you.'

227

I was almost overcome with the thought that she had needed to see me. I was about to reply when the foghorn sounded an inarticulate blast and the boat ungainly chugged off from the wharf. Emily pitched forward in her seat with a sudden motion, and I instinctively brought my arm up and across her chest to stop her. She caught it across her breast and held it there for a moment, an instant, before I politely pulled it away.

'Did Cartwright come up to see you yesterday?'

'Yes.'

I waited for her to go on, but her eyes fell away from mine, to the emerald green water of the harbour parting before us in foamy white waves.

'And . . . what happened?'

'I'd rather not say, Peter. Except that . . . he didn't get what he came for,' she said, an unmistakable flavour of insult in her tone.

'I suspected as much.'

'Did you talk to him?'

'No,' I said into the wind that was buffeting us head-on. I edged closer to her in the seat and bent my squinting face to her ear. 'He looked at me from across a room.'

The trip to Devonport was a short one, no more than ten minutes, and already we were drawing close to the wharf.

'I'm glad you came, Emily.'

She looked up at me, her porcelain skin pinkish around her cheekbones from the cold wind.

'So am I,' she said.

Devonport was home to the joint New Zealand and U.S. naval bases. The village itself was a timeless little place with a cinema, a couple of pubs and restaurants, and a sandy coastline that looked directly back to Auckland City. We got a table beside a cosy fireplace at one of the public houses, where I watched as Emily gracefully but determinedly dispatched a plate of roast beef with gooey gravy and baked vegetables. She observed a rigorous code of European table manners, but had the stamina of a lumberjack. The icy nerves in my gut left me with no appetite, and I did little more than play with the dry meat on my plate.

'You must think I'm a glutton,' she said, placing her knife and fork together on the plate and gently dabbing at her mouth with a starched linen napkin. She didn't seem to be as embarrassed as the remark would have suggested.

'Not at all. I'm just admiring your manners. You make eating look as difficult as playing a harp. I wouldn't know where to begin.'

'My manners?'

'Sorry,' I said, waving my hand in the air. 'I don't expect you to understand. I'm from Brooklyn originally. They're still trialling the knife and fork out there.'

The publican, a strawberry-nosed man in his mid-fifties, plonked a pot of tea and a pair of stained cups and saucers down on our table and cleared the dinner plates away. We both watched the teapot for a moment, waiting for the leaves to draw.

'I take it, then,' Emily said, a little playfully, 'that good manners are a matter of geography.'

'Not just geography.'

'But one's background, I suppose.'

'Right.'

'Do you think people can change their manners, Peter?' I noticed that the tone had changed slightly; it was edgier, challenging, but only just so. She had an artful ability to skip through certain states or moods as if she were running her fingers up and down a scale.

'I think people can certainly change their manners,' I said, pouring the tea.

'And if people can change their manners, I assume that means they can become . . .'

'Different people.'

'Yes. Do you think that's possible, Peter?'

'I hope so,' I said, after a pause. I looked around the room, at the smattering of young sailors in blue and white uniforms doing exactly as I was doing, buying a pretty local girl some lunch. They were all biding their time, waiting to get lucky. I envied them the simplicity of their purpose, the keen and clear eye they had for their target. 'I think, I don't know, I think that happiness kind of depends on it, don't you? I don't think I would want to live in a world where I didn't have the freedom to change myself.'

She looked at me openly for a long moment before responding, her eyes glazed with thought.

'Neither would I,' she said quietly, almost to herself.

We left the pub and walked through the narrow streets for a while, slowly heading back down towards the beach. By the time we arrived at the sand, a few rays of watery sunlight were managing to poke through the dense clouds. The harbour water looked leathery under the bruised sky, the grey of which was now flecked with highlights of lemon yellow and alizarin crimson. We walked along a path that followed the curve of the short beach around the cone of the small peninsula. To the left was the grim aspect of the U.S. Naval shipyard. They were busy doing repair work on the *Mount Vernon*, the Third's vessel – a steely reminder in case I needed one that time was short.

'Do you remember, Peter,' she said, looking absently up at the yard, 'when I found you in the library that day? When you first came to visit with Colonel Cartwright?'

'Yes?' I was unsure where she was going with this; as I recalled the situation, she had caught me with the open journal, the one I wasn't supposed to read.

'Do you remember what I said to you?'

'You said a few things.'

'But there was something in particular.'

'You said that I have a reassuring face. Is that it?'

She laughed. We were walking side by side along the narrow path, and at the very moment of her laughter the backs of our hands lightly brushed together.

'Yes. And you do. I just wanted to tell you again,' she said with a radiant smile that I hadn't seen before.

She seemed lighter out there in the bleached sea air. I felt in that moment a closeness that I don't think I'd ever felt with another person, a kind of proximity that defied logic, as if I could step straight through her, or wear her skin.

'Well,' I said, 'I guess reassuring is better than nothing.' I was only kidding around, but she pounced on my words with an ardour that caught me off-guard.

'What are you saying? It's better than everything. It is the best imaginable thing, Peter.'

'All right. Okay. I just—'

'Trust me, there is nothing better than reassuring. I . . . I want to tell you things, for some reason. I want to confess. You're not a priest, are you?'

Now it was I who misread the joke. I stopped in my tracks and seized her by the arms, a little too forcefully maybe.

'Do,' I said urgently. 'Tell me everything. I know that there's . . . I mean, there's nothing you can't tell me. I promise you that.'

'Peter,' she said, her face creased in concern, 'what are you doing? Let me go.'

I held onto her for a few more dreadful moments as my heart hammered away in my throat and I realised that I'd made a stupid mistake. Eventually I was collected enough to let her go, but the hurt look on her face was like a knife in my heart.

'I'm sorry,' I said. 'I thought you were, I mean, I . . .'

She straightened out her cashmere coat and looked back

towards the ferry terminal in the direction we had come from.

'I'm sorry,' I said again. 'I was getting ahead of myself. I used to think I was good at knowing what people thought. Until I came to New Zealand, that is.'

She played out her pause for a moment longer before she eventually looked up at me with a cautious smile. We walked along the path a little further and looked out at the harbour as yet another Navy ship sailed in from the sea lane. It was the supply ship this time, the very one Mrs Walters had so cleverly teased me about. It was a sobering sight, all that iron and steel and engineering, and I think we were both caught by the gloomy pall it cast. We had to take a few steps in studied silence before the moment would pass.

'You said in your note that you wanted to see the shapes and colours.'

She smiled, looking straight ahead.

'You remembered,' she said. 'Although, that's not exactly what I said. I said I wanted you to show me the shapes and colours. I can already see my shapes and colours.'

'Oh, yeah? Show me then.'

'Now?'

'Now.'

We stopped at a park bench, which was dug into a grass slope above the path, and sat down. I could see she was reluctant, but I pressed her anyway.

'Well,' she said slowly, looking out at the emerald harbour. 'That dreadful thing out there, the one coming into the harbour . . .'

'The supply ship?'

She turned to look at me. 'Yes. It's simply an illusion of perspective.' She paused self-consciously, but I kept my mouth shut. 'I think that's what you meant when you said you paint shapes. That isn't a supply ship we're looking at; it's a jumble of squares and cubes and triangles and so on. And when you say colour, I think what you meant was that that horrible thing out there isn't just green. It's also blue and red and brown and yellow and . . .'

'I think you're giving me too much credit. How do you know all this?'

'Mother encouraged cultural interests. She used to take me to the Tate and other galleries most weeks. I remember seeing Braque's *Man with a Guitar* one morning, and it . . . I don't know, it changed me. Mother disapproved of any sort of abstraction, any straying from realism, but I didn't care. I started buying used books from a dealer in Camden and hid them in my room, reading late into the night. I would have liked to have painted myself, if that sort of thing had been allowed.'

'Why wasn't it allowed?' I said, feeling obtuse.

'You wouldn't understand. In England, women . . . women of a certain breeding, do not *do* things. It's not like America, Peter. There are always certain . . . restraints. But she couldn't stop me buying the books. I bought everything on Picasso and Braque and Gris I could get my hands on. So when you said you paint colours and shapes, I . . . I thought I understood what you meant.'

Although I was thrilled at the extraordinary words that had just come out of her mouth, thrilled in a fundamental way, I had the distinct impression that she wanted to say something more; that there was a torrent of words waiting to tip out of her at the slightest encouragement. But with the embarrassment I'd caused myself back there on the lane, I felt too guarded to push further.

'Of course, colours and shapes are only part of it,' I said. 'There's also got to be a pulse in it somewhere, an artery running through all that geometry.'

'Yes, that's right,' she said softly. I was flattered by her agreement and the keen interest in her tone, almost inviting me or willing me to continue.

I moved closer towards her on the bench so that our hips touched.

'See up there,' I said, pointing my gloved hand at a row of pohutukawa trees at the edge of the grass slope.

'Yes.'

'There's a way of seeing that scene, a way of . . . I don't know, a way of looking at it that has to go beyond perspective. Beyond dimension, and even colour. There's a certain way I feel about those three trees in a row, with the sky above, and the harbour just there. It's a feeling I get as soon as I look at it, put it into a frame.'

'I understand,' she said, her voice little more than a whisper.

'That feeling is what I try to paint.'

'It's like a broken heart,' she said.

'It's like you're already dead.'

The silence that followed this was almost suffocating. My body was giddy with desire for her, something almost like a rage, and without any thinking or calculation I placed my hand on her thigh, bent my face towards her and tried to kiss her. I had closed my eyes and was waiting for the moment that my tongue was inside her mouth, but before I could get there she placed her hand on my cheek and pushed me back. I opened my eyes, my mouth frozen wide open, stunned. It took all my powers of concentration to understand that she'd rejected the advance, and that she was waiting for me to get off her. I slowly peeled myself off and sat back, feeling utterly nauseous.

'I think I should get home now, Peter.'

'I understand.'

'No, it's not that. It's just . . . Mother will—'

I held my hand up. 'I understand.'

She tried to smile at me, but the effort was lame, her eyes refusing to join in. I was still bewildered by the cold fact that she'd refused the kiss. I had thought that we'd been leading to it for a long time. She stood up and smoothed out the back of her coat with her hand. I offered her my arm again as we headed back towards the ferry terminal, but it was a hollow gesture, and when she took it I felt as miserable as I'd ever felt in my life.

We were the only passengers on the top deck of the ferry as it started off on the short passage back to the city. We stood holding the rails of the bow, a respectful distance apart, and watched as the grim aspect of the city inched towards us. The wind had picked up and the old boat was making hard work of it in the choppy water. I knew I only had ten or fifteen minutes until we arrived, and that this may be the last opportunity I would have to speak to her alone, unencumbered. I was already feeling nostalgic for the period, not half an hour ago, when we walked arm in arm along the sandy beach, free of context. But now everything was context-laden again: my uniform; her woollen coat, worn at the elbows, frayed around the hem; Auckland; the war.

We caught ourselves looking at each other a couple of times, and the feeling was like the force-field collision of two positively charged magnets. I still wasn't sure what had happened, what I had said or done to cause this distance. I willed myself to take a sideways step towards her. She noted my move, plainly, neutrally. We were five minutes from the city. I could see soldiers from the Second Marine Division on the warship coming up on our right. They were going through some sort of an exercise and were making quick, efficient movements in small groups, darting back and forth across the deck like miniature bee swarms, simulating battle.

'What are they doing?' she asked quietly. I could tell from her tone that she didn't care in the slightest, that the question was simply designed to cut the tension.

'Exercises. They're shipping out next week.'

'To . . . to the Pacific?' The idea of it seemed to stun her.

'To the war.'

She looked back at the warship before turning to me. 'I suppose that will be you soon,' she said miserably, her tone choked and desperate. 'When your time comes. When you have to leave.'

I took a step towards her. 'Marry me.'

'Pardon?'

She hadn't heard. The wind was strong; my softly spoken words, my shells of words, had been flung over her shoulder before they even had a chance to reach her ears. I looked at her, studied her profile hard, and to my surprise the knot in my gut began to unravel. I realised, out of nowhere, inexplicably, that I felt light and confident.

'I'm sorry, Peter,' she said, her eyes half-closed against the wind blowing in her face. 'I didn't catch what you said.'

'Will you marry me?'

This time she heard. It took her a while to register the question, as if she were trying to translate the words into a language she could understand. Finally she got it. The belated recognition flashed in her bottle green eyes, and for one delicious moment an adorable smile lit up her face. She moved her hand up to my chest, and I believe she was about to place it there when something caught her, some instinct of nature or environment, and she pulled the hand away at the last moment. The smile, so innocent and pure in its coming, had faded.

The captain cut the revs on the boat and everything went quiet all of a sudden, the only sounds coming from the primitive whirr of the idling engine and the fizz of the parting water just below us.

'Marry me,' I said again, utterly sure of myself now. I said it again, and was struck by how right the words sounded, a sensation I could feel in my chest, like a complicated melody resolving to its tonic.

'Peter,' she said, looking back out at the wharf and squinting. 'You don't understand.'

'No, I do. I want you to marry me. I've never been so sure of—'

'Peter, no. You don't . . . you just can't understand. I'm so sorry. It's not your fault.'

'Whatever it is, it doesn't matter. Just marry me. Everything will sort itself out afterwards. I don't care what happens afterwards. Just say you'll marry me.'

'I can't. You just . . . I'm sorry, Peter. But you just don't understand.'

I grabbed her by the lapels of her coat and kissed her, hard, our teeth clanging together like cymbals. She hesitated at first, but then I felt her kiss me back. I had her pressed into the very nose of the bow. We were nudging into the terminal now, but I kept a hold of her coat and wouldn't let her move. We stopped kissing.

'There's nothing you could say that would make me want to change my mind,' I said. I spoke fast, one eye on the approaching wharf and the crowd of people waiting to board the ferry to make the return trip. I had until the deckhand threw his rope and lowered the plank. 'Just say you'll marry me. And that you'll come back to California with me. Nothing else is important.'

She started crying, a few silent tears at first, but soon I felt the heave of her chest, and she buried her face into the crook of my neck. I waited, grimly holding on to her quivering body as the new passengers started to climb aboard.

She didn't say no.

CHAPTER 27

Eddie and I sat inside a Howard Johnson's in Anaheim. It was a quarter to five, exactly one hour and fifteen minutes before Sturgis's lecture began. As we had made our way through Irvine and Santa Ana I had tried to steer the De Ville in as generic a direction as possible, heading in a very unspecific way into the centre of Los Angeles. It was clear that neither of us wanted to make a decision about where we were going, so when I saw the restaurant it seemed only natural to ask Eddie if he was hungry. He seemed tremendously relieved at my offer of a meal. Although he hadn't said it, I got the impression he'd been living pretty rough the past few weeks.

I sat opposite him in a cherry-coloured booth as he very deliberately went about demolishing a cheeseburger, fries, and a chocolate malted. I was in no mood for food, so I ordered a cup of coffee and gazed blankly out through the filmy windows at the approaching orange haze of another L.A. dusk.

Just before we had got out of the car, Eddie had said something about Sturgis's book that made me realise what was wrong with it. He said that the marriage was slightly unbelievable; that it was unrealistic that the main character would marry the New Zealand woman when he barely knew her. I didn't agree with this, of course. Even if you took Emily and me out of it, the enlisted men were knocking over the local girls with marriage proposals like bowling pins. There is something about war, something about the threat of death that inclines young men to wedlock. I'm sure the same thing is happening in Vietnam right now. A wife represents stability. It's not as easy to kill a married man.

But it wasn't a lack of reality that damaged the book in my eyes. It was that the author saw the marriage as merely incidental rather than part of a wider shift in momentum or motive. The problem was that the marriage of the main character isn't tied to what happens later. It isn't seen as an antagonising event, a catalyst for things to come. And in a way, I suppose, I understood why Sturgis would have viewed it that way. He couldn't have known of the tension that existed between Cartwright and me, the depth of ill-feeling that made him relish the opportunity to see me go down. Sturgis saw Cartwright, in his relationship with me, as merely a cuckold. A man who'd been outdone, beaten to the punch.

And then there was also Beth, of course. Unless you're from a family like the Cartwrights, it's difficult to appreciate the indignity that comes with having a name and reputation besmirched. But I knew it was more than that. It was something that had started in that surgery class at Stanford all those years ago. I had a foreign name and an immigrant's brooding, unappreciative manners. I wasn't one of his sort, yet for one reason or another we kept getting thrown together. And, finally, I wasn't a Marine. I didn't live the code, and I didn't deserve to be an officer. I was simply a competent surgeon, perhaps a slightly better one than him, and they were forced to take me because they were short on numbers. His outranking of me was the opportunity he'd been wanting for years. It allowed him to remind me of the many things I wasn't; that no matter what, the plain fact was that I was below him. My decline was inevitable, it always had been, and now he was in a position to steer me down as I fell. After this, Beth and Emily hardly mattered to him at all.

Sturgis didn't know these things back then, and he clearly didn't know them now, and that is why I felt the story was a little shallow. He couldn't see the importance of my having forged the authorisation form required by the Department of the Navy before permitting an active-duty officer to marry. He still couldn't see the consequences that naturally followed it, the ruinous course it put in motion.

I ordered more fries for Eddie and another cup of coffee for myself. The waitress was young and cute, and she smiled at Eddie as she delivered our order. When she went away he looked at me with a comically raised eyebrow. He was all swollen nose and static hair. I laughed quietly and looked back out the grimy window.

Perhaps because I had actively suppressed the memory for so long, the thought of that day was hard to order in my mind, and would only come to me as a dream does, in fragmented bursts of colour and sensation. When I forced myself to think of it as a narrative, which was rare, I never lost the sense of wonder I felt about the sheer audacity of my actions. When we got off that ferryboat, and she still hadn't said no, I immediately abandoned all trace of rational perspective. I understood how delicate she was, and that she would fly away if I didn't properly catch her in my uncouth hands first.

With an imperative will that kept me awake for three straight days, I paid off Sturgis to pay off Diddle to get me the authorisation form that I needed before the unit's padre would sanction the marriage. The form was an acknowledgement that the prospective wife's family had been vetted and that the marriage was not a threat to American morality. I had to steal the form because both Green and Ford were in Australia that morning, planning our imminent Pacific landing; we were going to war for real, and soon. In their absence, Cartwright was acting C.O. for the next five days. I simply couldn't wait that long. I hadn't even got her to say yes yet, just a dubious omission where 'no' would otherwise have been. And in any event, there was no guarantee of a positive answer from Green or Ford even if I had waited. There was a whisper going around camp that we would be gone in less than a month. They would have had every right to refuse me. Plus I didn't know how well the Walters would stand up to the vetting process. I'd only poked my nose into their affairs and already I'd happened upon more than one skeleton. So I figured that if I just did it, they would have to accept it. It would be a marriage made before God, and who was the Navy to annul God's work?

Quarter past five. Forty-five minutes. Eddie caught me looking at my watch.

'Zero hour,' he said resignedly.

The food had taken the edge off his jumpy nerves. I think he was only just recognising the fact that he was back home, back to simmering reality.

'The point of no return,' I said, trying to make light, regretting it straight away.

It was his turn to look out the window now. He lit a Camel and blew out a jet of blue smoke followed by three perfectly formed rings that he made by popping his lips. It was an insouciant gesture, a small piece of careless bravado, but I knew Eddie better than that now.

'How's the nose?' I asked.

'Good. Just dull.'

'Dullness is good. If it's dull, it's good.'

'What do you paint, Peter? Back there in San Diego.'

I shrugged and drained the last splash of coffee left in my cup, its bitterness lashing the back of my tongue like the snap of a whip.

'You must know what you paint.'

'Things that aren't there. Things that aren't as they seem.

Things of indeterminate provenance,' I said, enunciating the last two words very slowly, syllable by syllable. 'All rendered in murky colour.'

He smiled and crushed out his cigarette in an ashtray.

'I wish I was a painter. You guys get to stand up while you work. Standing up is an advantage.'

'I know what you mean. When the big day comes, I'd rather be standing.'

'I guess you can stand up to write,' he said, 'but it's not the same. It would be like you're trying to prove something.'

'It would be like a flaw that would carry through to your work. Every sentence would seem unbelievable. People would recognise it, think it strange, think there was something amiss.'

'All because I was standing up.'

'Right.'

We both laughed, miserably so, I thought. Five-thirty. When we stopped laughing there seemed to be nothing left to say. We were dry and we both knew it; to go on talking would have been a lie, an affront to dignity. I looked around the restaurant for a pay phone, finally spotting one on the wall next to the john. I tapped my hip pocket for coins, hearing the loose jangle of so many dimes and quarters.

'Excuse me for a minute,' I said, standing up slowly. 'I've got to make a call.'

'Who to?' He was looking out the window and lighting another cigarette, hands trembling a little.

'My wife.'

He looked up at me quickly. 'But I thought you said you weren't—'

'I wasn't. But that's about to change.'

CHAPTER 28

I married Emily on a Saturday afternoon, three days after she hadn't said no on the top deck of the Devonport ferry, two hours after she and her mother had finished their day's work at the Japanese internment camp. It had started raining at dawn that day and didn't stop until late that night; hard, unforgiving rain that I should have seen as a portent for what was to come, but I was too drugged on sleeplessness and certainty to notice much that day.

Because Cartwright was in charge, I could only secure leave until eight that evening, and getting both Sturgis and Father O'Shea out of camp with me unnoticed had taken some co-ordination. Sturgis drove us up to Parnell in the pouring rain, large drops of it hitting the canvas top of the jeep like rapid machine-gun fire. Father O'Shea was circumspect about the whole thing, but I was a doctor and an officer, which in the Corps made me the technical definition of probity. He had little choice but to take me at my word.

We married on the Saturday because it was the first available day we knew Oscar would be out of the house. He was generally secretive with his movements, but Emily had learned, via Winston, that he was travelling to Wellington that day for a chess tournament. I had nothing to do with this decision, and at that point still wasn't sure why we had to keep it a secret from him. I knew he detested Americans, especially ones in imperialistic drag, and so I half-heartedly assumed this was the reason. Neither Emily nor Mrs Walters said anything in particular. I was just given to understand that no wedding would take place while Oscar was in the house.

The ceremony, which was brief, took place in the living room where Emily had played Debussy for Cartwright and me less than a month ago. I had asked Emily whether she wanted a Hebrew wedding, and had made Mrs Walters weep with an offer to convert if that's what it would take. They were both shocked that I knew their religion, shocked and delighted all at once, but the offer was turned down. The Third Division didn't have a rabbi who could conduct the ceremony, and neither Emily nor Mrs Walters wanted to look for one around town for fear of exposure. Father O'Shea asked us to read the formal vows, which Emily did with tears streaming down her face. Sturgis, my only witness, my best man, handed me the plain white-gold ring I'd stumped for from a city jeweller the day before. I'd bought a matching one for Emily to slip onto my middle finger, which she did with a shaking hand. We were Mr and Mrs Peter Sokol. I gave Mrs Walters and Winston twenty bucks to spend on an afternoon lunch at a place of their choosing.

When everybody had gone we slowly climbed the stairs to the garret at the top of the house, the place where she had woken me in the middle of that stormy night and made me promise I would come back for her. I closed the door and we looked at each other from across the room for a long time, the hard rain assaulting the roof just above our heads. Then we kissed, still standing, moving slowly, doing a small dance to the rain's hectic music. When I undressed her, gently easing the dress from her ivory body, releasing her long, chestnut hair from its complex network of pins, she started to cry again. She cried as we made love, cried and laughed. We laughed for long stretches at a time, lying naked together in the single bed.

We didn't leave that tiny room for six hours. We didn't eat or drink anything.

Nothing more was needed.

CHAPTER 29

I sat back down in the booth. Eddie was slumped back in his seat, his eyes glassy with what I assumed was the constant ache in his reset nose. Dappled ochre sunlight was shining in through the window, its glow sharpening the determined whiteness of his skin. I felt totally charged, alive to every nuance and detail.

'You took your time,' he said as I settled into my seat.

'Good things take time.'

'Yeah?'

'Yeah.'

I was sixty years old and alive for the first time in years. I was ecstatic, literally ecstatic to be sitting in a Howard Johnson's with this broken-nosed kid I'd found on the side of the road. I could see that my expression, my demeanour was troubling him. He leaned forward and squinted through the brilliant light shining on his face.

'Well?' he said.

'Well what?'

He lifted his hands up either side of him, palms turned up, the scales of justice.

'Are you going to tell me what this is all about?'

'What do you mean?'

His face creased in exasperation. 'You said you weren't married. And then—'

'What happens,' I said, cutting him off, 'what happens if you go back home?'

It took him a moment to absorb the question, the change of tack.

'I've told you.'

'You get sent straight down to the recruitment office.'

'I get driven down to the recruitment office.'

'No two ways?'

He scrunched up his face again. 'What is this? You look happy about it.'

'Sorry. I'm not happy about it, Eddie.' He nodded cautiously at me, but I still couldn't wipe the smile from my face. My feet were busy tapping a foxtrot on the ground. Every fibre of my body was reeling. 'But what I'm asking is, you go home and it's what? The war or the door?'

'Save the poetry, Peter,' he said, smiling, the lame little rhyme distracting him for a couple of loose seconds. Something quick and distant flashed in his dark eyes, a look that I recognized at once; it was the look of a person who took any opportunity to dive from the battlefield of the present, who took any chance to retreat from the austerity of practical cause and effect and consequence. It was a look I'd worn most of my adult life.

'And so tell me, Eddie. What's so bad about the door?'

He shrugged. 'You mean, what, apart from not going to college?'

'Right.'

'Apart from applying for a job here before we leave?'

I raised my hand in concession. 'Okay, okay. Stupid question. I just thought you might have been on one of those Jack Kerouac rides is all.'

'The whole finger to authority thing?'

'Right. I mean, I'm a teacher. I've seen it happen.'

'Nah. I guess I tried, but . . . I'm too uptight for that kind of thing, anyway. I can't stand the sight of bare feet. Wear some shoes, for Christ's sake. Plus you've got to be a cool guy to pull that sort of thing off. Women are supposed to find your brooding ways attractive. I can't even grow a proper beard.' He looked across the table, at my wrist which was laid flat in front of me, at my watch. 'Your lecture starts in ten minutes,' he said timidly.

I didn't respond for a few long seconds.

'My wife is Dean of Admissions at San Diego State. I just spoke to her. She said it's possible you could get in for the start of the fall semester. Three weeks' time.'

He was motionless for what seemed like a long time, not even a blink or a twitch. I had to nod at him a couple of times to get his eyes to focus.

'So?' I said.

He came to, leaning back in his seat again, slowly, deliberately.

'Wow,' he said softly, shaking his head. 'But, I mean, there's still the problem of tuition though.'

'There are scholarships and grants available. I'll write you a letter of recommendation. Show me some of your writing and we'll work something out.'

He still looked pale and a little shell-shocked. The hollows beneath his eyes were shaded black and a strange kind of dirty yellow now. The waitress came over and cleared our plates away. I slid her a fifty-dollar bill and nodded, feeling extremely large.

'Gee, thanks, mister,' she said, pocketing the money and turning away from the table with an adorable grin, unable to believe her luck.

I looked back at Eddie, who still hadn't taken his eyes off me.

'So?' I asked. 'What do you say?'

CHAPTER 30

The fortnight that followed our secret wedding still seems unreal to me, like a lingering memory from childhood whose blurry outlines have come to resemble a dream. The ordinary rules and conventions didn't seem to apply any more; afternoons went on forever, dark late nights contained an element of something undefined in them, as if we were getting closer to an answer. I felt as though I had been picked up by an ancient wind and had no control over where I would land. I had ceded control for the first time I could remember and it didn't bother me in the slightest. For a blissful two weeks I was an amnesiac, a man who'd forgotten inevitable disappointment, an innocent, a man bewildered to find himself in love.

I did strange things, was given to flourishing gestures of kindness and goodwill. I was jovial with my patients, caring and attentive with the nurses, retiring with my superiors. I took great relish in organising our clandestine meetings, which were all wordlessly scheduled around the comings and goings of Oscar Walters. I was bold and assuming. I did preposterous things. On an unexpectedly fine and warm July day I paid off the unit's cook to roast me a couple of chickens and bake an apple pie, which I served to my wife and her mother on the back porch of their Parnell mansion. I was Peter Sokol, provider.

We couldn't keep our hands off each other. I learned every corner, every dimple and freckle of her lovely lily-white body. We made love whenever we could, on a whim in the morning, for the fourth exhausted time on a dreary afternoon as dripping condensation clouded up the garret window. A look would be enough to instigate a fuck; a chance meeting of gazes in the sitting room while Winston poured the tea with his shaky, crippled hand. We'd flee the room without explanation and bound up the stairs trying to suppress the giddy laugher bubbling out of our mouths. And then, within the space of a minute, I would be inside her again. When we made love like this I could never get close enough to her, even when our faces and bodies were pressed madly together as if in a vice. I seemed to pine for her, for her body, for the elusive thing behind her eyes, even while I was in the act of having her.

This neediness slowly turned toxic, though. Pretty soon my passion started to turn sour and morbid. The flourishing gestures abated, the goodwill to others turned to nasty malice, and a royal lovers' tension, thick with desire and dread, quickly developed between us. The lovemaking didn't slow down one bit, but we became impetuous with each other. I was irascible whenever I was at camp and away from her, but as soon as I arrived at the house, shortly after fucking, I would grow moody and sullen. It was the first and only time I'd ever sulked in my life. I wanted her so badly that my eyes hurt, but nothing she could do would please me. The same applied to Emily. She would go from smothering and doting to angry and irrational within the space of a heartbeat. We had outrageous arguments that seemed to spring out of the air, arguments without a source or a starting point, arguments about nothing at all, the very act of raising our voices sexual somehow, arousing even.

When we were together we didn't leave the house. Mrs Walters spent large swathes of time at the Parnell library attending to her International Chess Association correspondence. She was fanatical about it, playing up to ten games at a time with other members in Melbourne, Toronto and Cape Town. Each letter, so she told me, would describe only one move at a time. Depending on the location of the correspondent, it could take up to three months before either player was able to take a single piece. She often enlisted me to deliver the bundles of letters to the post office on my way back to camp. Naturally, I wondered why she bothered going to the effort, but the names that appeared on the envelopes seemed to provide the answer: Schwartzman, Goldwater, Feldman, Heifetz.

Aside from the local library, neither Emily nor Mrs Walters ventured from the house unless there was an urgent need. I didn't ask any questions, but I knew there was a reputation outside the four walls of their home that haunted them. And so they imposed a kind of house-arrest on themselves and lived in an ascetic state of privation and decay, having long given up hope on Oscar, their rightful breadwinner, their young man who frittered away his days on theory and dope.

But the isolation suited me fine. As the days passed and the reality of being married to this beautiful woman started to sink in, I grew increasingly agitated. I couldn't stand the thought of her looking at anyone else, talking to other men, even thinking about them. I came to resent Sturgis's innocent questions about her; I thought it presumptuous of him to mention her name, as if he were claiming some sort of association or connection with her. Even the short walks we took around the neighbourhood presented themselves as a possible threat. The plain fact of her attractiveness was like an accusation, a sardonic statement designed to belittle me. Out in the street men couldn't help turning their heads, lowering their eyes. This ugly insecurity was the cross I had to bear for having her.

251

It is easy for me to look back on this time and see the fatalism in everything we did and said. But I think it's correct to say that in those brief few weeks we had together we shared a hard-bitten knowledge that we were living on borrowed time. If I had really believed she was my wife, in the possessory way that term is ordinarily used, I think I would have been even more miserable than I was. I would have felt compelled to ask more questions, any questions, about the Agatha Christie mystery of her family. Why she looked so different from the rest of them for a start. And why we had to hide from her brother. More importantly, I think I would have done something with the signed marriage certificate that I kept in the footlocker under my cot. If I truly believed she was my wife I would have sent the thing to Washington, where a grey-skinned clerk in the Navy Department would have registered the union and sent a notarized copy of the certificate back to Colonel Green. It wasn't that I was afraid of the consequences if the brass found out; even at that stage I felt I had begun my irrevocable drift from their jurisdiction. It was just that, in my marrow, I somehow knew that it wasn't real, that we were playing out a fantasy, and that the great edifice of fate would sooner or later cast its inevitable shadow. Until it arrived, though, I was happy to pretend.

Over time I've come to appreciate that I wasn't the only one who carried this sorry awareness. I imagine Mrs Walters was able to delude herself with hope, but I'm sure that Emily never truly believed she would meet me in America. We danced around the subject often, the unspoken words lashed to every discussion that happened to slip out of the here and now to the subjunctive, the wished for. But with all this tiptoeing, we only spoke of it once with anything like directness.

It was getting towards the end of July, or what I would normally think of as January, and the past few days had been one long, solid stretch of bleak skies and rain. The weather in Auckland has a way of closing in on you, demanding your attention. But this day was a reprieve, a bright, watery yellow morning that steamed the sodden city like damp laundry before a fire. I had been on night duty until two in the morning, so it was no problem securing leave. I commandeered a jeep and picked Emily up at nine, armed with a musette bag of terrible leftovers from the previous night's chow and a couple of bottles of beer. We had thought we would picnic at the top of Mount Eden, a small cone-shaped hill that was more like a large nipple than a mountain, and which was located close to Parnell. It was a delightful feeling driving through the empty city, top down, the Wednesday morning air blowing in our faces, almost as if we were the only people alive.

I strapped the bag to my back and we set off on foot up the goat's track to the summit. The top was like a wide rim, from which you could look down into a deep, perfectly formed volcanic crater that hollowed out the cone of the hill. The path wasn't steep, but it was narrow and rocky with only enough room to walk in cramped single-file.

As a painter, I should have been enchanted by the luscious, luminous green grass that coated the hill, each blade of which seemed identifiable and distinct with electric colour. The ground was still wet from all the rain, so that a gentle cloud of steam hovered poetically over the whole scene. As a painter, I should have noticed the bleached sky, enormous and unforgiving and impossible to render with any truth. I should also have noticed the fawn mud that splashed up the back of Emily's thick white cotton dress, coating its hem as if she were some latter-day Elizabeth Bennett.

But I saw these things only in passing, in soft focus. All I could see for sure were the looks she was getting from the G.I.s and other servicemen who passed us going down the track. It was a truly brilliant morning, and it seemed that every Yankee bastard in the country had the same idea as us.

They were all young kids, ungainly and gawky in their too-big uniforms, spots on their faces and johnsons, holding the hands of pretty local girls in bright pumps. They just couldn't resist looking at a beautiful woman was all. They were utterly harmless, but I hated every last one of them. I especially hated the sly little looks they gave me as I brought up the rear, the looks that said, 'Gee, Cap'n, nice goin'.' By the time we got to the glary summit I was in a frothy rage.

There were more people at the summit too, groups of doughboys standing together in large circles, talking loudly, smoking their Luckies, legs spread wide apart, hands thrust into their khaki pockets. Local girls minced around in flocks, handbags at the ready, giggling into their bosomy chests.

We went off away from the crater to a ridge that ran to the south-east and found a small bench to sit on. From there we had an uninterrupted view of the archipelago of small islands that littered the glistening gulf. I unpacked the food and beer in silence, still sulking, but the day was just too glorious to remain unhappy for long. Emily stretched her lithe body out in a series of windmill poses, and even skipped around the bench as if she were about to burst into song. I laughed and handed her a sloppily arranged roast-beef sandwich and a tin mug of beer.

'So, husband,' she said, taking a hearty sip of beer.

'So, wife.'

She caught sight of a brown rabbit bouncing through the long grass and pointed excitedly, her mouth too full to talk. The sun felt glorious on my face, as if it were burning away a thick layer of impurity. I was leaning back on the bench with my eyes closed, but I could feel her looking at me.

'Are you tired, Peter?'

I kept my eyes closed, revelling in the blind feel of her gaze upon me.

'I had to do some unexpected surgery late last night. There

was another training accident at Shelly Beach,' I said. 'They're not having much luck out there. Somebody had left potholes all over the foreshore and a few of the men fell into them in the dark. Nothing serious. Just some broken bones. It's strange, though, because—'

'Shush,' she said, cutting me off.

I sat up and looked into her face, my vision taking a while to adjust to the searing white light of the approaching noon. 'What?'

She hesitated for a moment; I could see her brain doing calculations behind her green eyes. 'I don't want you to talk about the war any more. Or anything to do with . . . whatever it is you do. It upsets me, Peter.'

'Okay,' I said cautiously, putting down my mug. 'What do you want to talk about instead?'

The response was immediate. 'San Francisco. I want to know what it's like. Can you tell me?'

I took a moment to ponder the question. She'd never asked anything like this before; she'd never even mentioned the States, or anything to do with what would happen to us once I left Auckland. And so I knew that whatever I said in response would be important, that it would set the tone for a much larger conversation to come. But I was blank. I was too conscious of the potential secondary meaning – the critical sub-text that she would quietly tear apart in her own time – to even deliver a coherent answer.

'It's big,' I said blandly. 'It's big and it's bright and it's loud.'

She didn't say anything for a couple of minutes. Instead she helped herself to some of the dark cooking chocolate I'd managed to smuggle out of the kitchen. I waited anxiously for her next move, the warm sun still on my face.

'That's not much of an answer,' she said. 'I thought you were a painter.'

'I am.'

'Well then, give me a painter's answer.'

'All right, then. Let me see.' I poured out another two mugs of beer, draining every last foamy drop from the brown quart bottle. 'It's full of undulating streets for a start. Steep slopes, strange-angled houses. There are the tram tracks and cars, as well. The bell ringing as the tram passes, the growl of the steel wheels on the tracks. There are businessmen in suits and ties, but the colours are all ancient in a way, kind of earthy and Mayan. I think that's what I like about it. Like everything's old and new at the same time.' I paused for a moment as the day gathered around us, and then added, almost as an afterthought, 'And nothing is surprising.'

When I had finished, I fell into a deep, heavy-hearted silence.

'It sounds wonderful,' Emily said quietly, delicately.

'It is. Now that you say it.'

Neither of us spoke for a moment, but there was an oppressive feeling of words in the air, hovering, waiting for a voice. I knew that I had to speak, to say something, anything, to stop the brooding momentum of silence.

'Have you thought about what you want to do? When you get there?'

She looked at me with a quick, birdlike reflex, her green eyes glistening like jewels in the morning light.

'What do you mean?'

'You know, after all of this. When you meet me there.'

'I . . . I don't . . . I mean, I haven't thought . . .'

She stumbled nervously in response, and the sight of her face downcast, her thick, rumpled hair concealing her eyes from me, was almost too much to bear. I had never seen her flustered like this before. It was an act of cruelty, what I had said, or the flippant manner in which I'd said it, and I could see the pain it had caused her. I took her hand and moved closer to her.

256

'We don't have to talk about this now,' I said, feeling desperate and foolish.

She pulled herself away from my grip and stood up, taking a few quick steps away from the seat and out towards the point of the ridge. Even in the foreground she was still a small figure, set as she was against the ultramarine of the gulf below. I was seized by the image she had unwittingly made, standing there with her back to me. But turning her into a muse felt cheap. I got out of my seat and walked up gently behind her. I put my arms around her slender waist but she wriggled out of my embrace and moved a couple of steps forward.

'You think I'm naïve, don't you?' she said. 'Like one of those stupid girls back there.'

'No. Of course I don't—'

'Well, I'm not, Peter. You don't know me. I've lived. I've done . . .' She trailed off, but I could see the frustration written on her face.

I came up behind her and tried to put my arms around her again, but she wouldn't have it.

'You don't know the half of it, Peter. I told you, I keep telling you, but you don't want to listen.'

'You can tell me or not. I don't care what—'

'No!' she yelled. 'No. Stop. I'm not who you think I am. I just, I just can't explain it to you yet. Not now. Not yet.'

She still wouldn't let me touch her, but I got up close enough to see that she was silently crying, a determined, frustrated stream of tears soaking her cheeks. As soon as she was composed enough to speak she demanded that I take her home. We flew back down the goat's track like a pair of mountaineers, pushing past the kids coming up, indifferent to the loose rocks and other potential dangers. When we pulled up outside her house, I made to get out of the jeep and follow her inside, but she put her hand on my arm to stop me. Her touch was cold, distant.

'Please, Peter. I just think I need to be alone today. I'm sorry I ruined your morning.'

'Are you sure? Listen, I've got the jeep for the day so I'll swing by later if you like.'

'No. Not today.' Her tone was tender now. She brought her hand up to my face and leaned across the seat, gently kissing me on the lips. Her face was still damp with tears.

'So, um, when do you think I should come back? I probably won't be able to get leave until Friday now. Maybe even Saturday.'

'I'm sorry, Peter. There's just a . . . there's just a few things I have to . . . consider.'

I felt as though I was drowning. My breath was coming hard and what little air I could get in was shallow and bubbled.

'So I'll come back Saturday then?'

'Yes.'

'Are you sure?'

'Yes. I'm sorry, Peter. I really am.'

I couldn't read her tone, couldn't even recognise the look in her eyes. I was struck by the hard, brittle distance in her body, the way it seemed to contort away from me.

'All right, so I'll be back on Saturday then. First thing.' I was madly trying to get to the life raft, but every time I got close it bobbed just out of reach.

'Yes.'

'Saturday, then.'

'Goodbye, Peter.'

She kissed me again and got out of the jeep. I watched as she walked up the long path to the front door, the hem of her cotton dress caked in mud. When she made it to the top of the enclosed veranda she turned around to wave, but it was a stiff and formal act. Something had changed, something had been dramatically altered, but I just didn't know what. I waved back, but it was hard to see her through the glare, standing alone, up there in the darkness of the porch. I brought my hand up to my eyes as a visor only to see the front door close behind her.

CHAPTER 31

After chow the following morning I decided to walk to the public library in the city. I'd barely slept the previous night thinking about Emily and our sudden, strange parting. I'd played the scene over and over in my mind, but I still didn't know what I had said or done that had so upset her. She knew that I knew she was Jewish, so it couldn't have been that. Perhaps it was just the impossibility of our situation; there was, of course, the small issue of the war that I had to fight before we would be in a position to resolve anything. The fact of the war, and of my going to it, made everything else provisional. It would be only natural for her to find such a state of affairs distressing.

As dawn had started to break something else began to bother me: Dr Walters's journal article. A few days after the wedding, while Emily slept on the couch beside the fire in the sitting room, and while Mrs Walters was busy playing long-distance chess in the Parnell library, I happened to recall the conversation I'd had with Dr Foster at the Ambassador a few weeks back. As I was dozily going over it in my mind, half-asleep in front of the fire, I suddenly remembered the second clause of Dr Walters's title, which Emily had curiously failed to mention.

Treatment of Fixated Latency Period: A Case Study of a German Boy. I checked to see that Emily was still asleep and quietly crept out the door, down the cold hallway, and into the library. It was the first time I'd been in the room since she had caught me there with the journal all those months ago. Nothing had changed. The ceramic ornaments were still there, and Dr Walters's Rembrandtesque portrait still scared the wits out of me from above the mantelpiece. Everything was exactly as it had been. Everything, that is, except that one slim volume.

The librarian in the public library showed me to the medical section, and it didn't take long to find the *London Review of Medicine*. I couldn't quite remember the date or volume number, but knew that it was somewhere between 1934 and '37. I tried a couple before I found it, bold and proud in black and white, volume IX, 1936.

I took a seat at a large oak table in the reading room and cracked the stiff book open to page ninety-seven. The piece was written in a florid, overly technical style that made it difficult to comprehend the actual thesis. From what I could glean, however, it appeared that Dr Walters had taken issue with Freud's assessment of the stages of psychosexual development. Freud and his followers had assumed that at each stage of psychosexual development – the oral, anal, phallic and genital – it was possible for subjects to fixate, or in another words, stop. If development stopped in, say, the phallic stage, the subject would fail to mature past his primitive oedipal urges and instincts. He would become aggressive and hostile, and be prone to displays of sexual violence. Freud had posited that during a subject's development, and typically between the phallic and the genital phase, a period of latency ensued, for sometimes up to five or six years. During this phase, or 'non-phase' as Walters described it, the subject becomes as close to asexual as is possible in a human being, where he experiences neither sexual urges nor hatreds or envies based on deep-seated frustrations.

What Dr Walters had set out to do was disprove the widely held assumption that a subject could not fixate during the latency phase. Puberty was a biological inevitability according to strict Freudians, and with puberty the latency period naturally ended, whereupon the subject began his genital struggle. While Dr Walters acknowledged the 'charming logic' of this, his own observations seemed to reject the assumption. And one boy in particular. A German boy.

The child was not named, of course, but it was noted that Dr Walters had had the opportunity to observe him 'these past fourteen years'. The boy, it was claimed, had passed easily enough through the oral and anal phases, but slowed down during the phallic, failing to display the customary oedipal urges. Dr Walters noted that whatever 'drive instinct' the boy had was not directed at his mother, and that he maintained a cool, yet perfectly respectful distance from his father.

Walters hypothesised that due to the failure of oedipal desire for his mother, the boy's drive-instinct had been turned inward. This was exacerbated by environmental factors, such as the boy's status as an only child, the fact that he was educated not in a school with other fellows, but by 'wizened Berliner tutors', and that he rarely, if ever, had the opportunity to socialise with children his own age. The result of all this was that the boy, even though he physically passed the puberty line, failed to develop psychologically from his pre-puberty state. The danger in this was that the drive-instinct, if not used or called to attention, would eventually atrophy and waste away, leaving the boy (medically at least) a eunuch.

I admit that I failed to properly understand what followed, but from what I could gather it seemed that Dr Walters believed the condition could be treated on an environmental basis alone. To prove the point, the boy was placed under strict, laboratory-like conditions and was subjected to the introduction of an 'exotic outsider' who masqueraded as a family member. The fact that the outsider was, at least from the boy's perspective, a relation (and, ergo, forbidden) meant that the resuscitation of his drive-instinct would be checked by the boy's highly developed superego, which would, in theory, restrain him.

The trial lasted six months, during which time the boy's drive-instinct did spring back to life. Dr Walters claimed the study was a success as it had apparently proven two hitherto unknowns: first, that individuals can fixate during the latency period; and, secondly, that such fixation can be treated solely by adjustments in environmental conditions.

The article failed to mention what became of the exotic outsider, or whether the boy ever discovered she was not a relation. Science did not require that we know.

That afternoon, Sturgis and I were back on P.R. detail. Perhaps out of spite, Cartwright had assigned us to visit Mrs Taylor again to thank her for her daily pound cake offering. Although I wasn't convinced that the P.R. programme did anything for the American reputation in the city – by and large we were visiting people who liked us anyway, old ladies and school children in the main – I was aware of the general resentment, which seemed to have got worse in the past few weeks. Just a few days ago a group of combat soldiers from the Third had got into a brawl on Queen Street with a crew of Maoris that just about turned into a riot. The M.P.s weren't able to control the situation, and the Auckland home guard had to be called in to stop the bloodshed. But it wasn't just the fights. Even the local press, usually so mindful of the censorship agreement the New Zealand government had struck with Washington, had started to flout the rules and publish incidents of American stupidity and drunkenness. The welcome mat was fast being rolled back in.

Mrs Taylor was in better spirits for us this time. Her reticence had given way to a kind of everyday loquaciousness, and she seemed genuinely pleased to see us. We learned that she volunteered at a munitions factory in Te Atatu and taught Sunday school classes to children at Saint Paul's on Richmond Road. She was pleasant enough to me, but reserved the few smiles she had for Sturgis. She sat next to him at the kitchen table, topped up his tea after every mouthful he took, and pushed slice after slice of cake in front of him with such a pitifully hopeful expression that it was impossible for him to say no.

I didn't mind being ignored, though. I couldn't get my mind off Dr Walters's article. It seemed obvious that Emily was the 'exotic outsider' he'd referred to. Emily had even said as much herself, the night when she came to me in the garret and told me she wasn't one of them. It seemed to fit, but at that stage I still had no idea what the implications of it were. It threw up so many problems, not least of which was how it came about that Dr Walters could lay his hands on such a compliant individual. Whatever it was, I told myself that it would be natural to want to hide such a thing. I just had to find a way of delicately telling her that I knew, and that whatever she did or was forced to do, it didn't matter to me. I needed to reassure her that the past wouldn't follow her to California, and that once we were together we could both start anew.

Sturgis's stomach finally got the better of him and he politely declined the fourth offering of pound cake and cream. I couldn't help looking up at the picture of Mrs Taylor's uniformed son on the wall. She caught me looking at it a couple of times, and although I felt ashamed I couldn't resist the tendency of my eyes to drift up to it every other minute. I watched her as she tended to Sturgis, the grieving mother given a chance to play-act her maternal instinct on a spotty stranger who, if she blurred her eyes just enough, could almost have been her son come back. I wondered at all the mothers out there now, from New Zealand to New England, baking food that nobody would eat, their hearts breaking every time they looked at dog-eared photographs of ghosts, the boys that went away to strange, unknowable places and never came back.

On our way out neither of us could help casting a guilty look at the closed door that had caused so much grief last time. The sealed bedroom. She caught us looking at it, and we spent a few awkward, static moments in the narrow hallway not looking at each other or moving. Finally she waddled her compact little body past Sturgis and opened the front door. The light poured mercifully into the grim thoroughfare, like the opening of church doors on a bright Sunday morning, freeing us to live and breathe and curse again.

We bounded up Richmond Road like a pair of gazelles, almost wallowing in the bracing fresh air. Without thinking, we crossed Ponsonby heading back down towards Franklin. Just before we reached the intersection at Collingwood I could hear a strange noise dancing in the thin air, high-spirited and exotic. This was followed by the growls of a couple of baritone voices, queer guttural sounds that I couldn't place. Sturgis grabbed me by the arm, a look of panic or excited agitation in his eyes.

'The cathouse!' he hissed.

I looked up ahead; the noises were certainly coming from that direction. I hadn't even realised we were walking past it. The sopranos and the baritones kept at it, the noises they were making now suddenly recognisable as something Oriental, Chinese perhaps. As we jogged ahead to the tunnel that was cut into the redbrick block of shops, the shouts of English voices began to ring out above the unfathomable Chinese.

When we had made it into the clearing of the courtyard,

our progress was stopped by a jostling ring of people, at least four or five rows deep. I could only make out the odd face through all the backs of hatted heads, but the crowd seemed to be almost exclusively local. They'd formed a circle around what sounded like an all-in brawl. I couldn't see the fighters themselves, but whoever was shouting in Chinese had refined his discourse to a single shrieked note, repeated over and over again like a persistent crow's call.

'Look up yonder, Captain,' Sturgis said, over the noise of the cheering crowd.

He was pointing up at the landing that jutted out from the steel door of the cathouse, situated at the top of the sagging wooden staircase that ran diagonally up the mossy redbrick wall. Two Orientals in blue suits came bounding down the stairs and burrowed their way through the crowd like moles through topsoil. I stood up on my tiptoes just in time to see them burst through the ring and into the centre of the action.

'Come on,' I said to Sturgis, pulling him through the crowd.

A few of the locals tried to block our progress. There was an ugly feeling of blood in the air, and the sight of our Marine uniforms seemed to bring the letting of it that much closer.

'Sir,' said Sturgis, frantically tugging at my arm. 'Upstairs, sir. Look upstairs!'

I looked up at the landing again to see O'Keefe this time, dressed only in an unbuttoned shirt and his khaki draws, a docile, almost amused expression on his doughy face.

'What the hell's he doing up there?' I said, unable to control the flicker of panic in my tone.

'You want me to tell you?'

'You don't suppose,' I said, nodding my head towards the unseen fighters, 'that Timmins is in there, do you?'

'One way to find out.'

Sturgis knelt down and attempted an approximation of the jungle crawl we'd been taught at Elliot, trying to work his way through the legs of the people in front of him. He didn't make it far. One of the spectators, catching Sturgis between his legs, tried to grab him in a headlock, but the little bastard was nimble enough to make a scurried retreat. Just then the fanatical sound of two screaming Oriental women broke the air asunder. They were up on the landing, two whores in flimsy silk nightgowns, their coal-black hair glistening in the weak sunlight, as strange and mysterious as if they'd stepped off the moon. The sound coming out of their mouths was utterly alien, devoid of provenance or source. I recalled what Sturgis had told me a while back, that he thought they were Nips. I couldn't tell the difference, but the sound of their shrieking was certainly different from the men.

The distinction, if there was one, seemed to be lost on the assembled crowd though, which heaved a collective gasp at the sight of them. I got bumped in the commotion and lost my balance, almost tipping over completely. When I looked back up the giant Chinaman, the thin ghost I'd seen at Western Park and outside the chess club, had taken the women by their hair and was dragging them back inside. O'Keefe looked placidly on at all this like a lost boy on a busy pavement, patiently waiting for his mommy to do her thing and whisk him back to safety. While everybody's attention was diverted, Sturgis and I made a play for the front, bursting through the shoulders and flailing forearms to be spat out into the ring of the action.

'Holy shit!' said Sturgis, almost to himself.

Timmins was nowhere in sight; instead, Oscar Walters and two of his black-suited buddies were locked in a vicious battle with four of the giant's Oriental underlings.

'I thought they were on the same side,' I said, a little dazed at the spectacle of a battle to the death between committed chess players. And it was a battle to the death all right. The Orientals were employing an array of impressive techniques – jumping kicks and swishing hand chops – that the black-suits were struggling to combat. Oscar had a stream of blood running from a cut above his left eye, and one of his comrades was staggering perilously on his shaky legs after fielding a thwacking kick to the ribs.

I pulled Sturgis towards me to get his attention. 'Go get O'Keefe, would you? Before the lid on this thing blows. The cops will be here any minute.'

'Not to mention the M.P.s.'

'Right. Get going,' I said, pushing him off in the direction of the staircase.

There were M.P.s crawling all over Ponsonby, and it was only a matter of time before they, or the local constabulary, decided to join us for the entertainment. As a doctor I had an uncomplicated duty to tend to injured people, but there was no way of getting to anybody without breaking another ancient maxim: first do no harm. And this applied to me.

Suddenly the secret gate in the paling fence opposite the whorehouse sprung open, introducing two more black-clad chessmen into the programme. They were making their way through the crowd when the whistles started blowing. First there was one, then they seemed to sound from every direction. Local police. I looked up anxiously at the landing and was relieved to see that Sturgis had managed to get O'Keefe's attention. He was still on the landing, though, and he kept making funny, hopeless motions with his chubby arms. It took me a second to realise he was referring to his pants, or the lack of them. The whistles grew louder, and suddenly the steel door swung open, just about knocking O'Keefe clean off his perch. It was the giant again. He gripped the wooden railing and yelled something down to his charges, a single syllable, deep, resonant, calm. At the sound of it the fighting Orientals stopped, as sudden as a jammed film reel. One of them had grabbed Oscar from behind and had been delivering short, hammer-like blows to his kidneys. He had his clenched fist raised ready to drive in another blow, but had the self-control to drop Oscar's ragged, beaten body to the loose gravel. And then they were gone. They were there and then they were gone, up the rickety wooden staircase, all five of them in a row like nimble-footed firemen pouring into a flaming building. The steel door closed behind them with a thud.

Everybody in the crowd remained focused on the landing, but there was nothing more to see – nothing more, that is, than the pantless, paunch-bellied O'Keefe. He sheepishly made his way down the stairs as the whistles sounded louder. They would be here any second. I motioned to Sturgis to meet me in the driveway, and was about to push my way through the crowd when a voice called out behind me, a gurgled voice rattling with liquid, blood perhaps.

'Wait,' he said, louder now, authoritative.

I turned around, but I already knew who it was.

'Wait!' Oscar shouted.

I felt the crowd gather round behind me, restless, excited, unsatisfied. I had the distinct, claustrophobic feeling I was trapped. There was a drawing-in and compression of space and energy. Dozens of people stood behind me, shuffling, advancing.

Oscar was on his feet now. The left side of his face was covered in rich, cardinal red blood. He walked towards me, gingerly clutching his left elbow with his right hand.

'Do you know who I am, Captain?' he said in a quiet, forceful whisper so that the crowd behind me couldn't hear. 'Do you have any idea who I am?'

'No,' I said, casting a wary glance back over my shoulder at the advancing crowd. He came within three feet of me, so close that I could see the nostrils on his generous nose flaring like mad. I braced myself for the attack I felt certain would come.

'I'm Oswald Mosley's son, you piece of shit.'

'Who?'

He stopped and looked up at me in wide-eyed amazement. He searched my face for signs I might have been fucking with him, but couldn't find anything because the truth was I had never heard of Oswald Mosley.

'My fucking God, you're kidding me. Tell me you're joking,' he said, laughing bitterly to himself and taking a couple of steps back to survey the crowd of locals over my shoulder.

I shook my head, still feeling an attack was imminent. 'What? Who is he?'

'It's their fault, you know,' he bellowed to the crowd, his voice declarative, professorial. 'It's the stupid fucking Yanks that are the cause of all this. They're the ones who are stealing your women, causing all the fights. They're even taking your work down at the wharf!'

I stood motionless, watching him edge closer towards me again. He studiously avoided making eye contact with me. A couple of his buddies were disappearing through the gap in the fence behind him. A whistle blasted, not more than sixty feet away.

'We don't want them here, do we?' shouted Oscar, still orating.

I heard somebody in the crowd, a lone voice, say 'No!' A ripple of laugher followed, and a couple more echoed the sentiment. 'No. No.'

Oscar said, 'And what good are they, anyway? Do you really think these cowards, these degenerates, would protect you from the Japanese?' He laughed again, his eyes wild, all the time inching closer to me in tiny, choreographed baby steps. He had a wonderful sense of drama to match the rhetoric.

With impeccable timing O'Keefe lumbered past Oscar, his pale white legs flashing under his draws, methodically buttoning his shirt.

'Exhibit A' declared Oscar, and with a shunt of his good arm sent O'Keefe flying into the crowd, which parted and let him fall to the loose gravel in an ungainly heap. He lolled face down for a moment like a seal, or a pig in a muddy sty. The crowd burst into raucous, derisive laughter. The shrill whistle sounded again.

'And this one is the worst,' said Oscar, pointing directly at me, quieting the crowd. 'He's supposed to be an officer. A doctor, no less. But do you know what this man is?'

He was three feet away from me now. Somebody in the crowd behind yelled 'Tell us,' and everybody burst into laughter again. Oscar stopped and finally looked at me.

'He's a whoremaster,' he shouted. 'He's married to a filthy whore!'

First I saw a flash of white light, then my hand suddenly hurt like hell. When I came to, Oscar was lying on the ground in front of me, his nose spread across his gaunt face. It wasn't until I saw him lying there that my brain registered what my fist had done. I felt sick. I was about to bend down and help him up when something heavy hit me from behind, knocking the wind out of my chest, and sending me crashing face first into the ground. Before I knew what was happening my hands were being forced up behind my back.

'You're nicked!' said an urgent, aggressive voice just behind my ear, the accent unmistakably Kiwi.

I was still flat on my front, writhing with the pain burning in my shoulders as the cop pushed my hands farther and farther up my back, when another voice said, 'Stop that! He's ours.'

I recognised the voice, even amidst all the confusion. All of a sudden I was hoisted up off the ground, two strong hands clutching me under either armpit. The hands belonged to a six-foot-four American M.P. Cartwright stood next to him, looking immaculate in his khaki uniform.

'He's a United States Marine,' he said to the local cop. 'He's under the jurisdiction of the Department of the Navy, and United States military law.'

The cop, a huckery fellah of around fifty with snow-white hair, looked decidedly confused.

'I can assure you he'll be punished,' Cartwright said over the jeers of the crowd. 'I saw everything, and he will be punished accordingly.'

'Right you are then,' said the cop good-naturedly.

The M.P. had me in a pretty good grip, but I still managed to crane my neck to see two of the black-suited chessmen dragging Oscar through the gate in the fence.

'Hey,' I said, rousing myself enough to protest, 'they're getting away! Behind you, they're—'

'That'll be all, Sokol,' Cartwright said, three inches from my face. 'Guard: take him away.'

I was thrown into the back of Cartwright's jeep along with Sturgis and O'Keefe. Cartwright hadn't said another word to me, but I couldn't be bothered trying to explain myself. That son-of-a-bitch Walters deserved a smack in the mouth. It also occurred to me that if Cartwright had 'seen everything' as he so confidently proclaimed, then he must surely know that I had married Emily. I wondered how Oscar had found out – whether Emily had summoned the courage to tell him, or whether there was an informer in the household. We were heading down Franklin back towards camp, the jeep travelling at a good clip. The swirling wind was making me feel nauseous. I was still having trouble piecing together what had just happened.

'O'Keefe,' I said, leaning close to him in the cramped back seat, straining a whisper through the gusting wind. 'What happened back there, anyway?'

'You mean you getting arrested and all?'

'No, you dumbass. Before that. What was the ruckus about to begin with?'

'Oh. Um. I think one of the chink whores took it.'

'What do you mean?'

'I mean, dead. Brown bread. I think it was one of them queers in the black suits that did it.'

'Who? Which one?'

'How the hell should I know? They're all in black, sir. I just heard some crashing and when I got up and went down the hall one of the chink whores was bleeding. Pretty bad. And she was just kind of lying there, on the mattress like.'

'Dead?'

'As a doornail, sir.'

I turned to Sturgis who was smugly assessing me with a raised eyebrow, as if he'd just been vindicated by something. I gave him a scowl in return and lent in close to him so Cartwright and his goon couldn't hear.

'Who the hell is Oswald Mosley?' I whispered.

'Who?'

'Oswald Mosley.'

He hunched his shoulders and looked back out at the rows of cottages slipping by.

'No idea,' he said. 'Why?'

CHAPTER 32

The three of us were taken directly to Colonel Ford's office. Not quite his office, but the outer office where Diddle, the company clerk, had his desk and switchboard. There was nowhere to sit so we leaned against the flimsy plywood walls under the watchful glare of the M.P., Sergeant Adams, who in another life could have played starting forward for the Celtics. Cartwright had gone into Ford's office, closing the door behind him. It had been ten minutes already. I wanted to question O'Keefe further about the dead prostitute, but it had been made clear that talking was out of the question. As I reconstructed the scene in my mind, it seemed to me that during the fight all of the Orientals had been trying one way or another to get at Oscar, but that his comrades were blocking their paths. Out of all of the chessmen, he was the only one who wasn't dressed properly, entirely in black that is. It was as if he'd been in a hurry to get away and had got caught.

Ford's door swung open and O'Keefe was summoned. As Adams led him to the door, Sturgis tapped me on the wrist.

'What's the story?' he asked out of the side of his mouth.

'Huh?'

'The story?' He was impatient, a little anxious even. 'What are we going to say?'

'You just tell them what happened. It's me they're after. Just tell them straight.'

'But that asshole – he said you were married. What if they . . .'

Adams had delivered O'Keefe and was making his way back to us.

'Just don't lie to them,' I whispered. 'I'll be fine.'

Sergeant Adams stood in front of us and loudly cleared his throat. 'The Colonel says you're to go back to your tent, Corporal. And that you're to stay there until further notice.'

'Me?' Sturgis pointlessly asked, jerking his thumb into his chest.

'You. Get moving.'

O'Keefe was out five minutes later and then it was my turn. Ford sat behind his desk, straight as a ramrod in his high-back chair. His eyes were icy and his mouth appeared to have contracted to the size of a nickel on the wide expanse of his craggy, grey face. To the side of his desk stood Cartwright, the pindick deputy with a flair for paperwork, who raised his eyebrows at me as I walked in, a 'well-well' expression on his smug face. His relish for the situation was naked, almost pornographic.

Ford let a pregnant silence hang in the heavy air for a moment before he spoke.

'Captain Sokol,' he said, cutting the words up into four distinct syllables.

'Yes, sir.'

He threw his gold-plated pen down onto the desk in front of him.

'Mind telling me why you're out on the streets punching locals in the mouth? Why you're doing this when everybody else is working overtime to appease these bastards?'

I tried not to look at Cartwright. There was a hint of resignation in Ford's voice. I knew that if I could play on this, the old dark-horse Sokol legend, and keep the truck between me and him, I might get away unscathed.

'I don't know what you've been told, sir, but I—'

He banged his fist down on the desk, hard, the resignation turned now to fiery rage.

'Jesus fucking Christ, Sokol! I don't give a goddamn horse's ass what I've been told. I asked you a question, for Christ's sake.'

He was half out of his chair, arms spread across the desk like a sprinter waiting for the starter's gun.

'Well, I, um, Corporal Sturgis and me were coming back to camp from—'

'Get to the goddamn point, man!'

'Well, we came across a fight,' I said, my voice sounding thin, tinny. 'And, um, one of the guys fighting pushed O'Keefe down. Then he just started raving at me.'

'So, genius that you are, you thought it would be a good idea to hit him. In front of all those people.'

'It just sort of happened, sir.'

'What are you, a fraternity boy?' He was on his feet now. He grasped his large, silver belt buckle with both hands, tugging at it like a nervous cowboy waiting for the gate to open.

'Why did you hit him, though?' asked Cartwright, his tone level, bureaucratic.

Ford and I both looked at him.

'Like I said. It just happened.'

I knew he was trying to work an angle here, trying to build up to something, but fortunately Ford was in no mood for subtlety.

'Colonel Cartwright tells me you know this guy?' Ford said to me, calmer now. 'This asshole chess player or whatever he is.'

'I've met his family, sir. You have too. At the British Med—'

'Whatever,' he said, waving his hand and walking around

276

behind me. 'He sounds like a royal prick, but that's no excuse, Sokol. Jesus, man, you're a surgeon, and an officer.' He closed his eyes and breathed in. 'One week's tent arrest.'

He said it as though he was showing me clemency, but it was the worst punishment he could have delivered. I would have rather had a full morning's lashings with a cat-o-nine-tails than to have to spend a week apart from Emily. I wanted to say something, but by the look on Ford's face I was already in the past tense. I made towards the door without acknowledging Cartwright.

'Before you go,' he said gravely, reaching out to take me by the shoulder.

I stopped dead, his firm old-man grasp making me shiver. I looked up at him, fearing the worst, but he didn't look angry. In fact, he looked kind of sad.

'Colonel Cartwright and I think you should know this, before the rumours start to fly around camp.'

'What is it?' I said.

Ford paused and muttered something to himself, shaking his head at my impudence.

'Corporal Timmins was in an accident this afternoon,' he said, his icy blue eyes dull and resigned. 'He was picking up a load of supplies from the wharf. On the way back the dumb son-of-a-bitch failed to stop at an intersection on Fanshawe Street. Nobody knows why yet. He got side-swiped by a bus coming down the hill on Nelson.'

'Jesus,' I said. I could tell from Ford's tone, the sorry demeanour and droop of his shoulders that it was bad. 'Is he . . . I mean, is he okay?'

'He's dead, Sokol.'

I didn't know what to say, so instead I flopped back down into the chair I'd just recently vacated. Everything was silent for a few moments before Cartwright cleared his throat.

'While it's tragic,' he said, in a businesslike tone, 'it's not our only problem.' He paused and looked at Ford, who gave him an unwilling nod before moving back round behind his desk and easing himself into his seat. 'The supply truck was a total wreck,' Cartwright continued. 'We've lost a month's worth of plasma, penicillin, catgut, scalpels, bandages—'

'I get the picture!' I yelled, surprising everyone in the room, including myself. I was still struggling to come to terms with the news, and the sound of Cartwright rattling off a supply inventory was more than I could take. 'So we'll scrimp and save. We'll borrow from the Army. Jesus Christ, Cartwright, a man's dead.'

His face went white with anger and he took a few quick steps towards me, leaning over my chair.

'I don't need to remind you, Captain, that this is a military hospital and—'

'That's enough!' Ford cried in a murderous tone. 'Get the hell out of here! Both of you!'

I didn't need to be told twice. I got up and made for the door. I tried to make it out of the outer office before Cartwright caught up with me, but I was too slow.

'Sokol,' he hissed urgently.

I turned around to face him. He made a show of excusing his M.P., who glared at me nastily on the way out.

'I have a question for you,' he said, coming right up to me, two feet away, within receptor range of the molecules coming off his sugary French cologne. It was his old trick, the crowding out of space, and it worked too; I felt as though all the air had been sucked out of the room, and that I was as trapped as if I had been nailed to the floor. But I forced myself to respond, and took a small, purely symbolic step towards him. I could see his nostrils flaring, the flickering tremor in his upper lip.

'He doesn't like Americans, does he?'

'Ford?'

He closed his eyes and smiled sardonically. 'That queer you hit.'

'He plays chess, you know.'

'I'm warning you, Sokol.'

'No, I don't think he likes us Americans. As you well saw. Jesus, Cartwright, can't this wait? Timmins is dead. One of your men is dead.'

'Yes, it's very sad, but you'll call me Colonel or I'll have you on latrine duty for a month.'

For some reason I couldn't help laughing. 'Do your worst.'

He swallowed hard. I could see he had something to say, and was prepared to put aside any indiscretion to get to it.

'Just out of curiosity, Captain. Why would this queer say you were married? It just seems, I don't know, a strange thing to say. Don't you think?'

'I have no idea what he was talking about.'

'Sure about that?'

My stomach felt completely uncoiled and hollow. What if he knew? What if Sturgis had told O'Keefe, and O'Keefe had spilled? What if the padre had said something about that oddball family in Parnell? I still hadn't done anything with the marriage certificate, so he couldn't have known that way. I had to call his bluff.

'I'm sure,' I said, stepping past him on my way out.

I spent a wretched afternoon and night in my stinking canvas cell, pacing what little floor there was until I was almost in a frenzy. I was shocked by the news about Timmins, but for all I cared about the poor bastard I just couldn't get Emily out of my mind. I had promised to see her on Saturday, and there was no way of contacting her. The only telephones on the camp were in Ford's office and in Diddle's outer office. There was also the small matter of Adams guarding my door.

I started to feel sick with wanting; it had been two days since I had last seen her, touched her creamy skin, and even longer since I'd made love to her. I kept pacing until my legs would no longer hold me and I was forced to flop down onto my cot.

I tried reading a week-old edition of *Stars and Stripes* to settle my mind, but it was no good. In my quiet funk the fragments of the morning started to piece together. Oscar had said that I was married to a 'whore'. I hadn't dwelt too closely on his word choice until now. I might have put it down to his soul-hate for Americans, and the plain fact that his sister had chosen to connect herself to one. But I wasn't convinced. He was an extreme guy, but to call his sister a *whore* seemed a step too far, even for him.

The following morning I did a seven-hour stretch in the post-op. The mood was sombre; everybody knew about Timmins, and nobody felt like talking. The worst thing about it was the feeling, the bitter knowledge that he would be just the first in a long chain of us to die. Everything looked slightly different that morning – the khaki camp more drab, the food bleaker, the wounded men that much sicker. The business of war, the business of dying had started for real now.

I buried myself in my tasks, examining the four amputees we had for gas-bacillus infections, adjusting the various traction frames that several patients were awkwardly attached to – the Bohler-Braun, the Bradford, and the Stryker. Most of the compound fracture wounds couldn't be closed in the definitive surgery, so post-op duty often involved monitoring whole-blood transfusions where the patients showed signs of anaemia. I was absorbed in the work, not allowing my mind to wander from the immediate task in front of me. I spent an excessive amount of time, over an hour, removing the sutures from an excellent pedicle graft a ship doctor had performed on a kid who'd been wounded in the Philippines. It was a beautiful job, and almost certainly saved the tendons in the kid's hand from wasting. I worked without a break and without a scrap of food in my stomach, and it was a grave disappointment when Cartwright finally came to replace me. We passed each other in the scrub room without saying a word, without even making eye contact. He was set against me now, and that's how it would stay.

I had barely been back in my tent five minutes when there was a knock at the door. The M.P. opened it to let in Diddle along with a cool gust of sooty air. Young Diddle was wielding a bulging leather sack filled with mail. The door closed behind him and he timidly stepped towards my cot, where I was sitting up, unlacing my boots.

'Mail for me?'

'Ah, no, sir. I mean . . .' He nervously looked back over his shoulder.

'What is it, Diddle? Do you want to talk about Timmins?'

Diddle couldn't have been a day older than eighteen, and the sight of him in his shabbily kept khaki uniform bordered on the tragic. He was morning fresh, so fresh his skin was almost green. He bowed his head quickly and sniffed, perhaps to suppress some tears.

'No,' he said softly.

'Any word from intel on the accident?' I asked delicately, knowing that Diddle generally knew more about Intel's investigations than they did themselves.

'I don't know,' he said, dropping his eyes to the floor again. For once he didn't want to talk about it. 'They're examining the truck at the moment. Scooter over at Devonport reckons there was something up with the brakes, but nobody knows for sure yet.'

I nodded my head and wearily kicked off my boondockers.

'Um, excuse me, sir, but Corporal Sturgis asked me to give this to you.'

He handed me an envelope, plain white, with the moniker

Captain Sokol written on it. My heart sank as soon as I recognised that it wasn't her handwriting.

'Thank you, Diddle,' I said quietly.

'Um, Captain?'

'Yes.'

'Corporal Sturgis said for me to say that the old butler gave it to him.'

'The butler?'

'Yessir. I don't know what it all means, sir. But that Sturgis was in the Birdcage and someone called the old butler came in and done handed it to him. The letter and all. Right there in the Birdcage, sir.'

I waited for a few moments after Diddle had gone, waited for the dank air to settle before accustoming myself to the immediacy of the thing in my hand. I knew the handwriting wasn't Emily's. The fact that the writer had sent Winston to deliver it gave me pause. He was a frail, lumbering old man for whom a doorknob, let alone the real world, was a dangerous prospect. To send him out on an errand like this, so far from his home, was an act of desperation, a step taken in last resort. I opened the envelope with my pocketknife, slowly running the blade down the crest of the fold.

Captain Sokol,

Please do me the honour of joining me for tea tomorrow at the Village Tearooms on Parnell Road. I will be seated there at three in the afternoon.

Respectfully,
Mrs Gertrude Walters

I knew the place – it was three or four streets over from their house, on the main road in Parnell. I read the note over and over, trying to find a clue, a buried meaning or inference in the combination of the words, but there was nothing. I had broken her son's nose; I had struck at him in anger. I had spent the past few weeks in her confidence, a secret family member free to roam her long, draughty hallways, gaze upon the family portraits and other possessions with a degree of entitlement, and fuck her daughter with impunity. But now I was a stranger, a dangerous one at that – one you meet in public, in a populated space, one you keep distant from the dusty vault of your family's shameful secrets. I crushed the note in my hand and flung it to the far corner of the tent.

I got up and opened the door, telling Adams, the guard, in a sonorous tone that I needed to speak to Corporal Sturgis concerning a medical matter to do with a patient, an emergency. I said that it was potentially a matter of life and death and that Corporal Sturgis was the only one who would know what to do. I was freewheeling now. I had crossed a line, taken a final step from which I would never be able to retreat.

Adams looked at me blankly, his stony eyes cold and sceptical. He nodded his head.

CHAPTER 33

Mrs Walters was sitting inside the tearooms as promised. I lingered for a moment on the threshold of the door, watching her through the large plate-glass window. She sat in the far corner, alone. There was no food or drink on the table in front of her, not even any condiments or napkins. I was a few minutes late, and I guessed she must have been wondering whether I would show at all.

I'd arranged for Sturgis to sneak into my tent while I was on duty and the guard was off doing whatever else it was he did. I'd then feigned a sudden illness just before my shift ended, and got Nurse Muller to tell the M.P. I'd gone back to my tent early. When he looked in all he would have seen was the unidentifiable form of Sturgis, blankets pulled up over his head, asleep in my cot. Sturgis agreed to do it, to be my sleeping doppelgänger, but it was obvious that my wanting to leave the camp so soon after Timmins's death hurt him. He didn't say anything, but I knew that in his eyes I'd made a decision at a crucial moment. I had chosen Emily over the unit. I had chosen Emily over him.

I pushed open the door, which set off the glassy tinkling of a small bell hanging from the frame. Everybody in the tearooms turned to look at me. I nodded, almost apologetically, and made my way over to Mrs Walters's table. The air in the small room was thick with the smoke and smell of fried bacon.

Aside from Mrs Walters's, there were another five occupied tables in the joint, but the place was almost silent save for the clinking of cups and saucers, and the odd hushed observation.

'Captain Sokol,' Mrs Walters said, her voice clanging in the repressed quietness like an ill-struck cymbal. 'Would you please order something. I cannot bear the looks any longer.'

She looked over at the woman behind the counter, a portly specimen with a yellow and white striped apron and a thick crop of blue-rinsed hair atop a face that lacked even the suggestion of a chin. 'I'll take tea if you don't mind,' she said.

I made an order of tea and an assortment of the cakes and slices that were arranged next to the mechanical cash register.

'I'm sorry I'm late,' I said, taking a seat opposite her. It was immediately very strange and awkward to be sitting so close to her, so in front of her. She had an intangible force or presence about her that was almost like a wind, threatening to knock me off my seat.

She waved a dismissive hand in front of her face. 'That's the thing about this country,' she said, looking up at the counter-lady who was now standing at the side of our table pouring the tea. 'You have to pay for everything in advance. If you can believe that. It shows a certain mean-spiritedness, don't you think? A lack of trust or civility. A society cannot function properly if one is made to pay before one does anything.'

I nodded obliquely and took my hat off. I could see that she was upset. Her face wore a tense, almost brittle expression, and the air around her was heavy with sadness. But I was in no mood to tread carefully around her sensibilities; like a man in a movie, my time was short and I needed answers.

'Why are we meeting here?' I said, the harsh crispness of my words surprising me.

The question clearly caught Mrs Walters on the hop as well, and she responded as if a challenge had just been laid down.

'Where would you have us meet, Captain?'

'Where is she? Why isn't she here?'

She looked over my shoulder at the other diners, who must have been gawking at us.

'Your manners surprise me, Captain. I'd always thought—'

'She's my wife!' I hadn't realised how angry I was until I opened my mouth. I felt the blood pulsing in my ears. 'Just tell me why I can't see my own wife.'

'But is she? Is she really your wife? When all's said and done. When you're back at your hospital in San Francisco. Will she still be your wife then?'

We both looked up to see the blue-haired woman standing over us with a tray of cakes. She studiously avoided our looks, but seemed to take great relish placing the items on the table, slowly, one by one.

Mrs Walters said, 'that will be all' without looking at her. It was a beautifully cutting remark. The woman lingered for a moment in defiance before leaving us.

'These people,' Mrs Walters muttered under her breath.

I poured some more tea and watched her eat. It was a painful sight. The anger or sadness was still in her eyes, but her empty stomach was compelling her, in spite of her cherished European dignity, to order her animal priorities. I felt ashamed of myself for watching, but there was nowhere else to look. When she'd finished, a long silence followed, during which I could feel all of the venom seeping out of me.

'You broke my son's nose,' she said, matter of fact, taking a sip of tea.

'You heard.'

'I've seen the thing spread across his face.'

'Is that what this is about?'

She leaned forward in her chair, her head cocked to one side as though she hadn't quite caught what I'd said.

'And pray, Captain, what exactly is "this"?'

'This place. Why are we here? Why can't I see Emily?'

'One thing at a time, now. In answer to your original question, no, my son is not the reason why we're here. But that doesn't change the fact that you broke his nose.'

'He deserved it.'

'I dare say he did.' She sat back again and I thought I could see a smile forming in the furrowed lines around her almond eyes. 'You don't know my son that well, Captain. But believe me, he's had it coming for quite some time.'

I was taken by her frankness, by the detachment with which she seemed able to speak of her beaten son. I think my reaction must have registered with her, because she quickly attempted to clarify her remarks.

'I mean,' she said, a little urgently, 'from what I've heard. You see, he's very political, but his education was frustrated. He was accepted into Cambridge and was about to leave when . . .' She trailed off again, but it wasn't a half-finished thought this time. I got the impression that she had spoken in haste, and had unwittingly backed herself into a corner. She made a show of pushing the cake plates away as if the very sight of them disgusted her.

'Who is Oswald Mosley?' I asked.

She caught her breath, even jumped a little in her chair before quickly scanning the other patrons. It didn't appear that any of them had heard. She turned back to look at me, her eyes as razor sharp as a hawk's, her face narrowing in front of me.

'My,' she said in a tone of fake nonchalance, touching her open palm to her chest, 'what a bizarre question, Captain. Where on earth does this come from?'

'Your son. Yesterday. Just before I popped him. He said he was Oswald Mosley's son. Like it meant something, as if I was supposed to be impressed by it.'

'And you . . . you don't know who he is?'

'Never heard of him. Should I have?'

She paused before answering. I could see that what I had said had rattled her, had shaken her from her haughty carriage. She forced a smile at me, but her eyes refused to soften.

'You Americans are precious, aren't you?'

'So, who is he?'

'It doesn't matter any more,' she said, nervously looking up at the counter-lady who was prying again. 'I'm not sure it ever really did.'

'So, you're not going to tell me.'

'Oswald Mosley is irrelevant, Captain. As you've probably figured out, I cannot control what my son thinks, but I can assure you he's not that gentleman's son. And in any event, I didn't ask you to meet me here to discuss my son and his fantasies.'

'Spit it out then.'

She let the words hang in the air, along with the bacon fat and cigarette smoke. 'Wonderfully direct. Most Europeans detest that very quality in Americans. They think it artless and crude. But I must say I've grown to admire it.'

'I'm glad.'

She looked guardedly around the room. I could sense that what she was about to say came at a cost to her, one way or another.

'Captain, I . . . I think it best if you . . .'

'Yes?'

'I think it best if you stay away for a while. From the house. From Emily.'

Her words, so soft and tentatively spoken, hit me in the chest with an almighty thud. I felt winded for a moment, felt a surge of blood run into my face and burn the back of my eyes.

'Why?'

'I just think that—'

'No. No!' I was critically aware of the attention we were attracting. The counter-lady shot us another one of her eagle-like glares. I moved to the edge of my seat and leaned across the table towards Mrs Walters. 'She's my wife,' I spat through clenched teeth. 'You've got no right to keep her from me.'

I expected an argument in response, a well-crafted rejoinder, but all she could do was look at me. And in that forlorn, doleful expression I thought I caught the only resemblance to Emily she'd ever betrayed. It wasn't a physical thing at all; it was just a look, a certain ironic resignation, a fraught acceptance of something. I wanted her to argue back. I wanted a scrap, I wanted to rant and rave and bang the table with my fist; I wanted to do something to demonstrate to her that my love for Emily was real, that I wasn't just another Yank out to get his leg over, but somehow I knew we'd gone beyond all that.

She said, 'If you do love Emily, Captain, then please keep away from her,' and for some reason, I understood what she meant. I didn't know the details, but it had to be related to the article, to Dr Walters's little gift to psychoanalysis. I could taste at least the flavour of their secret, and in doing so I had to accept that perhaps she was right.

I buried my face in my hands for a moment, thinking of absolutely nothing, and when I looked back up I saw clearly how frail and tired she actually was. Poverty and exile had hollowed her out. Poverty and exile and something else.

'What are you trying to hide?' I asked, unable to resist. 'I've read the article, you know. Your husband's experiment. It was Oscar, wasn't it? And Emily?'

My revelation didn't seem to surprise her at all. She just looked over my shoulder, at the curious and withering looks I assumed she was getting from the other patrons. Her eyes had gone dull, listless.

'My husband was a genius, you know.' She paused for a long time, still looking at something over my shoulder, at something that wasn't there. 'He was a genius and that's why people hated him. None of us want to be truly challenged, Captain. The truth is . . . uncomfortable. A genius must wait, he must die before his ideas can be accepted. You know that, don't you? History loves the pioneer, but his contemporaries despise him. Especially in outposts like this.' She paused again and looked up at me, a vague kind of look that seemed to stop an inch before my face.

'He had a continental mind,' she continued. 'Only on the Continent could his ideas be received properly, without the sanctimony and pious umbrage. The Continent is . . . was the only place where the idea was separate from the man. We're all of us victims of the new Puritanism, Captain. One way or another.'

'Excuse me,' said the counter-lady, who was suddenly, inexplicably standing over our table.

She bent her barrel of a chest across the table and fastidiously stacked our cups and plates onto a tray. I felt as though I had just been awoken from a dream, mid-image. The damned woman was pointedly taking her time and I could see Mrs Walters pick up her small handbag from the ground beside her chair. She started to button her coat.

'Please,' I said, as the counter-lady finally removed herself. 'Don't go. You were going to tell me something about her – weren't you? About Emily. You were about to say something.'

'No.'

'Please.'

'I must go now, Captain. You don't . . . you cannot understand.'

'I'll follow you. She's my wife. I'll beat down the door if I have to.'

'You'll do no such thing, Captain, and you know it.' She stood up, her expression hardening into a frosty, defensive glare. 'You're an honourable man. I know you've tried to do your best for us. But please, leave us now.'

As she made her way through the tables I turned and saw for the first time the gaping looks of our audience. Even the cook, a skinny bald man in a greasy black apron, had come out to watch. Mrs Walters opened the door slowly, the small bell tinkling its bright, merry tune.

'Why?' I said across the room before she stepped through the open frame.

She didn't turn around. She kept her hand on the doorknob, her eyes cast to the ground.

'You wouldn't understand.'

I waited in the tearooms for twenty or thirty minutes before I was able to bring myself to leave. Nobody bothered me. The other diners left soon after Mrs Walters, and the turkey-necked counter-lady set about cleaning the joint around me, giving me a wide berth, not saying a word. I couldn't think of a single thing. There was a messy, inarticulate pain in my chest and head, but it refused definition. I just knew that it hurt and that there was nothing I could do about it.

I found myself walking out of the shop to the bell's glassy music and into the cold, fragrant evening air. A beautiful silvery light glistened in the bleached sky and on the damp grass and trees, and gave the spacious old wooden houses of Parnell a mournful quality.

In New Zealand things were left unsaid.

I walked through the village in a fugue, past pinched old women armed with parcels of meat wrapped in newspaper, past big-eared children dutifully schlepping sacks of potatoes, trays of eggs. I walked on air, on a road made of foam, and eventually found myself back on Ponsonby Road. I had no idea how it happened, how I'd got back so quickly on foot. I started to hear voices again, cars motoring down the centre of the road, people bent together in conversation at a bus stop, the canned roar of a public bar, its hazy orange windows illuminating the murky night like a lighthouse in a squally harbour. I went in.

I sat at the horn end of the horseshoe bar and ordered a scotch. The place was about half full. A group of young Kiwi guys in uniform were standing around a piano singing 'We'll Meet Again' in big, loud, tuneless voices. The heavy air in the room was laced with the usual cocktail of sugary beer fumes, smoke and sweat. I hit my drink and ordered another. My mouth burned with the familiar taste of rotten apples and smoky wood, and as the creature trickled down my throat I could feel myself starting to come back together. A flow of words started to bubble up from somewhere beneath my feet. Pretty soon they were harmonising with the ache in my chest and I started to feel miserable very quickly. I ordered another and told the barkeep to leave the bottle.

I didn't know what to make of it all. When she'd demanded that I take her home that morning on Mount Eden something had happened. I racked my brain, but I couldn't put it down to anything either one of us had said. Even though she had acted queerly, I didn't think I'd heard anything like finality in her voice. And it wouldn't have been like her – what I knew of her – to cast me off without an explanation. But then this. I needed to talk to Emily in person, away from that wretched house, away from her goddamn family. There was something rotten about them, but I knew Emily well enough now to know that she was distant from it somehow. She was a marginal creature like me, and she had all the same marginal resilience. I could see it in her the moment we met. I just needed to get her off her sinking ship.

I had to piss, but as I shuffled off my barstool the scotch ran to my legs and they buckled like a boxer's. I only just managed to catch myself on the rail of the bar, and from that ant's-eye perspective I was surprised to find the bottle of scotch empty.

The Kiwi guys over at the piano cheered loudly.

I looked over and nodded, feeling for the floor with my rubbery feet. I hadn't realised how drunk I was, and it took me a moment to focus my eyes.

I did a scarecrow's stiff-limbed shuffle across the floor. I think I had the vague intention of finding the head, but the door I pushed on blew back an unexpected gust of delicious cold air, and I somehow found myself battling for verticality on Ponsonby Road. I took a couple of baby giraffe steps and felt myself pitch forward into the hood of a parked car. I lay there for an instant, my mind totally clear, and foggily remembered that only a few months ago I had seen the giant Oriental, that enigma of Ponsonby, similarly splayed outside the chess club. As I started to laugh at the symmetry of it, I got a taste of the salty warm tang of blood on my tongue. I wiped my hand across my face and felt a long, thin cut in the middle of my top lip. I gagged for breath, and in doing so took a good gulp of the tepid blood in my mouth. My stomach began to churn. I stood up, seeing everything in threefold, and stumbled my way through the grumbling throng of pedestrians to a nearby trashcan.

The last thing I could remember was the echoey sound of their shouts of disapproval as I buried my head into the stinky tin can, trying for dear life to spit out the roiling contents of my stomach.

CHAPTER 34

Somehow I woke up in my own tent. I had no idea how I got there, and it took me a few seconds to figure out exactly where I was. For a brief, seductive moment I was in the small garret at the top of the Walterses' house, roused from one of those deep, grateful sleeps we often descended into after a bout of lovemaking. But the feeling didn't last long. My stomach was fragile, and as I made to sit up the pillowcase stuck to my cheek so that the pillow lifted clean off the cot. I peeled the thing off the side of my mouth and was concerned to see an archipelago of blood drops on the starched white cotton.

I touched at my face gently and felt a painful, bulbous mound where my lip used to be. I tried to figure it out, but my mind was as blank as a newborn's. Slowly, fitfully, images of the previous night started to flash back to me, each of them coming with a sharp thud to my temples. I remembered the tearooms, the walk back through town to Ponsonby, the pity I had felt for myself as I trudged through the smoky winter evening. I even faintly recalled the glowing orange windows of a public bar, but that was as far as I could get. The fat lip and the fortuitous arrival back at camp were a panicky mystery.

I looked at my watch. The numbers seemed significant somehow, but I was having trouble placing them in any context. And then it came: morning duty; five minutes late already.

I battled my way through the shift, avoiding small talk with the nurses and the few patients who required my attention. I kept myself busy so that I didn't have to think, but some memories – in sepia tinge, worn-out and faded – were determined to foist themselves on me. They were the obvious ones: Mrs Walters demanding that I stay away from her daughter; the sudden change in Emily; both of them telling me I wouldn't understand, without saying what it was I was supposed to not know.

At noon Dr Connors came in to relieve me. Connors was a recent addition to the unit. He'd trained with us at Elliot but had stayed behind in the States while he recovered from a broken ankle he suffered after falling off a high beam on the obstacle course. Something about his neat features and uncomplicated ease with the world around him brought out in me a strange compulsion for mockery.

'You're done here, Sokol,' he said, striding into the post-op where I was feeling the swollen appendix of a nineteen-year-old Marine, who just five days ago had his left leg amputated below the knee. Every time I mentioned the word appendix to him he would burst into uncontrollable, helpless laughter.

'You're always striding, Connors. Whenever I see you, you're striding into a room, striding around the camp. You're a man who strides.'

'And you're a . . . Whoa, what the hell happened to your face?'

'Oh.' The lip was numb and sore, but I'd been too tied up in my own misery to bother with it. 'I, ah, I just tripped.'

'Sounds likely.'

'Yeah, well . . . Hey, what are you doing here, anyway? This is Cartwright's shift.'

'The Colonel's indisposed,' he said, his tone frosting quickly into disapproval. 'Something's afoot. I think it has to do with Timmins. They're all in Ford's office sorting it out. So here I am.'

'What is it?' I asked, feeling brittle and nauseous.

He eyed me carefully before answering, a little piece of individual drama he liked to flash from time to time, his own item of mannered style.

'I don't have the full story,' he said, taking a step towards me and lowering his voice. 'But from what I can gather, it sounds like the dumb asshole's accident may not have been an accident after all.'

'What do you mean?'

He looked over his shoulder and took another small step towards me. 'Apparently,' he whispered, his eyes darting all over the shop as if he were a sparrow with a crust of bread. 'Apparently the brake cable on the truck had been cut. Intentionally.' After a dramatic pause he stepped back, smiled, and straightened up his posture; he'd exhausted his fill of gossipy scandal for one day. 'But don't ask me anything more, Sokol, because I don't know. I'm just a doctor.'

I slung my field coat over my shoulders and stepped outside, trying not to think for a moment. It had gone noon, but the sky still had that dewy morning quality to it, full of watery sunlight and mist. There'd been a lot of rain lately and the camp, or at least the thoroughfares between the tents, had turned into a bog. The air was choked with the stench of stagnant mud and garbage smoke from Perfectus. I was about to step into the mess-hall for a cup of coffee when I heard footsteps behind me, quickly followed by the sharp panting of somebody in a hurry.

'Captain Sokol!'

The voice was without body, trying to be quiet but urgent all at the same time. I turned around to see Sturgis, his face red with exertion, blowing hard in the thick air. He put his damp hand on my shoulder and had to suck a couple of big breaths before he was able to talk.

'Captain Sokol, I'm glad I found you.'

'What is it, Sturgis?' I was in a fragile state and the desperation in his voice rattled me. He'd come to talk about Timmins, I presumed, but I didn't know if I could handle it at that point.

'I was just speaking to . . . Hey, what happened to your face?'

I instinctively brought my hand up to my mouth. 'It's nothing. I just tripped.'

He seemed to lose his train of thought for a moment, and it was all he could do to stand there and stare at my fat purple lip.

'It's nothing. It's fine,' I said. 'Is this about Timmins?'

'What? No. What about him?'

'I just . . . nothing,' I said tiredly, glad that he hadn't yet heard the latest. Not that I believed the latest. I didn't have much faith in Connors's ability to sniff out information; he was too righteous, too clean and honourable – too good a Yankee – to come across that kind of ripe information. If such a thing had happened, Sturgis and Diddle, with their dirty ears perennially to the ground, would have been the first to hear about it. 'I just thought you may have wanted to talk is all,' I said. 'I know I kind of ran out on you yesterday.'

He looked around himself, furtively, and, seeing no one in particular, took me by the arm and shepherded me around the back of the mess-hall where we were out of sight from the rest of the camp.

'What the hell are you doing, man?'

With me safely stowed behind the back of the mess he looked around again, and this time stepped back onto a guy rope running off the corner of the large tent. He stumbled and only just managed to recover his balance. I couldn't help a laugh.

'Listen, Captain,' he whispered and then stopped, looking ominously at my lip again. The look frightened me.

'Jesus, Sturgis, what is it?'

'It's all over Ponsonby, sir. I was up there this morning and all hell's breaking loose. The local cops are everywhere, crawling all over the chink cathouse and the chess club and whatnot.'

He spoke so fast that he was actually stammering over his words, a thing I'd never seen the garrulous bastard do before.

'Slow down, slow down. What's all over Ponsonby?'

'Oscar Walters, sir.'

'What about him?'

'He's dead.'

I felt tired and cold, cold in the mass of my bones, in the gristle of my muscles. The pungent river smell of the camp mud was almost too much to take, and I thought for a moment that I was going to heave. I could feel the burn tickling the back of my throat, but I worked hard to suppress it, drawing a couple of quick deep breaths.

'Dead?'

'Dead, sir.'

I had never seen Sturgis look so young before; it was almost as though I were seeing him for the first time. I shook my head.

'I know, sir. I couldn't believe it either. First Timmins and then this.'

'How . . . I mean, what happened?'

'Nobody knows. His body was found somewhere out back of the garbage depot this morning. Just over yonder,' he said, pointing his arm in the wrong direction. 'Not even a hundred yards away. I can't say for sure, but rumour has it he was stabbed. Get this, in the neck.'

'Jesus.'

'You said it.'

I didn't know what to think. It was shocking, obviously, but for some reason I wasn't all that surprised. It may have been the hangover slowing my reflexes down, but I just couldn't work up the requisite level of surprise I knew I ought to be displaying. If one thought about it long enough, Oscar Walters was always going to end up stabbed in the neck. What with the strange, angry politics, the opium and the whores, it seemed only natural his cold body should be found in a dump in the dead of winter. But he wasn't just any ordinary malcontent, my addled brain started to realise with dismay. He was my wife's brother.

'Sir.'

'What?' I snapped. I'd almost forgotten Sturgis was there in front of me.

'Um, sir. This is, ah, how should I put this?'

'Put what, for chrissake?'

I recognised the look on his innocent face and it worried the hell out of me. It was the look that doctors reserve for telling a mother that her son hadn't survived the surgery.

'Um,' he continued, contorting his face into an anxious wince, 'it's like . . . ah, hell, I hate to say this Captain. But a lot of people up in Ponsonby just now – well, they were talking about the fight the other day. About how you kind of, you know, hit him. Walters, that is.'

He said the last sentence almost as if he were apologising. I had been so wrapped up in thinking about Emily that the fight hadn't even occurred to me. But I could see the terrible logic of it, though, the preponderance of evidence, even if it were only circumstantial.

'Who was talking about it?' I asked, my throat tightening.

'Most everybody, sir.'

I looked at him but didn't know what to say.

'It's more than that, though,' Sturgis said. He took a step towards me and checked over his shoulder for the third time. 'Listen, I was just speaking to Diddle, and, well, one of the local cops is in there with Ford now. As we speak.'

'In with Ford?'

'And Colonel Cartwright. Ford got Diddle to patch a call through to Colonel Green as well. He's, ah, he's on his way.'

'And ... and what are they talking about, Sturgis?' I listened to the words as they left my mouth, all brittle and dislocated. The poor kid was having a hell of a time breaking it to me.

'They know you were out last night; that you snuck out. They think,' he said, now looking as if he were expecting a blow to the face, 'they think it might have been you that done it.'

I didn't say anything. I couldn't even motivate myself to search the black hole in my memory.

'Diddle said that, well, it looks as though they'll want to talk to you. Pretty soon like.'

I brought my hand up to my face, slowly and deliberately, and felt with dread the bulbous, tender mound on my lip. I knew how it looked; I could see that it looked bad even to Sturgis. To Ford and Cartwright it would be as good as a signed confession.

'Were you in my tent when I got back last night?' I asked.

'What?' The question seemed to strike him as particularly bizarre. 'No. You don't remember?'

'So you weren't there?'

'No. I mean, I heard the M.P. look in at midnight. He must have got tired of standing out there in the cold and took off. I went back to the dorm about fifteen minutes later. I won't lie to you, Captain. I was pretty damn upset last night. Oki's a fucking disaster zone, can't stop blubbering.'

We both spent a tense few seconds looking at the boggy ground. I badly wanted to lie down for a few minutes, just so I could put my head back together, but when I looked up I could see that Sturgis still had more to say.

'What is it, Sturgis? Just get it over with.'

'I think,' he said, scrunching up his face into a prune again, 'I think Colonel Cartwright knows about the wedding.'

'Oh, Jesus. You're kidding me, right?'

''Fraid not, sir.'

'How?'

'It was after the fight the other day. What Oscar Walters said about you being married to a whore and all. He started asking round and eventually got to the padre.'

I closed my eyes and breathed in the pungent air. I listened to the sounds of a few of the men playing touch football in the muddy yard just on the other side of the mess. The harder I tried to recall the events of the previous night the more I seemed to forget. I had managed to trace my steps into the bar, and to the sugary burn of my first scotch, but that was it. From that point there was nothing but a yawning black hole until my heathen awakening this morning. I could see that Sturgis was waiting, hoping for me to say something in my defence, anything to redeem his misguided faith in me.

'I, um, I better get going, Sturgis,' I said pathetically. 'I need to get some shut-eye for a bit.'

I patted him on the shoulder. The look in his eyes was almost more than I could bear. For some reason the kid looked up to me as a kind of role model, an avuncular figure who indulged his idiosyncrasies and premature talents. He wanted an assurance that he hadn't been let down.

'I didn't do this, Sturgis,' I said, as much for his sake as anything else. It seemed to do the job. I just hoped I was right.

'Oh, sir,' he duly protested, 'I wasn't, you know, I never meant to suggest that—'

'I know.'

I started to walk away without any thought as to where I would go. I wanted to sleep, but I knew I couldn't just go back to my tent and wait, like a rabbit in headlights, for the onslaught.

'Are you going to see Colonel Ford, sir?'

I stopped, my back to Sturgis, and felt at my lip again. The math was simple and it had the kind of economical elegance that a guy like Ford would warm to: the secret wedding plus the fight plus the break from tent arrest plus the mangled face. Plus the dipshit accused, who mysteriously didn't have the memory to confirm or deny a single thing.

'Because if you're not,' Sturgis continued, his tone back to its cryptic, cunning best, 'Private Yardley is taking the ambulance up to the Thirty-ninth to drop off some bedding. He'll be leaving in like, I don't know, three or four minutes.'

I waited a moment before responding. It would mean going AWOL for the second time in twenty-four hours. It would, in their eyes, be tantamount to guilt. If I left they could put me before a firing squad without so much as a trial. But if I stayed. If I stayed I was as good as guilty anyway; I had nothing with which to meet the accusation when it came. If I stayed, I would never see Emily again.

'From the east gate?'

'From the east gate, sir.'

CHAPTER 35

Private Yardley didn't suspect a thing. I wedged myself into a triangle of space between the side of the ambulance and a stack of upright mattresses. When the vehicle came to a stop and Yardley cut the engine I simply let myself out and walked quickly away in whatever direction it was I was facing. I moved fast, head down, hands thrust deep into my pockets, heedless of the direction I was taking. After a few minutes I finally looked up, and to my surprise and dumb good fortune, I found that I'd managed to walk straight out of the Thirty-ninth hospital grounds and into the undulating green of Cornwall Park itself.

It wasn't until I stood on the side of that hill, staring directly back at the misty aspect of Freemans Bay and the direction I'd come from, that it occurred to me that I may have made the wrong decision. I didn't know where I was heading or what I was going to do, but I kept moving, getting myself onto a dirt path that wound down to the bottom of the hill.

There were so many thoughts exploding in my head all at once that it was difficult to follow a single one through. But for the first time since Sturgis had broken the news to me a little less than an hour ago, I made myself confront the obvious question. The idea that I could kill a man, even a man like Oscar Walters, seemed laughable. I hadn't, before coming to New Zealand, had anything like the kind of constitution required to stab another man in the neck. That sort of thing demanded a certain wilfulness, a recklessness or passion that I simply didn't have. But what troubled me, in the absence of memory, were the changes I'd noticed in myself since I'd fallen in love with Emily. Ugly things like manic possessiveness, rabid and irrational jealousy, a general dimming of my view of human nature now that I had something to lose. Maybe the elemental need that coursed through me daily, making me sick with wanting, had turned me into a person capable of murder. I couldn't rule it out.

But whether I did the thing or not was only part of the problem. They thought it was me. The evidence made it look as though it was me.

I thought it more likely Oscar had come to his grisly end at the hands of one or another of the Orientals he'd been fighting. If he had killed that whore, it would go a long way to explaining his sudden departure. I just had to find something – something tangible – that I could use to convince the people that mattered that my hunch was right. It was my only shot.

At the bottom of the hill the dirt track levelled off into a flat expanse of green, where a few black and white dairy cows were happily grazing. About twenty or thirty yards ahead were the busy sounds of Remuera Road. I slowed down; I needed a plan before I put myself back into the world. I still felt terribly hung-over, and the willing of an idea or a course of action didn't come easy. I made myself stop and think, reduce the situation down to its bare bones, its constituent parts. If they didn't know already, it wouldn't be long before Cartwright and Ford, and the local constabulary, figured out that I had gone AWOL. Which meant that pretty soon they'd be out looking for me. Which meant that I had no choice but to see Emily now. The Walterses' house would be the first place that Cartwright would look, especially now that he knew we were married. I searched my pockets for the money I had quickly stuffed in them before fleeing the camp. Twenty-two bucks U.S.

I ran to Remuera Road, suddenly fired with a plan, and weaved my way through the foot traffic of shoppers until I found a cab.

I rang the front doorbell a few times but nobody answered. I tried the handle but the door was locked. They had to know by now. Perhaps they were at the police station still, being grilled about their dealings with me these past months, my state of mind, my queer characteristics and predilections. I trusted Emily but had no doubt that Mrs Walters would leave me for dead. I would be shorn from her experience and memory like the culture and religion she had so clinically left behind.

I peered in through the front windows, but there were no signs of life. If they were at home they would be in the sitting room out back. I checked the driveway for police cars before heading up the long, narrow path that cut through the tall hedgerows at the side of the house. When I came into the clearing at the far end, I made my way to the steps leading up to the sagging back porch. The deep, sloping yard had turned into a swampland of muck and rainwater. I was about to put my muddied boot onto the first step when I heard a loud clanging sound somewhere behind me. I looked around, fearing the worst, but there was nothing there. This is what life would be like for me now; I would be a man scared of noises, hearing in every unexpected sound the cold voice of fate.

I made to spring up the stairs when I heard another noise, loud and clear this time, coming from the direction of the shed. It had to be Winston. I tracked back across the sodden stretch of lawn, careful not to come upon him too quickly. As

I approached I heard the soft murmur of a voice, but couldn't quite make out the words.

'Winston,' I called apprehensively. 'It's me, Peter Sokol.' There was no response, but I heard a scurrying sound come from within the shed. I went around to the front, where two wide, barn-like doors were swung open. 'Winston?'

It was him all right, and I got the distinct impression I'd caught him in the act of something he would rather have kept concealed.

'Oh. Yes. Hullo. Captain Sokol,' he said from behind his dark glasses.

I couldn't see his face in the murky darkness of the cluttered shed, but what I did see surprised me. He was trying to secure an enormous black throw-cloth over a car of some description, a Whippet perhaps. Just then I thought I saw something move behind him, something quick and flickering in the dingy gloom.

'Is somebody in there, Winston?'

He clamped his mouth shut and puffed up his gaunt, sallow cheeks, the gnarled patch of paralysis holding firm.

'Somebody in shed? Just me in shed.'

I looked over his shoulder but couldn't see anything. I waved my question away with a flap of my hand. I looked down at my feet, down at the deep indentations the wheels had made on the boggy ground, like trenches in the Somme. He must have just been out.

'I didn't know you had a motor,' I said.

He finished covering the thing and slowly emerged from the darkness, his generous frame bent forward in weariness. He looked like a benign giant in one of those English fairytales, strangely bespectacled and looming. He used an oily, soiled rag to wipe his hands.

'Yes,' he said guardedly. 'Motor vehicle.'

'Right. Have you just been out?'

'Errand. For Mrs Walters.'

We were both standing away from the shed now and in the light, where I could see the reflection of my tired face in his black lenses. I wondered whether he saw what I was seeing. Whatever he could make out, I could tell he wasn't all that pleased to see me; in fact, I thought for a moment he might offer to escort me off the grounds.

'This way,' he said, pointing up at the back porch. 'Mrs Walters. Upset.'

I nodded gravely and followed him in silence up to the porch. For some reason he didn't open the door, but knocked a couple of times on one of the dining room windows. I looked in to see if anyone was coming, and when I finally heard a stirring from within, I turned back to see that Winston had left me, and was lumbering back across the sodden lawn to the shed.

I waited for the back door to open, but nothing happened. Perhaps they hadn't heard. I made my way down to the far end of the porch, which stopped just shy of the large sash windows of the sitting room. As I approached the windows I could see the glow of the fire in the small iron hearth. I stretched my torso over the porch railing and craned my neck to look in. They were both there. Emily was sitting up on the chaise longue, her face buried in her hands. I could see from the way that she rocked back and forth that she was crying. The sight of her like that made me feel sick. Mrs Walters stood next to her, one hand resting gingerly on Emily's shoulder. She was saying something to her, talking passionately, emphatically, her free hand cutting out a whole grammar of punctuation in the air.

They gave every appearance of not wanting to be disturbed, but my time was tight. I knew that this would be the last chance I would have to see her before facing the music, one way or another. I gently tapped on the grimy windowpane. They both jumped in fright, and it took them a moment to

307

recover themselves and identify me. It was dark and gloomy outside, and Mrs Walters was having a difficult time making out the lonely figure in the window. She took a few tentative steps towards the window before she realised who it was. I tried to see behind her to Emily, but the old woman had effectively blocked my view. She was mouthing words that I couldn't make out, but whatever they were they didn't seem to be at all welcoming.

Suddenly I heard the door swing open back down the far end of the porch.

'Oh, Peter. Peter!'

It was Emily. We looked at each other for a tense moment, the length of a back porch between us. Her verdigris eyes lit up the steely evening gloom like a pair of pilot lights at sea. She was wearing a pleated formal dress, black for mourning I supposed. I took a step towards her and stopped.

'Peter.'

'Yes.'

She ran towards me and tackled me in a desperate embrace. Her cheeks were damp and sticky with tears. She cupped my face in her hands and pulled me down into a hot, hurried kiss. Her thin, willowy body was familiar in my arms and I pulled her tight, feeling the taut wiriness of her limbs press against me. The sensation of holding her again was enough to make me burst.

'Peter,' she said again, burying her face into the crook of my neck. 'Thank God you came. I'm so sorry for—'

'Captain!'

I looked up in fright. Mrs Walters, also dressed entirely in black, was standing at the other end of the porch, arms hanging tensely at her sides as if she were about to draw a six-shooter on me.

'Captain, you should leave immediately,' she said spitefully. 'Don't you know what has happened?'

308

I thought I heard in her tone a half-formed accusation, but I couldn't be sure. I had no skill in reading these people at all.

'I'm sorry,' I said. 'I have heard.'

Emily still clung to me, the side of her face pressed against my chest. Maybe she was just upset, but it seemed to me that she was keeping her back turned on her mother for a reason. It was as if she were making a decision.

'Then you shouldn't be here,' Mrs Walters cried. 'You know what the police are saying about you? Don't you?'

'Mother!' Emily pulled away from me and squared off against Mrs Walters. She held my hand tightly. 'Mother, go back inside.'

'You know you have to let him go.'

'Now!'

I wasn't quite sure what I was witnessing. I'd known that Emily maintained a certain independence from her mother, but I hadn't encountered anything like this before. Mrs Walters hovered for a moment, unsure of her ground. She was just about to reluctantly step back inside when she looked back at us.

'I imagine you rue the day you met this family, Captain.' It was like a challenge, a slap in the face with a leather glove.

'No, I don't, ma'am,' I said firmly.

Emily's grip on my hand tightened. I pulled her closer to me.

'Then you are a fool. A blind American fool.' And then, as an afterthought, she added, 'Perhaps my son was right. You Americans are too innocent for your own good. Your motives can never be impeached, can they? Yes. I think he may have been right. You'll end up ruining us all with your wretched innocence.'

The door closed behind her. Before I had a chance to swallow what she'd said, though, Emily was pulling me by the hand across the porch and down the stairs. We ran through the muck like giddy children, back past Winston's shed and into the cover of the hedgerows. When we'd made it to the side of the house she literally flung me up against the wet, prickly face of the hedge and pinned me there in a bear hug.

'I'm so sorry, Peter.'

'Don't apologise.'

'You know I love you. I wouldn't have married you if I didn't. Please . . . just please believe that.'

Hearing those few words was, and probably still remains, the singular moment of my life. I squeezed her tightly, trying to pull her inside of me, unable to get close enough.

'I love you too.'

'I didn't think you would come back,' she said, trying to suppress another round of tears.

'Listen,' I said, pushing her back slightly so I could see her face. 'I don't have much time. They think I killed Oscar, but I promise you, I didn't. You probably heard about the fight I had with him, but—'

She put her hand up to my mouth to stop me talking. Her forefinger rested gently on the swollen mound of my top lip, but curiously she didn't remark upon it. It didn't seem unusual to her. I could see she wanted to say something, was about to say something, but her beautiful face just creased in confusion and nothing came. I gently took her hand away from my face.

'I can't stay,' I said, looking anxiously up and down the path. I had a shadowy feeling that a hand was about to reach out at any moment and grab me. 'I promise you I didn't do it, but I've got a fair idea who did. He was mixed up with some Orientals in Ponsonby, and I'm pretty sure—'

'No,' she said, and left it at that.

I waited for her to continue, but she just looked at me, her eyes glassy and vacant.

'Emily. I need you to know that I didn't do it. You've got to—'

310

'I know you didn't, Peter.' Her voice was calm, but I was too frantic to properly appreciate the change that had come over her.

'I think he may have killed one of their women,' I said, unable to control the trilling panic in my voice. 'One of their prostitutes.'

Everything went silent for a moment. She looked up at me, open-mouthed, ashen. I could almost see the blood draining from her face. I had a horrible feeling that I'd overstepped the mark, but I couldn't wait any longer, I didn't have time for subtlety. She had to understand it wasn't me.

'I have to go,' I said, taking her by both thin arms and making her look into my eyes.

The news I had just delivered, perhaps a little irresponsibly, had deeply shaken her. She seemed to be floating in a kind of daze. 'They'll look for me here for sure. But I'll be back as soon as I can. I just need to clear myself is all. Then I'll be back, I promise.'

I kissed her again, but she was barely responsive. It took all my strength to let her go, but when I did, and had actually taken a few steps back down the path, she called out.

'Peter.'

I turned back to face her. 'Yes?'

'I want to paint.'

'What?'

'Remember the other day? On Mount Eden. You asked me what I wanted to do when I got to San Francisco.'

Her voice seemed disembodied, all tinny and hollow. She seemed barely in control of herself, as if a gust of wind would send her up and over the hedgerows. I didn't recognise her at that moment – the voice, the posture, the vacant look in her eyes; she was foreign to me.

'Yes,' I said.

'Well, I've decided. I want you to teach me how to paint.

I want to be your apprentice.'

'I would be honoured.' I backed down the path, unable to take my eyes off her. When I got to the front of the house she was still facing me, the wind blowing her thick chestnut hair, already a ghost.

CHAPTER 36

I made my way back to Parnell Village on foot, and headed straight for the nearest menswear store. The clerk was a wheezy fellah of around seventy who wore a tweed three-piece suit, thick eyeglasses, and a tape measure draped across his shoulders like a scarf. He regarded me with a kind of cool, formal politeness that I nervously interpreted as suspicion, but turned out to be little more than that peculiar brand of Kiwi deadpan that most U.S. servicemen had such a difficult time understanding.

I shelled out for a pair of navy blue slacks, a woollen charcoal overcoat that would cover my olive-drab shirt, and a black fedora. The clothes cleaned me out, and by the time I left the store I had barely enough money left for the cross-town tram.

I rode the tram back to Ponsonby in studied anonymity, taking a seat in the back corner, where a couple of war-age local males slouched invisibly, a morose blight on their country's national spirit. While it may have been heading back into the eye of the storm, I felt I had little choice but to go back to Ponsonby. If I was going to have any hope of clearing myself I needed help, and the only people I knew who could help me were all there. Seeing Emily, knowing that she did love me, had a galvanising effect. The risk I was taking was no longer in vain. I had something to work for other than just self-preservation.

I got out at the top of K' Road and walked anonymously through the evening crowd. Before I knew it, before I'd even had a chance to let the dust settle in my whirling head, I realised I'd stumbled blindly halfway up Ponsonby Road. I looked around at the familiar setting, at the ridge of the gully that swept down into Western Park, down towards the dump, and panicked. This was it. I'd wandered back into the scene of the crime. I chastened myself for being so careless, and quickly ducked down the next available side street. It was a quarter-to-five. I knew that Sturgis would be coming off duty in fifteen minutes, and, all things being equal, he would be heading straight for the Birdcage.

I zigzagged my way down through the cottaged side streets of Freemans Bay, cutting through Paget and Heke until I was three-quarters of the way down Franklin Road. I couldn't get too close to the camp, but needed to catch Sturgis on the hop. I made my way around to the alleyway, which was sandwiched between the east wall of the garbage depot and the back of the Birdcage's lounge bar. I was gambling on him crossing College Hill from the west gate of the camp and breaking to the left, which he occasionally did, rather than taking the more direct route through the east gate.

I waited for twenty minutes, but nothing. It had started to rain, and the sky had gone almost completely black now, making it hard to get a clear sight of the scores of people coming across the busy intersection at College Hill. By quarter to six I was wet and cold, and about ready to throw the towel in when it dawned on me that I had nowhere to go. I was so bent up with this thought, and with the hunger pains stinging my stomach, that I felt like collapsing. And I may have done so if I hadn't heard the footsteps coming up the pavement beside the depot. I moved up a little closer to the dim paraffin street lamp, which threw off a limp, blood-orange, haloed light, barely enough for me to make out the silhouette coming my way. I recognised the gait, the controlled swagger of the spindly legs, the hands buried in hip pockets, shoulders hunched forward as if he were walking into a Chicago breeze.

'Sturgis,' I whispered into the night.

The figure stopped and I held my breath, the blood ringing a symphony in my ears, my heart almost jumping out of my new coat.

'Captain?'

The relief was beyond measure, a feeling of true weightlessness. I was thrilled to hear everything about that voice – its uncertain timbre, the childish raised inflection at the end.

'Captain,' he said again. 'Is that you?'

'Sturgis. It's me. Come back here.'

When I saw him come I moved back myself, away from the glow of the streetlamp.

'Captain,' he said again, taking my hand and squeezing it in both of his. He seemed happy to see me at first, but as I moved round to get a better look at him in the light something in his expression changed. 'I knew I'd find you here. I just knew it,' he said, the tone unreadable, his expression a little distant.

We were about halfway down the alley now and standing in total darkness. It was difficult to even make out the features on his baby face.

'What's the latest?' I asked, trying to regulate my breathing.

'It's gone fucking nuts here today, man.'

'Are they looking for me?'

'You bet your ass they're looking for you. Ford's got M.P.s out combing every place in town. Local cops too. Everybody's in. Plus the reporters. I swear to God, I've never seen anything like it. Ford's tearing his hair out. The local press guys are refusing to adhere to the blackout, and the word is they're going to print your name and picture on the evening edition. Radio as well. Diddle's got the whole fucking scoop.'

He was so swept up in the story, in the narrative of my hunting, that I think he forgot I was there for a second. I'd anticipated the local cops investigating, but the press coverage was unexpected and worrying. New clothes or not, if my mug was on the evening paper then there was nowhere I could go.

'That's not all, though,' he said, eyeing me queerly, unsure of himself.

'What?'

He looked up the long dark alley and blew a cloud of steam out into the sepia-tinged night. It seemed to take an age for him to turn back to me, and when he did so, I didn't like the mistrust I saw in his saucer eyes.

'It's about Timmins,' he said slowly. He appeared to be trying to gauge my response. 'I just got this from Diddle a half-hour ago, so nothing is confirmed.'

'What are you telling me?'

He looked back over his shoulder, but it was an empty gesture; he knew there was nobody there.

'The brake cable on the truck was cut. Somebody tried to murder him. Somebody did fucking murder him.'

This was too much. I didn't know what to make of it. If Connors, Diddle and Sturgis were all singing from the same hymn sheet, it had to be genuine.

'This is New Zealand. I mean, why the hell would anybody do that?'

'You tell me,' he said quietly, challengingly.

All of a sudden I was deeply, bitterly angry. I didn't need any light to see what the little fucker was thinking. 'Be careful, Sturgis. Be careful about what you say here, buddy.'

'I'm not saying anything, Captain. I—'

I grabbed him by the lapels of his fatigue coat and threw him up against the brick wall that backed onto the garbage depot. I held him up a few inches off the ground, alarmed at my own strength, the force of my anger.

316

'What are you telling me, Sturgis? Do you think I killed Timmins? Is that—'

'Put me down you son-of-a-bitch!'

The words sucked the air out of my chest, choking me in a kind of waking night terror, and just like that my spell of rage was over. I eased him down off the wall and removed my hands from his coat, terrified of myself, sick to the stomach.

'Jesus Christ,' I whispered, looking up and down the alley in a daze. 'Jesus, I . . . I'm sorry, Sturgis. I'm . . .'

He stood where he was and straightened himself up. His eyes had lost their challenging daring and were only filled with hurt now.

'Sturgis, I'm sorry . . . I'm sorry, buddy, I—'

'Why did you leave yesterday?' he asked angrily, all wounded and nineteen years old. 'I mean, you just found out he'd been killed. And all you can think of is busting camp to fuck your girlfriend. I . . . I thought you cared about us, Captain.'

This was better than him thinking I killed Timmins, but just as bad time-wise. As much as I wanted to console the poor bastard, I knew I was a sitting duck out there in the open like that.

'It's complicated,' I said, realising I had tried unsuccessfully to use this fob-off on him once before. 'Of course I give a damn about Timmins. And I didn't leave to go and fuck anybody. I just . . . I just had to go. You've got to trust me on this one.'

He looked at the ground, but I could see by the loose fall of his shoulders that I'd mollified him.

'Listen,' I said with an urgent tone, trying to steer him back. 'You know I can't be hanging around out here like this. I need you to tell me what you know. About this Oscar Walters business, I mean.'

He looked up at me, his baby face all puffy and sullen. 'I

317

can tell you that the locals are foaming at the mouth. Guys with bats and shit out looking for you.'

'Jesus.'

'You said it.'

'Does Yardley know that he helped me escape?'

'Dumb bastard doesn't have a clue. No one knows how you got out.' He even allowed himself a laugh here, a short diabolical chuckle. 'No one but me, that is.'

'Why are the locals after me?' It was a stupid question, but I had to remind myself that I was innocent, or that at least I hoped I was. The response was as expected.

'What, are you kidding? Think about how pissed they got with us stealing their women – times that by ten. You're the face of American whatever. Arrogance. Assholeness. They want to crucify you.'

'All right, all right,' I said, placing my hand on his shoulder. 'That's enough. I get the picture.'

It seemed to me a fait accompli now. I was the guilty man; I would be found and shot to appease the ally. There was no point continuing with this hare-brained scheme anyway, not if vigilante groups were after me.

He was silent for a moment.

'Sorry, Captain. I just . . .'

'Don't worry.'

'But all the guys – everybody back at the hospital – they all know you didn't do it.'

'Listen, I can't stick around here. Have you got any money on you?'

'Not a dime, sorry.'

'How are you planning on drinking?'

'I ain't out here to drink. Even if I wanted to. All leave's been cancelled.'

'What are you doing then?'

'What do you think? I'm looking for you.'

318

'Jesus Christ,' I muttered, hearing in my small voice a tone of helplessness that I hadn't realised was coming. 'What the hell am I going to do?'

'Oki knows that giant chink son-of-a-bitch, and reckons he had a thing against Oscar Walters and all those chess sons-of-bitches. There's one whore he sees regular and she speaks a bit of English. She must have learned it off all the G.I.s she's banged, if you can fathom that. A sentimental education. He's going to try to see her tomorrow to get the word. He reckons she'll spill, seeing as she hates that giant. He's a pimp and all, Captain.'

'That's good, right? I mean, it had to be them. You saw the way they were trying to get at him the other day.'

'Right.'

'And if O'Keefe can dig up something then, well, case closed. Right?'

'Right,' he said, as earnestly as a boy scout.

'This has got to go through the local police, though,' I said, checking my enthusiasm for a moment. 'The M.P.s and Ford will never buy it. We've got to get O'Keefe to tell the cops, so they'll look in on the brothel and question all those Orientals.'

'That's exactly what we got to do, sir.'

He was excited, exuberant even, and he was my only hope, but I still couldn't help resenting the drama in his voice, the sense of high adventure. While he was living out his Hemingway fantasy, I was the one who had no place to sleep. And on cue, the drizzle that had been falling for a while now turned into rain, hard straight rain like in the movies.

'Ah, hell,' I said, looking skyward, holding my palms up to the heavens. 'Where am I going to go?'

'You can't go to . . . I mean, your wife?'

'No, they'll be watching that place like hawks.'

'Hey, what about Mrs Taylor? The cake lady. They mightn't think to look there.'

I thought about it for a moment, suspended in the miserable night, and couldn't think of an obvious counter-argument.

'That's not a bad idea,' I said cautiously, watching the steam cloud in front of my mouth, still trying to mull the implications.

'I think it'll work,' Sturgis said, highly pleased with himself again.

There was no other option. 'All right. Meet me there at six tomorrow morning. And bring O'Keefe.'

'What if she doesn't let you in?'

'Just meet me there anyway. If I have to sleep rough I'll go back there at six.'

'All right. It's a plan.'

'And bring O'Keefe.'

'Yes, sir.'

I slapped him on the shoulder and headed up the alleyway in the opposite direction, hugging the depot wall to avoid the full force of the rain.

'Captain,' called Sturgis.

I turned and could only just make out the outline of his figure against the shallow light of the streetlamp. He hadn't moved.

'Good luck,' he said.

CHAPTER 37

She let me in. I was sodden wet, and I had to spend three minutes explaining who I was through the closed front door, but in the end she let me in. When she finally opened the frosted glass door a magnificent wave of cooking smells flooded out of the house and enveloped me in the bitter night air, almost bringing me to my knees. She held a pair of kitchen tongs in her hand. Her round cheeks were flushed scarlet and there was a thin film of sweat on her brow.

'I'm sorry to call on you like this,' I said, trying to swallow the deep awkwardness I felt standing shivering in the dark at her front door. 'But it's just that, ah, I'm—'

'The police came here this morning.' She spoke slowly, her vowels crunched down to grist. 'They asked me if I'd seen you.'

'The police? You mean the M.P.s. Americans.'

'No. The police. The Auckland police.'

I wasn't sure how to take this. If the local cops had thought to come here, then there was a good chance they would keep watching the place. On the other hand, they may have simply crossed it off their list and moved on.

'Right,' I said, taking off my hat and running my wet hand through my flattened hair, trying not too subtly to drop the hint. 'As I was saying, I'm in a spot at the moment and I'd be awful grateful if—'

'I'm sorry,' she said, her tone measured and cautious. 'You're wet. Do come in.'

She led me straight into the bathroom off to the left of the hallway, and switched on a light that buzzed like a small engine. The icy air in the bathroom was stung with the metallic smell of soap and ammonia. She handed me a towel, all stiff and scratchy from its air-drying, and watched as I dried off my face and hands. I then followed her into the warm, glowing kitchen at the end of the hall, where a roasted leg of what looked like mutton was cooling on the stovetop. The windows looking out into the back garden were white with condensation.

'Please, sit down, Captain.'

The oppressiveness in the house I'd felt on my previous two visits was still there, dense in the close atmosphere. I was conscious of every breath, every movement. She poured me a mug of tea from a pale blue enamel pot and sat down opposite me at the small kitchen table. The smell of the meat was making my mouth water, and I had to swallow hard to get the tepid tea down. I couldn't help taking a look at the framed picture of her son on the wall behind her, and wondered whether she had been cooking for him.

'I'm sorry to barge in on you like this,' I began, 'but I just didn't know where else to go.' She was looking at me intently, but the expression was so nondescript that I couldn't even begin to guess what she was thinking. 'I'm not sure what the police told you, ma'am, but I—'

'Please, Captain,' she interjected, her open hand up in the air as if she were stopping a vehicle. 'You don't have to tell me anything.'

I leant back in my chair. I felt exhausted. 'Thank you.'

I watched her in a daze as she considered what to say next, feeling curiously absent from the scene.

'Are you hungry?'

Thank God. 'Yes, ma'am.'

She looked mildly elated as she padded her way over to the stove and carved off some slices of meat. She loaded a plate full of roasted vegetables – potatoes and parsnips and pumpkin.

'Do you like gravy?' she asked, looking at me sideways with an almost mischievous grin. She looked happy in the way she'd been happy stuffing Sturgis's face with cakes, taking pleasure in seeing to a man's hunger.

'You bet,' I said, getting in on the act.

'Good.'

For all her proportions, her generous girth, the squat frame, she moved around the kitchen like a dancer in the Bolshoi, nimble and swift with tea towels and meat forks and carving knives. It was a pleasure to see her happy, or at least happily distracted, but it was a feeling laced with heartbreak. I couldn't help thinking that I was probably the first person she'd cooked for since her son had sailed away from her on his abstract mission.

'Do you like the radio, Captain?' she asked, eagerly.

'Sure.'

'Sometimes I like to listen at night. It's nice hearing the voices.'

'I know what you mean.'

She was looking up at the black lacquered beast at the far end of the kitchen, an old RCA model perhaps, which was housed in a glass-fronted cabinet.

'Why don't you put it on?' I encouraged.

She looked at me nervously, the tips of her fingers touching the side of her glowing cheek. She genuinely seemed to need my approval.

'Should I?'

'Absolutely.'

This seemed to please her immensely. She wiped her hand on the fawn apron wrapped around her bubble waist and snapped the old thing on with a resonant click. It was marginally off-tune, and she had to play around with one of the knobs to hit the station. Finally a chorus of horns emerged through the crackle.

' "Little Brown Jug",' I said.

'The gravy?'

'No. The song. That's the name of the song.'

'Oh.' She brought her fingers to her cheek again and looked at the ground, not knowing what to say.

'It's a good one,' I said, feeling faint.

I ate the Everest of food she'd piled on my plate with my head down, shoulders hunched forward as if I were outdoors, just finished hunting some magnificent beast, sitting beside a campfire in the open air. I ate without chewing at times, and it wasn't until I'd scaled half the plate that I realised she wasn't joining me. She sat at the opposite end of the table watching me shovel one load of food into my mouth after another. The colour in her cheeks had gone down and she looked almost serene.

The radio had been busy pushing out the syrupy tunes, but at the end of one of them came a series of five short beeps followed by a long, drawn-out one. And then the dulcet tones of a newsreader. Naturally, I was the lead story.

Murder of a Parnell man, Oscar Michael Walters, otherwise known as Oscar Mykel Wasserman. Found early this morning near the municipal rubbish depot. Captain Peter Sokol, Third Division of the United States Marine Corps. Stationed at Victoria Park. Surgeon. Suspect. On the run. Manhunt.

The food I'd stuffed in my mouth was still sitting in my chest. I laid down my knife and fork, and it took all my will to bring my eyes up to her face. She was looking at me as if I were a cancer patient, with a mixture of pity and naked fear. Her eyes were almost perfectly circular in her head, a cow's eyes, and her lips were slightly parted, jaw gone slack.

324

I cleared my throat and pushed my plate away.

'I can leave. If you want me to. I would understand.'

She seemed so confused by my words that I half wondered whether I'd said them in a foreign tongue. She seemed to fall into something, some mental drift or void, a disappearance I could see in her glazed eyes. I cleared my throat again, the food starting to repeat on me, and she came back with a shake of the head, as if somebody had just pinched a nerve in her spine, or stepped on her grave.

'No. No, please don't go.'

'I don't want to get you in trouble,' I said, and meant it. I knew enough about the law to realise that she'd now become an accessory after the fact. I didn't want to have her on my conscience, but my body was spent. Now that I'd stopped eating I could barely move my arms. I pushed my chair back and made to stand up.

'No, Captain. Please stay. I want you to stay,' she said, getting to her feet.

I believed her too. When she saw that I had relented – it hadn't taken much – she sat back down. For a moment I thought she was going to smile.

'I guess you know my secret,' I said. I couldn't be bothered defending myself, declaring my innocence and all the rest, and to be honest I don't think she was particularly interested one way or the other. I had the impression that I could have cut the throat of every man in Ponsonby and she still would have fed me.

There was absolutely nothing to say, and the bald fact of this was like a corpse sitting at the table with us. Finally she stood up and started to clear the table, taking my plate. The introduction of movement into the room, the stirring of molecules in the air around us, seemed to release the pressure valve slightly. I stood up as well, automatically, and helped her with the washing up, being more of a nuisance than anything, but I had to move, to shake out the rot of tiredness seeping into my bones. I kept getting in her way, and after a while I could see that my intrusion into her domain was upsetting her more than my radio legend.

'You sit down, dear,' she said. 'You look tired.'

Dear. I was a fugitive, for all she knew a murderer, but out of nowhere I had become dear. I didn't want to sit down again, but there was nowhere else to go. Without thinking I started looking at things on the walls, a clock with roman numerals, a pocket-sized icon of the Virgin Mary, the portrait of her dead son. I turned guiltily to the right; she was standing at the kitchen sink, her chubby arms buried in soapy water, looking at me.

'I'm sorry,' I said and lowered my eyes.

She rattled some cutlery at the bottom of the sink, the dishwater gone murky brown now.

'You don't have to be sorry.'

I quietly sat back down again, in the chair that she'd just been in. It seemed important to sit down, as if it were an act of contrition, a mark of respect. As I waited for her to say something, Emily inexplicably popped in to my mind, as sudden and unexpected as a stranger at a window. The image seemed important, but I couldn't follow it.

'His name was Peter. Like yours,' she said, her arms still submerged, but she wasn't washing anything now. 'That photograph was taken on his eighteenth birthday. He was killed three months later, to the day.'

I waited for the outpouring like last time, the crumbling into raw grief, but she held herself. In fact, her voice was strangely measured and controlled, even a little distant. She must have pulled out the plug in the sink because there was a sharp gurgling sound of spinning water that took me off-guard.

She dried her hands and sat down opposite me, hesitating

before she did so, letting me know that this wasn't her chair.

'I raised him by myself. His father, Norman, died when Peter was only four. A work accident on the wharf. I used to take Peter down to the harbour on the anniversary of his death every year. He loved ships and boats.' She smiled briefly and touched her eye with the side of her forefinger, just one dab. 'He was so excited when he enlisted. All he could talk about was North Africa. Places I'd never heard of, never dreamed existed. El Alamein. Sidi Rezegh.'

She looked at me and smiled hopelessly, still confounded by the exotic place names, as if they held a certain secret about her son that she couldn't understand. I imagined her alone in this tiny house, receiving the news, the telegram, the knock at the door. She'd borne it in silence. Silence was the only way to manage the unfathomable grief, but silence had made her its prisoner. I could see, even with her head bowed, the rich well of words swirling in every fibre of her body, just waiting to be liberated.

'Some of the patients at the hospital,' I said and paused, carefully feeling the uncertain waters. 'The wounded men from the Pacific. They tell me where they've been. Tarawa. Palau. The Solomons. And I just can't imagine that they're real places. The names seem too strange to be real.'

She nodded and looked away, twisting her body around in her chair so that she was looking out of the large misted window behind her. She ran a line with her finger across the condensation on the glass, sending small beads of water running out like tributaries across the map of mist.

'He did all the training,' she said softly, 'and acted like the other men, but he wasn't one of them. Not really. When Norman died I just clung on to him and couldn't let him go. I tried to hide him from the world, but it only made him awkward. I think he was desperate to get away from me when

327

he left. He was just a boy, Captain. He didn't have any real idea about what a war actually was. It was just place names to him. Strange, beautiful place names.'

She paused, but I knew she hadn't finished. She twisted even further round in her chair now, so that the better part of her back was facing me. It occurred to me that in all the times I'd been at her house I had never once seen her on that side of the room. The reason, now that I thought about it, was obvious: the photograph. She couldn't bear to talk about him while he watched her from the wall behind me, so she had to hide her eyes.

'It was a Tuesday morning when they came. Ten-thirty. Three loud knocks on the door. I knew when he left, when he boarded the ship – I knew that if there was a loud knock on my door one morning, he would be dead. And so it was.'

She was silent now, and in that empty space I could sense the event happening, the gathering fragments and momentum, the critical mass, the ridiculous coincidence. I could hear the knocks before they came, a syncopated half-beat in advance. Mrs Taylor jumped, her arms raised like a bird preparing for flight. We looked at each other for a frozen moment. And then, slowly, we both stood up and walked towards the kitchen door that led into the hallway.

When I had gathered myself, and had recovered from the surprise, I seemed to confidently know that the person responsible for the knocks was Sturgis. He would be coming armed with new information, charged with exuberant drama. I was so convinced of this I just about stumbled out into the hallway, but as I was rounding her to get past, Mrs Taylor grabbed me by the arm. I stopped, feeling the queer sensation of her firm grip upon me.

'Who is it?' she called out from the threshold of the kitchen, down into the dark hallway.

The response was immediate. 'Lieutenant Colonel Cartwright, Third United States Marine Division, Victoria Park. I'm here with Sergeant Adams, military police. I'd like to ask you some questions, ma'am.'

This was it; the end. Once I was in their custody I would have no chance to prove my innocence. They'd assign me a Marine-Advocate who would rubber stamp the government case. I'd be shot by the end of the week. I felt my stomach hollow out, as if the yards of my intestines were unravelling. I felt like going to the door and opening it myself, just to make things quicker. To end it.

I could still hear the reverberations of Cartwright's voice echoing in the cold hallway. The words were bubbling up from my chest now, full, ripe words, and they were about to pop out of my mouth, clearly enunciated, when Mrs Taylor tightened her clammy grip and pulled me into the hallway and pushed me up against the first door on the right. I put my hand on the doorknob out of sheer instinct and was about to twist it when I realised what I was doing, what she was forcing me to do. I craned my neck to look around at her, at the silhouette of her head in the darkness, but all she did was push me again, hard, willing me through the door. The latch clicked, faintly, almost imperceptibly, and before I knew it I was on the other side and the door was closed again. I stood panting and aghast in the stale, rancid air of her son's mausoleum.

The curtains were drawn, making it completely black, but I didn't want to turn the light on. The air in the room was thick with mould, and as I breathed I could feel the spores entering my lungs. I heard Mrs Taylor unhinging the chain lock on the front door. It creaked slightly as she opened it. Cartwright's voice was clear and true, full of dismal purpose.

'I'm sorry to intrude on you so late, ma'am, but you've probably heard the news about Captain Sokol.'

'Ah yes, yes I have.'

She sounded nervous. I could almost see the haughty, officious expression on Cartwright's face, eyebrows raised, interested.

'So you've heard?' he said flatly.

'It was on the radio just now.'

Pause. I was finding it hard to stand still, but I didn't want to move in case I knocked something. My eyes still hadn't adjusted to the dark, and I had no sense of the objects around me.

'Do you mind if we come in, ma'am?' asked Cartwright after what I assumed had been a silent deliberation between him and Adams, a look and a shrug.

'Now? You mean, come in now?'

Her voice was brittle, and I could sense that Cartwright wanted to take advantage of her nerves. I pictured him taking a step towards her, crowding the marginal space around her thick, vulnerable body, imposing himself.

'It's nothing to worry about,' he said, trying to muster a tone of reassurance. 'We're checking every place we know he's visited in Auckland. It's important that we find him, ma'am.'

'Yes, of course. Come in please, gentlemen.'

She said this loudly, above her usual range, perhaps as a signal to me. She needn't have bothered though; the door was thin and I could hear everything. I took a step back into the room, but it was like wading into the shallows of a beach at night, each step loaded with dread. I decided I couldn't risk it. If they opened the door they would find me, and that would be the end of it. I tried to remain completely still. My breathing sounded thunderous in my ears, even though I was trying to make it as shallow as possible.

She led them past the door and into the kitchen and dining area, all three of them silent. About a minute passed before they returned to the hallway. I could hear their breathing, the rustle of their clothes, six feet away.

330

'Do you mind if we look in these rooms, Mrs Taylor?' asked Cartwright.

She didn't say anything, and I felt my heart surge up to the back of my tongue. I heard the flick of a light switch; the bedroom opposite on the left.

Cartwright said, 'Sergeant Adams will just take a quick look. For your protection.'

A few seconds passed before Adams said, 'Nothing,' in a deep, mechanical voice.

'Try the next one down,' said Cartwright. 'This won't take long, ma'am.'

Again the flick of a light switch followed by a few hard footsteps. I could hear him opening and closing closet doors.

'Nothing,' said Adams.

There was only one room left. I listened as Adams stepped back out into the hallway. The silence of waiting punctured the air like a drum roll. Emily had said that she loved me and I knew she meant it. It was only one thing, but as I stood in that dark, dead bedroom, my quivering legs barely able to support my weight, I felt it was enough. She loved me and that was all that I had, but it was enough. At least I was a man who was loved by someone.

'Check it,' said Cartwright, his tone soft, uncertain. He knew the mystery of the door to the right, and I thought I could hear in his voice a suggestion of unwillingness.

There was a loud step towards the door. Adams's, I assumed. I could feel his presence, feel the weight of his antagonism getting closer. He put his hand on the doorknob and I closed my eyes.

She screamed. She screamed like the first time, perhaps for Cartwright's benefit, to refresh his memory. There was a rattle and bang on the door, but it didn't open. The scream persisted agonisingly. I could feel its shrill falsetto in my teeth. Finally it stopped, and in the stunned aftermath there was only the sound of heavy breathing. There was a pause before something loud hit the wall beside the door.

'Jesus,' hissed Cartwright. 'Are you okay?' I heard his knee click as he bent down, the old football injury he carried with him like a trophy. 'Come on now,' he said softly, sounding like a doctor for once. 'Just breathe, big breaths, slowly now.'

I could still sense Adams's presence on the other side of the door. He would have been looking down at Mrs Taylor on the ground, but there was still a chance he could open the door. I felt as though I had lived a score of years in that bedroom, standing rigid on that one spot.

Mrs Taylor started to cry, a slow, hiccupping sob, but it had all the hallmarks of an impending wail.

'It's her son's room,' whispered Cartwright. 'I don't know. I think he must have . . . you know.'

'Oh,' said Adams, and I could hear him take a step away from the door.

'Come on,' Cartwright said, still whispering. 'Let's get out of here.'

He must have stood up because I heard his knee click again.

'Well, ma'am,' he said, sounding ridiculous. 'We'll be on our way now. Sorry to bother you.'

I held my breath and waited. Finally the door clicked shut with a glassy rattle. They were gone.

I stood completely still, waiting for her to move. Eventually she pulled herself up with a groan and shuffled over to the door.

'Captain,' she said, her voice barely audible.

'Yes.'

'Please sleep in that room. You will be safe there.'

Before I had a chance to respond I saw the light of the hallway vanish from the base of my door. Then the door directly opposite me closed shut. I badly wanted out of the room, but I had sense enough to know she was right. Besides, I wouldn't dare step around her house while she slept. I patted the wall for the light switch, but when I found it I suddenly lost the desire for light. I didn't want to see the dead boy's bedroom if I didn't have to.

My eyes had adjusted to the light well enough to make out the narrow single bed on the opposite side of the room. I tiptoed across the floorboards, kicked my boots off, and lay down.

The bedclothes were damp to the point of being wet, but I was too tired to care. I rested my head on the rubber pillow and felt every muscle in my body dissolve, so that I was nothing more than a sack of bones. I closed my eyes and saw Emily's face, her peculiar expression as she waved to me from the hedgerows. The image was blurred at the margins and I was too weak to focus. I realised I'd been playing this image on a continuous loop in my mind all day, but I'd just been too busy to follow it. Something in her eyes, her bowed head. She had wanted to tell me something.

I fell asleep.

CHAPTER 38

I awoke with the queer sensation of knowing exactly where I was before I opened my eyes. The sporey air in the bedroom was cold and moist. It was still dark. I knew the house I was in and what had delivered me here, but I was still passive in the cloud of a dream whose filmy vapour trails were taking a moment to dissipate. There were images and impressions but nothing concrete. Every time I tried to burrow down into the slipstream of a thought it would disappear.

I pulled back the curtain beside the bed and brought my watch up to the glass. I could just make it out: quarter past three. It would be another three hours before Sturgis would arrive. I laced up my boots and crept over to the door, hesitating before I opened it. On an impulse I went back to the window and quietly drew back the curtains. The glass was frosted with mist. I made myself stop for a moment to heed the consequences of this inevitable forward motion, but there was no point; I couldn't think any more. I could only act. I tried to ease the window open, but it creaked like hell. I held my breath for a few seconds until the noise settled in the stunned air. I leapt out of the window and landed in the still and ominous night. The rain had stopped.

I made my way up Richmond Road and across Ponsonby, not thinking but acting. It only occurred to me that I was heading to the chink cathouse when I was a few blocks from it. I crept up the tunnelled driveway to the gravel clearing out back. I had seen a military police jeep up on the corner of Collingwood, but there didn't seem to be anybody else around. The moon lit up the courtyard in glowing, painterly chrome. The steel door at the top of the landing was shut. I winced every time my feet crunched the gravel, feeling certain I would be struck or grabbed from behind at any moment. I made my way over to the old oil drums where Sturgis and I had hidden only a month or two ago. As I crouched down behind their stinky cover, a rat dashed out from one of them, its nasty little claws scratching on the rusty tin before it disappeared somewhere in the blackness.

I was breathing hard and the fibres in my muscles were twitching like hell, compelling movement, but there was nothing to do but wait. Something was bound to happen sooner or later. It was a whorehouse, after all; half-past three in the morning was right in the middle of business hours. I sat there breathing vapour for twenty minutes, still no closer to figuring out what in the hell I was going to do. I was convinced that for whatever reason Oscar Walters had met his end, it was at the hands of one of these Oriental whoremasters, and most likely the giant one. I had seen the way his underlings had tried to tear Oscar apart the other day. That was no garden-variety scrap – it was bitter and bloody, a fight to the end. They had wanted to kill him. If Oki was right that he had knocked-off one of their whores, then it all seemed obvious.

Another twenty minutes passed with no stirring, in which time I came to understand that if I was going to learn anything about the whores and their purveyors I would have to fashion myself into a paying customer. I had no money on me, but I did have my bars. I was a captain; they would know I'd be good for it. I eased myself up from behind the drums, my knees straining under my weight. I was just about to step out into the clearing when a shrill report of metal scratching on metal sounded in the thick, misty air. I immediately crouched back down, but in my panic I kicked one of the drums. I closed my eyes tight and gritted my teeth in a childish attempt to silence the noise, but the warbling echo seemed to go on and on. Finally I willed myself to look up. Fortunately the door hadn't yet opened. There seemed to be a delay for some reason, but after a tense few moments it finally swung open a few feet, releasing a dim, pinkish light out onto the landing along with two figures who proceeded down the rickety staircase. I could see in the moonlight that one of them was definitely the giant Chinaman, but it was impossible to make out the other.

At the bottom of the staircase both men stopped. They exchanged a few whispered words in a cloud of steam before the giant shook the other man's hand and climbed back up the stairs, taking in four, five steps at a time. Before my eyes could adjust he had already stepped off the landing and in through the door, which quickly closed behind him. He was so expert at vanishing that I hardly believed I had seen him at all. Even when he was in front of your eyes, he was in the process of vanishing.

When I looked back the other man was already halfway across the courtyard. He was big and broad and walked with a stiff, bobbing kind of gait. I briefly wondered where he was going until it occurred to me that he was making for the gate in the fence. The gate that led to the path that led to the chess club. It had to be one of Oscar's chessmen. And, if this guy was still in cahoots with the giant chink, then perhaps the story of Oscar's sudden end lay on the other side of the fence. In any event it would be easier to get answers out of somebody I knew for certain would speak English. Even in that light he seemed to know precisely where the gate was, reaching over the exact paling in the fence to release the latch.

As soon as the gate closed behind him I crept across the

gravel as fast and as quietly as I could. Even though I had just seen him do it, it took me a few scrambled seconds to find the latch on the other side of the palings. The path was dark and narrow, overhung by a row of low branches from a series of conifer trees to the right. The chessman was well up ahead, but I could still make out his shadowy figure in the distance. I moved quickly up behind him, holding my breath, clenching my fists until we both came within a sad pool of light thrown from a bulb affixed to the corner of a white building. The back of the chess club cottage. The path stopped dead at a low iron gate that led onto a small, damp patch of grass that I assumed was the back yard. I kept my distance as the chessman wearily climbed the three steps to the back door and, after wiping his feet in the dark a couple of times, went inside.

I knew if I thought about it too long I would lose my nerve, so before all the loose shards of information and doubt and fear had a chance to cohere in my mind, I opened the iron gate and padded up the back steps. I tried the handle on the door. Unlocked. I looked behind me one last time, a seaman's rueful glance back at the safe port he has just left, and stepped inside.

I slowly crept up the passageway running off the door, the pulse in my ears ringing like mad. The passage wasn't directly lit, but a narrow band of light from an open door to the left did just enough to cut the dark and enable me to charter my way forward. The place smelt musty and damp with an edge of something ripe about it, like old meat or rotten fruit. I came to the door that was set ajar, the one from which the shaft of light shone. I placed a trembling hand on the face of the door and was just about to push it when a sound came from the room, not five yards away, a sound of rustling papers followed by the clunk and screech of a chair being repositioned on bare floorboards. I whipped my hand away from the door so fast that it just about cracked the air with a snap. A noise, a cry of fright had surged up my throat and sat at the base of my tongue, so clear and present I had to bring my hand up to my mouth to suppress it.

By the time I had recovered, the laborious sound of a phone dial was ringing from the room. I eased my ear to the small open gap in the door and held my breath. Presently the dialling stopped and the man cleared his throat.

'It's me,' he said in an urbane, articulate tone. I couldn't pick the accent, but it certainly wasn't Kiwi. There was a short pause before he said, 'What did I tell you? Nothing good will come of it.'

I managed to silently open the door another few inches before hitting a creaky sweet-spot in the hinges. But I still couldn't see the speaker through the widened gap. All I could make out was the edge of a desk, a stack of papers and folders arranged carelessly around the base of it.

'It's done,' he said tiredly. 'Two hundred and fifty. Needless to say they're happy with the . . . Who's there?'

This last was not spoken into the phone, but directed at the door. I heard the click of the receiver being placed back in its cradle. A chair screeched across the floorboards again. 'Who's there?' said the man, the voice different now, somehow familiar.

Before I knew what I was doing, before I even had a chance to panic or freeze, my hand instinctively reached up to the door and pushed at it, the hinges singing a surprised metal tune as it opened in an expansive arc. I saw the whole room at once – the worn armchairs beside the fireplace, the nondescript desk in the corner, the green velvet curtains, the papers and pamphlets scattered across the chipped and dotted floorboards, the rows of books on a set of mahogany shelves, the portrait of the Führer hanging on the near wall. I saw the whole room so completely at once that it took me an age, a truncated eternity to see the man, the animate object

338

leaping out of his chair, his electric white hair glowing yellow in the soft, gaseous light of a reading lamp.

He wasn't wearing the dark glasses, and although I hadn't ever seen his cobalt blue eyes before I recognised them at once. They were the eyes from the painting. They were Dr Walters's eyes.

'Winston?' I said, barely aloud, the air dying before it had passed my lips. He was as surprised to see me as I was him. For a moment he attempted to shed the proud, eloquent bearing and crumple back into the butler I had hitherto known, but in the end he couldn't bring himself to do it. The eyes were remarkable, a dazzling baby blue that seemed to penetrate all the way through me, past skin and flesh and into bone.

'Captain Sokol,' he said eventually, creasing his face into a bitter smirk. As good as his transformation from crippled butler to European gentleman was, he couldn't shake the twisted knot of paralysed stroke-sinew on his cheek. It remained unmoved throughout his initial shock and recovery, undermining the diabolical irony I think he was going for. 'How good of you to come,' he said, a lingering trace of German harshness colouring his Etonian English.

We both stood in the middle of the room, suspended in the dreamy unreality of the moment. I wasn't even close to being able to talk. It was obvious that he, that Winston, was Dr Walters, but that was as far as my addled brain would let me go. The rest was just static. Eventually he recovered his composure and, quite calmly and very deliberately, motioned for me to sit in one of the armchairs. I instinctively shook my head.

'Very well,' he said. 'But you'll have to excuse me, Captain. As you know, I have been working hard lately.'

He sat back down in the chair next to the desk without taking his burning eyes off me. He retrieved a tin of cigarettes from the desk and offered me one. Again I shook my head, feeling like a dazed, slack-jawed child watching a magic show at a carnival. He lit a cigarette, the puffy white smoke clouding beautifully around his head.

'You are a smart man, Captain. I have observed this. Smart, but a little naïve perhaps.' He shrugged his shoulders and blew out a thin stream of smoke. 'Like many of your countrymen, no doubt.' He looked at me and laughed. 'Still, I don't suppose I need to explain anything to you here. I suppose you are . . . astute enough to piece it together. No?'

'You killed your own son,' I said, taking a step back towards the door out of caution. I could outrun him every day of the week, but I needed to know the escape route was there. I could see my backing away amused him.

'Believe me, Captain, you are safe here,' he said, allowing himself the faintest ripple of a laugh. He crushed his cigarette out in an ashtray that looked as though it had been fashioned from a cartridge shell. He immediately lit another one, extinguishing his match with a long, slow brushing motion of his wrist.

'So, you killed him then?' It was a stupid question, playing right into his assessment of my naïvety, but I figured if he had the nerve or cavalier daring to tell me I would simply dash out the door and grab the nearest M.P.

'And if I had, Captain,' he said smiling, and then trailed off. His teeth were brown and decayed, but all of them large and perfectly in place. When he smiled it looked as though he'd been assigned too many of them for his tight little mouth. 'If I had, do you think I would tell you?'

'All right then,' I said thinly, taking another step across to the open door. My legs were heavy and unresponsive. 'Why don't you tell me what you were doing with that Chinaman over yonder.'

'You mean Mr Quan?' he said thoughtfully. I nodded. 'Mr Quan has been, how should I put this, very good to our family,

Captain. I dare say if we hadn't met Mr Quan your wife would have starved to death a long time ago.'

'You leave her out of this,' I said, his reference to her stinging me sharply.

'Why should I?'

'She's my wife.'

'She's my daughter.'

'No she's not,' I said, no longer nervous. 'I've read your little article. I know what she is to you.'

He crushed out the second cigarette and stood up slowly, pointedly not acknowledging my thinly veiled whatever it was – accusation. He walked over to the portrait of Hitler beside the bookshelf.

'That is the thing with you people, isn't it? You are meddlers. You stick your big noses into people's business. You lend people money, you hoard it in your banks, you accuse people in your newspapers, and yet have the nerve to ask why they hate you. Why everybody hates you. Isn't it obvious, Captain?'

I looked at him closely, at his sorcerer's eyes and crippled cheek, but I was a thousand miles away. The pieces, the fragments were starting to collect, and as they did so I could feel my stomach slowly starting to unravel.

'Do you mean to tell me,' I said, feeling my cheeks burn, my forehead slicken with sweat, 'that Emily is . . . that you all are . . .'

He took a large stride towards me and stopped. The smile had gone from his eyes now. He was no longer delighting in the situation, the theatrical revelation. He was Dr Walters again.

'Japan is our only hope now, Captain. Japan can still win us this war. And I would like you to know – I insist that you know – it has been my family's great honour to serve them. My son died because he failed to act like a man. He was a thespian, like his great absurd hero in England. Given to puffy, hollow nonsense. Our information, the information my family has provided over the years; it has great strategic value. But my son was a clod. He was more interested in cutting brake cables and sabotaging your training games. Which, in the end, amounts to nothing. He couldn't seem to understand that his petty terrorism placed the whole operation at risk.'

'You mean you . . .'

'What I mean, Captain, is that my son always thought he was something he was not.'

'He killed Timmins,' I said to myself, winded, almost gasping for breath.

'Yes. Your driver,' he said absently, inconsequentially. 'He did that. But now, Captain, I would like you to meet Arthur.' It took me a heavy moment to realise that he was looking past me and at the open doorway to my right.

I spun around to see a man in a black suit. It only took me a second to recognise him as the guy who had wanted to crush my face in a few months ago, just out front of this cottage, when I had uselessly tried to come to O'Keefe and Diddle's rescue. Arthur stood motionless in the doorframe, a stocky barrel of a man with a doughy, expressionless face. His fat fists were clenched and he was champing at the bit to get at me, a vicious pit bull of a man straining at his leash. Dr Walters stepped around to my side, as light and nimble as a dancer, boxing me in.

'We all wear disguises, don't we, Captain? I wore one, my wife and daughter each wear one, my son even believed in his. And, I think that perhaps you, Captain, are also a man under-cover. No? But in the end, we are what we are.' He paused for a second and squinted at me thoughtfully. I could feel Arthur slowly advancing on me, but even so I couldn't bring myself to look away from Dr Walters. 'You know, death does not recognise our disguises, Dr Sokol.'

342

Just then there was a hammering sound on the window behind me, quickly followed by an even louder hammering on the front door of the house. All three of us seemed to jump forward and gasp, as if we were playing some sort of childhood game. An enormous bright light shone in the window, penetrating right through the thick velvet curtains.

'This is the Police,' cried the voice outside the door, six, seven yards from where we stood.

Dr Walters kept his icy eyes on me, neither one of us moving, locked in a stalemate. After a brief pause, Arthur fled from the doorway and darted off up the hallway, his clanging footsteps resounding throughout the house. A couple of cars pulled up outside, their sirens wailing.

'You are all wanted for criminal conspiracy with the enemy, collusion with the enemy, and treason,' said the voice at the door, slowly, fastidiously, as if he were reading from a script.

Dr Walters looked at me again and shrugged. He slowly turned and sat back down at the desk, lighting another cigarette as if he were on a cruise and had all the time in the world.

'This doesn't look good for you, Captain. I wonder how you will explain this to your colonels.' He blew two streams of smoke out of his nostrils and extinguished his match with that same, relaxed, brushing motion of his wrist. He was prepared to wait, come what may. 'First you kill my son. Then you are caught here. It looks bad, no?' He laughed, a nasty chuckle that caused him to cough a little. 'Maybe you were the one who killed that poor Marine. Cut his brake cables, no? Who can tell?'

'If you don't come out immediately, we will break the door down,' cried the voice outside. Another patrol car arrived, its siren blaring in the night. There was a hubbub outside the window, a sparkly buzz of low voices, footsteps, intrigue.

I wanted to say something to Walters, something concise

and truthful and cutting, but words have never come easily to me. Instead I took one last look at him, at the watery turquoise eyes, at his twisted and gnarled face, sitting peacefully, almost contentedly under a portrait of his black-haired leader. As I backed out of the room he smiled at me one last time, the mad doctor, the father of my bride.

Somehow I made it out of the house and back down the path without being noticed. Clearly the Auckland police weren't familiar with the strategy of surrounding a house before announcing their presence. I couldn't for the life of me find the latch for the gate that led onto the whorehouse's courtyard. I could see the dancing flicker of torches back down the path towards the house. They were coming now. The opposite direction was nothing more than a coal-black void, a leap of faith that even at that time, in the crucible of my descent, I wasn't prepared to take. I told myself not to think, took a few paces back into the thick of the conifer branches, and leapt at the paling fence. I made it over in two desperate movements, but not before sounding off an almighty racket. By the time I landed on the familiar gravel on the other side I could hear the cops' plodding footsteps and collective heaving coming up the path towards me. As I ran across the courtyard to the tunnel driveway something caught my eye in the moonlit dark and made me stop abruptly – the giant Chinaman, or Nip, or whatever the fuck he was, standing up on the landing with a pipe in his hand, looking directly down on me. He casually drew on the pipe, causing the gold and red embers in its bowl to glow magically. I believe, although I could have been imagining it, that I caught a glimpse of his dark face then in the fiery light of his tightly packed, glowing opium. He seemed to be smiling at me, derisively, mockingly, and I couldn't help feeling that this man, this myth of a man, this legend slinking around in the blurry margins of Ponsonby, had known me all along.

I told myself not to think.

I ran out through the tunnel and up towards Collingwood where I had seen the M.P. an hour or so ago. The road was desolate but full of eyes, unseen eyes. The gas lamps threw out a weak, buttery yellow light, but nothing was illuminated. The M.P. wasn't there any more – he'd obviously been drawn to the commotion at the chess club on Franklin – but the dumb bastard had left the key in his jeep. I jumped in and started it up, oblivious to the noise now, oblivious to consequence, and sped away up Ponsonby Road, past another two patrol cars whose sirens were tearing the night apart.

I told myself not to think, but the injunction was redundant by the time I made it to Parnell. I was beyond thought, beyond simple cause and effect. I just had to see her; if I could see her, maybe I would be able to understand. But whatever understanding I may attain, I knew it would have to be backdated. There was no future now, no problem to be solved, no question to be answered. All of this, this mad running up the front path, this dash up the steps and in through the front door – it was the pathetic frantic energy of a grief not yet felt, the need to see the loved one's dead body, if for no other reason than to verify that the end had come. That it was over.

I didn't need a light to make it up the long, pitch-black hallway; I knew every inch of it by heart now and treaded with steely confidence down past the formal lounge where Emily had played Debussy for me, past the office where we had first kissed, past the library where her Nazi father's portrait hung from the wall. Mrs Walters was in the sitting room alone, seated on the uncomfortable edge of the chaise longue. The room was plunged in gloom, lit only by the red spectrum of the fire burning in the hearth and a solitary candle on the cherrywood coffee table. She wasn't in the least surprised to see me, standing crumpled by the fire, out of breath, out of life. She stood up and faced me, her hands cupped in front of her belly as if we were about to play out something from Ibsen, some sordid reckoning of grubby reality spoken in calm, modulated tones.

'Where is she?' I demanded, unable to look at her.

'We were just trying to survive, Captain,' she said without hesitation, a well-worn justification she'd clearly been convincing herself of for months, years even.

'I don't give a damn. Tell me where she is.'

'It wasn't her fault. She was not to know. You must—'

'Where the fuck is she?'

This caught her good and proper, wrenching her from the stagey scene she was trying to create. I looked at her for the first time, at her powdered, egg-shell face glowing in the dark like some portrait of Queen Bess. The detached austerity of her expression only fanned my rage. She had lied and cheated like the lowest teamster, yet she had the audacity to give me calm resignation.

'Where the fuck is she?' I said again through gritted teeth, taking a couple of menacing steps towards her. She didn't move an inch, though.

'We were women in a man's house, Captain. You must understand this. We were just trying to survive.'

She braced herself for the spray in response, but I couldn't find anything to say. My silence emboldened her, and it was she who took a step towards me this time.

'Whatever you know of me, Captain. Whatever you may have heard of me in the past, just believe this. The only thing I believe in now is bread. The only thing . . . the only reason . . .' For the first time since I'd entered the room her hardened expression began to crack. Her chin quivered, but her eyes were dry. Whatever crying she had done, there would be no more. There is only one thing left after the crying stops, and her eyes seemed to tell me that she knew this. 'We just wanted to survive.'

I couldn't look at her again; even rats should be allowed to die in peace. I made to move past her towards the dining room, towards the stairs, but she gamely stepped into my path, so close and firm that I had to balance on one foot to prevent myself toppling right into her.

'Don't hurt her, Captain,' she said as I manhandled her to one side and moved on past. 'She is not like us. She is not one of us.'

As I made my way up the blackened staircase I could hear something primitive in the distance, something out there in the night, blaring, wailing. By the time I made it to the first floor I knew what it was. Sirens. I checked the bedrooms, but they were all in complete darkness. There was only one place left, the obvious place. I climbed the attic stairs feeling my heart hammer a nauseating *prestissimo* in my chest. A thin line of light glowed beneath the closed oak door. I foolishly closed my eyes and an ugly vision clouded my brain – my wife lying peacefully on our austere single bed, our marital bed, her white cotton dress soaked with ruby-red blood. But instead she stood with her back to me, staring out of the black window with her beautiful chocolate hair clamped and clipped in a metal nest of pins, her long neck glowing creamily in the dim yellow light, unwittingly making a painting of herself again. I closed the door behind me but still she didn't turn.

The bedclothes were rumpled and the room was thick with hot air, wet tears, and the heaviness of desperation. I looked at her, at the back of her, at the painting of her, and felt myself succumbing to something, to weakness, to plain old love. But just then she turned, and for whatever reason the tears rolling down the svelte plains of her cheeks inflamed me. I had recovered my breath and I was frothy. Her beautiful face was like the final dagger and it was all I could do to fight back.

'You used me!' I cried, my voice cracking as I tried to hold the guttural notes. 'You lied to me. You used me!'

'No . . . no, Peter.' She crumpled, falling into herself in a torrent of tears.

'You . . . you strung me along. You betrayed me. You've turned me into a fucking traitor!'

It was only as I said this that I realised it was true. Even in my rage the logical sphere of my mind was ticking away at the consequences, the inevitable fallout. And what was I if I wasn't a traitor? Dumb? Stupid? I certainly was, but would anybody believe it?

The sirens were closer now. No, not closer. They were here, they had arrived. I could hear doors slamming, shouted voices, banging on the front door.

'No, Peter. I love you,' she said, rushing towards me and stopping a couple of feet away. She put her hand out to my chest but I battered it away, denying myself a final touch, a final feel of her warm flesh.

I said it again, but quietly this time. 'You used me and turned me into a traitor.'

The footsteps were coming up the stairs now, a swell of voices, urgent sounds.

'I . . . I tried,' she said, choking on the words, her mouth stretched into a wide grimace of pain. 'I tried to push you away. I tried, Peter, but I couldn't. I fell in love with you. I couldn't help it.'

Coming up the garret stairs now. The moment of final things, the end. She had heard them too, and in that moment she seemed to pass over some kind of threshold of emotion, tipped over the tipping point, so that she appeared almost calm again, stately even, with her flushed milky cheeks and hopeless eyes. She straightened herself up and looked at me as if I were a memory. She was framed perfectly in the black window behind her, the yellow light catching her proud brow and fine nose, a painting again. And perhaps that was all she had ever been – something imagined, something constructed by the raw materials of my painter's brain. A beautiful mystery. An ugly lie.

They were at the door now.

CHAPTER 39

The day of my release, a little over two years later, I spent the afternoon in the reading room of the Sacramento public library, assiduously poring over the dozen or so editions of the *New Zealand Herald* that covered Dr Walters's trial in the Auckland Supreme Court.

The proceeding ran for fifteen days, and at the end of it all he was sentenced to death. Not for the murder of his son, though. That act, the newspaper reported, had been carried out by the young man's legally adopted sister – the late Emily Katherine Walters, who had stabbed him in the neck with a steak knife as he tried to rape her on the family's eighteenth-century walnut dining table. It was solemnly added that Miss Walters, a former London prostitute, had been taken into the family for reasons unknown.

Instead, Walters was tried and convicted of the murder of Corporal Irvine J. Timmins, the attempted murder of the five Marines who had been injured when the Shelley Beach pier collapsed, criminal conspiracy involving the enemy, colluding with the enemy, running an illegal brothel, and immigration fraud.

Walters, or Wasserman as the Crown prosecutor liked to call him, admitted everything bar the murder and attempted murder raps. His counsel had sought to rely on the police transcript of an interview with a Captain Peter R. Sokol of the

United States Marines, taken on the night of Wasserman's own arrest. The transcript seemed to suggest that this Captain, who had been linked to the family's adopted daughter, had been told by Wasserman that Oscar Walters had been responsible for the murder and attempted murders. The judge had ruled this evidence inadmissible, as the Captain was in combat in the Pacific, and therefore unable to be subpoenaed. In any event, the Crown successfully argued that it had sufficient evidence to prove Wasserman himself was responsible.

On the stand the 'undeniably charismatic' psychiatrist made it clear that his game was not 'petty terrorism', a phrase I remembered well. His business was the simple provision of information to the Japanese, to whom he, as a proud, 'red-blooded' German, was bound to under the Tripartite Pact. His son, he made plain under cross-examination, had indeed been committed to a campaign of local sabotage. But then again his son was an 'idiot'.

The trial was a scandal, sharing the front page with the Italian campaign and Hitler's losses in the Soviet Union. At every corner, under every innocuous rock, lay a kind of perverse intrigue that New Zealanders generally weren't accustomed to. The editorials piously wondered how 'our tiny island nation' could fall victim to such wickedness. But while the editors mourned the loss of innocence, the hacks on the front page wallowed in the grubby facts.

It seemed that the Wasserman family had, after leaving Berlin in mysterious circumstances in 1932, fallen in with Oswald Mosley and his B.U.F. movement in London. It was established that Gertrude Walters was a distant relative of Mosley's, but the suggestion that the two had once been young lovers never managed to elevate itself from the cheapest of the scandal pages. Dr Wasserman referred to his late son's boasts of having been sired by Mosley as merely the sad pathology of his psychological retardation. Following the invasion of

Poland the family had, again under mysterious circumstances, fled Britain in a hurry, eventually arriving in New Zealand in early 1940, at the same time Mosley and the rest of the B.U.F. were being interned in London under regulation 18D.

The background was colourful, but it was almost tame compared with what followed once the family had set up in New Zealand. The reports never really fleshed out the connections, but from what I could gather, the chess club had acted as a front for an organised espionage operation that supplied information to Japanese agents across the world. The information largely consisted of the comings and goings of the U.S. forces in New Zealand. The family made various 'connections' with U.S. servicemen in New Zealand, prising information out of the unwitting soldiers and then forwarding it on. The information was sent out of the country in coded letters that purported to be chess games played by correspondence. The moves and pieces described in the letters corresponded to certain troop divisions, camps and officers. Mrs Walters had sent the letters for over a year before they were caught out by a clever intelligence officer from the Australian Army.

The Walterses' connection in New Zealand was a Chinese soldier of fortune known only as Mr Quan. Mr Quan had allegedly been on Matsu Kikan's payroll in Australia, and had decided to branch out to New Zealand once the U.S. forces arrived. Mr Quan ran a brothel that employed Japanese whores who had either escaped or been released from the internment facility in South Auckland, the internment facility where Mrs and Miss Walters so generously volunteered their services, teaching the women English, among other things. The whores themselves were an excellent source of information, but their target subjects were invariably lowly enlisted men. Mr Quan was prepared to pay over the fist for the Walterses' ability to infiltrate the American officer class, who, strangely enough, were just as careless with their lips as the coarse doughboys and leathernecks under their control. Nobody was able to find Mr Quan or his Nip whores after the family's arrest. All that was left behind the steel door of the brothel were a few sunken mattresses and abandoned opium pipes.

On the last day of the trial, when he must have known that his conviction was assured, Wasserman withdrew his defence and admitted everything. I assumed this was a last ditch attempt at dignity, a kind of hara-kiri his Japanese paymasters would have been proud of. He had had the soapbox of a trial, and now he wanted to die for his country. Which he did, swinging from a rope in Mount Eden prison on the sixth day of June, 1944, the very same day the Allies invaded Normandy.

He would have rued the timing. His death only made it to page four.

CHAPTER 40

Los Angeles at dusk, all hazy ochre and cadmium reds and yellows. Eddie and I drove north from Wentwood up to the San Fernando Valley in open-windowed silence. It was a quarter to six. The time was like a third passenger in the car, a brooding, troubled type whose determined quietness made conversation difficult. The breeze was whipping at the loose strands of what was left of my hair. I felt great, light and alive. I felt as though I had just shed twenty years.

I couldn't say the same for Eddie, though. He had taken some persuading to get back in the car, and now that we were driving to his house, weaving our way through the neat little streets of the Valley heading to Northridge, he'd assumed his regular slouched, sullen position. But I was doing the right thing; for the first time in years there wasn't a doubt in my mind.

'I don't get it,' he said, sitting up in his seat, feeling his chest pocket for the box of Camels.

'You don't get what?'

'You drive all the way up from San Diego. You have his book. But you don't go to see him.'

I stopped at an orange light, even though there was time to skirt through. I wanted to slow this down a fraction; I wanted to pause for a moment.

'It's complicated.'

'That's a bullshit answer.'

It was. 'You're right,' I said.

He lit his cigarette and tossed the match out the open window.

'Is it the war?' he said. 'Like, like all the killing and stuff? You just don't want to remember it?'

I watched as an elderly couple crossed the road in front of us, hand in hand. The guy was wearing a lemon summer shirt and beige pants, and his wife was decked out in some sort of garish purple jumpsuit. They seemed to notice nothing.

'Maybe it's that.' The light changed and I pulled away slowly, enjoying the sensation of the low width of the De Ville on the road, enjoying the space and the suburban hum. 'I've spent years thinking that I had to see him,' I continued. 'In a strange kind of way, everything I've done since has been on the assumption that I would see him again, that I would have to explain myself to him. And still, I never really believed it would happen. I think I've spent my life preparing for it, though. Just in case.'

'I don't get it.'

'Neither do I.'

I looked across at him, at the swollen proboscis, the Steve Allan glasses, and the steel-wool hair. Here was a bright, talented boy, I thought. I'm driving with a bright, talented boy who has yet to understand the cold, middle-of-the-night reality that he must die one day. We were somewhere in the sprawl of Northridge, at another intersection.

'Left or right?' I asked.

'Left.'

He was giving me the bare minimum of directions. It was like a deal we had struck. He refused to map out the entire route and would only direct me on a street-by-street basis, so that whenever we got to a fork in the road or a binary intersection I had to stop and ask. I could see his hand shaking as he brought the cigarette up to his lips.

'I didn't see Sturgis,' I said, looking straight at the road ahead, 'because I don't have to any more. And you know what? I've got you to thank for that.'

'Me?' he said, as if he'd just been accused of something.

'You. Left or right?'

'Left again.'

I turned the De Ville into a perfect tree-lined street with two never-ending rows of perfect little houses.

'What's in front of you is always the most important thing, Eddie. I haven't always known this, but I believe it to be true.'

He threw the butt of his cigarette out the window and wiped his hand against the thigh of his dirty jeans.

'Yeah,' he said dismissively, 'well what's in front of me is some Viet Cong motherfucker who wants to blow my head off.'

'What about my offer? Come on, I thought you were going to consider it.'

'I am,' he said, a little high-pitched and desperate. 'I have. I've considered it and I want to do it. Which is why I don't understand the reason for me having to go home.'

'Classes don't start for another three weeks. Besides, there are things to sort out. Paperwork. It can't happen overnight. You know that.'

'Be that as it may, I don't see why I have to wait here while the paperwork is done. There are other places I can go, man.'

He fumbled around with the box of Camels and shakily lit another cigarette. He was clearly anxious, but there was something artificial about his protest, a whiff of the high drama the young Sturgis used to employ. I got the feeling that he knew there was no other option, but that he just couldn't bring himself to acknowledge it yet.

'You can't run away, Eddie. I don't want you to come down

to San Diego to run away. I'm just giving you another option is all. If you run away now you'll never stop.'

'Hey, thanks for the cliché. That's a great help.'

I laughed in spite of myself. 'Listen, just take it from somebody who knows. Running away is like a cancer. It'll be in your bones in no time if you're not careful.'

A heavy, expectant pause followed. And then he said, 'Pull over here. On the right. That white place there.'

It was a single-level ranch-style house with the standard low-pitched gable roof and deep-set eaves. It was identical in everything but colour to the houses immediately either side of it. A small patch of burnt summer grass sloped down from the front door to the street, studded with a couple of plum trees bearing fruit, and surrounded by an immaculate garden fringe. Eddie's humble home. I let the car idle for a moment, not sure what to do.

'This is it then,' said Eddie, his voice flat and expressionless.

'All you have to do is tell him the truth. And stand your ground.'

He looked at me and raised his eyebrows.

'You've got my number,' I said. 'Just give me a call when you've sorted everything out.'

He leaned forward in his seat and pulled the rear-view mirror towards him, checking out his nose.

'You did a good job of this thing,' he said, lightly touching the bridge of it with his pinky finger. 'I mean, for a painter.'

I smiled and tried to ignore the insinuation. He readjusted the mirror back to where it had been and slumped back in his seat, letting out a resigned sigh.

'You're him, aren't you?'

'Who?'

'The doctor in the book. It's you.'

I thought about it for a moment, looking into Eddie's house. There appeared to be somebody standing in one of the front windows waving out at us. Eddie saw the person as well, but he chose not to return the wave. He wanted an answer.

'You can tell me now. This is the end of the road, Peter,' he said. 'You're him, aren't you?'

I smiled and looked out of the windscreen, my eyes tired and out of focus, alive to nothing but the muddy-gold hush of the approaching night.

'Not any more,' I said. 'Not any more.'

CHAPTER 41

I was released without charge from Auckland central police station a little after dawn, released to the custody of the United States Marines. I may not have killed Oscar Walters, but I was still up to my neck in shit with the brass. I spent five straight hours in Ford's office being grilled by every colonel and ass-kissing U.S. intelligence man in the country. They shone a light in my eyes and told me I had betrayed my country. They told me the men believed I was responsible for Timmins's death. I meekly gave them my side of the story, the dumb, unreasonably stupid side, and perhaps in the end they believed me. In their marrow, both Ford and Green knew that I lacked the cunning to be a spy. If I had been any other man they would have shot me on the spot, but I had lived with these guys for over a year now. They knew what I was – a sap, an unwitting dolt for whom the real world, the unpainted world, would always be just out of reach.

Either way, they didn't have time to figure out the charge. While I'd been on the lam the unit had been given its orders to sail to the Solomon Islands. We were to leave the following day. The Third Marines were going to war, and they couldn't afford to lose an experienced surgeon, not even a naïve pinko asshole like me. War makes exceptions of us all.

It rained the day we left Auckland.

It took two weeks to sail from Auckland to Bougainville. The atmosphere on the ship was toxic. I was quartered as an officer but treated like a pariah, essentially under bed arrest. The interrogation continued at sea, but only half-heartedly. There were bigger things now. I would have given anything to hand back my bars and bunk with the enlisted men, the real Marines, but I didn't get the chance to see Sturgis or his buddies once on the entire trip. Not that they wanted to see me anyway.

Every time I closed my eyes I saw her face, but I didn't let myself dwell on what I had lost (or never had). I had seen the faces of the men who'd come back from the Philippines, from Guadalcanal and Tarawa. I could feel death around the corner, in the rank air of my cabin, drawing closer with every nautical mile, every choppy, gut-wrenching wave. I didn't welcome it, but nor did I have reason to fear it any more. I was a man without a family and a history. I was a set of dog tags. I would quietly disappear.

The day we passed Noumea and sailed up into the eerie transparent waters of the Coral Sea, Cartwright came to my locked cabin to tell me what I somehow already knew.

He spoke through the steel door, but I could hear him as clearly as the crashing sea outside my portal. He said, 'Your Nazi wife is dead, Sokol.'

His flattened Yankee tone made it plain that he took no great pleasure in delivering the news. But it was his job as an American, as a Marine officer, to deal in cold, unvarnished facts.

He said, 'She hung herself in a cell.'

The Third Marine Division landed on Cape Torokina on the first day of November 1943 in a blaze of heat and light. The bleached white and turquoise colours of the lagoon have haunted me the rest of my life, haunted me more than the blood and the bodies. The air was so pure it was hard to believe anybody had ever breathed it before. We dropped anchor in Hell's little oasis and waited for the blood to flow.

The Japs had held Empress Augusta Bay for almost a year and had fortified themselves to the teeth with ammunition, gunner placements, pillboxes, caves and makeshift trenches. It had been easy for me to be distant from the code in New Zealand, where V.D. was the biggest threat to the men's health, but this was different. I could have wept as I watched those cropped-haired boys climb down the rope nets thrown over the starboard side of the ship, down into the amphibious landing crafts that would deliver them to their fates. I didn't dare look at any of them in the face.

Until the beach landing was achieved, and the lower slopes of the jungle secured, the medical personnel were to operate out of three cramped O.R.s aboard the ship. It was the job of the enlisted men of the Third Medical Battalion, Sturgis and O'Keefe and Yardley and others, to follow behind the infantry once the shooting had started and bring back the wounded men who had a chance at survival. The rest they were to stack on the beach until further notice. The dead were to remain where they fell.

The landing was only supposed to take four hours, and the beachhead, according to the generals, was supposed to be secured by nightfall. But the Pacific was a place that baulked at plans and grand stratagems. And then there were the Japanese. None of the surgeons spoke as from the deck we watched the shallows of the lagoon turn red. The tide had stayed out longer than expected and the landing crafts couldn't make it over the reef. The infantrymen proceeded to wade through the shallows, at first in tropical quiet, then to the accompaniment of machine-gun fire. The air filled with sand and debris from all the shelling, creating a hazy cloud over the killing, as if God couldn't bring himself to watch.

It took three days to secure the beach, in which time we lost hundreds of men. We operated in a floating theatre of carnage, up to our knees in blood and guts. O'Keefe was killed on the second day, hit by an invisible sniper as he was trying to drag a sergeant with a gut wound through the wet sand. There were dead Marines everywhere, corpses piled three or four high in cairns of flesh, monuments to something they never really understood.

One by one the orderlies were picked off, so that pretty soon we didn't have enough medical personnel to retrieve the wounded. Late on the second day, and without asking, I climbed overboard and scaled down the rope netting, jumping into the first landing craft that came along. As we made it over the reef, our path was forever being blocked by corpses. The knowable world had been reduced to the stink of cordite and flesh. I trudged through the pink shallows and dragged kids of eighteen back to the craft by their limp arms. It wasn't that I wanted to die; I didn't. But I am ashamed to say that I didn't mind the bullets flying past my body, and that I perversely liked the queer space I inhabited for those few moments. It was almost peaceful in a way, waiting for the inevitable bullet to hit. I was free from consequence, distant, not really human any more.

But for some reason the snipers and the mortars missed and I made it back safely. Nobody said anything when I boarded the ship again. It was yet another breach of the code, but we were living by something more fundamental at that point. Cartwright, who didn't understand despair, interpreted my act as a cheap attempt at heroism, and, not to be outdone, one hour later he climbed down the ropes himself. He stood on a landmine buried in the sludgy sand three feet from where his craft landed. He was the first officer to be killed on Cape Torokina.

When the beach and the lower slopes were finally secured the whole outfit moved in proper. The engineers built an airstrip, which enabled the merciful delivery of supplies like plasma and bandages, tinned beef and condensed milk. They built a series of rickety medical tents that were routinely bombed. The sun never ended; even in the cool of night you could feel it, the anticipation of it. The only thing that upset the pristine azure sky was the occasional flack cloud, as surprisingly black as an ink smudge on a crisp sheet of white bond.

I never thought it would end, and if it did end, I didn't know if I would be able to live again. To live without the heat, the malaria, the chlorinated drinking water taken from brown rivers, the tinned food, the bully beef, the sound of Nip banzai charges in the night, the sea of blood, the fear, the nightmare.

We wore the Japs down. We expanded the beachhead and took the Piva Trail, Coconut Grove and Hill 600. We travelled elsewhere, but I lost interest in the names after a while. Sturgis told me it was 1945 and I laughed. It was the first time he had spoken to me since we left Auckland. I was down to a hundred and twenty pounds and losing fast. They shipped Ford home at some point and sent out another colonel, some hard-ass whose name I can never remember. We learned the jungle, its sounds and its smells, its lore and custom. We knew it and in a strange way we accepted it.

And then one day the earth shook, the sky went bright, and it was all over.

CHAPTER 42

They couldn't deny my service. But nor could they ignore my flagrant breaches of the code. We arrived back in San Francisco on the tenth of September, 1945. I only managed three steps on American soil before I was whisked away to the stockade at Elliot. I spent eight tormented days inside a cage while they figured out what to do with me. After they caught me hanging from a sheet I was sent to a classified psychiatric hospital on the outskirts of Sacramento for a battery of tests. A number of the men came forward to speak on my behalf. Even Colonel Ford wrote a letter to the Judge-Advocate, counselling leniency.

In the end they decided I wasn't insane. I was dishonourably discharged for desertion and falsifying an official document, and set free into the world. Two weeks later the California State Medical Board revoked my licence to practise. Apparently my military record had the potential to bring the profession into disrepute.

This is the story of how I became a painter. This is the story of how I became a free man.

CHAPTER 43

A week after my trip to L.A., Missy and I got married under the spidery shade of the California sycamore tree in the corner of our garden. We agreed for each other's sake that we would keep what was left of our families out of it, and limited the invites to some friends from the College and a few old acquaintances and neighbours. We had everybody stay on the property for a few days, and went out of our way to be good hosts, to be entertaining and engaged. It was a strange thing to do, as neither of us were the charming-host type. Although we didn't conceive of it this way, I think the long party must have had something to do with trying to delay the realisation of marriage – the plain, Monday morning fact of it. It was something that had always stood between us, and now that it had happened we would have to confront its meaning, its daily significance. We would need to know that it changed things, that it changed us.

By the time the last of the guests had left I think we were both exhausted and more than ready to return to our quiet way of life. In the still silence of our big old house, our new status seemed to follow us into every corner, demanding recognition. We were married now, and so we actively imputed a glow to the hundred little things we did every day. We forced ourselves to sit longer over meals, to ask one another earnest, redundant questions and nod vigorously in response, to make a certain theatrical light of things barely worth mentioning in the first place. But we were hardly what you would call newlyweds. We both knew we were old and impatient with anything that ate into precious routine. Ours was a love built on the steady hum of a lived life. Our real pleasure came from catching each other by chance in the hallway or the kitchen, from seeing one another across a bed of rosebushes, secateurs in hand, our faces sun-licked and slick with perspiration. We couldn't pretend to be what we were not. And so pretty soon Missy went back to her morning slog at the Steinway, and I went back out to the studio.

But for the second time in my life I found I couldn't paint anything. I meticulously coated my canvases with layer after layer of titanium white primer, but the colour just wouldn't flow. I tried not to think about it for a few days on the assumption that it would eventually come back. But as the weeks passed, and as the colours still refused to present themselves, I began to realise that I no longer cared. Ever since the war I had always somehow known exactly what it was I wanted to say. There had always been a shape that I felt could be seen anew, a tangle of forms at the edge of my vision, a daydream of bright primaries, a nightmare of black. There had always been something elusive out there at the extent of my reach, revealing itself in the desperate pause of a hollow afternoon, or in the ordinary panic of a sleepless night. And while the images may still have been there if I had really looked, I just didn't have the energy to chase them any more. I had painted all the colours I could, and now I was back to white.

A few months after the wedding, I woke particularly early one morning. Missy was still asleep, so I crept out of bed and padded my way over the waxed Douglas-fir to the kitchen. A soft, caramel light shone in through the windows, which were streaked with the rain that had fallen in the night. I brewed some coffee on the stove and looked out at the studio through the small panes of glass in the French doors. It was getting into fall, and the long grass surrounding the shed was coated in a silky cloth of shimmering dew. I had been preparing for this day for years, and as I looked out at my little shed, so stark and alone in the dawn light, I was relieved to find myself happy that it had come.

I finished my coffee and went back into the bedroom to wake Missy, but found her already up, standing in front of the tallboy mirror, tying her gunmetal hair into a ferocious bun.

'Come with me,' I said, my voice still a little raspy and clogged with phlegm.

'What is it?' she said into her chest, still tying her hair.

'Today is your first day.'

She finished what she was doing by skewering the arrangement at the back of her head with an eraser-tipped yellow pencil. Her movements were brisk and formal. I could see she wanted to get to her piano.

'Today is my what?' she said, turning to look at me for the first time.

I creased my face into a smile and ran my hand, hard and callused from years of sandpaper and turpentine, across the stubble on my cheek. 'Follow me,' I said.

I led her out through the French doors of the kitchen and across the gravel path. The sun was low in the sky, but I could feel its approaching warmth through the misty morning air. Everything was damp and golden. I listened to her footsteps behind me, in step at first, then slackening as I got closer to the studio door. By the time I arrived she had stopped, halfway between the house and the shed.

'What is this all about, Peter?' Her tone was measured and pure. Even in her confusion she was stately. She belonged to a different time, to a more dignified order and code.

I put the rusty key into the loose lock and pushed the door open. The old familiar stench hit me, a heady mix of solvents and resins that instantly overpowered the delicate fragrance wafting off the long, wet grass.

'Come inside.'

She didn't take her eyes off me as she passed over the threshold. I closed the door behind her and hit the light switch. She looked cautiously around the room, uneasy on her feet, as if she expected a rat to dart out from one of the cluttered corners.

'It's yours,' I said, feeling light and a just little bit grand.

'What's mine?'

I pointed over at my second easel, positioned just opposite mine. The easel she'd pinned the news clipping to all those months back. I'd stretched and primed a canvas for her and it sat waiting in the cradle, burning the dark room with a blistering egg-shell white. On a stool beside the easel I'd left a fresh palette board and a range of sable and soft hog-hair brushes. She looked at me neutrally for a moment before taking a very deliberate step towards the easel. She picked up one of the brushes and ran the pad of her thumb across its stiff bristles. She wasn't one to make a fuss, my Missy. I felt my heart ache as she took the palette board in her hand, placed her thumb through the hole, and rested it like a pro against the inside of her wrist.

I watched her from behind as she stood facing the sterile slab of white in front of her. I watched the yellow pencil wedged into her hair bob up and down a few times before she straightened her shoulders and looked back round at me. The silence in that dank little room was immense.

'Where do we start, Peter?' she said.

Eddie didn't come to San Diego in the end. I got a letter from him a couple of weeks after the wedding to say that his father had relented and had agreed to continue paying his tuition at U.C.L.A. The war for him would remain a theoretical thing, part of his generational experience, a subject. I was glad that he got the deferment, but I admit to being a touch disappointed that I wouldn't see him around the campus. I think I would have enjoyed his company, being around to see what kind of a man he'd turn out to be. And then about a year later I heard from him again. Enclosed in a large envelope was a copy of *The New Yorker*. His letter simply read, 'See page 54. Thank you, Peter.'

It was a good story, but I won't bother describing it here. It involved a Second World War veteran who lived a rudderless, disaffected sort of a life in a changing world. The veteran encounters a young kid on the hustle for ideas, and the two enjoy an afternoon together, talking at cross-purposes, trying in vain to understand each other. He had a nice grasp of tone, and his prose had a certain laconic, elliptical quality to it that I enjoyed.

But like most stories it left me cold in the end. It wasn't his fault; it was simply a matter of form, an old dog's stubborn preference. Maybe it's just the painter in me talking, but I don't like the feeling that I'm being pushed to a conclusion, that I'm being prevailed upon to have a certain response. I want to be left alone is my problem. I want to look at a thing every day and feel different every time I look at it. Like the way I look at my wife. I watch her in the mornings, at her piano, or reading her journals in one of the tattered armchairs by the sunroom windows. I watch her in the studio beside me, as we lose ourselves in intervals of colour. I watch her in the evenings, when we walk together through the orange grove out the back of our property, the rustle of flaxy grass beneath our feet, a flaming sunset in the dusky sky. I look at her and I feel different every time.

This is all I choose to paint and care about now. This is what my life has resolved to.

The small changes. The small steps we take together, quietly, towards the end.

ACKNOWLEDGEMENTS

In writing this novel, I have drawn on the following sources: Harry Bioletti *The Yanks are Coming: The American Invasion of New Zealand 1942–1944* (1989); D. Beaven *United States Forces in New Zealand 1942–1945* (1992); Ed Gilbert *US Marine Corps Raider 1942–1943* (2006); Colonel Eugene T. Lyons's chapter 'Australia and New Zealand' in *Preventive Medicine in World War II, Volume VIII: Civil Affairs/Military Government Public Health Activities*, Medical Department, United States Army (1976); the entry entitled 'US Forces in New Zealand', which contains a good overview of the period, on the New Zealand History Online website (www. nzhistory.net.nz); Barbara Rose *American Art Since 1900: A Critical History* (1967); Richard Stevens *Sigmund Freud: Examining the Essence of his Contribution* (2008); the following documentary programmes: *With the Marines at Tarawa* (1944), and *Pacific: The Lost Evidence: Tarawa* (The History Channel): and, the results for the following Wikipedia entries (www.wikipedia.org): 'Oswald Mosley', 'Velvalee Dickinson' (whose conviction in 1944 for espionage provided a starting point for Mrs Walters's coded letters), 'Axis Naval Activity in Australian Waters', 'Bougainville Campaign', '3rd Marine Division (United States)', 'Fascism (and, in particular, the quote from Alfredo Rocco)', 'Tripartite Pact'; and 'Psychosexual Development'.

The surgery scenes depicted in the novel are largely paraphrased from the following two reports of the Medical Department, United States Army – Surgery in World War II series: *Orthopedic Surgery in the European Theater of Operations* (1956), edited by Mather Cleveland, M.D.; and, *Vascular Surgery in World War II* (1955), edited by Daniel C. Elkin, M.D. and Michael E. Debakey, M.D. The reports also provided useful information about the general nature of military medicine. I am indebted to the various authors of these two works.

On a personal note, I would like to thank the following people: Geoff Walker, Catherine O'Loughlin and Jeremy Sherlock of Penguin NZ, for all of their advice and efforts on behalf of the book; Louise Armstrong, for her excellent editorial guidance and eye for detail; my agent, Michael Gifkins, for agreeing to champion the book, and for his generosity, intelligence and support; my family; and, of course, Helen.

I would also like to thank Patrick Evans, not only for his comments on this book, but for all the years of insight and encouragement.